ONLY

CALL US

FAITHFUL

———————※———————

BOOKS BY MARIE JAKOBER

THE MIND GODS

SANDINISTA

A PEOPLE IN ARMS

HIGH KAMILAN

THE BLACK CHALICE

ONLY CALL US FAITHFUL*

*A FORGE BOOK

ONLY

CALL US

FAITHFUL

———— ✳ ————

A NOVEL OF THE
UNION UNDERGROUND

————————

MARIE JAKOBER

A TOM DOHERTY ASSOCIATES BOOK

NEW YORK

This is a work of fiction. All the characters and events portrayed in this novel are either fictitious or are used fictitiously.

ONLY CALL US FAITHFUL: A NOVEL OF THE UNION UNDERGROUND

Copyright © 2002 by Marie Jakober

This book is printed on acid-free paper.

Edited by James Frenkel

A Forge Book
Published by Tom Doherty Associates, LLC
175 Fifth Avenue
New York, NY 10010

www.tor.com

Forge® is a registered trademark of Tom Doherty Associates, LLC.

ISBN: 0-765-30316-7

First Edition: December 2002

Printed in the United States of America

0 9 8 7 6 5 4 3 2 1

To Sarah, with love.

Whatever I might know about politics,
power, and the struggle for freedom,
you taught me most of it.

ACKNOWLEDGMENTS

I would like to thank Thomas P. Lowry, whose fascinating work, *The Story the Soldiers Wouldn't Tell: Sex in the Civil War*, alerted me to the existence of the Van Lew property in Locust Alley, and who subsequently put me in touch with Robert Waitt in Richmond. Thanks are also due to Mr. Waitt, who corresponded with me in a most helpful fashion, and kindly forwarded to me the unpublished reminiscences to Thomas McNiven, excerpts from the diary of "Madame Clara," and miscellaneous materials.

I would like to thank the staff of the University of Calgary's Document Delivery Service, who succeeded in locating every book and article I asked for, no matter how rare and obscure; and the staffs of the numerous libraries and archives who searched dusty shelves and stood over hot photocopiers to provide me with my mountain of research materials.

A special vote of thanks is due to my agent, Shawna McCarthy, and to my editor, James Frenkel, for believing in the novel, and to James M. McPherson, for reading a portion of the work-in-progress and giving me encouragement at a time when I needed it most.

This novel was completed with financial assistance from the Alberta Foundation for the Arts, for which I am deeply grateful.

ONLY

CALL US

FAITHFUL

———— ✳ ————

ONE

———— ✳

THE FEW STARS LEFT
WERE SET IN BLOOD

The triumph of the Confederacy would be a victory of the powers of evil.

John Stuart Mill, English philosopher

. . . That cause was, I believe, one of the worst for which a people ever fought, and one for which there was the least excuse.

Ulysses S. Grant

The azure on our flag was gone. The few stars left were set in blood.

Elizabeth Van Lew

The past is always with me now. And I can see it, sometimes, with remarkable clarity, as though I were standing just beyond the footlights of a vast stage. Not an actor anymore, nor properly an audience, and yet somehow both. Inescapably both. We are always part of what we look upon, and we change it, however slightly, just by being there.

I won't apologize for that. If I should apologize, we all should; you are changing me even as you read my words. Sherman said it as well as anyone: *These are my memoirs, not someone else's. This is what I remember. If you remember something different, go ahead and write your own.* An arrogant man, William Tecumseh Sherman. A divided man, belonging nowhere. Half his soul was forged in the century before he was born, and half in the century after. No wonder he went crazy.

But that was later. During the war he was as sane as any of us, and saner than many. He had a gift for seeing the future. New kinds of nations, new kinds of warfare. I wonder if he knew that seeing the future is often the first act in creating it.

Just like seeing the past. There is a history that really happened, but none of us will ever know exactly what it was. The other one, the one we think we know, is made by us, and we remake it every time we look at it. In the summer of '65 I thought the war was over. Before five years had gone by, I knew it would never be over. It would be fought again and again, and every time it was fought, it would be a different war. Oh, people's names would be the same, and the dates, and the lonely river crossings and country towns where the battles took place. People would agree on those. They would agree on very little else.

So you're free to tell me I'm remembering it wrong, or even making it up. I know some of you think there were no Southern Unionists at all—none worth mentioning, just a few fools and criminal opportunists. You think the whole South rose as one, proud and resolute, to try to forge a nation.

It wasn't like that at all.

It was like the August night in '64, when Kershaw's infantry slipped through Richmond in the dark dead of night. One might have thought they were ghosts already, they went so quietly, crowded into unlit cars in a pouring rainstorm, at two in the morning, with the whole weary city trying to steal a little sleep.

But some of us were not asleep. Every single hour of the day, someone watched the railroad depots. By day they idled nearby, chatting with the workers; by night they watched from sheds and tall windows, or from the streets, wrapped up in ragged blankets pretending to be refugees.

I was awake, too, that night, in my house on Church Hill. . . .

AUGUST, 1864 . . .

The depot of the Virginia Central wasn't very far from our house; sometimes, in the summer, if my windows were open and the breeze was right, I could hear the trains chugging away, bound for the Shenandoah. But that night I heard nothing except rain hammering on the walls, and wind tugging at the rafters, and the strange sounds houses make at night when one is sleepless and afraid.

I was sitting in the library, with one small lamp burning and the heavy drapes pulled shut. Small papers were scattered about the desk in front of me—notes from friends, and from strangers, and a couple I had written to myself, earlier that afternoon, jotting down things I'd been told by word of mouth. Any one of those papers could have got me hanged.

So it shook me badly when I thought I heard pounding on the door. I listened, and heard nothing more, only the clamor of the storm. I went back to work . . . and a few moments later, I heard it again.

I didn't hesitate. I swept all the papers together, stuffed them into the hollow head of the ornamental lion on the mantel, turned out the gas lamp, and fled to my room. If the provost's men came, they would find me where I belonged at four o'clock in the morning, quietly abed. I waited for the shouts of angry men, the tramp of hurrying feet. People came often to our house at night. Most times they were friends; yet every time, until I knew for sure, I wondered: Was this the end?

But when Josey tapped on my door about five minutes later, the tap was gentle, and so was her voice: "Miss Liza?"

I wrapped myself in a dressing gown and opened the door. Josey was alone.

"Was someone at the door?" I asked.

"A black man brung you this." She held out something wrapped in foil. "Young feller. He just took it out of his shoe and skedaddled."

"Thank you."

I went back to the library. Whatever was inside the foil, I knew it would be important. I lit the gasolier again and peeled the foil open, full of eagerness and hope.

It was one of those times in the war when we desperately needed hope. The previous year, three splendid Union victories had given us—or so we thought—a truly decisive edge; final victory seemed only a matter of time. Now it began to look like time was running out. Grant's Union army was bogged down outside of Petersburg, and Sherman's outside of Atlanta. Jubal Early's Rebels were reclaiming the Shenandoah Valley, threatening Washington itself; and the elections were three months away. If the Northern people, disheartened by the stalemate, voted for a different government—a government willing to let the Confederacy go—then the Union was finished, and all the long struggle had been for nothing.

The key to everything, just then, was the Shenandoah, where Early and Union general Philip Sheridan played feint and run. Tucked between the Alleghenies and the Blue Ridge, the Shenandoah country was a grand place to live if you were a farmer or a villager. If you were a military commander, it was a grand place to court disaster, a maze of highlands and valleys and passes where—as someone told me, not entirely in jest—one army could easily surround the other, and maybe both of them at the same time.

It might not take much to tip the balance in the Valley, and a defeat in the Valley could tip the balance of the war.

I opened the folded note inside the foil. It was from Samuel Ruth, superintendent of the Richmond, Fredericksburg and Potomac Railroad. He had obviously written it in haste, since he had coded nothing except the signature. *Large numbers of CS infantry embarked on V. Central tonight in great secrecy. Believed to be Kershaw's division joining Early. J. M. Hills.*

I felt as if I were holding a bomb. I put it down very carefully, and went to fetch the papers I had secreted on the mantel, and with them my cipher code and the half-finished letter I'd been writing to Colonel Sharpe at City Point. An hour ago, everything in the letter had seemed important. Now it all seemed trifling indeed. I rewrote it, putting Sam's message at the start, and ciphered it. By then dawn light was creeping in around the curtains, and the servants were starting to get up. . . .

How many nights did I spend in this fashion, through those four years of war? Truly, I don't remember. And there were others like me; don't ever believe different. Every man and woman who gave me information had sources of their own, supplying *them*. We weren't legion, perhaps, but we were thousands, all through Richmond, all across Virginia. Much later, I learned that my message to City Point was confirmed three times, from three different agents on the way to Orange Court House. Sheridan knew exactly when Kershaw arrived; and later in the summer, thanks to a loyalist schoolteacher in Winchester, he knew exactly when Kershaw left. And that was the end of the Rebels in the Valley.

But it isn't part of the myth, and some of you will say I'm just making it up: all the resistance, all the people who never believed in the glorious Confederacy. All the forgotten stories I still remember, and want to tell—about the loyalists, yes, but many other things as well—the courage we saw in the war, and the cleverness, and all the craziness, too. Five-course dinners at the Spotswood Hotel, served with music and candlelight, while Lee's half-starved men were gnawing on the corn the army bought for their horses. A young Northern prisoner, a tailor in private life, toadying up to the Rebel officers something shameful, until one of them actually gave him a uniform to mend—which uniform the prisoner quietly put on, and so, transformed into a good Confederate major, walked out of Libby Prison in broad daylight, and never bothered to go back again. Abel Streight, cavalry colonel from Indiana, watching in the same Libby Prison while the names of his junior officers were scrawled on bits of paper and thrown into a dirty cardboard box.

I wasn't there, of course, and so I can only tell it the way it was told to me, the way I see it sometimes, pageant-like, the faces and the deeds played out again, always familiar, and yet never quite the same. . . .

MAY, 1863 . . .

Colonel Streight was a big man, with a westerner's occasional rough edges, and a tendency to bluntly speak his mind. No one would ever have called him soft or sentimental, but on a day like this one, he would have found it easy to cry. He was hungry right down to his toes. He was exhausted. It was impossible to sleep in Libby, two hundred bodies in a single room, all squashed together like sausages in a tray, some mumbling and some coughing and some yelling at everyone else to shut up, and one damn fool or another always having to go, and always managing to step on somebody's ankle or in somebody's face on the way . . . no, the dead couldn't have slept there, unless you shot them two or three more times. Sometimes, when Abel Streight longed for home, he didn't even think about his wife's warm body or his two winsome children; he just wanted a big feather bed, far away in a darkened house on an utterly deserted street, not a sound for twenty miles, not even a cat out, just black Indiana night and sleep.

Just sleep. Just one night to forget where he was, and how he came to be there. He had led a raid out of Nashville in April, a diversionary action deep into enemy territory. By early May he was in Georgia; the horses and mules were giving out, and his supplies were almost gone. The forces of Nathan Bedford Forrest were all around him, outnumbering him more than two to one.

Or so Bedford Forrest had led him to believe.

It was all deception, all huffery and puffery, the same little bands of Rebel cavalry riding around in circles, seeming to be thousands when they were only hundreds. Had Streight chosen to fight instead of surrender, it might have been Forrest, rather than himself, who would have found the situation hopeless. Every time Streight remembered it, he felt another stab of dark humiliation and regret.

Especially on a summer day in '63, the day they drew the names. The day Captain Turner took his little clerk Erasmus Ross into Libby Prison, the pair of them flanked by armed guards, and called the prisoners to order. There had been a hanging in Kentucky, he told them, a vile and unconscionable murder by their vile and unconscionable army of invasion. Two Confederate captains had been falsely accused of being spies, and put to death. Now, by order of the Confederate government, two men of the same rank would be chosen by lot from among the prisoners, and hanged in retaliation.

Turner shouted to silence the outburst of rage and disbelief. He had not come here to discuss the matter. There was nothing to discuss. The decision had been made; the decision was final.

Justice according to King Jeff.

Clumsily, painstakingly, the way he did everything, Little Ross wrote out the names—all the company commanders in seven regiments, including Streight's Fifty-first Indiana Cavalry. Ross could have done it before they came. The prison officers had all the information in their records. But he did it in front of them, offering them his vile little grin sometimes, his knowing look: *You're in for it now, Yankees, oh, yes, indeed, you're in for it now . . . !*

Richard Turner was undoubtedly the most hated man in Libby, but Ross ran a very close second. The prisoners called him Little Ross when they were being nice. Most times they called him Erasmus Rat, and the little worm, and a great variety of things unprintable. Ross never walked past a shelf without knocking some precious personal treasure onto the floor, and if it broke, he smiled. He rarely opened his mouth without insulting someone. He lost mail and bragged about it. Perhaps he had a natural talent for nastiness, Streight thought, or perhaps he worked at it. He could picture Ross sitting up nights thinking about his charges, and how to get them good; meditating on them with his lonely sandwich and his comfortless bowl of soup. He had no wife; he had no friends. He had only the secret life of his warped, cold, incomprehensible mind.

Abel Streight didn't swear much, but he swore all the time when he talked about Ross. "It's like he never blinks. The little son of a bitch got eyes all around his head, and he never blinks."

Ross had all the names written, finally; the papers were carefully folded and tossed into a box.

"You." Captain Turner pointed to a skinny, underage second lieutenant. "Come here."

The lieutenant swallowed, his pale face growing paler. He was one of the most timid men there, probably, one who would find this especially horrible to remember. Streight no longer wanted to cry. He wanted to strangle Richard Turner.

"Captain." His voice was louder than he intended, and harsher. "This is no task for a boy."

Turner shifted his attention to Streight. That one again. Cavalry raider, cattle thief, destroyer of railroads and bridges and barns, trampler of sacred Southern soil. The man who lured half the Southern cavalry out of Mississippi for Grant, led them on a devil's chase into Georgia, while that other hellion Grierson ran the rest to Baton Rouge. Had it not been for those two, the Yankee general and his army would have ended in the river. They'd have been wrecked and gone now, instead of blasting cannonballs into the streets of Vicksburg, morning, noon, and night. It was reason enough to detest Colonel Streight, but Turner had another reason. Prisoners were supposed to act like prisoners, and Streight never did. He was aggressive and mouthy, always looking for trouble, always stirring things up. Damnable dog of a Yankee.

"Well, then." Turner was rather pleased by his interruption, this time. "Then you will have to oblige us, Colonel Streight."

"No," Streight replied. "It's no task for a man, either."

Casually, he linked his hands behind him, and a ripple passed swiftly through the room. A ripple of fourteen hundred hands slithering out of sight behind seven hundred sullen Yankee backs. It had not been planned, but between two blinks of Richard Turner's black eyes, every prisoner in Libby looked like Venus de Milo in blue, only grubbier, without the nice curves.

"*Atten-shun!*"

The Rebel guards went ramrod-straight at Turner's shout. So did the Federal prisoners. But their arms were still behind their backs. Life wasn't easy for the black-haired, beadle-faced creature who ran the jail there.

He swore then, stringing together a long list of vile names, the worst he could think of, all of them for the man from Indiana. But in the end, he let the Yankees have their little moment of defiance, because he knew it changed nothing. Someone else could draw the names.

Someone else did. . . .

I drift along the riverbank, just above the edge of the water. I don't feel the cold anymore, in any physical sense, yet somehow remembering the Rebel prisons makes me notice how chilly the night has become. Libby is gone now. They took it apart and shipped it to Chicago, and made it into a museum. Yet I see it still, as though its lines were carved upon the air; as though its great brutal bulk still took up space, and its barred windows still rang with hundreds of defiant voices: "Oh, may that cuss, Jeff Davis, float, Glory Hallelujah! On a stormy sea in an open boat, In Iceland's cold without a coat, Glory Hallelujah . . . !"

Or with one voice, bawling softly in the dead of night: "Spoon left!" or perhaps "Spoon right!" And the rows of sore and tired bodies would roll over as one, and lay still again, until their other side was numb.

A lot of Union men died in Libby, and more of them on Belle Isle, where the enlisted men were kept. The provost marshal's office hired a grave digger especially to bury them, a man I happened to know rather well; he made a good living doing it. Some of them are still here. There's one who doesn't know his name, and can't go home because he doesn't remember where he came from. He only remembers the island, and shivering in a ragged blanket with snow blowing in through the cracks of the tent, half a cup of raw cornmeal as a ration with no wood to cook it, and dead men lying stiff as boards until their comrades stumbled over them in the morning. One morning in '64 it was himself.

"They told us it was warm at the South." It's all he ever says. "They told us it was warm." He doesn't walk, as others do; he sits under a ledge by the river like a broken patch of fog, and cries sometimes for sheer despair. There is a coldness always by his ledge, and living folk avoid it.

I came to know the Rebel prisons well, although they never let me near Belle Isle, or into any part of Libby except the hospital wing. And even this much only when I insisted, and cajoled, and flattered, and went on about Christian charity, and being kind to one's enemies, and I don't remember what else. I had to go all the way to Secretary of the Treasury Memminger, who was appalled. He reminded me how dirty these men were, how uncouth. They were totally unfit to be allowed in the same room with a lady.

What he didn't say, and didn't need to say, was that he couldn't imagine why any lady would want anything to do with them. The Northern people were mudsills: conscienceless, humorless, money-grubbing Yankees; brutal westerners without breeding or culture—and, of course, immigrants, who were the worst of all, the leavings and scourings of all the rest of the world.

And here was I in my bonnet and lace, with my immaculate spinster's reputation, with my pillared house on Church Street where Edgar Allan Poe once read poetry, and where a handsome army captain named Robert E. Lee sipped brandy and danced . . . no. There was something wrong, something terribly and inexpressibly *wrong* in my wanting to go anywhere near those men.

He knew, of course, that I was a loyal Unionist. I had never hidden the fact; indeed, I was notorious for it. But I was something far more important than anything I believed in. I was a lady, a Southern lady, a creature made of angel silk, untouchable, untouched. White, of course. Parasol white: no sun, no cuss words, no degrading knowledge. No body at all, really, except for mothering. Black people had to use their bodies in place of mine, fetch and carry for me, soak up the sun and the rain. Black women had to lie down in the darkness for me, take the hot desires of my father, my brothers, my husband, my lovers—the lovers I could never have, and was never supposed to think about, not ever. And neither were they.

Would they think about it, those vile unwashed men in Libby Prison? Would they soil me somehow, merely by taking my gifts of oranges and books? Memminger didn't voice the question, not even to himself. The question was part of everything we did, and everything we were. It was part of the war, though the men of the Confederacy mostly misunderstood it, and the men of the Union ignored it altogether.

Without the lady, there could have been no South at all.

Being a lady had its advantages, though. Not advantages I would ever choose again, if God were to send me back to live another life. But advantages nonetheless, and when the war came I used them all. I was a lady to my tender feet, to the tips of my sharpened fingernails, cutting flowers from my garden in the dead of night, wrapping their stems in a drenched linen handkerchief, and sending them through the lines with my couriers. They were always flowers for a wedding, of course, or for a grave site, or convalescing aunt. Imagine if some Rebel picket had been told the honest truth: *Actually, they're for General Grant, sir, over at City Point. Something to brighten his table in the morning. And really, you don't need to pick them apart; all the military stuff is in my shoe. The flowers are exactly what they seem. They're a gift, a compliment, a lady's tribute to a warrior hero.*

Heaven preserve us all, what Richmond would have thought of that!

But no one knew. There were so many things about me Richmond didn't know—couldn't be allowed to know, when it mattered, and didn't want to know, afterward. Richmond and I, well, if one can speak of unrequited love affairs between a person and a place, Richmond and I would surely rank as legends among them. I cherished this city while I lived, whatever my enemies may believe. And I still do. It's a wonderful brave old city, full of dreams and memories and history; and full of ghosts, too, sometimes, on certain chosen nights.

Tonight, I think, is such a night. It hasn't been dark long, but already there's excitement in the air, and definite whispers of uneasiness. Not among the living, who always seem quite distant to me, and quite peculiar, but among the dead, the reveners, who are starting to whisper out from every rock and tree. Several hurry away before I notice who they are. If they notice me, most of them act as though I weren't there—just as they did when I was in the world.

But Will Rowley is out, too, and I'm shamelessly relieved to discover him. One warm face at least; one old comrade to walk beside. He's leaning against a lamp post by the old Danville depot, obviously waiting for me. Beard and bowler and all, if you can imagine what the ghost of a bowler hat is like. He smiles and doffs it, bowing with more grace than he ever had as a man.

"Miss Liza."

"Hello, Will. What a pleasure to see you again."

He is a tall man. With his long dark beard and his austere clothing, he has a distinctly puritan, almost clerical look. But he has imps in his eyes, and in his soul. I knew few men I could have tolerated being married to for longer than a fortnight; Will Rowley was always one of them. Pity he already had a wife when I met him.

"A fair night, Miss Liza."

"Yes."

"You been uptown yet? Place is absolutely crawling with Rebs."

"I'm getting that impression. Do you have any idea what's afoot? Are they celebrating something?"

"This time in October? Only thing I can recall is General Grant being sent down to take charge at Chattanooga. I'd sure be surprised if they were celebrating that."

We exchange a small, celestial grin.

"They're Jennie Rebs, most of 'em," he adds. "Maybe the Daughters of the Confederacy are holding a convention."

"Maybe I should go."

"Nnnhh."

"Well, we could at least drift over and see what they're up to."

Will gives me a wry look. We may be dead, but we aren't crazy. There are places even ghosts don't go alone.

"Reckon we could. But I think we should scare up some reinforcements first. McNiven and the Lohmanns are over at New Market. And Marty the Shovel is down by Winder's office, hiding under a hedge."

Marty the Shovel. Will Rowley does have a way with nicknames, and some of them aren't nice at all. He always detested Martin Lipscomb—Martin the grave digger, the con man, the shameless eccentric. He ran seven times for mayor of Richmond, and never got enough votes, in seven tries together, to count as respectable in one. I didn't like him much, either, to tell the truth. But he was very useful.

"We'd best find Mr. Lipscomb first," I suggest. "Or we mightn't find him at all."

So we start off toward the provost marshal's office—or rather to where it used to be. General Winder won't be there, of course. He died in the Deep South, and I think the ghosts of Andersonville must have got him, because no one has ever seen him or heard of him since. Will takes my arm, a totally unnecessary bit of gallantry, but comforting. There is a chilly wind coming off the river, and to the southwest, directly above the valley of the Appomattox, a sliver of moon hangs in the sky like the shard of some broken, godly bayonet. We don't speak at all for a time, lost in our memories, sad and triumphant by turns, as we have been since the war; as we will be forever. Then, very suddenly, we are jarred by the harsh sound of laughter. A dozen or so young men swing around the corner and come toward us. They're very much alive, dressed in what I'm told are army colors now, some kind of ugly mottled green, and they're carrying the battle flag of the old Confederacy.

I have seen such things before, of course, but I'm always bothered by it. And always curious, too, wondering if they know what that banner really stood for.

The men are loud, vulgar, and drunk. We slink back into the shadows to let them pass. But the last one stops, listens, and then calls to his companions, "What the devil is that?"

He doesn't actually say devil. He says something far more rude, a word I never heard spoken by a living man while I was still alive.

"What is what?"

"I thought I heard something."

Perhaps he has. Will is whistling. The boys won't know the song, I suppose. No one seems to know our songs anymore, except a few poor artists, performing them as background noise in theatres. I think the world has forgotten what songs can mean.

One night in '62, the whole Union army sang "The Battle Cry of Freedom," camped in the rain during the Seven Days fighting. A few began, and others joined in; it spread all down the line, from bivouac to bivouac; seventy thousand voices all became a single voice: *"The Union forever, hurrah, boys, hurrah! Down with the traitors, up with the stars!"* At least one Rebel officer, listening on the other side of the picket line, never recovered from the experience. "We licked them six days running," he said afterward, "and here they were, singing rally round the flag, in that cold and freezing rain, loud enough to wake the very dead. I'm not superstitious, but it sounded like a knell of doom, and my heart went into my boots. . . ."

All of that's forgotten now. These brassy young men, if they were ever to hear the name of George Root, would probably think he was a vegetable. But even they have heard of Sherman. At least Will thinks so, swinging into a tree above their heads, whistling *that* song, the one that still can start a riot in most any Southern bar, whistling it marvelously loud, by afterworld standards, and tapping its jaunty drumbeat against the tree. *Da-dadada-dada-da.* . . . A great song, "Marching Through Georgia," though after a hundred and nineteen western regiments marched past in the Grand Review in '65, every one of them playing it in honor of their chief, poor Sherman, they say, leaned over and muttered to his good friend Ulys Grant: "If I hear that wretched tune one more time I'm going to be sick."

The young men mill briefly on the sidewalk. Two of them, I notice, are wearing armbands, with a peculiar crooked insignia I have never seen before. They curse ferociously. "There's something here," one of them insists. Leaves scatter onto their heads, and he actually draws and brandishes a gun.

Some things haven't changed much at all in the South.

Will is enjoying himself enormously. He reminds me of the Will I knew during the war; and of another man, whom I must admit I never really knew at all, but whose every spoken word I still remember.

"We are all born," he told me, "with an incurable appetite for mischief. And it's a good thing, too. If we weren't, humankind would sink into a bog of tyranny, and never come out again."

John Fairfield. Virginia cavalier, swamp runner, freedom fighter, thief. I met him only once, and I never forgot him. If Will Rowley was a man I might have married, John Fairfield was surely a man I might have loved. But I was a lady, and I loved no one until it was too late.

"Let's go, Will."

I am bored with these ill-bred young men. I belong somewhere else: the one place, the one time, the one reality to which I ever truly belonged: Richmond in the Great Rebellion, a peaceful city transformed overnight into a national capital and a war camp; quiet old houses made over into noisy hives of treason and disorder; armies of functionaries, armies of soldiery, armies of thieves, all colliding in the once tranquil streets. And old General Winder trying desperately to control it, like an aging despot with bad eyesight and untrustworthy friends.

His office was on Broad Street, just ahead of us now. . . .

MAY, 1863 . . .

It was the ugliest building in the city, the provost marshal's office, a plain frame structure that glared down like a prison on everyone who came. It was always crowded. The halls smelled of unwashed bodies, and the fountain glasses smelled of whiskey. People waited in long lines, right out into the street. General Winder must have thought sometimes that every living soul in Richmond wanted something from him: a pass to leave the city; a disorderly son set free from jail; a nice job away from the fighting. Or certain arrangements, perhaps; certain rare and lucrative privileges; certain harmless and not so harmless bendings of the rules. And then, once in a while, things over which he could only shake his head.

"That one again? God in heaven, Major, didn't you say I was too busy?"

"I tried, sir. I've been trying for an hour."

Winder waved a weary assent, and leaned back in his chair. As he waited, he noticed the fly. It was huge, shimmering, and ugly, and it was sitting directly on his appointment book, rubbing two of its skinny legs together in a manner that he couldn't help considering obscene. He was fascinated just the same. As the war went on, he grew more and more fascinated by ugly things, and more and more distressed by them. He wanted very much to kill the fly, to smash it with his inkwell or even with his fist. But the splatter would have been uglier still. He shrugged and brushed it away.

The general was considered attractive. He had a great shock of white hair, shaggy brows, and a finely chiseled mouth which, depending on your preference, you might have called either sensual or cruel. He was brusque and even abusive toward other men, but he could be charming to women. Despite his modest station, and his father's disgrace, he had married extremely well. Twice.

Yet if it is possible to speak of a man being utterly without character, then this was such a man. Where his soul should have been, he had a sieve. Where other men and women through the years accumulated good things, conscience and judgment and understanding of the world, he accumulated nothing. He was empty even of true wickedness. Evil merely passed through him, like everything else, without difficulty, without resistance. Over and over again.

He was provost marshal of Richmond. He was responsible for the confinement of Federal prisoners, for military security, for public order, and, ultimately, for the safety of the Confederate government. These tasks were far beyond his competence, and the whole of Richmond knew it. Whether he knew it or not, he would never consider stepping down; he had a name to redeem. His father was disgraced in the War of 1812, allowing a small British force to capture Washington and burn it, after routing his troops in thirty minutes. The Bladensburg Races, people called it, and said the only Americans who died there had run themselves to death.

General Winder the First was not a coward, just a hopelessly inept and irresponsible commander. It should have crossed his son's mind that the family simply wasn't cut out for the military life. He should have been a baker, perhaps, or a bricklayer. But no. Like a singed moth, he came back to the fire, giving up his retirement to demand a place. The wrong place, redeeming nothing. By 1863, men already spat at the mention of his name. A year later, he would build Andersonville.

But he smiled at the woman who came in and sat across from him. Though he was annoyed at her presence, he was also amused. She was a silly little thing, but her very unreasonableness touched him, made him feel wise and rather fatherly, something he wasn't allowed to feel very often anymore.

"Well, madam, how can I be of service to you?"

"Oh, General!" She leaned forward slightly, lifting her hands from her prim lap onto his desk. "Can you not speak to Captain Turner? He insulted me terribly yesterday!"

"Insulted you? Surely not." This was the South; when a man insulted a woman, it was a serious matter.

"Yes." Her eyelids fluttered. He couldn't tell if she was about to cry, or if she was trying to flirt with him, or both. "He confiscated my pudding!"

With great difficulty, Winder managed not to smile.

"Can you believe it, General? He took away my pudding because he said it would be bad for the prisoners. In front of everyone, he said it! I was never so mortified in my life! I'm sure his wife put him up to it; she's been jealous of me since we were little girls!"

She leaned forward even farther. She barely stopped for breath, telling him how awful it was, how humiliated she felt, when she was such a *good* cook. There were tears in the corners of her eyes. There was also a tiny smudge of egg yolk on the front of her dress. It was a very fine dress, made of the best materials, but he hadn't seen one like it since the Mexican War.

He felt genuinely sorry for her. She wasn't a bad-looking woman. She had beautiful hair, poking out in soft ringlets from beneath a bonnet that, like her dress, was a relic of her lost youth. Something sad happened to women when they didn't marry, he reflected; something died in them; it wilted and shriveled like the unused womb. Even her face was growing pinched and thin. She reminded him of a small blond ferret.

"Imagine him thinking my pudding would make the prisoners sick! I shouldn't bring them any food whatever, he said. For their own good, he said. And then he took it home, and do you want to know what he did, General? *He ate it himself!*"

"But, madam," Winder protested gently, "if he thought the pudding would make the prisoners sick, he wouldn't have eaten it, now would he?"

"Oh." She was bewildered. Something that seemed very simple to her had suddenly been made difficult. "But he said it was for their own good. What other reason could there possibly be?"

"It's a question of discipline. Libby is a military prison, madam; it must be run like an army."

This was not a useful answer. She stared at him with the blank incomprehension of a child. He knotted and unknotted his hands, and began again.

"The prisoners get used to a certain way of doing things, don't you see? Certain rules, certain structures, a certain diet. When you interfere with these things, you only make it harder for them in the long run. That's what Captain Turner was trying to say."

"But it was just a pudding. What difference can a pudding possibly make to the rules?"

He had already answered the question, as clearly as he knew how, and it was as if he hadn't said a word. Dealing with the ignorant in the world, he thought, was as hopeless as dealing with the ugly. The problem just came back again, like the fly perched on the rim of his desk, rubbing its legs together as rudely as before.

The woman leaned forward again, eagerly.

"General, they're just boys, most of them. They're hungry; they have nothing to do. It can't possibly matter if I give them some food and a few books. Captain Turner is just doing it because his wife doesn't like me. He ate my pudding and then he took my permit and he tore it up. The one you signed yourself. You *will* give me another one, General, won't you? You wouldn't be unkind just because of some silly rules. I think you should be the one who makes the rules."

There was genuine pleading in her voice and her eyes, an unfeigned softness. The damn Yankees were the only thing she could find to mother, so she wanted to mother them. Make puddings for them, bring them Bibles and Shakespeare. He sighed inwardly. Perhaps that was as it should be, after all. What would the world of men become if women weren't driven by this constant need for taking care of everything? He was annoyed with her because she chose the enemy as the object of her charity. Yet he understood the impulse. And he understood that she wasn't, as they say, driving her buggy with all four wheels on the road.

He opened his desk drawer. Already paper was scarce in the Confederacy; he rummaged for a small piece, and wrote on it, in a fine, flowing hand: *Miss Elizabeth Van Lew is hereby permitted to deliver, for the use of Federal prisoners within my jurisdiction, items of food, clothing, and reading material. By order of Brig. Gen. John H. Winder, Provost Marshal.*

He handed it across the desk with a smile. "There. Will that do?" It felt good. Turner did have a habit of forgetting who made the rules.

"Oh, yes. Oh, thank you, General. I knew you'd understand. You've always been such a kind man. Do you know, my mother says you have the kindest face she's ever seen!"

"Does she really?"

The woman got to her feet, but didn't immediately leave. She babbled on, saying nice things, but saying them badly. Like an actor, he thought, who remembered all the lines, but forgot where they belonged. She even invited him and Mrs. Winder to dinner, and wilted a little when he declined.

"Oh, that is too bad. My mother would so enjoy it. People just don't socialize anymore, since the war started. It's very sad."

He didn't bother to contradict her. People were socializing just as much as ever, and maybe even more. But the big house on Church Street might as well have had a plague warning on its gates, as far as the decent folk of Richmond were concerned.

It had been a bright place once, when John Van Lew was alive. There were gay parties and elegant dinners, and everyone who was anyone came. Randolphs, Carys, Custises, and Lees. Poets and princes and orators. Frederika Bremer, the Swedish novelist, and Jenny Lind, the Swedish nightingale. John Van Lew had been a remarkable man, talented and tough, a man who made a fortune in business, lost it all through no fault of his own, honorably paid off his debts, and made another.

Perhaps, Winder thought, perhaps he'd been too busy with his business to watch over his children, because they all took after their mother's side of the family. The Philadelphia side. Abolitionists, every one of them, all Quakerized and sentimental. And two of them, at least, a little soft in the head.

He didn't know much about the youngest daughter. She married in Philadelphia and stayed there. But John Van Lew's son, named after his father, never amounted to anything. Even his wife gave up on him, and went back to Mississippi. All he did now was run his father's faltering store, and try to keep himself out of the Confederate army. He claimed to be unwell, but Winder suspected his only serious disability was a weakness of the spine.

And then there was poor Liza. Well over forty now, without a hope of ever finding a husband, and with so little understanding of the world. The first thing she did, before her father was cold in his grave, was turn loose the family slaves. Every single one, no matter how young they were, or how valuable. Then she started going to the auctions, and buying up their children, and their lovers, and their cousins, and turning them loose, too. Richmond watched in astonishment, and shook its head at the extravagance, and wondered what John Van Lew would have thought, being such a sensible man himself.

Still, no one minded especially. She was a respectable lady, and if she didn't want to own slaves, it was her own affair. If she wanted to waste her inheritance, that was her own affair, too. It was her talk that slowly wore away the patience of the community, and deprived her of her friends. She talked about freeing all the slaves. She said there should be a law against owning them. It made a mockery of the Declaration of Independence, a mockery of everything America stood for. It was evil.

Evil.

Winder shook his head. In a perfect world, like as not, there wouldn't be any slavery. There wouldn't be any sickness, either, or any wars, or any damn flies crawling over his desk. But to call it

31

evil was just plain silly. Every civilized society in the history of the world had slaves; it was a practical institution for dealing with practical necessities, just like government and taxes. Somebody had to do the work. God himself knew as much. He didn't forbid owning slaves in his commandments. Didn't preach against it on the mountain, either, or in any other place. One might as well have called it evil for men to grow a beard—which they did, in Boston, when John Winder was a very young man. He read about it in the papers. Read about the poor fellow who had his windows broken, and his garden trampled, and who was finally beaten senseless on the street, merely because he wouldn't shave. He was evil, too, presumably. And now that beards were fashionable at last, how long would it be till the Northern fanatics decided shaving was a sin?

That's what happened when a society lost its hard grip on order. When the mob took over. When people started thinking religions were alike, and social classes were alike, and races were alike, and even men and women, God help us, were alike. Then every lunacy was listened to, and every passion unleashed, and every damned ism ran wild in the streets.

That's how we got Lincoln, Winder thought grimly. *How we got this rotten war.*

Elizabeth Van Lew was saying good-bye, thanking him yet again. He realized, without embarrassment, that he must have stopped listening to her several minutes ago. He was vaguely angry now, made so by his own reflections, and he wished he'd never given her the permit. She was a Unionist after all, another confounded abolitionist crazy woman. But he couldn't take it back without seeming a fool. He saw her politely to the door, and allowed himself an audible sigh of relief when she was finally gone.

His adjutant brought him coffee and lit his cigar. Lieutenant Todd was waiting to see him, he said. With the names.

"Names?" Winder frowned through a great coil of smoke. "What names?"

"The Yankees who are to be hanged, sir."

"Oh, yes. Send him in."

David Todd marched in smartly, saluted, placed a paper on the general's desk, and stood erect again. Like a pillar. Or, perhaps, like a man who felt he was always being watched. Which he was. Not consciously, of course. Nobody wondered about his loyalty, not in the front of their minds, and certainly never out loud. He belonged to one of the oldest and finest Kentucky families; he had three brothers and all manner of cousins in Confederate gray.

But there was, alas, his half sister Mary, who went to stay with kin in Illinois and married a Black Republican named Abraham Lincoln. . . .

Winder read the names without much interest. Captain Henry Sawyer, First New Jersey Cavalry. Captain John Flinn, Fifty-first Indiana Volunteers.

"Have they been placed in special custody, Lieutenant?"

"Yes, sir. In the lower level."

"Keep them there. They may write to their families, and receive the services of a minister of the gospel. They are to have no other visitors."

Winder put considerable emphasis on the last sentence. He'd been through this process before. The first time, he let Elizabeth Van Lew visit the condemned, and her meddling and whining all but drove him crazy.

"That will be all, Lieutenant, thank you."

Winder rummaged for another piece of stationery, a clean piece with proper letterhead. He would inform President Davis, who would in turn inform the Yankee government in Washington. Last year, the Federals backed down, and no executions were necessary. This time it was too late; the two Confederates were already dead, hanged like dogs in the street. Two splendid officers, sons of the finest Southern blood . . . no, they would be avenged, and notice would be served to the barbarians. Spies were spies, and honorable men were honorable men; perhaps after this the Yankees would not confuse the two.

The fly was back, right in front of him, crawling up the side of his coffee cup. He was thoroughly tired of it now, and decided to kill it.

As usual, he missed.

When Liza Van Lew emerged from General Winder's office, she almost flinched from the fierceness of the morning sun. Immediately she hoisted a parasol, and began to make her way down the boardwalk, past the gauntlet of people who were waiting in line.

They all watched her, some idly, some with sharp interest. She was born in Richmond, and thought of herself as a Virginian, but nearly everyone who knew her thought of her as Northern. There were cold stares, and bent heads, and whispers. Natives pointed her out to strangers. *That's Lizzie Van Lew. She's always hanging around the Yankee prisoners, bringing them stuff. And she won't even knit so much as a sock for our poor boys, would you believe it, not even a sock, and she has piles of money, she lives in a big house on Church Street. She'll be sorry for it one day, I promise you. Lord, she dresses funny. A lot of people do, since the blockade. It's not the blockade; she's been dressing like that for years. If she likes the Northern savages so much, why doesn't she go live with them? Maybe she's a spy. Crazy Bet? Naw, she ain't no spy, she's just a dumb old maid. . . .*

Everything about the woman was slightly mismatched. Her gestures were uneasy sometimes, even timid, yet she swept along the street as though she owned it. Her body was slight, her blond hair beautifully feminine, yet children who met her eyes would sometimes freeze, and swallow, and run as though they'd seen a witch. A few people wondered if maybe she was a witch, if she learned dark and horrid things from her niggers, living as she did in that big house with hardly any friends, and the whole family gone a little batty since the old man died.

A black man waited for her at the street corner, holding a small wheelbarrow, on which a huge basket had been fitted.

He straightened like a soldier as she approached; he was eleven inches taller, and easily twice her weight.

"New Market, Miss Liza?" he asked.

"Yes, Nelson."

They moved on. The day was hot, and their progress was slow. When the Confederate government came to Richmond, half the world's noise and crowding and dust and disorder came with it. There were always carriages and wagons and galloping horsemen clattering through the streets. There were always mobs on the sidewalks. Before the war, this early on a hot summer day, only slaves were likely to be out. Now there were clerks and soldiers and hurrying functionaries everywhere. There were paper boys and hawkers and stumbling drunks and homeless refugees sitting on the ground. There were even a great many respectable citizens, some of whom were forced to do their own marketing, and run their own errands, because of the desperate shortage of black labor.

Even the most careful couldn't help getting dirt on their clothing and dung on their footwear. Even the most passionately rebellious couldn't help thinking, at least occasionally, that the honor of being the capital city of the Great Rebellion was an honor they would rather do without.

But on this day, perhaps, they were happy, even though the streets were more impassable than ever. The crushing Confederate victory at Chancellorsville was barely two weeks old. Flags were everywhere, and music: the doombeat of drums, the mesmerizing tramp of marching feet. Regiment after regiment was parading through Richmond, and wherever they moved, hardly anything else moved at all. Great, cheering crowds lined the streets. They waved hats and scarves, blew kisses, and stepped out eagerly with gifts of food and drink.

Nothing official had been said, and nothing would be, but Richmond knew where these men were going. They were going north, across the Potomac into the free states, and God willing all the way to Boston. And when they came back the Yankees would be finished and the war would be over.

Not everyone, though, had flowers in their hands, or in their eyes. Off to Liza's left, the second-story window of an old house snapped shut, despite the heat, and a pair of silk-draped wrists yanked the curtain closed. Here and there quiet citizens shouldered through the crowd as best they could, some sorrowfully, some with defiant urgency, as though there were hundreds of things in the world more interesting to them than the Rebel army. Right beside Liza stood a man of obviously Slavic blood, bearded and muscled like a blacksmith, and very tense. Over and over he wiped his face, and put his handkerchief away, and took it out again. An officer trotted by them, a major in glistening knee boots and a uniform tailored to perfection, finished off with a silk sash and miles of gold braid. The Slav cursed viciously under his breath. Viciously, but very low, with an accent so heavy Liza barely understood: *God damn something something boyars . . . !*

Boyars. The hereditary lords who ran everything in Russia, even, most of the time, the czar.

She had heard such curses before. Unionist immigrants spoke of the Rebellion with a bitterness even the most passionate native-born rarely expressed. They felt as if they'd come here for nothing. They had abandoned their homeland and their kin; they had hungered and sickened on stinking ships on an ocean that went on forever, for a dream of free land and free men, and now their dream was being torn apart before their eyes.

Liza and Nelson stood by in silence. The black man was almost fifty, and built of brick. He was noticed everywhere he went, as fine horses were noticed, or fine hounds. He would have been worth a considerable sum of money, despite his age, except for the small piece of paper he carried in his breast pocket. It had Mrs. Van Lew's signature on it, and it said he was free. He was grateful for the paper, but he knew exactly what it was. It was scrip. The army tramping before him would determine what it was worth.

This army, and one other.

Liza watched the passing troops with careful attention. The men looked fit and ready, but they seemed too young to be soldiers. Half of them, at least, had no shoes. Their uniforms were dirty, patched everywhere, and tattered where they didn't bother patching. In fact, they mostly weren't uniforms at all, just homespun shirts and trousers of various drab colors, often butternut, but sometimes even blue—a fact that would invariably get one or another of them killed by his own comrades. They had no proper packs, only their bedrolls slung over one shoulder and a burlap bag bobbing at the opposite hip, tied on with a piece of twine. Although most of them carried good Enfield rifles, a few had only old, smoothbore muskets, unlikely to hit an elephant farther away than eighty yards.

But they marched like heroes. They were proud of their tatterdemalion look; they compared themselves to the men of Yorktown and Valley Forge. Washington's men. She prayed Washington was sleeping sound in his tomb, and couldn't see.

There were tears in her eyes, and a painful, hard knot in her stomach. It happened every time, since the first ones came from Georgia in '61. She knew half of these men couldn't read, and most of them owned no slaves. She knew they had been lied to; they were tearing their country apart for a lie. But her tears did not blind her. She took careful note of their weapons, of the artillery and supply wagons that accompanied them. She took note of the condition of the horses. Two years ago, when she began, she had little idea of what to look for, or how to evaluate anything she saw. Now she had a practiced eye—unprofessional still, but practiced and relentless. She missed little that any well-trained army scout would have seen.

"You take a real good look at them now, Miss Lizzie."

The voice at her shoulder was soft, but it cut through all the drums and cheering like a bayonet through a bag of feathers.

"You take yourself a real good look, and tell Old Abe how many are coming. It won't matter none."

She knew the voice, knew the face it belonged to: Reginald Cleary, a hard-boned, straggly-haired horror from Baltimore; Winder's man. She wondered how he found her in this crowd, if he followed her from Winder's office, or if he followed her from home.

She turned slightly, and gave him the most withering look she could manage.

"You are quite right, Detective," she said icily. "It won't matter. They can all go, every last man of them Jeff Davis can find, and they're still going to get whipped."

He pulled a plug of chewing tobacco from his pocket, bit off the end, and spat it onto the ground.

"Do you know, Miss Lizzie, a man mostly shouldn't want to fight with a woman. But I am going to *enjoy* seeing you hang."

She laughed. A loud harsh cackle that made other people look away from the soldiers, just for a moment, to look at her.

"You go on back to Maryland, you vile little man. Nobody wants your kind here, picking on decent people all the time. Stealing from everybody. Beating up on old men who buy a little brandy for their poor lame bones. Just go on back where you came from, why don't you, you miserable hired thug!"

Now she had the attention of people all around. Not everyone in Richmond hated Provost Marshal Winder, but they all hated his imported policemen. The Plug Uglies, Richmond called them. The Baltimore Bullies. And here was crazy Liza Van Lew practically screaming at one of them. In public.

The citizens exchanged brief looks, small fluttering smiles. The devil and Beelzebub had fallen out. It wasn't a matter of great importance, not today, not with this glittering array of war passing through their streets. But they would talk about it, even while they marveled at the spirit and élan of their troops, and wondered where Lee might be right now, and where he might be going. Even while they hoped that, wherever he might go, he would plunder and wreck and burn and humiliate everything he marched over, just like the damned Yankees were doing down here.

They would talk about all these things, and in the midst of it they would tell each other how Lizzie Van Lew was heard shrieking like a fishwife at one of General Winder's detectives. And it was dreadful, of course it was, how could a lady behave like that? But it was all right. It would serve. Just like it served Levi Coffin back in Cincinnati, admitting to the whole world that he harbored runaway slaves in his house—a serious crime, according to the law. And then he would smile.

"Leastways," he would say, "the poor things claimed to be slaves. But everybody says Negroes are always making things up; there isn't a courtroom in the land will take their testimony. So I'd be a great fool to believe them myself, now wouldn't I? I'm a Christian, that's all; when poor hungry people come to my door, I give them food and shelter. Where do they go afterward? I haven't the faintest idea. I never ask."

Brazen, they were, those Underground Railroad people. Brazen as a noonday sun, and secret as a fogbound, moonless night. What they spoke, they shouted from the housetops. What they kept to themselves, even God might never come to know.

But they lived among friends. It was different here, and every time, facing down another of Winder's men, another group of angry neighbors, Liza was afraid it was the last time. Afraid she'd never get away with it again.

She would have changed, if she had known another way, if she could have become another person. She would have been a proper spy, the kind she'd read about in books, the kind no one noticed and no one suspected. How safe it would feel, how comforting, to be a spy whom no one suspected.

But this way was all she knew; this person was the only person she knew how to be. Crazy Bet. Rich old spinster. Loudmouthed Yankee lover. Poor little fool.

It would work, or it wouldn't, and that was all.

TWO

————— ✳

LOYALTY WAS
CALLED TREASON

There is little doubt in my mind that the prevailing sentiment in
the south would have been opposed to secession in 1860 and
1861, if there had been a fair and calm expression of opinion,
unbiased by threats, and if the ballot of one legal voter had
counted for as much as that of any other.

Ulysses S. Grant

I do not believe the common people understand it, in fact I know
that they do not understand it, but whoever waited for the
common people when a great move was to be made? We must
make the move and force them to follow.

A. P. Aldrich, Member, South Carolina legislature, 1860

Finally the State was surrendered, and we cried out for the blood
of Summers and Carlisle and other Union members of the
Convention, who fled for their lives. . . . Mobs went to private
houses to harry the true of heart. Loyalty was called treason, and
cursed. If you spoke in your parlor or chamber to your next of
heart, you whispered . . .

Elizabeth Van Lew

I should have warned you at the outset: I'm not going to tell this story straight through from the beginning to the end. To begin with, it doesn't have a beginning. People will tell you the war started on April 12, 1861, when Rebel batteries opened fire on Fort Sumter in South Carolina. But that only made it official. The Union was already divided—divided in fact for months, and in spirit for years. Blood had already been shed in Kansas and Missouri, at Harper's Ferry, and even in the chambers of the United States Senate. The fight over slavery and freedom was well under way by the spring of '61, and it hasn't ended yet.

So I can only tell you bits and pieces. I was born and raised in Virginia. The state where Nat Turner led a slave revolt in '31. The state where John Brown came raising holy hell a quarter century later. He meant to arm the slaves and set them free, and I suppose in a way he did, though he never lived to see it. We hanged him after the briefest mockery of a trial, and from that day on, we lived in a palpable state of war.

I'm told my world is much discussed in yours. There is a certain nostalgia, apparently, for the Old South. For a world of elegance and honor, as you imagine it, stately and well ordered and refined. You have come to see it as it tried so desperately to see itself, in those years before the war. Everyone believed in it, even when they didn't. The South was a special place, a chosen people, the best of all possible worlds. Only now and then, in quiet places, would come a whisper of malaise: a sudden burst of uncertainty in a letter to a friend; a savage whimper of loneliness in a diary; a brandied tale of boredom on a midnight street, shared with an equally brandied friend. Then the window snapped shut; the light went out; the well-bred face smiled serenely into the chaos of the world. Nothing was wrong in Dixie. The men were brave, the women were chaste, the cotton was higher than the housetops, the Negroes wore pretty cotton kerchiefs and sang as they worked; they all loved Old Massa, and if they didn't, nobody was going to mention it. Nothing whatever was wrong in Dixie.

You cannot imagine how many rules had to be kept, to create a society where nothing was wrong. Even for the powerful and the indolent, rules governed every waking hour. *Obey your father in everything he considers important. Offend no one, not even in trifles, and permit none to offend you. Marry correctly. Maintain thereafter a vast network of familial and social obligations. Question few things, and nothing very closely, least of all your own superiority.*

All the things that make life exciting vanished quickly. Love was bridled from infancy. Creativity hesitated at every step, and checked the opinions in the room. Even daring, that mainstay of at least male self-respect, was reduced to the racetrack and the field of honor.

Then we leveled the guns of Charleston harbor at a small black rock in the sea, and a shudder of ecstasy swept across the land. The streets exploded with torches and song. Men and women alike screamed for the joy of it, the freedom, the defiance. Nobody asked if the guns were pointed in the right direction, if the great intolerable figure of authority might be closer to home. It was enough to strike, to dream, to see the sky ablaze with fire.

Who can ever forget Secession night in Richmond? The torchlight parade, the long streets hammering with drums and drunken with flags, the proud and soaring songs, the great devouring greed for an identity that didn't quite exist—could never quite exist, bleeding at birth from its own impossible contradictions. Who can forget the terror of it? The mobs dragged abolitionists from their homes and tore off their clothes. They painted their skin with steaming hot tar and stuck them full of feathers. The police did nothing, and the militiamen laughed. Secession radicals ran respectable Northern businessmen headlong out of town, and the lucky ones left with their coats and their bones in one piece. Windows were broken, and wagons overturned and set afire; harmless strangers were clubbed senseless in the streets, accused of being Yankee spies. Many who had spoken publicly against Secession fled in the dead of night, and some who did not, afterward wished they had.

The cry was for Unity! Unity! everywhere, and that was the most unthinking cry of all. We weren't unified in Richmond, or anywhere else in Virginia. For every slaveholding planter with an aristocratic name, there was a German or a Scot who despised not merely slavery itself, but all forms of aristocratic power. For every poor working man who approved of slavery because it kept the Negroes in their place, there was another poor working man who knew that slavery kept his wages low. Despite all the passion in the streets, despite all the battle flags and screaming, I was never personally satisfied that the vote for Secession was a fair one. It was not a secret vote, and many people whispered to me afterward of threats and twisted arms. On the day itself, Governor Wise took the floor of the Convention brandishing his pistol, which he laid on the desk before him as he railed against the Unionists and called for the show of hands.

Thus the vote carried. We were out of the Union and into the Confederacy, and the many Virginians who were appalled by it stayed quietly at home, or met even more quietly at night, talking in whispers with their curtains carefully drawn. . . .

SPRING, 1861 . . .

Six of us met in Will Rowley's house about a week after the vote. I would love to tell you we set up an elaborate resistance network on the spot, but we didn't. All we did was talk. My brother John was there, and Lucy Rice with her husband Ethan; he was twenty-six and had militia experience; he was a prime target for recruitment by the Rebel army. All of us, without exception, believed we were targets for surveillance and possible arrest. We'd all met at least one

Rebel who knew for a fact that Lincoln's vice president was half nigger and the pair of them wanted to set up an African kingdom below the Potomac. The white men would all be killed and the young women given to the blacks for their harems. So the only thing to do was shoot every Yankee they could find, and hang every Yankee sympathizer, and flog every damn Cuffee who even suspected what the quarrel was about. After you listen to a few people like that, you get a little crazy yourself.

So we said a lot of reckless things, as I recall, and Will Rowley mostly listened. Then he leaned his bony elbows on his table and said, rather softly, like he was talking to himself: "Don't much matter what happens in Virginia."

We all stared at him, shocked to silence.

"Oh, it matters to us," he said. "And to the kids. Lord knows I don't want my kids hurt. But it isn't going to matter a fig to the Union. The war won't be settled here."

"Then where do you think it's going to be settled?" my brother John demanded.

"Kentucky. Tennessee. Ohio, maybe."

"You're not serious."

He was entirely serious, as we would learn. But he was also trying to take our minds off our own fears for a while.

"Fetch me that book, will you, Merry? The one we were looking at before."

His eldest son Merritt darted away, and came back with a large, lavishly illustrated volume; in the back of it was a folded map, half the size of the table. Will had big hands, with long knobby fingers. He spread the map out carefully and traced one by one the great rivers of America. The Mississippi cut the Confederacy in two. The Tennessee and the Cumberland went like arrows into its heart. The Ohio, likewise, led deep into the Union. Whoever controlled those rivers, he said, would win the war.

His family had heard it all before. They were not surprised. But

John frowned, and Ethan Rice shook his head emphatically.

"No chance, Will. There's nothing out there but Indians and bush. All the big cities are here, all the industry, the governments, the money. No chance."

"But the rivers are roads," argued Merritt. "Like Papa says, they lead right through everything."

"If they do," I said, "neither government seems to have noticed."

"They're going to," Will replied. "And everything's likely to depend on which one notices first."

Will was a shrewd man, and my head saw a lot of sense in what he said. But my heart couldn't quite believe it. The west was much too far away, and the war was all around us.

It closed more and more tightly around us as the months went by. None of us were arrested, but we all knew someone else who was. We found ourselves increasingly isolated from our neighbors, and increasingly dependent on each other, not merely for company, but also for courage. It's one of the hardest things imaginable, to find yourself an enemy in your own country. To walk into your own churches, and hear your friends and your leaders condemned. To walk down your own streets and know you aren't safe there.

Events on the battlefield didn't help. The first big skirmishes were fought, and the Union lost badly. Then a dashing young man named George McClellan was placed in command of the Federal army. They called him the Young Napoleon, and I have to admit that, patriotically speaking, I fell in love with him right off. So did several million other people. John and I promptly cleared out our finest guest room, and covered it with fresh wallpaper and stocked it with our best furniture, so we could offer him fine quarters when he led his triumphant army into Richmond.

I got teased about it for the rest of my life. *What are you doing with McClellan's room, Miss Liza? Just how many bales of cobwebs you got in there now? Why don't you put that room to some good use, Miss Liza?—take in a boarder.*

45

I could only smile and shrug. God knows I had a weakness for proud things, for bold men and wild songs and riders in the wind. I always did, and I always will. But all through '61 my pretty room stayed empty. McClellan didn't come.

Richmond was turned into a veritable camp of war. Soldiers tramped through the streets every hour of the day and night. One morning Nelson went out to buy firewood and didn't come back. We searched frantically for him, and discovered that hundreds of Negro men had been collared off the streets like so many stray animals, and put to work on the city's defenses. Poor Nelson came back a week later, exhausted and half starved. McClellan, he said, had better be ready for a fight.

McClellan, alas, looked as though he might never be ready for a fight. Like the old cat who wouldn't hunt until his tail got longer, the Young Napoleon always had a reason for staying home. He organized the Federal army; he trained it and groomed it and polished it, until his army dazzled the eyes of everyone who saw it. But he wouldn't take it into combat. He needed more men first, he said, more horses, more wagons, more supplies.

"More nerve," Will grumbled to me, two or three different times. He was one of those people who never liked dash. He distrusted all flamboyant men on principle, until they'd properly proven themselves. There was wisdom in it, of course, but I always suspected there was a tiny bit of jealousy. "Cold, hard nerve, Miss Liza. That's all Little Mac really needs, and I don't reckon Mr. Lincoln's got any factories for making none."

While all of this was happening, the Confederacy quickly whipped its own armies into shape. Most of the best known officers in the pre-war army were Southerners, and they'd gone out with their states: Beauregard, Joe Johnston, Robert E. Lee. No one doubted their ability to lead. Abroad, we were told, foreign governments cast increasingly skeptical eyes on the future of the United States. In Washington, Lincoln took to wandering the White House halls in his nightshirt and slippers at three A.M., and began to look old. In

Richmond we waited and prayed, and sometimes asked ourselves if the Rebel boasts were just, if the Northern armies truly had no leaders and no pride.

The thunderbolt came in February of '62, from a place called Donelson, in Tennessee, a place very few of us had heard of, and a man we hadn't heard of at all. Two strategic Rebel forts were gobbled up in a mere ten days, one on the Cumberland River, one on the Tennessee; twelve thousand prisoners were taken, and a vast hinterland suddenly laid open to Federal invasion—all the work of an obscure young brigadier general from Illinois, named Ulysses S. Grant.

For weeks the Northern papers talked of nothing else. They dug up every scrap of information they could find about the general. They sent reporters out to Galena and St. Louis to talk to people who knew him before the war. They made a slogan out of his initials: Unconditional Surrender Grant.

Then suddenly the talk turned ugly. Certain career men took it badly, all this attention being given to a scruffy leather clerk from a scruffy western town. All the glory, all the sudden possibilities for power and promotion. Grant, they said now, was a drunkard. Lazy, insubordinate, a failure at everything. Forced to resign from the peacetime army because of his drinking, and no damn good for anything since.

Three weeks after his splendid victory, the hero of Donelson was stripped of his command. . . .

"Will." I smile, and tug ever so lightly at my companion's arm. "Do you remember when they relieved General Grant, back in Tennessee? In all the years I've known you, I don't think I ever saw you so mad."

"Nobody ever saw me so mad. Poor Kitty. She took the kids right out of the house, the first time. She said there wasn't any need for them to hear a grown man carry on so. But they deserved to be cussed at—Halleck, McClellan, the whole lot of 'em. McClellan, especially.

Talking about a court martial, the pretentious little fop. He just couldn't tolerate it that some nobody from Galena had shoved him off the front page. God in heaven, Liza, where would we have been without Mr. Lincoln? I try to imagine it. If the Rebs had killed him right at the start, like they wanted to. Or if he'd been a whole other kind of man. Someone like Halleck, with all that book learning and no sense. Or someone like Jefferson Davis."

"An emancipationist Jeff Davis? That's a bit like a vegetarian bobcat."

"Suppose he had been. Just for the heck of it, Miss Liza. Suppose he'd been a free-soiler and he'd been our president, and everything else about him was the same? Lincoln saw through all the smoke and mirrors. He didn't care where Grant came from, or what he did for a living. Didn't care if his uniform was pressed. Didn't even care if he got drunk sometimes, as long as he fought sober. If it'd been Davis . . ."

Will shook his head. "He never would've figured out who was good, and who just knew all the right ways to pose and all the right things to say. No more than he ever did with his own army. He only cottoned on to Lee when there was nobody else left, and he only liked him because he never talked back."

I think about Will's notion for a time. Jeff Davis in Washington, leading the poor Union. I even think about the opposite: Lincoln in Richmond, leading the Confederacy. Couldn't have happened, of course. He'd have had to own slaves, and owning slaves would have made him a different man. A good man still, no doubt, but different, seeing the world, and other men, and violence, and power, all differently.

For a time, though, I embrace the contradiction as if it were possible. An exchange of presidents, everything else the same. And I wonder which would have hurt the Union more: the loss of the one president, or the acquisition of the other.

Fortunately, we never found out. We had Lincoln, and he took a dim view of Grant's removal. He demanded evidence. *This man has* neglected his duty? He's been insubordinate? Very well. I want the facts. Dates, places, circumstances. Of course, there weren't any. Grant did get howling drunk on occasion—though, of course, in those days of temperance and camp meetings, all his friends pretended he didn't. The rest, like Will said, was nothing but smoke and mirrors. I can still remember his face the night we made our bet. . . .

MARCH, 1862 . . .

We could get Northern papers from time to time, and the story was front page in all of them. *General Grant Returns to the Army of the Tennessee. With full confidence of the President and the War Department, etc., etc.* Will Rowley so pleased with himself. The biggest victory of the war had come in the west, just like he said. Along those two fatal rivers, just like he said. And now Grant was back with his army, with yet another fatal river on his mind. Will sat at his kitchen table like a big brown cat, canary feathers still clinging to the corners of his mouth.

"Are you a betting woman, Miss Elizabeth?"

"I certainly am not."

"What a pity. I was going to wager you one of these Rebel shinplasters here. Maybe the whole passel of 'em. Have you ever seen the like of it? Confederate States of America money. Bank of Virginia money. Fairfax County money. Before we know it, the dogcatchers and the milkmen will be printing the stuff, and none of it'll be worth half a cent."

"And what were you going to wager this treasure on, Will Rowley, tell me?"

"That you're going to have to rename your little back room. The one you papered and prettied up for General McClellan. Grant's going to get to Richmond first."

"All the way from Tennessee?"

"All the way from a warmer place yet, if he has to."

I was the kind of person who had hunches. Will Rowley was not. He always had reasons for his opinions. They were strange reasons, sometimes, but he could always pick them out and name them.

"Well, since I'm not going to bet in any case," I said, "you may as well tell me why I shouldn't."

"It seems there was an old farmer in Galena who lost his mule. He owed some debts he couldn't pay, and the sheriff come all pompous and preachy and took his onliest mule away. So he goes to see Captain Grant. Grant the man who can't do anything right. Can't hold his liquor. Can't farm. Can't sell real estate. Can't remember the prices in his brother's leather store—"

"Didn't Sherman find him in St. Louis, Papa?" Merritt asked. "Before the war? Peddling firewood in the streets?"

"So they say. Dirt broke and freezing cold, still wearing his ratty old army overcoat with the shoulder straps cut off. Yet somehow he's always the man people turn to when they're in trouble. You've got to wonder about it, don't you? Anyhow, it seems Grant told the old farmer he'd do what he could. Come Saturday, the mule went up for auction. It cost him twenty dollars, most of which he had to borrow, but he bought the mule and gave it back."

"That," observed the youngest child, "is an awful lot of money to give away."

"Especially for a man who didn't have any. But the story's just beginning, Roe. The sheriff was marvelously displeased; he figured this was making a mockery of the law. So he confiscated the mule all over again. Come next Saturday, what do you suppose happened?"

"Another auction?"

"Uh-huh. And Grant bought the critter again. For five dollars this time, since his neighbors wouldn't bid against him now. A few days later, blamed if the sheriff didn't haul it off a third time. Seems as long as the same old man had the same old mule, the law still wasn't properly enforced—"

"That sheriff wasn't from South Carolina, was he?" I murmured.

"Saturday came round again. Grant got the mule for a dollar this time. And he took it halfways across the next county, traded it off, and brought another mule back, and leased this one to the old man for ten cents a year. With papers and all, just as legal as can be. And that did it; the sheriff was finally beat. They say the mule's still plowing, and the general's never collected a penny for it yet."

The children thought this was marvelous. So did I.

"I *like* that story, Will."

"It's one of several, Miss Liza. And they all kind of fit together and make a pattern. When nothing much is happening, nobody much notices Ulys Grant. And some look down their noses at him, maybe. But not for very long, and not when they need help. A neighbor goes berserk and barricades himself inside his house with a double-barreled shotgun? Right away, everybody's shouting, go get Captain Grant."

"Did that happen?"

"It did."

"What did he do?"

"Kicked the door down, rassled the gun away from the fellow, went home again."

Will put his elbows on the table and wound his thumbs in his beard.

"When there's trouble, the way I figure, people don't send for the town drunk, or the town loser. They send for somebody they know they can depend on. If that's how General Grant's old neighbors look on him, that tells me something mighty important. He's a West Pointer, too, and they say he sparkled in that little war in Mexico. So he's got the training, and some experience, too. Now, while we're all talking and parading here in the east, and parading and talking, he gobbles up half of Tennessee and half of Kentucky, before anybody notices he's got his mouth open. And that tells me a whole lot more. Put it all together, and I think we have ourselves a general. A real one this time, not the Sunday dress-up kind.

"So. As I said, a fair wager. One of my shinplasters against . . .

51

what? What will you risk, Miss Liza, on behalf of your Young Napoleon?"

"*My* Young Napoleon? Really, Will. General McClellan hardly belongs to me."

"I wish he did. I'd buy him off you and give him to the Rebs."

This was rather harsh. I wondered about McClellan myself, sometimes; it was impossible not to. But I still hoped his long preparation might be followed by some brilliant stroke of action, all the more successful for being carefully planned.

"Oh, come now," I said. "We shouldn't hang him before he fights a major campaign."

"And why hasn't he fought a major campaign, tell me that? The war's a year old already, and he's still diddling his mustache and polishing his buttons. Come on, Miss Liza. Make me a tiny, harmless, little wager."

So we bet. His Henrico County ten-cent bill against my splendid, full-page woodcut of George Brinton McClellan, carefully cut out of a smuggled New York magazine. Which two items, by the time we settled our bet, were just about equal in value.

THREE

———— ✳

THE EDUCATION
OF OUR DAUGHTERS

My parents were both intellectual and devoted to books. . . .
From the time I knew right from wrong, it was my sad privilege to
differ in many things from the perceived opinions and principles in
my locality.

Elizabeth Van Lew

. . . [As] these female petitioners are, I do not doubt, old maids,
not exceeding twenty-five, for they never get beyond that age, I
would recommend him to take one of these interesting, charming
ladies for his wife, and in doing so, I have no doubt he would
lessen the ranks of the abolitionists by one, at least. . . .

James Garland, Virginia Congressman, 1835

It is not safe, wise, or prudent to commit the education of our
daughters to Northern schools, nor to female teachers brought
from the North.

George Fitzhugh, Southern pro-slavery writer

Perhaps you find it peculiar, being addressed so directly by a ghost.
Or perhaps you wonder about the other ghosts, the ones who died
long after the war, the ones who die in your own day. To tell you

the truth, I wonder about them, too. They're timid creatures, most of them; they almost seem to think they shouldn't be here. But there are always a few who come and talk to us, eager to tell us how much the world has changed. They like the changes, usually, especially the women. They say it isn't a disgrace anymore to have a lover, to get divorced, or even not to marry in the first place. The word "spinster," they say, is all but disappearing from the language.

I don't know how I feel about that. I hated the word when I lived, but now I can't decide if it should be buried and forgotten, or taken back and decked with flowers. Reclaimed, the way the black folks have reclaimed their color.

It won't be an easy reclamation for some of us. Can you imagine what nothingness was embodied in the word, here in the South of my growing? Here in a world that was founded so utterly on blood? Even a married woman, childless, was an object of pity. Ask Mary Chestnut; she felt its teeth. She wept softly in the dead of night, when no one could hear. Took to her bed in the sweltering, child-filled Carolina summers. Railed at the family patriarch in her journals—a man who was, as patriarchs should be, marvelously prolific himself, and mortally offended by her barrenness.

And if she, beautiful and clever as she was, moving in the highest ranks of Southern society, was made to feel a failure, you may judge what I was expected to feel. Did feel, sometimes. Insubstantial. Not there at all, perhaps, an accident of light; a ghost while I still lived, slipping in and out of the crowded, clamorous places where other people lived. I recall driving in from the farm on a rainy afternoon back in the fifties, the wagon laden with harvest. . . .

AUTUMN, 1853 . . .

I came in the back way, telling Nelson where to put things, and threw off my gloves and bonnet in a single fling. I thought how pleasant a cool drink would be, and then a good book. I heard voices and laughter. There was an edge to the laughter, the wonderful hard edge it takes on in polite society when someone, bored with being polite, says something deliciously wicked.

We had company. Well, that was all right, too. I was almost at the parlor door when I remembered I'd been out in the rain, and looked it. I stopped still, wondering whether to go in anyway, or to go upstairs and change.

"Well, Lizzie won't marry now, that's for certain. She's gone past thirty-five."

Oh. We're talking of marrying again, are we? I stood utterly still; the rainwater began to trickle down my face from my hair.

"She might." My mother's voice, low and sorrowful. What else could she possibly say?

"You should never have sent her back to Philadelphia. She got her head full of crazy ideas up there, and scared all the young men off. I wouldn't dream of sending any of my children to a Northern school."

"You're forgetting, Carleen. I went to school in Philadelphia myself. My father was the mayor there."

Very good, Mother. Remind them. We are people of substance, too, if only from a troublesome Quaker town.

"That was a whole other generation. Good heavens, Eliza, that was before Nat Turner, before the nullification fight, before *everything!* The North has changed since then. I ought to know. Warren and I go every summer. The abolitionists are getting completely out of hand. And there's so many immigrants, especially after all those troubles in Europe. They tried to wreck everything over there, and got kicked out. Now they want to come and wreck everything here."

"We go back, too, sometimes," my mother said. "It isn't that bad. Most people at the North just want to live decently and raise their families and be left alone. The immigrants most of all, probably."

"Then why don't they mind their own business, and stop telling us what to do with our Negroes? Warren says he doesn't even trust West Point anymore. As for the other schools, well . . . ! I mean no unkindness saying this, Eliza, but Lizzie's whole life was spoiled up there. She's a nice young lady. She's even pretty, or she could be if she tried. But she came back changed, and we all saw it. It happens all the time, when the youngsters go to school there. The abolitionists get to them, and the atheists get to them, and those howling women radicals get to them. And they come home not knowing right from left, or good sense from bad."

"Or a hawk from a handsaw."

Giggles.

Watch it, Millie Franklin; the wind's from the northwest, and rising. . . .

My mother got to her feet. She would check on the refreshments. She would give them a chance to discreetly change the subject. She moved with a great dignity and a consuming sadness. Social gatherings so often reminded her that her family never turned out right. A lot of times, in these last years, social gatherings seemed to have little other purpose.

She stepped into the hall. She saw me, saw the rainwater trickling down my face, dribbling off my boots, dragging at the hem of my skirt.

"Oh, Elizabeth. . . ." Sympathy and bitterness struggled in her, and for a brief moment, bitterness won. She shook her head. "Elizabeth, for heaven's *sake* go up and change!"

But I didn't go. I waited to hear what they would say about me when my mother wasn't there. As it happened, they didn't say anything more at all. Except for Millie Franklin, these women were all my mother's friends. *My* friends, more or less. They meant well.

I think I would have found it easier to forgive them if they hadn't.

I was thirty-six then. I had fifteen years of marriage talk behind me, fifteen years of when Lizzie, why Lizzie, really Lizzie, poor Lizzie. It didn't hurt much anymore. Nor did the loneliness—the permanent, enveloping loneliness that was to serve me so well in the war, when a person less used to loneliness than I was might have crumbled and blown away in the wind.

When I was younger, though, it was a kind of permanent ache, like a broken bone that never healed. Seeing all the young women I knew with their beaux on their arms, so proud and so admired, flashing their rings like battle flags; hearing carriages passing all night long, and music spilling out from the parties on Church Hill, everything beautiful and alive, the air drenched with honeysuckle and the May night as warm around me as a lover's bed. . . . It was all I could bear, sometimes, to be alone. Virginia was full of handsome men, and over the years I coveted one or another of them quite desperately, and quite in vain.

Oh, I had suitors, of course. I had three proposals of marriage, all in the manner of ship chandlers searching for a warehouse. Another woman, rolling downhill from thirty, might well have shrugged and taken what she could get. Spinsterhood was more than a personal failure, after all; it was a moral failure. God intended women to be wives.

I simply couldn't do it. Marriage was for mating—for intimacy and passion and all those other terribly powerful and terribly personal things. I couldn't see any other use for it. If I didn't want a man in my bed, I didn't want him at my breakfast table. Still less did I want him in my conscience, telling me what to think, governing the smallest actions of my life. I would give up my freedom for a great love affair, perhaps; I wasn't about to give it up for less.

But somehow the great love affair never came, never even approached. Perhaps here, among the patriarchs, freedom had to be surrendered first. Kneel, and I will raise you, saith the lord.

I stood upright from the start, and to the bitter end I stood alone.

But there. It doesn't do to dwell on such things very much. I can brood and feel sorry for myself with the best of them, but I can shrug it all off, too. Always could. I can gather it up like a passel of unmended socks and stuff it in a basket and shove it under the bed. You wouldn't believe how many strange things gradually accumulated under my bed. . . .

I look up sharply as Will stops motionless along the sidewalk. There is clamor everywhere up ahead. More Rebels are abroad. One of them bounds out of a side street, right in front of us. He glares at us for the briefest moment, and then hurries on his way. Living, he had a personality made entirely of porcupine quills and vinegar. Dying didn't improve him a bit.

"Jubal Early," I mutter. "Nothing ever happens in Richmond without that old scoundrel having his nose in it."

"One of your favorite people, I take it."

Oh, yes. Old Jube is one of my *very* favorite people—not for anything he did during the war, but for all the things he did after. He was a one-man canonization board, raising up saints all over the landscape. And devils. And, of course, one god: General Robert E. Lee.

Jube was always rather gaunt-looking, and he had a high squeaky voice; he always reminded me of somebody's mean grandmother, sitting in an old rocker with the needles just flying, knitting up that incredible wall hanging they call the Lost Cause, in which a third of the South's population and two-thirds of its history simply . . . disappeared.

When Old Jube has that look on his face, something is definitely afoot.

We start searching for our comrades in earnest now. Obviously, reveners can't be killed, or even hurt in ordinary human terms. But we have minds and spirits; we can suffer terrible psychic pain. Reveners in groups, with their passions roused, can be every bit as fierce as their living counterparts. And while we're all hard to catch, and harder to hold down, sometimes it happens. I'm sure it's what happened to Winder. He's pinned under a rock somewhere in Georgia, encircled by a thousand starving, fever-eyed prisoners from the charnel house of Andersonville, reminded every mortal second of their hatred, and of his guilt. As close a thing to hell as anyone could imagine.

We make a wide circle around Shockoe Hill, cutting through the Burnt District. It's all been rebuilt, of course, but the scent of smoke still lingers in my throat. Will closes in on himself a little, like a man walking in a cold wind. From the northeast comes the sound of hoof-beats and marching, and a sudden great shout of voices, singing at the top of their spectral lungs: "I rode with bold Jeb Stuart and his band of Southern horse. There never were no Yankees who could beat us force to force. . . ."

"Lord above," Will murmurs, "I haven't heard that one for a mighty long time. They really are on the prod tonight, aren't they?"

Shafts of wind carry the singing away, and carry it back. "We rode our worn-out horses and we ate on plain cornmeal, And we licked 'em where we caught 'em, with Southern guts and steel. . . ."

It's a wonderfully stirring song, and I always feel a tug of admiration when I hear it. But it's all stuff and nonsense. We did beat them—force to force lots of times, and twenty other ways. We beat them good.

By the time we reach New Market, there is no sign of Rebels any-where. In the war, this area was the center of Federal resistance in Richmond, in so far as such a center physically existed. Facing the market was the grocery store and restaurant of Willy and Angelina Lohmann. Behind Lohmann's was the tavern of Christian Burging. Two blocks away was the depot of the Richmond, Fredericksburg and Potomac Railroad, whose superintendent, Samuel Ruth, visited the Lohmann place regularly to eat, and the tavern occasionally to drink. The market itself consisted of rows of wooden stalls, clamorous with different accents. There were German bakers and Hungarian butch-ers, a Connecticut blacksmith, and a small, handsome Turk who mended harnesses. There were scores of free blacks, staffing other people's booths or, quite often, operating their own. There were local farmers selling produce, and a Cajun from Louisiana who made won-derful fish pies. You could buy pretty scarves or small toys for pennies, get your boots polished, or your hair cut, or, if you were brave enough, an aching tooth pulled out. There were several shoemakers who by 1862 rarely saw, much less sold, anything made of leather. There was a tea-leaf reader who was cheap and therefore did extremely well. There was even an amanuensis who read and wrote letters and other documents for the illiterate.

Here, on any given day, could be found various members of the Union underground, quietly going about their businesses. Or, on this occasion, gathered in a circle around the tea-leaf reader's table, waiting for the rest of us to turn up.

It must be five or six years, as living people count them, since I've seen Angelina Lohmann. She was lean and hard-bodied in life, and she still has the same look about her. Once, in desperation, Chris Burging got her to help him break up a brawl in his tavern; they say she did a memorable job. She greets Will Rowley and myself with obvious delight, wrings our hands, and startles us, as always, with the thickness of her Prussian accent.

"Ach, is vunderful, *ja*, all uff us together again?"

Yes. Is wonderful. But we aren't all together yet. Martin Lipscomb, thankfully, is here. And so is Sam Ruth, whom I actually worry about a good deal more, since he has absolutely no sense of self-preservation when he gets depressed.

Here, too, is Tom McNiven, the Scottish baker who hated slavery enough to get involved with the Underground Railroad, right in Richmond. He was never part of my network, strictly speaking; the war was barely begun before he'd set up his own. But we shared information when we could, shared couriers many times, shared warnings. Like Will Rowley, McNiven was totally committed. He was indifferent to danger, difficult to fool, and impossible to bribe. He was also ruthless when he had to be—no more than I, perhaps, but differently. He had a singular gift for wrecking things.

"So what's going on?" I ask them. "What are the Rebels up to? Does anybody know?"

"Look at her, Villy. She does not change a bit. Is alvays the first thing on her mind: vat are *diese verdammte* Rebels up to?"

Sam, predictably, is the one who knows. Half of them probably came in on his trains.

"I gather it's a great big conference on Southern culture. And specifically on Southern womanhood."

"So what's the cavalry doing out, for heaven's sake?"

"Well, you can't expect the ladies to go abroad without protection, now can you?"

Indeed not. Should have thought of that myself.

"You von't belief who vill be master uff ceremonies, Liza. The young man vat writes all the books about the Rebels. *Wie heizt Er, Willy? Ich hab es doch vergessen.*"

"Cooper DeLeon."

"Cooper's in town?"

"He came in this morning," McNiven says. "I'm told he gets to name the quintessential Southern lady, when it's all over."

Oh my, oh my. Shades of Paris and the Golden Apple.

"He could start another war if he isn't careful."

We laugh, softly. We laugh a lot at the Rebels; we always did. The war was hard, and murderous, and went on for howling ever, and many times a laugh was all we had left, the last human thing remaining between ourselves and absolute despair.

Sometimes, even now, it still is.

I look around my little group, study their precious unselves one by one. I love them all, and yet if the truth is to be told, only Will Rowley was ever a personal friend. We were bound by something else, something that touched every one of us as persons, but somehow wasn't personal at all. When the war was finally over, those who survived it drifted quietly apart. By the time my mother died, there weren't enough Van Lew friends left in Richmond to carry away her coffin.

But why dwell on it, especially tonight? The chivalry is out, and I can hardly wait to discover who and what the quintessential Southern woman might prove to be.

"Are we waiting for anyone else?" I wonder. "Or might we edge on over to the picket lines?"

"You're in a decidedly provocative mood tonight, Miss Liza, aren't you?"

"Really, Will. Provocative? Me? Why, I'm the feeblest, silliest, most harmless little creature you ever saw. General Winder said so."

"Uh-huh."

"I vant to vait for Lucy. Martin says he might have seen her, earlier. Ach, Liza, you know who I vould luff to see again? The little black girl. The vun vat come from Boston, to vork for the Rebels. *Gott im Himmel,* she was brave."

God in heaven, she was brave. Angelina puts it rather well. Perhaps we should track down Cooper DeLeon and acquaint him with at least one quintessential Southern woman he doesn't know anything about.

Her name was Mariel. Short for Mary Elizabeth. A fairylike name for a small, fairylike little girl. There was already one Mary in the house when she came, and two Elizabeths. And my mother didn't think a slave's name should be taken off like a piece of wrapping paper, and replaced with whatever the new owner happened to like better. So she thought of "Mariel" as a kind of compromise.

We owned Mary Elizabeth Bowser for nearly twenty years. She became very attached to us, especially to my mother. Perhaps at times she even forgot she was a slave. I know I did. Then something would happen. Someone we knew in the community would be sold to the cotton lands. Or someone would run away, and the patrols would be out for days, ranging the countryside with rifles and dogs. Or a half dozen would be caught in the middle of the night in an empty shed, with a mouth organ and a bottle of contraband whiskey, dancing and partying, and they would all be taken down to the city jail and given thirty of the best for being out without a pass.

And a cold fog would pass through the house on Church Street. I don't know if my parents ever felt it; they never gave a sign. But I felt it. For days afterward our slaves grew quieter, their laughter less easy, their eyes more carefully veiled.

Our slaves. Our chubby, finely clad, extraordinarily *safe* slaves. . . .

Mariel, especially, grew quieter. Afterward, when she was older, we would talk sometimes about what happened, or even about slavery itself. I told her once that if it were up to me, all the Van Lew Negroes would have their freedom papers before the day was out. I know she didn't believe it until the papers were in her hands.

I never blamed her. Had I been a slave, I wouldn't have believed it, either.

There is no time after death. We're aware of the passing of a night, the passing of a decade, but the awareness is vague because the matter is of no possible importance. It is the past that fascinates us, and the past is always now. So even as I think of Mariel's arrival, and her twenty years among us, I think of her return. . . .

DECEMBER, 1862 . . .

The wide James River was gray with winter fog that day, the Virginia landscape gray with menace. Two great armies were gathering on the Rappahannock, yet there was a vast loneliness in the bleak, unchanging sky. Little bands of bundled refugees tramped along the roads, drawing aside for wagon trains and galloping horsemen. A few waved and cheered, "Give the Yankees hell, boys, give 'em hell!" Others only hugged their children or their goods, and wondered what would be left of Fredericksburg when they went back.

It was early December, and the cold was mortal, worse than almost anyone could remember. Travelers moved as fast as they were able, their hands and faces muffled against the wind. Few noticed the black woman at all, and none remembered her. She had friends in the countryside here, and a pass to visit them, but she mentioned to no one her actual destination: a farm on the James, a few miles downriver from Richmond. A farm she knew as well as she knew the house on Church Street.

It wasn't large by plantation standards. But there was a fine country house and a barn, several Negro cottages, a smokehouse, and some sheds. To the local folks, it seemed a rather sleepy place. Even a tad neglected, some would have said, with no white man in charge, and its owners living in town.

Despite the cold, Mariel stood at the gate a full minute before she opened it. When she was a child among the Van Lews, she was sure there were spirits in this house, and that Liza Van Lew was a witch. A good witch, she eventually concluded, but nonetheless a witch. And therefore always dangerous.

Well. There's no help for it, is there? You come this far, Mary Bowser, you best go all the way.

She walked briskly to the farmhouse and knocked. The door opened; another black woman, somewhat elderly, stood motionless and stared.

"Lord save us, Mariel, is I dreaming, or is that you?"

"It's me. Now are you going to ask me in, or you going to stand there and catch your death?"

The women laughed, and embraced. Inside, Mariel took off her coat, and unwrapped the scarf from her head. The older woman touched her face, ran her eyes from the thick black hair to the delicate small feet, and back again.

"Well, if you ain't still the prettiest child I ever saw. But you come on in the parlor now, and I'll make some tea. Miss 'Lizabeth's waiting for you. Oh, she'll be so pleased. You look just like a lady."

Mariel hesitated. "Do you know why she wants to see me, Esther?"

"Well, child, why on earth wouldn't she want to see you? You was always her favorite!"

Mariel said nothing more. Esther thought it was just a social call, then. Mistress and freed slave, tea and cookies for old times' sake, a little mutual self-congratulation. Obviously Esther didn't know about the letter. It didn't come by post. It came by messenger, and it was a very vague and peculiar letter to be sent to a favorite. It didn't even have Mariel's name on it. She burned it weeks ago, but she still remembered every word.

Dear Friend. If you can see your way clear, come home for a while. Don't come to the house in town. Send word, and I will see you at the farm. Evl.

A most curious letter, containing a most curious word: "home." A remarkable oversight, that word, coming from so sensible a woman as Liza Van Lew.

Mariel stepped into the parlor. Five years had passed since they last saw each other, five years frozen now into a moment of absolute silence. Then Liza swished across the hardwood floor. She was wearing high button shoes and a fussy, out-of-fashion dress, and she walked with the stride of a man. She hadn't changed a bit. She was still funny to look at, and she still had the most piercing, hard-to-meet eyes Mariel had ever seen. Demon eyes, Esther called them once. They were ice blue, and always too bright. People first meeting her sometimes wondered if she had a fever. Or if, perhaps, she might be slightly mad.

"Mariel! How very good to see you!"

"Miss Elizabeth."

They hugged each other a thousand times when Mariel was small. They did not embrace now, but they took each other's hands, briefly, cautiously.

"Are you well, Miss Elizabeth? And your mother?"

"Mother is weary. She can scarcely bear this awful war. You look splendid, Mariel. Please, come and sit."

Two large chairs were placed carefully by the window. A vase of beautifully dried flowers stood beside each. There was a cheerful fire in the hearth, and sherry in a crystal decanter on the table.

Liza poured two small glasses, and offered one to her guest.

"Lord save us, Miss Liza," Mariel murmured. "Serving liquor to a Negro? Whatever would the provost marshal say?"

Liza laughed. "I'd be in almost as much trouble for drinking it myself. Did you come through Richmond? Have you seen what our poor city has become? There's no end of brawling and thievery now, so General Winder is trying to stop everyone from drinking. Fancy trying to stop an army from drinking. You have to get a medical prescription to buy alcohol; that's the law. His henchmen buy it up with forged prescriptions, sell it on the black market or drink it themselves, and then arrest the poor devils who sold it to them." She raised her glass. "Welcome to the Confederacy."

Esther bustled in with a tray of chicken drumsticks, small cakes, and tea.

"You eat hearty now, child," she said. "I made this all just for you."

The food was delicious, like the sherry, like the warm fire. Mariel had almost forgotten how wealthy people lived. How wealthy Southerners lived, especially. She remembered that word in Liza's letter. "Home."

"So tell me how you've been," Liza said, leaning forward. "How did you find the North?"

"Which North?"

For the first time, they both honestly smiled.

"The puritan North?" Mariel went on. "The republican North? The poor immigrants' North? I thought we was a mixed-up folk down here. They're more mixed-up than anything I ever saw."

"But you got on all right?"

"I got on all right."

Liza's questions fell over themselves in their eagerness. More questions than Mariel could ever hope to answer. *Where did you go, who did you see, tell me about Lucy Mott, the Grimkés, Frederick Douglass, what are people saying in Boston, what are they doing in New York, how are they taking the war, what do they think about the Emancipation Proclamation?*

"The North is no paradise, Miss Liza. Not for black folks. Some of them want to treat us fair. And some just wish a big hole would open up in the middle of the country, and we'd all fall in it and disappear. The day Mr. Lincoln's Proclamation was in the papers, hundreds, maybe thousands of Yankee soldiers just threw down their guns and went home. Freeing the slaves has made a lot of people mad."

Liza picked up a piece of chicken. She held it delicately, but she bit into it as though it were she, not Mariel, who'd just walked all the way from Richmond in a winter wind.

"If you think it's made some Northern people mad, you don't want to see what it's done down here. For days all anyone would talk about was raising the black flag—they talked about it in the papers, in the streets, even in the pulpits, if you can believe it. The North is inciting servile insurrection. We're all going to be murdered in our beds. Lincoln should be shot, and the whole Union army should be hanged. And more such like, till a body hardly knew whether to laugh or to cry. The war has changed, Mariel. It's all different than it was a year ago."

"It wasn't a war a year ago. It was a brawl between a bunch of het-up neighbors. Now it's a war."

"Would you like to help win it?"

"Beg pardon, Miss Liza?"

"I ran into Millie Franklin a few weeks ago, down by the Treasury. Do you remember Miss Millie? She was a Calder, before—the youngest of the Calder girls, and surely the silliest. She was so upset. That's probably why she bothered to talk to me at all; she wanted someone to rail at. Did you know, Mariel, you just can't get good domestics in Richmond anymore; they're simply not to be had, neither slave nor free, not for any price. Some of the ungrateful creatures have actually run away, and the ones who're left aren't half enough to go around—not with Varina Davis and Mary Chestnut and every other *grande dame* of Dixie all living in the same little city and all having dinner at the same time.

"It got me thinking. You have all the qualifications necessary. You've served at as fine a table as was ever set in Richmond. If you could get a post in an important household—somebody in the government, or maybe even in the cabinet—well, all manner of interesting information might come into your hands."

Liza Van Lew's long, thin fingers were curled around the stem of her sherry glass, but the sherry had barely been touched.

"You want me to become a spy?" Mariel whispered.

"I don't see how you can be a spy, serving your own country inside its own borders. But yes, I want you to work for the Union. As I do."

"But . . ."

Mariel faltered. This was all terribly ridiculous, and terribly sad. Poor strange, romantic Elizabeth. It was her loneliness, no doubt, and the strain of the war. The terrible strain of being trapped here in this teeming nest of traitors, with her frail mother and her gentle younger brother, both of them needing comfort and protection themselves, rather than giving it.

"Miss Liza, it wouldn't work for a moment. Too many people know me. They know I went north, and they know why. My manumission papers have your mother's signature on them."

"What of it? You were given your freedom, and you went north. And there you discovered what they could have told you in the first place: it's an ugly, ill-bred, money-grubbing world up there. And, like you said yourself, no paradise for blacks. So you've come back, to work for civilized folks who know how to do things right."

It took Mariel a moment to find something to say.

"But I wouldn't want . . . I couldn't speak against you and your mother."

"No reason to. You're glad to be free. It's nice to go where you like, and have a little money in your pocket. Nice to think of maybe getting married. You're grateful to the Van Lews. But you don't see them anymore because, well, they just wouldn't understand. They're such idealists, after all. Such dreamers, especially the daughter; they don't see how things really are in the world. Of course, you never bring the subject up yourself. But it's what you tell people if they ask."

"My God, you're serious about this."

"I'm deadly serious."

There seemed to Mariel a bit of emphasis on the word "deadly." But perhaps it was only in her mind. She was no longer hungry. The audacity of the idea left her breathless. And frightened. And ever so slightly angry.

Poor romantic Elizabeth, indeed. Lord, Mary Bowser, you know better. She's always been different, maybe, but she's never been anything but clever. She was your mistress for twenty years, and if you take this on, she's going to be your mistress again.

Mariel stared into her teacup. Back in Massachusetts, dozens of her friends were tramping and cursing in the mud of Readville Camp, under the hard, watchful eyes of a blond aristocrat named Robert Gould Shaw. They were black soldiers, and proud of it, the first in the free states. But their officers were white. Their commander was white. An honest man, Shaw, as this one was an honest woman. But still white, and still in charge.

I should have ignored that damned letter. Two skinny little lines, come home, as if this or any place is home, and I come running, I don't even know why. We take it in with our mother's milk, I think, that impulse to come running. . . .

"It's just a suggestion," Liza murmured softly. "No one should take on a task like this, unless they really want to. But heaven knows, if anyone can do it, I think you can."

Mariel looked hard at Elizabeth Van Lew. She remembered the first time they met. She was only six years old. Her mother was dead, killed in the backlash after the Nat Turner rebellion. Murdered, really, though Virginia law would never call it murder. Virginia law would always call it an unfortunate mistake. Mariel's owners didn't want her. They felt perhaps that her mother's wickedness, although imaginary, might nonetheless be inherited. She could never remember being sold; she only remembered driving up to a beautiful three-storied house in town, in the back of a high-wheeled buggy, being lifted out, being taken in to meet Miss Elizabeth.

She remembered a slender girl in her teens, a mass of long, pale ringlets, an incomprehensible outburst of tears. White girls cried all the time, over absolutely anything.

"Oh, Papa, you didn't," the blond girl kept saying. "Not a child, oh, you couldn't have! Not a child!"

She remembered how unwanted she felt, and how desperately afraid. How much she disliked Miss Elizabeth, wondering what the girl might do to a slave whose very presence made her howl. She remembered how long it took to bridge the barriers between them. How frail and tentative the bridge always was, and always remained.

Yet she thought a great deal of Liza Van Lew. She knew it was Liza, and not her mother, who insisted on freeing all the family slaves, after the father and family patriarch was dead. Liza made up her mind about it years before, and if the rest of the family had objections, she simply argued them to pulp. She was always capable of bullying her mother, or most anyone else, into doing what she thought was right.

But her sense of what was right was deep, and clear, and steady. And that, Mariel thought, was deserving of respect. Deserving even, perhaps, of an occasional impulse to come running.

"If I were to get my hands on any . . . information . . . what on earth would I do with it?"

"It will depend on where you happen to be working. I doubt we'll be able to meet. The likeliest thing is that you'll write it on a small piece of paper, possibly in cipher, and leave it with a third party, in some place where it's perfectly reasonable for you to go."

"A third party? There are others, then?"

"Yes."

At this point, almost anyone else would have asked at least one indiscreet question. *How many people, what sort of people, where are they, are you the one in charge?* Mariel didn't ask. Liza noticed, and was pleased.

"Well . . . I hardly know what to say."

"Then don't say anything. Go back to Richmond and make yourself available for work. Even the rich are economizing now, keeping small staffs in their homes, and hiring extra people just for their levees. That's probably how you should start in any case: a dinner here, a wedding there. You'll soon be recommended to the best people. You can decide then, if you want to go ahead. If you think you can do it."

Intended or not, there was a challenge in those words. *If you think you can do it.* It was a challenge Mariel would find hard to resist, and they both knew it.

For a long time after Mariel was gone, Liza sat alone in the parlor. She knew she'd succeeded; she knew Mariel would try. And she knew it might cost the woman her life. She wondered if it felt like this to send an army into battle. Like this, only worse, because a battle could cost so many lives. Was there the same tug between confidence and terror, between faith in a well-made plan and one's knowledge that anything imaginable could go wrong? Was there the same impossible mix of pride and guilt?

Esther stuck her head inside the door, and withdrew instantly, without a word being said. There were times when a wise body just left Miss 'Lizabeth alone.

You want me to become a spy.

She flinched slightly, remembering. She hated the word. So did everyone else. Richmond turned out in great crowds to watch Timothy Webster hang. They cursed and jeered and screamed at him, although he was almost too crippled to walk, and in too much pain to care. In Washington or Boston, Union citizens would have done the same. Spies were the lowest form of life, and few even got the dignity of a trial and a formal execution. They were killed where they were found, and thrown by the roadside. Sheridan would lose ten in his Virginia campaign alone, none of them in combat, and none on a public gibbet.

It won't work for a moment; too many people know me.

It had seemed like such a good idea when it first occurred to her.

But Mariel was right. It was utterly mad. A freed slave of the most notorious Unionist in town? One who'd been these last four years in Boston, among all those abolitionist crazy people? Richmond knew her. The Rebels had spies in the North. A few questions asked, a few connections made, and it would all be over. And she was a Negro. They wouldn't bother with a trial.

They also wouldn't bother with the questions. Because she *was* a Negro. Because Negroes had no past life, had no links to anything meaningful in the world, had no opinions or philosophies, and hadn't half enough brains to try something like this. They would take her at face value because they took all Negroes at face value, the door-opening face, the brandy-serving face, the forever smiling Cuffee face. What, me, Massa? Abatis? Lord, Massa, I never heard of 'em, but if you can get me a recipe, I'll sure enough try and bake some for you. . . .

Or at least, Liza Van Lew, that's what you have to believe, if you're going to get through the night.

FOUR

———— ✳

THE SPIRIT
OF THE AGE

We must settle this question now, whether in a free government
the minority have the right to break up the government whenever
they choose. If we fail it will go far to prove the incapability of
the people to govern themselves.

Abraham Lincoln

We heard the Proclamation, master hush it as he will. . . .

Marching Song of the First Arkansas

It would not be enough to please the Southern states that we
should stop asking them to abolish slavery; what they demand of
us is nothing less than that we should abolish the spirit of the age.

James Russell Lowell, American poet

The sun was low when I started back toward Richmond, and the
roads were busier. The whole of Henrico County was trying to get
home before dark. Wisely so. Traveling by night was dangerous
now—a fact which I was never going to get used to.

And, of course, everyone had to travel on the turnpikes. By government order, all the railroads in northern Virginia were restricted to carrying military personnel and supplies. One railroad, the Richmond, Fredericksburg and Potomac, which led straight into the war zone, was nonetheless breaking down under the strain. It kept having all manner of stupid accidents. Trips that used to take three hours now took six or seven. Supplies for Lee's army piled up in warehouses while cars ran back and forth half empty, for lack of proper requisitions. Someone even forgot a whole carload of muskets on a siding, until the winter rain completely ruined them. The R.F. & P. was surely the most abominably run railroad in the history of the world. General Robert E. Lee was a patient man, but eventually he had enough. He wrote a confidential letter to President Davis. He wanted the superintendent fired.

Every night the Rebel president took home a mountain of paper, and went through it in his study. Lee's letter was there somewhere, among applications for military promotion, complaints about the impressment of goods, and twenty-seven separate reports on Lincoln's policy of Emancipation. By the time Davis got to the letter, it was two in the morning. His one good eye was hammering with pain. He read Lee's request and laid it quietly aside. Generals always complained; it was the nature of the beast. Railroads broke down; that was also the nature of the beast. Sam Ruth had fifteen years of experience running the R.F. & P; there was no earthly reason to relieve him.

Except one, of course, if only Davis had known it. . . .

It was well after suppertime when I got back to the house on Church Street. My brother was sitting by the library fire. He'd brought his favorite chair from his study. Firewood was scarce now, and terribly expensive; one fire had to do for everyone.

Like all of us, he was a smallish person, with pale hair and delicate bones. If he'd been hardy and aggressive, his size would not have mattered; men would have thought of him as a terrier or a bantam rooster, and looked up to him anyway. But he was gentle and easy to please; he liked books better than people, and dreams perhaps better than either.

People sometimes said God got us mixed up. I got the masculine soul intended for him, they said, and he got the soft and womanly soul intended for me. We weren't twins; we were a full six years apart in age. I thought God had little excuse for being so confused . . . unless of course the government in heaven and the government in Richmond operated at similar levels of efficiency.

Don't be cocky, Liza. That's their *great weakness, underestimating the enemy.*

John closed his book and rose to greet me.

"Well, hello. I was beginning to wonder if you'd be back tonight."

"Hello, John. Where's Mother?"

"She's lying down. I don't think she's sleeping, though. She told Josey to be sure to let her know when you came in."

I settled into a chair, allowing myself an audible sigh of weariness and relief. "Really, John, why must you all fret about me so much?"

"Because you don't have enough good sense to fret about yourself. Did the pickets give you any trouble?"

"The pickets never give me any trouble. The devil himself could come and go from Richmond with Winder's name on his papers."

"And probably does, my dear. Several times a week."

"Several times a day, more like it."

Josey brought a platter with a pot of tea, two cups, and a tiny pitcher of milk. No sugar. Since the Federal capture of New Orleans, sugar cost nearly two dollars a pound, and it kept going up. I was fond of sweetened tea, and I missed it. But it was a small price to pay for one end of the Mississippi River. Now if only that promising young man from Galena could get his hands on the other end. . . .

Josey poured the tea and served it. She was a graceful, middle-aged black woman. For many years she'd been in love with Nelson, and had two children by him. Now they were just friends, living quietly parallel lives.

"You want I should build up the fire, Miss Elizabeth? It's getting powerful cold out."

I hesitated. I loved a big fire, loved the warmth of it, the cheerfulness. But there were so many other things we needed the money for.

"No, thank you, Josey. We'll be fine. You can go to bed, if you like."

Josey bade us good night. For a time there was no sound in the room at all except the crackle of the fire, and the occasional tinkle of china.

"What were you reading when I came in, John?"

"*The Mill on the Floss.* George Eliot's new book."

"Is it any good?"

"Yes, actually. It's very good."

"I'll send it over to Libby, then."

"Not until I'm finished, if you don't mind."

I laughed softly. "Now, John, when did I ever take one of your books before you finished it?"

"Never," he replied. "Because I watch them like a hawk."

"Dear heavens, you make me sound like a thief."

"Where the Libby prisoners are concerned, I expect you could become one without batting an eyelash. No offense, my dear; I rather admire it. I just don't want to be the victim, that's all."

"Thieves can't always be choosers," I said. "But I'll try to do my best by you, seeing you're the only brother I've got."

He took a small sip of brandy, leaned back in his chair, and put his feet up. His face grew thoughtful, speculative, the way it often did when he'd been alone most of the day, and was hungering to talk. "You can be rather fine company of a winter's night, Liza. You really should have gotten married, you know."

I acknowledged the compliment with a smile. But even as I did so, his own smile faded, and he went on, moodily: "Then again, maybe not. There wasn't much hope of us marrying well, was there? Either one of us."

76

"What on earth do you mean?"

"Don't you remember what it was like? All the parties and the flirting. All the young women in Virginia looking for a cavalier, and all the young men looking for a belle with fluttering eyelashes. All the parents looking at the pedigrees and considering the property. Nobody ever sat down and actually *talked*—not about anything important. I expect the only difference between us was that I was a man, and chased after what I thought I wanted, until I caught it. And you were a woman, and couldn't do the same. If you had, you'd probably be just as sorry as I am."

"John," I told him, "you have no idea what I might have brought home, if I had chased after what I really wanted, and caught it."

"Oh, yes, I do. You're a child of your world, just like me. You'd have caught yourself a cavalier. Maybe an improbable one, but a cavalier nonetheless, sword and pistol and white charger and all."

"Indeed." *A bowie knife for a sword, and a flat-bottomed boat for a charger, and a thousand dead leaves in his hair. . . .*

My little brother was too sharp to be tolerated, sometimes.

"Do you still miss Catherine?" I asked him.

"Changing the subject, are we?" He finished off his glass of brandy. "The truth is, Liza, I've never missed her. I was glad when she left. And every morning when I wake up, and think of her not being here, I bow three times over my pillow and say: 'God is good.' Do I shock you?"

"No."

"No, you don't shock easily, do you? Well, let me have another stab at it. What would you say if I told you I'm beginning to understand why so many Southern men end up involved with their slaves?"

"I'd say it was time to put away the brandy."

"Lord, you can be superior when you take a notion. Maybe you don't care, being alone all the time. Having nobody. Watching the days pass, the years, always alone. Well, I care, Liza. I hate it. And I understand the temptation. That's all I'm saying: I understand. It isn't approving a sin, you know, to understand a temptation."

"You could always find yourself a mistress."

John had difficulty shocking me. I, on the other hand, could shock him rather easily.

"What did you say?"

"A mistress. A nice woman of your background and age, sensitive like yourself, lonely like yourself. There must be a few hundred of them in the world, at least."

"Liza." He had trouble finding words. "In the name of . . . Liza, no decent woman would dream of such a thing."

No, I suppose not. Oh, they dream about it, all right, but taking the risk, paying the price for it—that's another matter. What a nice little trap you men have built for yourselves. And we're all in it with you, aren't we? Your poor slaves, your ill-chosen wives, your angry, old maid sisters.

I ought to strangle you, John Van Lew. You understand temptation, do you? How many times do you think I've looked at a man and wanted nothing in the world except to lie down in the grass beside him? Not to marry him. Not to have his children. Only to lie down with him and be a woman and be free.

But if I were to tell you so, well, I know the look I would get. I wouldn't even shock you, because you wouldn't believe a word. I would just get that look: Oh, really, Elizabeth. Don't be vulgar, Elizabeth. You shouldn't read so many novels, Elizabeth.

Womanly purity is like the existence of God. Deny it, and all the underpinnings of heaven and earth come tumbling down.

"Who did you meet with?" he asked me. "At the farm?"

"Changing the subject, are we?"

He lifted the brandy glass, gracefully. "Touché. Now tell me, who was it?"

"General Burnside. He's taking me to the ball on Friday night."

He didn't say anything for at least a minute. Perhaps he couldn't decide if he wanted to be amused, or if he wanted to be angry. He settled on a little of both.

"I suppose he wants you to advise him on tactics."

"I most certainly hope not."

John laughed. We sparred sharply, now and then, but we never quarreled. He was really a very darling brother.

"I still want to know what's going on," he said. "There was nothing needing attention at the farm; I was out there three days ago. It's something do with this spy business, isn't it?"

"I'm not a spy. I merely do what I can for my country, and its lawfully elected government."

"Do you ever give a straight answer to a straight question?"

"Not if I can help it. I'm a child of my world, remember? Of all those parties, of all that endless, clever, marvelously evasive talk. Indirectness is a Southern virtue, John. Whatever we say, we have to be able to get out of it before the duel."

"If you'd been a man, you'd have provoked more duels than Jeff Davis."

"Ah, but he didn't fight any, did he? All those challenges, and never a drop of blood."

"Until now."

We looked at each other, and neither of us smiled. John's retort was too pointed to be funny. If you wanted to, I thought, you could trace the whole course of Secessionist politics in Jefferson Davis's hair-trigger life. The arrogance, the impossible sensitivity, the impossible demands. *Take that back, or meet me in the morning. Take back your free-soil farms, your free-soil politicians. Take back your compromises and petitions. Apologize for asking questions about anything we don't ask about. Apologize for stealing our property. Apologize for your newspapers and your books. Apologize for the whole of the nineteenth century. Or else.*

Like the boy who cried wolf, the duelists challenged once too often.

"He's in a fight now," John murmured.

"We all are."

"Liza." His hand moved toward the brandy bottle, and fell back.

He knew I disapproved of intemperance, not for moral reasons, but for practical ones. One should never get drunk on the front lines. Trouble was, the front lines were everywhere now, the whole of Richmond, the whole of Virginia. There was no rear in our war, and there were no furloughs.

"Liza, Mother thinks you've taken entirely too much on yourself."

"Did she tell you so?"

"Not in so many words. Confound it, you'd be doing quite enough just looking after the prisoners in Libby. Let somebody else do the . . . the other stuff."

"Like who?"

"Oh, for heaven's sake. There must be a couple of thousand Union men in Henrico Country alone—"

"Ah, yes. Men. Let the women look after the hungry and the imprisoned. Men can do all the other stuff."

"That's not what I meant."

"Of course it is. You're simply too much of a gentleman to actually say it." I put my teacup down. "I have a country, too, you know. I have a stake in all this, as much as any soldier in the field, and more than some. Haven't you noticed yet what this rotten little war is all about? It's about keeping everything and everybody in their place. Slaves, freedmen, poor folks, radicals, the government itself. Well, I don't much like my place, John. I never did. I wouldn't have started a war over it; somebody else was crazy enough to do that. But now it's been started, nobody's going back to the way things were before. Nobody."

I smiled. I think I meant to reassure him, but my smile appeared to have the opposite effect. Perhaps I intended that as well.

"People do the impossible in war," I went on. "Thereby proving it was never impossible in the first place, merely unheard of. Look at Grant. A scruffy little man with no money and no connections, coming out of the mud and grub of the west, out of absolute nowhere, looking like somebody's stable hand. Walking into the gold-braided world of McClellan and Beauregard and doing all the things they couldn't do, all the things they said couldn't be done—"

"He hasn't got Vicksburg yet, Liza."

"He's already done half a dozen things they said he couldn't do. And he'll have Vicksburg, too. He'll have it before the spring."

"Well, so what? It's got nothing to do with the subject under discussion."

"It's got everything to do with the subject under discussion."

John threw out his hand in frustration, and it found the brandy bottle. Hang the front lines. He was going to have another drink. He thought I should have one, too.

"Brandy?"

"Thank you, no."

He took a long sip, and considered me. Since he first learned of my work as a Federal agent, I knew he'd been trying to look on it as a kind of heroic obedience. I was a woman; I wasn't allowed in the army; I had to offer what loyalty I could to my country and my flag. And the loyalty was certainly there, as passionate as any in the camps or the trenches. But he could see there was more. There was also *dis*obedience. The gates had been kicked open, and there was more than loyalty spilling through them. There was rage, and possibility, and defiance, and dreams. The black people knew it. Lincoln and Sherman and Bedford Forrest knew it.

A lot of women knew it, too. *Nobody is going back to the way things were before.*

That was the thing about war. It always led to outcomes no one intended. When men chose to fight, they gave up their power over the world. They gave it back to God, or to Fate, or to Chaos—all of which, my brother suspected, were just different names for the same thing.

He smiled, and stretched out his thin legs toward the fire.

"Hang it, Liza, what's the use? You're not about to change your mind because of anything I might say."

"No. I am not."

"And perhaps it's just as well. I'm hardly the world's fountain of practical wisdom, am I?"

I said nothing. He cultivated melancholy sometimes, like a delicate plant. We all did. And melancholy was something I couldn't face tonight. Not with Mariel so heavy on my mind. Not with wind scratching hard at the windows, and snow already falling. Not with thirty-five hundred Union soldiers starved and shivering in the tents of Belle Isle prison. Some would be dead by morning, their ragged uniforms brittle as old paint, their boys' faces bearded with ice.

"I feel like a song or two, John, what do you say?"

I went over to the piano, sat down, played my hands across the keys. Began, loud and clear and defiant. *"Come all you true friends of the nation, Attend to humanity's call, Come aid in the slave's liberation, And roll on the liberty ball . . . !"*

"God in heaven, Liza, the neighbors."

"Piffle the neighbors. Come and sing with me. *And roll on the liberty ba-a-a-ll, And roll on the liberty ball. . . ."*

Oh, how we sang then, my brother and I. Till midnight and beyond, all the freedom songs we knew, one after another. I don't think the neighbors heard us. Houses were discreetly spaced on Church Hill, and everyone's windows were shut tight against the cold. When the war first began, I never would have dared, but now I didn't care anymore. We had need of our songs that night, and many a night thereafter.

It was the darkest time of the whole war, those five months from December to May, from Fredericksburg to Chancellorsville. Two horrible slaughters inflicted on our armies in the east, and nothing but stalemates in the west. Burnside up to his belt buckle in mud, and Grant up to his in swamp water. No Vicksburg by spring, as I had imagined. No victories anywhere, just blood and death and failure.

God was passing judgment on the Emancipation Proclamation.

Nothing made me angrier than hearing that, and I heard it every-

where I went. The Yankees had provoked the Lord beyond enduring. To restore the Union by force was bad enough. But to free the
slaves, to put black savages in arms, to make black rebellion a strategy of war . . . oh, Abe Lincoln was calling forth a holy wrath unseen since the days of Sodom. The hotheads didn't talk of
independence anymore; they talked of conquest. Raise the Bonnie
Blue Flag over Faneuil Hall in Boston, over the lighthouses in Maine,
over the gold fields of California. The Yankees had forfeited their
claim to a separate nation, even the scrawny rump of a nation they
had left. The Confederate States of America was going to *be* America.

As for people like me, well, we would be dealt with as well, pretty
soon. Ratty little street gangs took to following me for blocks, chant-
ing, "Hey, Crazy Bet, where you gonna run to? Hey, Crazy Bet,
where you gonna run to, All on that day?"

Then, after Chancellorsville, when it really began to look as
though the Union might have nowhere left to go but down, small
cracks appeared in the invincible Confederacy—very small cracks,
more noticeable in hindsight than at the time. Stonewall Jackson,
wounded at Chancellorsville, died ten days later, a loss in leadership
that the Rebels never found a way to replace. Triumphant Rebel
cavalry chased Abel Streight all the way to Georgia, and Ben Grierson all the way to Baton Rouge; but when they stopped and looked
back, Grant had marched his army down the wrong side of the
Mississippi, ferried it across on gunboats, taken Jackson and all
points between, five battles in twelve days and he won them all, and
finally laid siege to Vicksburg. We already had New Orleans, and
this high river fortress controlled the rest of the Mississippi River.
If Grant could capture it, he would cut the Confederacy in two.

I began to think: *Maybe. Maybe we aren't up against the wall.
Maybe we've just begun to fight.* June came. Jeb Stuart's cavalry put
on a grand review for General Lee. The next day, before the Rebels
even had a chance to scuff the fine new polish on their boots, Union

horsemen rode down on their camps, and all hell broke loose at a place called Brandy Station.

They said it was the biggest cavalry fight in the history of the world. Probably it wasn't. But it was the first cavalry fight we didn't lose. We didn't win, either; it was pretty much a standoff. Rebel casualties were high, though, and General Lee's son was among the wounded. For Stuart, the flawless cavalier who twice rode circles around McClellan's army, this standoff was an appalling shock.

I thought again: *Maybe.*

It's hard, I suppose, for you who know the history, to realize how scared we were, how our spirits went up and down like bits of driftwood at the bottom of a waterfall, how close defeat and ruin sometimes seemed, and sometimes was. We could have lost the war in half a dozen different places, half a dozen different times. Don't let anyone tell you otherwise, seduce you with high-flown words about the North's manpower and money and factories, or about the natural destinies of nations. Armies with all the advantages in manpower and money lose wars rather often. The whole British empire lost to thirteen backwoods colonies, just a little while before. And no nation has ever had a natural destiny, or ever will have. We fashion our destinies with our own hands, by deed or by default, one decade, one year, one hour at a time.

So, just like my Rebel neighbors, I was devastated by every setback, reassured by every small advance, and forever hungering for news. It was Lucy Rice who told me the most about Brandy Station. When her husband fled Virginia to escape being taken into the Rebel army, she pretended to be heartbroken at his cowardice, and made up for it by volunteering at Chimborazo Hospital. A lot of what she learned there was simply gossip, but some of it was singularly useful.

General Stuart was caught napping, she told me, and he was very, very upset about it. He would be looking for vindication in his next campaign; you could bet on it. The cavalrymen, she added with a smile, were popular patients. All the belles in town were bringing them little gifts, and offering to do them favors.

"Especially Rooney Lee, I suppose?"

Rooney Lee wasn't there, she told me. Apparently he hadn't been seriously hurt, after all, and must still be with the army.

"Too bad," I said, and she gave me a troubled look, which I met without flinching. War is war. Rooney Lee was a brigadier general, and although he was of modest talents, he was valuable to Stuart. And Stuart, along with Rooney Lee's father, was preparing to march some seventy thousand men into the free states, and smash the Union and its dreams of freedom forever. The fewer leaders they had for such an enterprise, the better.

I went home again. It had been scorching hot for days, and the streets were almost unbearable with dust, and noise, and glaring sunlight. A man in a shabby waistcoat and low-brimmed hat lounged in the yard of St. Paul's Church, across the street from our house. It was Patrick Henry's church, where long ago he talked of liberty or death. A sorry comedown for such a fine old place, I thought, to become the nesting ground for a Peeping Tom.

I still remember my mother's face when I walked through the door. My mother's words. "Gracious, Elizabeth! You look like a ghost!"

I didn't tell her I'd spoken to Lucy Rice. I never named my people to anyone who didn't have to know. But I did tell her I'd seen the chaplain who was looking after the condemned men in Libby Prison. I told her what he'd said.

"They're in a bad way, Miss Liza. Captain Sawyer, now, he's holding up as well as can be expected. But poor Flinn. . . . War or no war, I tell you there's no justice in it, to bind men to such a fate, in such a dreadful place. . . ."

The lower levels of Libby Prison were little more than cellars: dark, smelly, and full of vermin. If the prisoners sat still for a while, mice and rats emerged boldly from the piles of straw. Bugs of unknown origin and unspeakable ugliness crawled over their feet and into their empty food bowls. When Flinn slept at all, he did so sitting by the table, with his face pressed against his arm. That way, he hoped, nothing horrible would crawl into his mouth.

The table was only large enough for one man to use, and Henry Sawyer had it now. He was burning up the last of their small candle, writing something; his pen scratched and paused, and scratched and paused, like a desperate but exhausted rat.

Flinn thought about being hanged. About the vileness of it, the awful degradation. Hanged men gurgled and twisted and kicked in midair; they were laughed at and jeered; they soiled themselves like infants, and died sometimes very slowly. It was beyond his comprehension that this could happen to him. Beyond his endurance, perhaps. Among the many things he feared was the possibility that he would lose what was left of his courage, that he would struggle and scream and have to be dragged to the gallows like a bad child to his bed.

He did not understand it. He was an officer of the United States Army. He had been in combat and acquitted himself well; he was a brave man. Or he thought he was, until they pulled his name out of a box, and the world collapsed around him, lost its shape and its boundaries and all it ever had of meaning. He had been prepared for death in battle, for the sad but honored death of a hero. Nothing in his life had prepared him for the death of a felon. He told himself there was no difference, not really, the Rebs were traitors and this was war and if they blew him to hell in a cavalry charge or he caught pneumonia in a winter camp or they hung him out of sheer howling vengeance, it was all the same. He gave his life for his country and there was no disgrace in it; the only disgrace in it was theirs. He told himself over and over, but he never really believed it.

"Flinn! Chrissakes, Flinn, are you dead?"

He looked up, bewildered. Sawyer was framed in the pale light of the candle, shaking him lightly. He was holding a small piece of paper.

"Sorry. Didn't hear you. What is it?"

"Here." Sawyer shoved him the paper. "What do you think?"

The letter was addressed to General Winder. Flinn looked up, astonished. But Sawyer said nothing, and he read on.

We respectfully wish to draw to your attention the fact that the executions carried out in Kentucky were ordered by General Ambrose Burnside, and that we, the undersigned, do not belong to General Burnside's forces and should not be held accountable for his actions. Officers from General Burnside's command are, at present, in Confederate hands, and if retaliation for the said general's actions is to take place, these officers, and not the undersigned, should be executed. Yours very respectfully, Captain Henry Sawyer.

Flinn handed the paper back, silently. But instead of taking it, Sawyer offered him the pen.

"It just needs your signature," he said.

"I'm not signing that."

"What the devil do you mean, you're not signing it?"

"I'm not signing it. Burnside's men are just as innocent as we are; we can't ask the Rebs to kill them instead. God in heaven, Sawyer, what does that make us into?"

"Survivors, if we're lucky. Sign it."

"And go home and tell everyone how we stayed alive?"

"All right, then. Don't sign it. Go tell my wife and my three little kids that maybe we had a chance, a tiny, impossible chance, but we lost it because you were too pure, too gallant, too pretty prissy nice to even try. You know what you sound like, Flinn? Like *them*. A lot of fancy notions of honor and no God damn sense."

And do you know what you sound like? The very caricature of a Yankee. God help us, how the Rebs would smile, if they could hear us. How reassured they would be. We're just like they always said.

"It isn't a nice way to die, hanging," Sawyer muttered.

"Don't remind me."

Flinn put his head in his hands. It would have been easy to refuse if Henry Sawyer had been a scoundrel. But he wasn't. He was just an ordinary man. Not as strong as some, maybe, but just an ordinary man. Desperate now, and cracking at the edges.

This, too, was something no one had prepared him for: that men faltered under pressure, and broke, and did things no one expected of them. Upstairs, in the crowded dens of Libby, officers of the Union systematically cheated their fellow prisoners out of commissary stores. Precious belongings mysteriously disappeared. Even escape plans were betrayed for a blanket or a fine Virginia ham.

At first, when Flinn encountered such things, he could not believe it. They were officers, after all. Not riffraff off the streets, joining the army for a lack of better things to do. They were men who'd been to school, who had decent families, who had responsibilities to carry out and reputations to protect.

But it didn't work like that. Not in prison. Perhaps it didn't work like that anywhere. Perhaps all human beings were just animals, under a thin coat of civilized paint. Perhaps he was just an animal himself, and all his ideals were illusions and dreams.

Libby might have overwhelmed him altogether, if it hadn't been for Streight. Steady, clear-thinking Colonel Streight, who was surprised by nothing, rattled by nothing, and corrupted by nothing. There were good men and bad men, Streight told him, and plenty in between. Everywhere. In the officer corps, in the streets, in the countryside, in the gutter.

"I figure a man's character is like his coat, Flinn. Nobody knows if it's any damn good or not, until he's been a few days out in the rain."

Flinn would have given almost anything to have Streight here now, to talk to. But he had only the captain from New Jersey, who pulled the chair over near him and sat down.

"Listen to me a little, will you? I'm not crazy. I know it isn't right if they hang Burnside's men. We aren't talking about right. Right is the war ending and everybody going home. Hell, right is the war never happening at all. All we've got is a choice of bad. And you got to admit it, Flinn: if it's bad to hang anybody, it's worse to hang men from an army that wasn't even there. You got to admit it."

His hand was on Flinn's shoulder.

"I can see how you don't want to sign the letter. I didn't much want to write it. But if we don't both sign it, it's worthless. And I don't see as how you can run out on me, Flinn, when we're both in this together."

"You know what the Rebs will think?"

"I don't care a hair off a hog's back what the Rebs think."

"Sawyer, I can't. . . ."

"You can't let me down. Not in a mess like this. You think your pride is worth more than my life? Is that it? What happens to me, what happens to my wife and kids, none of it matters as long as you can sit there and feel noble?"

Is it all so simple, then? My self-esteem against your survival? An abstraction against a living man? What of those other living men? They're strangers, aren't they? Someone else's problem, someone else's grief. You're the one I know, we're in this together, and I can't let you down. . . .

How easy it all was, riding through the Indiana countryside with their flags high and spotless in the wind, the Union and liberty and everything covered in glory like a field of August wheat. They might die but they'd never be in Libby, nobody had ever heard of Libby; nobody had ever heard of hostages, or soldiers being hanged; nobody had ever dreamt of signing a little piece of paper explaining why one inhumanity should be substituted for another. . . .

"John, please."

Flinn signed the letter without lifting his head. He would never be certain if he did it out of kindness to Sawyer, out of sheer weakness of will, or even, God forgive him, out of the vile hope that the Rebels might, after all, hang someone else instead. With a small borrowed pen he scratched away a part of his soul, and nothing, until the day he died, would ever put it back.

FIVE

————— ✳

NO TIME CAN DO JUSTICE TO THE WRONGS

I looked to the South, and I looked to the West,
And I saw old slavery a-comin'
With four northern doughfaces hitched up in front
Driving freedom to the other side of Jordan.

Jesse Hutchinson

And I warn the abolitionists, ignorant, infatuated, barbarians as
they are, that if chance shall throw any of them into our hands he
may expect a felon's death.

James Henry Hammond, S.C. planter and former governor

I have always contended that the Underground Railroad, so called,
was a Southern Institution; that it had its origin in the slave states.

Levi Coffin, Underground Railroad leader

Slavery as it really is . . . no pen, no book, no time can do justice
to the wrongs. . . .

Elizabeth Van Lew

In your world, I have been told, spies are carefully chosen, and many are professionally trained. It was all quite different in the Great Rebellion. Most of us just drifted into it, and we really didn't have the foggiest notion of what we were taking on. If you had asked me before the war began, I would have described a secret agent rather like someone hunting for a cache of stolen gold—someone cloaked and daggered, listening at doorways and sneaking up dark stairwells in the dead of night.

As it turned out, we were more like California prospectors most of the time, walking around in plain broad daylight picking up grubby little rocks. Sitting hour upon hour with wet feet and cold hands, shaking sand through a sieve; scratching about for weeks and never finding so much as a decent nugget, only flakes—innumerable tiny flakes which, after I separated them from the mud and the rubbish, and weighed them all together, could maybe buy me dinner.

Sometimes, I didn't believe I was doing it. I didn't believe any grown-up person would spend so many hours of her irreplaceable, God-given life studying railroad schedules and daily newspapers. Decoding messages which, when I could finally read them, said nothing of any conceivable importance to anyone. Sending books away and getting them back. Marking words in *A Tale of Two Cities* with my fingernail. Searching for words so marked by other hands. Sick. Man. Die. Sun. Night. Tell. Grave. Man. Need. Clothes. Luck. Straight.

Suddenly, unexpectedly, a nugget.

Next Sunday night, if all went well, one of the sick prisoners in Libby would appear to die. He'd been getting worse for days, so no one would be surprised; and he'd be careful to give up the ghost in the middle of the night, when the sleepy guards were willing to take a Federal doctor's word for it, and even more willing to let someone else take care of his remains. His comrades would fetch in a coffin, and carry him to the storage shed, where Martin Lipscomb would collect him in the morning. In some quiet, secluded place, Mr. Lipscomb would supply the cheerful corpse with civilian clothing, money, and if possible, papers, all provided by myself and my friends. Five men got out of Libby that way, before the Rebels grew edgy and we had to give it up.

The grave man did extremely well on these transactions. He always kept a portion of the prisoner's money. He was paid by the provost marshal for the burial. And, in a few weeks' time, he would sell the empty coffin back to the Rebel commissary.

But the truth is, such sweet victories were few and far between. Most of my work was detail work, slow, tiresome, and wasteful. Every single day I read all the Richmond papers, and as many from out of town as I could get. They were full of valuable military information, as the generals on both sides had already discovered. I wondered, though, if the generals read the social pages as well as the news, if it would ever occur to them.

I read them very carefully. That was where the names were dropped, and sometimes behind the presence or absence of a few names was the presence or absence of a company, a regiment, even a brigade. Blunt accounts of theft and crime said a lot about rising or falling morale among ordinary people. The guest lists of dinner parties held clues to newly forming or declining political alliances.

The great difficulty was that there was always too much information—as on a certain occasion I still remember, in June of '63. I went over my papers three or four times that night, trying to sort things out. After a while, everything became a blur—what my agents told me, what the rumors were, what the newspapers speculated, what the Rebel government gave out . . . how could I possibly know what was true? More important, how could I determine what mattered? Hetty Cary was hosting a masque to raise money for the wounded from Brandy Station. Vicksburg was under daily bombardment but holding fast. The Fredericksburg trains were now running on time. Mrs. Robert E. Lee had gone to visit her daughter-in-law's family in Hanover County. The *Examiner* thought Johnston would attack Grant and rescue Vicksburg in a matter of days. Samuel Ruth, in a secret message, wondered how; no more than three or four thousand men, he said, had been sent west from the Carolinas. All the other reinforcements had gone north with General Lee.

I put down the last paper and closed my eyes. I was tired, I was bored, and I was terribly uneasy. Something was niggling at the back of my mind. Something was wrong, or perhaps right, but I wasn't catching it, I wasn't making the link. I read the papers again. I read all my friends' messages again. I looked at all my maps again.

"God in heaven, Elizabeth, do you know what time it is?"

Mother was standing in the doorway like an old castle ghost, draped in a white, fluttery nightgown and holding a tiny lamp.

"No. What time is it?"

"Four o'clock in the morning."

"Oh."

I believed it, because my mother said so, but I had no sense of the time having passed. I wondered how the parlor clock could have chimed so many times, every quarter hour, without my noticing.

"What will those detectives think, Liza, when our light is on all night?"

"Well, if they're staying up all night to spy on us, I don't see as how they have any business thinking anything."

"You're not very practical, my dear."

No. That was what everyone kept saying.

I gave Mother a peck on the cheek, and went to my room. I didn't sleep. I put out the light and stood for a long time by the window.

You know what you are, Liza Van Lew, don't you? You're a perfect howling fool. A bored spinster with nothing to do, chasing phantoms and shadows. Your brother is right. Help the men in Libby and Belle Isle, forget the rest. The army has scouts, and good ones; they know which troops are moving where. General Hooker

*can read the newspapers just as well as you can. For all you know,
you've never sent out a single scrap of information they didn't already have from someone else. A single suggestion they hadn't already figured out for themselves. No wonder Winder doesn't take
you seriously. Why should he? You're just a silly bat.*

A shadow moved in the streets. One of Winder's Plug Uglies,
probably, watching my window. Watching all the time, waiting for
the moment when he could drag us all to a cell in Castle Thunder,
John and poor Mother, too, all because of my ridiculous notion that
I could help in the war.

I needed someone to talk to. Someone to wrap an arm around
my shoulders and tell me it was all right. Someone to shut out the
darkness, and the thought of half a lifetime gone for nothing. Someone like Julia Grant, waiting four years to marry the young officer
her father considered too poor and too futureless, waiting a dozen
years more for him to find a road that he could walk on. Believing
in him against all the failures, against all the judgments of the world.
Braving storm and mud and even Rebel cavalry to visit him in camp,
one campaign after another, everywhere he went. Standing breathless on the deck of a gunboat as the whole sky shimmered and exploded with cannon fire, watching the Union flotilla run the batteries
at Vicksburg, knowing it was the biggest gamble any American general ever took, the flotilla and the army both lost if the gamble failed.
But he would make it work, she knew that, too; she had the certainty
of a mountain, and he leaned on it every hour of his life.

No one believed in me like that. Not in me, nor in any woman.
No one ever would. I drew the curtains against the coming of the
morning sun. I took off my shoes and my dress, moving slowly and
without thought, like a mechanical toy. The darkness settled in, and
there was no one and nothing to stand against it.

I woke to the sound of bells, remembered it was Sunday, and
pulled the covers over my head. I belonged to Old St. Paul's across
the street, but I didn't go there anymore—nor to any other church

where the wrath of God was summoned against my country, and where its enemies were prayed for.

I tried to go back to sleep, but I couldn't. I knew I ought to get up, but I couldn't. I didn't want to move. There wasn't any reason for moving; nothing good would ever come of my life. It was like one of those dreary, low river farms, where nobody could ever discover what would grow.

Since my childhood, it had been that way: a slow accumulation of wrong decisions, wrong emotions, wrong desires, none of it growing out of wickedness or deliberate defiance; quite the opposite. I wanted so very much to please, and to be good. I would spend two hours dressing for a party, just like all the other girls did. And they would still put their heads together after I'd passed, and whisper, and most times I had no idea why. Why my costume was never right. Why I myself was somehow never right.

"You're a throwback," Mother would tell me sometimes, and mean it as a compliment. A throwback to the pioneers, the revolutionaries. To my great aunt, who carried baskets of food to the soldiers of the Continental Army, hungry and shivering in the British prisons of New York. To further back still, perhaps, to the Dutch Huguenots who defied both church and empire, and actually got away with it.

My mother's words were sheltering, but they drew attention to the problem nonetheless. I was different. And I didn't want to be— not when I was young. So, for a long time, I tried even harder. It was the first of my long chain of wrong decisions, all that desperate trying, all those years of being good, being careful, being as much of a lady as I knew how to be, which was never quite enough, which only leached away my youth and gave me nothing of substance in return. I should have *been* a pioneer. Climbed on one of those bone-rattling trains and gone west, opened an opera house or, God help me, maybe a saloon, taken lovers as I pleased, learned how to cuss and to drink. . . .

I burrowed deeper into the pillow. No, I thought, it wouldn't have worked either, probably. I would have been every bit as lonely as a pioneer, just colder and hungrier. What I really should have done was get married and have children, like every woman did who wanted her life to count for something. But I failed there, too. I could never win the men I really wanted, could never want the few I might have won.

What went wrong? I was healthy, privileged, singularly intelligent, but the years went by. They were still going by, and nothing had come of my life. Forty-five years to be exact, disappearing slowly through a sieve like melting gelatine. What went wrong?

Tears ran heedlessly down my face. Perhaps it was like everyone said. God got me mixed up. Not with John; that was just nonsense; I wasn't a man, and I knew it very well. But he got something mixed up when he made me; got distracted, perhaps, and put all the wrong things together in the pot. An idle lady's soft body with a Viking's imagination and a chessmaster's mind. A republican conscience amid the luxuries of a slave state. An appetite for questions in a strait-blinkered world of believers. And all of it, may God forgive himself, to produce a woman, in a world run entirely by men.

Could such a recipe ever have turned out? If I had been wiser, or even just a little bit luckier? I didn't know, and I never would, but I knew the broth was quite beyond saving now. I myself had put into it the final ingredient, the last bitter fruit of unbelonging. I was an enemy in my own city, among my own neighbors. Everything else might yet have been forgiven me, if I hadn't gone over to the Yankees.

I didn't regret having done so. I couldn't imagine regretting it, any more than I could imagine never having done it. But I saw it for what it was—the final and absolute proof of my isolation.

You're unnatural, Elizabeth.

Catherine's words, a few years back. And yes, God knew Catherine wasn't exactly an authority on nature, or on anything else, but she was John's wife, she was supposed to be family, and even she finally had to say it. *You're unnatural.*

I ignored the knock on the door, ignored my mother's voice, asking if I'd like to come down to breakfast; ignored the receding steps, the half-muffled murmur of sympathy: "Poor dear, she must be sound asleep."

But eventually there was no help for it. I had things to take to Libby Prison. I had a letter drop to visit. I got dressed. I snatched a small muffin from the kitchen and disappeared with it, before Josey could start insisting on a proper meal. I heard Mother's voice behind me in the hall.

"Heavens, Elizabeth, you're not going out like that?"

"Like what?"

"You haven't combed your hair." Mother smiled, and brushed a wisp of something back from my face. "Poor dear, you should see yourself. You look like the witch of Endor."

There was a small mirror in my reticule. I took it out and regarded myself carefully. I had indeed forgotten to comb my hair.

I was amused. Not in a light-hearted manner, not at all. Amused as hunting cats were, and footpads on dark streets—and, I supposed, war leaders waiting in ambush behind some innocent, sun-wrapped line of trees.

"I look absolutely perfect, Mother. I wish I had thought of it myself."

"What on earth are you talking about?"

"Crazy Bet's going downhill fast, don't you think? It must be the war. Heaven knows but she'll soon be neglecting to bathe, and babbling to herself as she walks down the street."

"Liza, you wouldn't . . . ?"

Wouldn't I? Turn all the failures upside down? Take all the loneliness and differentness, and all the unbelonging, and turn them into gifts? Even gifts of war, since there's no others to be had?

Oh, Mother, you'd better believe I would!

✳ ✳ ✳

I took my packages to Libby Prison, and turned them over to the officer of the day. My permission to visit the men in the hospital, which I'd obtained from Memminger at the start of the war, had been revoked for the last time some months before. I could only bring my offerings now, and hope they were delivered intact. Sometimes they were. Sometimes they weren't. It was the same with the shipments that came from the North. They were piled up in huge sheds at the east end of the prison. They were searched. They were robbed. They sat for weeks, while the perishable food in them rotted. Sometimes, with a brazenness even my spies would have blushed at, Rebel guards sold the prisoners their own belongings, cakes made in some Northern mother's kitchen, blankets and underwear with the words "United States Sanitary Commission" stamped right on them.

Rebel honor was a fabric with a good deal of rubber in the weave.

I had tea at Lohmann's restaurant, and bought a paper from a Negro lad who hung about outside. I waited to open it until I was safe in my own study, but I needn't have bothered. There was nothing inside.

It was as if the whole world had ground to a halt, as if everyone and everything, from God on down, was just waiting now. Waiting as Grant's vise closed on Vicksburg and the Rebel force behind him gathered and grew. Waiting as gray legions moved across the Pennsylvania fields to no one knew where. Waiting for the crash that could mean the ending of the war, or the ending of the world.

Unbearable, that waiting. Like being buried in sand to the neck, wondering if your searching friends would find you before the tide came in.

"Miss Liza?"

It was Nelson, slipping into the study without pausing for an invitation, his face wreathed in the closest thing to excitement I'd ever seen there.

"Beg pardon, Miss Liza, but I got something powerful important to tell you. I been talking to Mariel."

"Talking to Mariel? For heaven's sake, Nelson, none of us is supposed to talk to Mariel. You know that!"

"Yes'm, Miss Liza. But she wouldn't have it no other way. And nobody saw us, I swear to you, we made sure of it. She was scared to write it down, she said. And I believe her, though I ain't sure if she was scared of somebody getting hold of it, or just scared you wouldn't believe it. She's got herself a job, Miss Liza. A real regular live-in job."

He paused then, baiting me.

"Well, don't just stand there, tell me! Who hired her? Somebody in the cabinet? Mallory? God knows he loves his fine dinners. Oh, Nelson, I'll hug her to death if she got Mallory! Tell me!"

"She got better'n Mallory, Miss Liza. She got the White House."

"*What?*"

"She's been hired by Varina Davis," Nelson said. And then added: "The president's wife." As if I didn't know.

The blood drained from my face. I could feel it. Feel my stomach curl up into a quivering little knot.

"You're serious, aren't you? She'll be serving in the White House? For Davis? For his cabinet? *His generals?*"

"Everyone who comes to dinner, I reckon. And yes'm, Miss Liza, I'm serious. Mariel was awful proud. And though she didn't let on, I think she's awful uneasy, too. She says Varina is nice, but Jeff Davis makes her think of them . . . I forget the word she used . . . them folks who die and come back with long teeth, all gray-faced and real dangerous—"

"Vampires?"

"Yes'm, that was it. And she says she doesn't know yet if she'll be doing any shopping for Mrs. Davis, but if she isn't, she doesn't think New Market is a place she should be seen at much. Seems there's too many people of dubious loyalty hanging about."

I smiled. That was a nice way of putting it.

"Anything else?"

"No, ma'am. Except she sends her regards to you and your mammy, and to Mister John."

"Well."

I got to my feet. It was astonishing, I thought, what one piece of good news could do to any number of bad feelings.

"Thank you, Nelson."

He was almost out the door when I added sharply: "And, Nelson? No more meetings with Mariel. Especially now. I mean it. You can never be sure what Winder's bloodhounds see and don't see."

"Yes'm."

The door closed. I walked back and forth, sat down, got up again. A part of me wanted to turn cartwheels, to run down to the piano in the parlor and sing "Glory, glory hallelujah!" at the top of my lungs. And a part of me was truly and honestly cold with dread. Mariel was in that man's *house*. That impeccably well-behaved and well-bred man who introduced into the Confederate Congress legislation calling for the execution of any white officers who led Negro soldiers against the South, and for the enslavement or death of the soldiers themselves. They weren't prisoners of war, according to Davis. They were criminals, guilty of something called servile insurrection. Something Mariel understood very well, having lived through Nat Turner's rising, and what came after: the night riders, the burned-out wooden huts, the country roads turned one by one to gibbets, with black bodies hanging in clusters from the trees; her young mother dragged away by a posse and never coming back. Now, every day, she would smile into the thin, ashen face of Jefferson Davis, and wish him a good evening. She would pour brandy for his cabinet ministers and his generals, as they dreamt and designed the great slave empire where no such insurrection would ever be dared again.

How would she do it? Where would she find the calmness, the patience, the sheer icy nerve? I didn't know. I couldn't have done it myself—not day after day, week after week. I'd have come apart, started screaming like a banshee, probably, and picked up one of his beautifully monogrammed knives and gone for his throat. . . .

Sometimes, looking back on those years of war, I myself no longer quite believe how bold we actually were. Mariel serving dinner in the Rebel White House. Tom McNiven burning down the Tredegar Iron Works, when the place was never empty and never unguarded, even for a second. Sam Ruth fouling up the supply of Lee's army so completely that Lee had to send a whole corps off down the peninsula, and couldn't get them back in time to fight at Chancellorsville. So did our battered Army of the Potomac survive to fight another day. A great deal of blame flew in all directions, but Sam wiped his sweating brow, and apologized, and cursed the weather and the workers and everything else a boss curses to distract blame from himself. And he got away with it.

Where did it all come from, the ingenuity, the energy, the endurance that made possible our long, bitter fight? Ours, and the soldiers', too? We dared the impossible, did the undoable, bore the unbearable, not merely once but over and over again. I don't believe in fate or inevitable destinies, as I keep telling folks. But I do believe in a certain kind of inevitability. When you plant a potato, you get a potato. When you plant a rose, you get a rose. There is a pattern already in the seed, and it will unfold according to its nature. And yes, plants can be cross-pollinated, mutated, grafted onto other plants, and in various manners changed. Which is exactly my point. When that happens, the pattern is broken, and a new pattern comes in its place. But the pattern in place at the beginning must be dealt with. It may flower and bear fruit in its own way, or it may with great effort or by accident be changed.

So with the seedling of a nation; so with the seedling of a human soul.

I can't speak for any of my agents. But for myself, the patterns that shaped my actions in the war, and that sustained them, were already in place long before the war began.

I went to school in Philadelphia, at Mrs. Hollingworth's terribly respectable Academy for Young Women. I had strong personal ties in the city. My grandfather had been mayor there, long years back. He died at his post during a yellow fever epidemic. He sent his young family away, but he himself wouldn't go. I think the whole town had something of his spirit. It was an abolition town. A Quaker town. An Underground Railroad town. School there was more than reading, writing, and arithmetic. When Mrs. Hollingworth allowed us out of her hands, we trooped off in terribly respectable bevies to Independence Hall, to hear Lucretia Mott speak on behalf of the Female Anti-Slavery Society. We went to rousing concerts offered by the Hutchinsons, where we paid half price for our tickets. As long as women earned half of what men earned, the Hutchinsons said, they should pay only half as much for anything they bought. It seemed a perfectly sensible idea to me, but it upset some people worse than murder. We went to the Great Philadelphia Abolition Fair, where we bought everything we coveted without a pang of conscience, until every penny we had was gone, because all the profits went to anti-slavery work.

Sometimes we met and heard the testimony of runaways. I was not surprised by anything they said. I was from the South; I had seen the Negroes stumbling out of the iron works in Richmond, bent and coughing and almost too weary to walk. I knew you could get a slave flogged at the city jail for thirty cents, if you were too squeamish to do it yourself, or if you didn't want your neighbors to hear the commotion. I knew light-skinned, blue-eyed slave children weren't accidents of nature. And I knew that everything we saw or ever heard of in Virginia just got worse as you moved south. Field hands in the sugar country lived maybe seven years; replacing them was a regular but accepted operating cost, like transportation and new machinery. They didn't work themselves to death without encouragement; the driver's lash patrolled every field like a prison guard's rifle. And no, it wasn't used all the time, of course not. It was used when needed. The stocks as well, the bucking rail, the manacles, the cages. Anything that got results. Slave management was a science, discussed in magazines and newspapers, just like the breeding of cattle and the breaking of horses.

So when the runaways talked about their hardships—or when they refused to do so—I understood. What I did not understand, for quite a while, was how so many of them got away. Because, as a Southerner, I also knew the difficulties they faced. I knew about the curfews and the patrols. I knew if you were black you couldn't go anywhere without a pass, and you probably couldn't even read what the wretched paper said. I knew about the rewards for captured runaways, about the bounty men and their packs of hunting dogs.

Yet escaped slaves kept arriving safely in the North—not just in Philadelphia and other eastern cities, but even more of them in Ohio and points west. And yes, I had heard about the Underground Railroad, of course I had. It was mentioned at every abolitionist event. The Hutchinsons wrote songs about it. But when I was a young girl, the Underground Railroad sounded to me rather like the old Jewish God, something mysterious off in the distance, behind a burning bush. What it actually was, and how it actually worked, was terribly unclear. No one seemed in any hurry to explain. So, being the kind of child I was, I asked.

It was the summer of 1832—a year after the Nat Turner uprising. Harsh new slave codes were being written into law all over the South, even in Virginia. Fifty years of inching toward emancipation were being rolled back in months. A year ago, there had been over a hundred anti-slavery organizations below the Potomac. Soon there would be none. This backlash would gradually polarize the American nation. It would create in the South a political culture rooted less and less in ideologies of freedom, and more and more in ideologies of control. It was one of the beginnings of the Civil War. But on that hot afternoon in Philadelphia, all these things were far in the future, and our minds were on something very immediate. . . .

SUMMER, 1832 . . .

Rebecca Foxe was sitting in the wooden rocker on her back porch. Her daughter Becky was sitting on the step, and I was on the swing. It was Sunday, and the whole city was talking about a runaway who'd come all the way from Louisiana, with slave catchers on her trail every step of the way. The bounty men had traced her to the edge of Philadelphia, and then lost her again.

"But how did she manage it?" I wondered. The air was full of honeysuckle, and my head was full of fantasies. I was fourteen, and small; I barely had breasts yet. People thought I was a child, but inside my head, I knew I wasn't. It's distinctly possible that I have never been a child at all.

"Louisiana is an awful long way to come," Becky added.

"That it is," Rebecca agreed.

She was a quiet woman, sympathetic to abolition as most Quakers were, but soft-voiced about it. Her husband was one of the directors of the Pennsylvania Farmers and Merchants Bank; as a matter of fact, they were entertaining the entire board at dinner the same evening.

"The slaves always say they get help," I persisted. "A branch broken off from a certain kind of tree, pointing to the right road. A basket of food left under a carefully marked bridge. A hideout in a barn on such and such a farm. But who arranges all those things, and how do the runaways know how to find them?"

"Well, Elizabeth. If I knew, I'd be tempted to tell thee, and one day thou would be tempted to tell someone else, and that person would surely tell someone else, and soon everyone would know. Especially the sheriffs and the slave catchers. So . . ." Rebecca smiled a little, to soften what was so clearly a reprimand. "I do not ask."

"Oh."

I was terribly disappointed. But after I thought about it a little, I was also rather pleased. Becky and I were best friends, and we prided ourselves on our ability to keep each other's secrets. So many of our peers loved to tattle. Male or female, it didn't matter; they got such an obvious jolt of pleasure out of having something to reveal. We felt so superior, Becky and I. We had discovered, even then, that a well-kept secret could be a very satisfying kind of power.

I was several years older when I learned the Foxe house was itself a station on the Underground Railroad. Josiah Foxe and his wife were among the pre-eminent Philadelphia conductors. The slave from Louisiana had been hiding in the attic while we talked, and while the Pennsylvania bank directors dined later in the parlor.

I began, in small ways, to work for the Railroad myself. After I finished my studies, I kept going back to Philadelphia, not only to visit my sister and my friends, but to keep alive my links to the active abolition movement.

Becky Foxe never married, and as her parents grew older she took over much of the work. A plain girl in her teens, she blossomed into a graceful and striking woman in her thirties. On one visit, the one in particular that I'll never forget, I found her confined to her bed with a badly broken leg, at the same time as her mother was recovering from pneumonia.

I brought her candy and fruit from the market, and a new English novel. We sat for hours, I recall, talking as easily and as freely as though we'd parted just the day before. We shared gossip about old friends, and discussed the news of the day. It was 1854; only a few weeks earlier, the passing of the Kansas-Nebraska Bill had opened all the western territories to the possibility of becoming slave states—another one of those horrid compromises the country kept making every time the South bared its teeth. Had we been inclined to bad language, Becky and I might well have turned the air blue on the subject of Kansas.

But we talked about other things, too, including young men—this one's elegant manners, and that one's beautiful hair. Becky was the only person in the world who could ask me if I still expected to marry, without a whisper of disapproval in the question.

"I don't know," I told her. I no longer recall the name of the man

I'd been admiring, the one with the beautiful hair, but I said I'd marry him in two seconds flat if he asked me. Since he never would, though, the answer to her question was probably no.

"It does seem men are frightened of us," Becky said. "Of any woman who thinks for herself. Many of our friends believe I am too willful for my own good, and for the good of the cause."

"And do you agree with them?"

"Sometimes. But I have never learned how to be different."

"If you ever find a way, let me know. I might want to try it myself."

"Oh, thou mustn't, Liza. It is good for the world, I think, when some of us are willful. And at least here we can be if we want to. I can't think how it must be in the South. Does thou know Angelina Grimké can't go home again, not even to visit her family? They won't let her back across the Carolina border."

"Yes, I know."

"And what of thee, dear Liza? We keep hearing these dreadful stories. I think a season does not go by without a lynching somewhere. Is thy family safe? I mean, really? Thou must tell me the truth now."

"Oh, safe enough, I expect. Mother's never said an objectionable thing to anyone in her life. As for John and I, we've never published anything, never joined anything, never brought a scrap of abolition print back into the state. We just talk. You can still do that, at least in private, and at least in Virginia. But it has cost us, Becky. I'd be a considerable liar if I said otherwise. A lot of Mother's old friends have drifted away. The store used to make us a small fortune every year; now it just limps along."

"And for most people," Becky said, "that is coercion enough, isn't it? I do not wonder that so many accept the South's ways, and so many others leave."

"A few go strange in the head, too," I said dryly. "It seems Liza Van Lew might be one of them."

"Strange in the head? Thou?"

"Yes, indeed. It's all been too much for her, you see. Her father's death, and the shame of spinsterhood, poor thing, and altogether too much book learning, and no man in the house strong enough to give her proper direction . . . well, a frail female brain could hardly be expected to keep itself together under such circumstances. Or so it is whispered, apparently, among some who used to be our friends."

"Oh, Liza, surely not!"

"Surely yes, my dear. What else can they do? I'm not a man; they can't take me out in the woods and tie me to a tree and whip me. They can't provoke me into a duel. They can't get the law after me, because I haven't broken it. And I won't leave town, and I won't shut up. Besides, what rational woman would want to set all the Negroes free? Especially a single woman, an unprotected woman. She, most of all, should know the risks."

Becky said nothing for some time. She simply sat wrapped in her bedclothes, shaking her head a little.

"It is all rotten, isn't it?" she said finally. "Rotten from the root to the seed. The whole system. And now it is going to spread. All over the west, and maybe up here, too. Has thou seen Parker's new pamphlet? He thinks it is only a matter of time until the slaveholders test our laws in the North. He thinks they will bring slaves here, and appeal to the Constitution for their right to keep them. And he thinks if it goes to the courts they will win."

"The free states will never stand for it," I said. "Never!"

"No, I think not. People are finally waking up. All these years we talked abolition, and worked and prayed and sheltered the runaways, and everybody laughed at us, and threw rotten tomatoes, and called us crazy. Now they are going to the Republican meetings in such numbers the halls cannot hold them. Even people who don't care at all about the Negroes are angry now. They want their hundred and sixty acres in the Territories, when they've saved up a bit of money to go west. They know there'll be nothing left if it all goes for big plantations. And they are worried about their freedom, too.

They see how things are in the slave states. One cannot teach this. One cannot publish that. Even the pulpits are censored. Even the mails. Dear heavens, Liza, I cannot write thee a letter without wondering if it will be opened in the post office, before thou ever gets it. And finally it is sinking in here. If slavery spreads, all these things will spread with it."

"You have a lot of work to do," I said.

"Far too much, I fear. Why does thou not come and live here for a while, and work with us? Thou would make a great stir, I think."

"And be banned from the South forever, just like Miss Grimké? It would break my mother's heart, Becky. And my own, too, I expect."

"Wouldn't thou be more at home here? Really, deep down?"

I pondered her question. I knew the answer was no, but I had to think about it awhile to understand why. I loved Virginia. I loved the landscape, the heat, the unhurried days, the fragrant and languorous nights. But there was something else, too; a sense of belonging that went beyond birth, that held me to a past beyond my own, to an identity I could no more discard than I could discard my skin. I was a Southerner, all the way through to the bone.

"Virginia is my home, Becky," I said. "I won't be driven out. I won't give them the pleasure."

"Well," she said, smiling, "if thou must stay there, thou could have a worse reason."

We laughed, and the conversation turned to other things. We heard the commotion downstairs, the opening and closing of doors, the voices and hurrying of feet. We didn't pay much attention. People were always coming and going in Becky's house. Then her father came into the room, closed the door, and pulled up a chair near the bed.

"Miss Elizabeth." Josiah Foxe was a man who didn't say much, and what little he did say was always formal as a sworn oath. "Thou has always shown much kindness to my family. Now, I fear, I must ask thee for a greater kindness still."

"I will be happy to do anything for you I can," I told him.

"Will thou guide a poor unfortunate to a place of refuge? I cannot go, and as thou can see, there is at the moment no one else."

My heart raced. Nothing more needed to be said; I knew exactly what he meant.

"Yes, sir," I said. "Most willingly."

"God bless thee."

Two runaways and their guide, he told me, had arrived at the Sheffield warehouse, near the edge of the city.

"I will have the team and wagon hitched. If thou can pick the strangers up, and take them to Friend Saltby's house, he will shelter them and see them on their way. I grieve to have to ask thee, Liza. If thou should be arrested, I fear thy family will be terribly angry with me."

"Well, then, I shall have to make sure it doesn't happen, shan't I?"

"Their guide is very capable. I've never met him, but men I trust have sworn to it. Thou will be in better hands than mine, I hope."

He said God bless again, and went off to his unavoidable appointment. I went off to meet one of the world's most extraordinary thieves.

The Sheffield warehouse belonged to a Quaker friend of the Foxes, who dealt in farm implements and tools. A quiet, well-spoken young Negro took me into a back room. There were no black runaways there that I could see, only a ragged white man, lean as a water moccasin and formidably armed. He needed a shave and a haircut and a bath. Even more, I thought, he needed a week of sleep and a month of square meals.

Immediately he got to his feet, but he waited for me to speak. I said what I'd been told to say.

"I am here for Friend Josiah. I have a team and wagon outside."

"Good," he said. There was a world of thankfulness in the simple word. He favored me with a small but very graceful bow. "John

Fairfield. Swamp runner and slave stealer, at your most gracious service, ma'am."

I was, I admit, taken somewhat aback by this introduction.

"I'm Liza Van Lew."

"I'm honored to meet you."

He pursed his lips, making a remarkably clear and delicate imitation of a whippoorwill. The cover lifted cautiously from a trunk beside him, and two small black faces peered out.

"Oh, heavens," I whispered. "Children."

"Yes, ma'am. These are Bandy and Jen. Their ma's in Nova Scotia. She's been trying nigh on three years to get them back."

His voice was soft, with a smoky slowness I would have recognized anywhere. I wasn't at home, or in the Foxe house, or anywhere that was considered polite society. It made me a good deal bolder than I might otherwise have been.

"You're from Virginia, aren't you, sir?"

He smiled a little. "I am. And I expect you are, too, or you wouldn't have noticed. Have you left the Old Dominion for good?"

"No. I'm just here on a visit. And you?"

"Oh, I leave and go back. I leave with Negroes, and I go back without them. I dare say it's not the sort of profession my family had in mind for me."

"Profession?" Nobody I knew had ever called it such a thing before.

"Absolutely. Slave stealer for hire. Rates negotiable, cash in advance, delivery more or less guaranteed."

"You take money for it?"

"Even an abolitionist has to eat, sweet lady. And drink occasionally, too, I'm afraid."

He didn't look as though he ate much. He couldn't have been over thirty-five, and he still moved with the grace of a woodsman. Yet there was a permanent weariness about him, the aura of a life already become spent and desperate.

"A gentleman's son can hardly be expected to take up a trade," he went on. "And under the circumstances, my chances of inheriting the family plantation are frightfully small. So I have to earn my living as best I can, in some manner suited to my talents and my breeding. Both of which, I assure you, are exceptional."

There was a trace of wry amusement in his voice, and in his eyes. Only a trace, though. He appreciated the irony of his role, but the role itself was pitiless. Already I understood that. Already I was halfway in love with him.

"Are you kin to old Josiah?" he asked me.

"No. Just a family friend. I went to school with his daughter."

"Ah. You choose your friends well. I wish more Virginians would." He turned to the children, who all this while had merely knelt in their trunk, staring cautiously at the three of us.

"All right, in you go." He snapped the trunk shut, and pulled on a long, well-worn coat, carefully concealing the pistol and bowie knife on his belt. He and the young Negro carried the trunk outside, and heaved it into Josiah's wagon. The exertion brought on a fit of violent coughing, and he almost collapsed, hanging onto the wagon wheel with one hand, the other pressed over his mouth.

I stood beside him, helpless and stricken. It was the young black man who had the wits to run back inside and fetch a canteen of whiskey. The slave stealer took a long drink, wiped his mouth and leaned against the wagon, and then took another. In the clear light of day he looked even more bedraggled. But he straightened, finally, gave the canteen back with thanks, and turned to me with as much of a smile as he could manage.

"Too many nights in too many country jails, I'm afraid. No need to look so alarmed, Miss Liza. A few weeks of Canadian sunshine and it'll disappear. It always does."

He helped me onto the wagon, climbed up himself, and took the reins. We moved slowly onto the road.

"Where are the children from?" I asked him.

"North Carolina. Nice plantation, too. Not all that big, but mighty nice. They served the best terrapin in brandy I've ever eaten. And they had the nicest feather beds."

"You were a guest there?"

"It's the only way, with the smaller places. You have to have some excuse for getting near the slaves."

"And the owners never suspect you?"

"Not until it's too late. You wouldn't believe what a hard-eyed, hard-souled, abolition-hating cottonmouth I turn into when I go south. Passed myself off as a Kentucky salt trader once, up along the Kanawha, with two of the most cowed-looking blacks you ever saw, acting as my slaves. They made friends with the Negroes there; I made friends with the masters. I made a deal to have a couple of boats built for my new business. When some of our mutual property stole one of the boats and took off, well, the sympathy and commiseration I got, it nigh on broke my heart. I've always wondered what they thought when the second boat disappeared a week later, with more slaves in it, and that fine Kentucky trader to boot."

I laughed. I was quite overwhelmed with admiration, and couldn't resist the impulse to keep turning my head to look at him. His hair was very dark; I liked that. I liked the lean, wilderness grace that he carried as naturally as a cat. He wasn't otherwise beautiful, I suppose, but I really didn't notice, and I certainly didn't care. I wondered how he would look groomed and dressed as a Virginia cavalier, and decided the change would add nothing to his appeal— would diminish it, more likely; make him seem ordinary. Ordinary was something this man would never be.

"How many slaves have you taken north?" I wondered.

"Altogether? I really don't know. Several hundred, I guess."

"And you've never been caught?"

"Oh, I've been caught. Not hanged yet, though. Rank has its privileges, Miss Liza. Blood. Breeding. Money, even when you don't have any left. The appearances of things. Especially in the South. If I'd been born a Cracker, I'd be long dead."

That voice had its privileges, too. It was lazy, sensual, laced clean through with hot sun and honey. Perhaps it was what I liked best of all. He could have walked into my house, and walked out again with everything I owned, and purred it all into the sweetest compliment.

"Did your family ever own slaves?" he asked.

"Yes. For more than twenty years."

"And what made you an abolitionist?"

"Living in a slave state, probably."

He nodded. "I reckon so, Miss Liza. And that's something the slaveholders will never understand. Their very existence creates people like us. Not Yankees. Not troublemakers from outside. Slavery itself does it. Most of the white folks I work with in Ohio are Southerners."

It made me proud, hearing that. It made me proud, too, that he was talking to me like an ally.

"You said you've been caught," I asked. "How did you manage to . . . to get out of it?"

"I was acquitted once. I persuaded them I was a victim of bad luck and hasty judgment. The other two times I had to break out."

"You're very brave, to keep going back."

His answer was singularly dry. "Then I can assume you don't disapprove?"

"Disapprove? Dear heavens, how could anyone disapprove? I mean anyone here."

"The Quakers disapprove. Levi Coffin in Cincinnati thinks I'm a wicked man."

"But don't you work with the Quakers?"

"All the time. They shelter my runaways. They give me money when I need it. I'm sure they'd do most anything to help me if I got in trouble. But they do disapprove."

"Because you ask for money from the Negroes?"

"No. And I should tell you, Miss Liza, I only ask for money because I need it to do the job. Every run I make, I have to buy things—food, ammunition, disguises, railroad and boat tickets.

Bribes too, sometimes. It all has to be paid for somehow. And I've never refused a job because the kin couldn't pay. No. The Quakers object because I steal the Negroes. I don't wait for them to come. I go and fetch them. And I do whatever I have to, to get them out."

"But . . . but what else could you do?"

"Wait for God, I suppose." After a brief silence, he added: "Don't misunderstand me, Miss Liza. I think the world of the Quakers. We wouldn't have an Underground Railroad if it wasn't for them. But I'm a fighter, I guess, and I always will be. And you know, sometimes I wonder if they disapprove near as much as they let on."

I wondered, too. The majority of white Railroad workers were just like my friends the Foxes. They were devout and respectable people, almost to excess. Church choirmasters. City elders. Quiet schoolteachers. Honest, hardworking farmers. All in all, the most upright people in the land.

So it ought to have bothered them a little, breaking the law. Lying to their neighbors, and even to their spouses, sometimes. Fashioning secret rooms in their houses, and secret floors in their wagons, and secret pockets in their hats. Forging documents, or stealing them; and even, once in a while, using a crowbar on a law-abiding lock.

It didn't bother them a bit—rather the opposite. I had always felt the excitement in the Foxe house when a rescue was under way. And once, just a year or two ago, as I sat with the family in the same backyard, on a dreamy, mellow summer night, Josiah let it all slip. He told me how much it tickled him sometimes, driving down the broad streets of Philadelphia in his somber black cape with the stiff white collar, with food or clothing or papers for the runaways hidden in his wagon, or maybe the runaways themselves, and himself a gray-haired bank director and a man who hardly ever smiled. Smiling all over inside. *I am not what I seem. Nothing is quite what it seems, and therein lies one of the marvels of God.*

John Fairfield's languorous voice broke into my thoughts, and echoed them.

"I think we're all born with an incurable appetite for mischief.

And it's a good thing, too. If we weren't, humankind would sink into a bog of tyranny, and never come out again."

We were approaching a crossroads, and he asked me for directions. To the left, a few miles down the road, was the Saltby farm. I was dreadfully tempted to point him right, so the journey could continue. So I could talk to him some more, and look at him. So I could charm him, perhaps, make him want to come to Philadelphia again, or even to Richmond, just to see me.

But he was hungry, and tired, and there was always the possibility of encountering some overzealous official who might wonder why such a well-dressed young woman was traveling with such a disreputable-looking man, and what they might be packing in their trunk. . . .

"Left," I said. "It's not far now."

Never did time or distance pass so quickly. Before I knew it we were standing in the Saltby yard, surrounded by barking dogs and eager children. I couldn't bring myself to say good-bye. I accepted the Saltbys' invitation to come in. I drank tea with them, and ate a bit of cake. Till the day I died, I would never be able to call to mind who else was in the house that day, who else was in the room, only John Fairfield. I could not take my eyes off him, except by the rudest force of will. I wondered if he noticed; if anyone else noticed. I didn't especially care.

But finally I had to leave. The Foxes would begin to worry about me. John Fairfield walked back into the yard with me. His eyes were soft and melancholy. I wish so much, now, that I had kissed him good-bye.

"Fair Virginian, it has been a pleasure and an honor to meet you."

He bowed, and took my hand, and touched it to his lips. His hair was so long it spilled over my sleeve, and so tangled that little bits of leaf and rubbish were caught in it like burrs.

Through all my life, I would remember the moment, and the man. The incongruousness of it, and the perfect beauty. Drawing room gallantry and raw violence. Slavery at any cost, and freedom also.

The best of my beloved South, and the worst, framed as in a photograph, forever. Years after, people would ask me when I became a Union agent. I never told them, but I know it was that very afternoon.

"I am honored to have met you also," I told him. "It's a meeting I'll never forget."

I wanted to wrap him in my arms. I wanted to send the wagon away with someone else, and stay with him. Go back with him to the cane country, to the rivers and the swamps, the boats loading in the dead of night, the half-hidden trails with strange and secret markings, *when the sun comes up and the first quail calls, follow the drinking gourd. . . .*

He helped me onto the wagon and handed me the reins.

"Tell that Quaker Josiah to pray for me," he said. "I don't reckon on having much time to do it for myself."

He wasn't thinking of his death, probably, when he said it; he was thinking of his work, of his turbulent, fugitive life. But his words had ice all around them, and they chilled me to the heart.

I never saw him again.

I never forgot him, either. I won't say I was in love with him, since you wouldn't believe me. It was only a single meeting, after all, a single afternoon. You'd smile, the way my sister did, when I was foolish enough to tell her, mellowed with Christmas brandy and an overdose of trust. *You don't fall in love with men,* she said. *You fall in love with ideals.*

It may be so. But something about the man's proud spirit caught hold of my own, and through all the rest of my life it never let go. I wrapped every memory I had in golden foil, and took them out sometimes at night, and stroked them with my fingers, and held them in my arms. I never came north, or talked to anyone from the movement, without trying to discover if anyone had seen him, if anyone knew where he might be, or what he might be doing. It was Levi Coffin from Cincinnati who finally told me what became of him. What probably became of him. Years had passed by then, and some things weren't secret anymore.

Friend Levi still thought he was a wicked man. He shook his head half a dozen times, talking about John Fairfield; shook his head and smiled, both at the same time.

"He was something of a rogue, Liza, and I tell thee truly, I don't know what God is going to do with him, in the other life. I truly don't."

He drank, apparently. He blasphemed. He consorted with lewd women. He believed in very little, if indeed he believed in anything at all. And he killed, with cool efficiency and without guilt, every slave-catcher unwise enough to go after him, and unlucky enough to get within his reach. He left poisoned bait for the dogs. He shot the men from ambush, and set deadly snares to trap them in the swamps.

Yet his whole life was given over to freeing slaves. Giving women back to their husbands, and men to their wives, and children to their families. Giving hope to the desperate, and a future to those who had none. What indeed was God going to do with such a man?

He disappeared about three years after I met him. It was natural in his work to just slip quietly away, telling no one where he was headed. Only this time he didn't come back. Months passed. Rumors drifted north of a failed uprising in Tennessee, of blacks in arms, of a white man who led them, and was killed. His friends in Ohio wondered and feared the worst. Months stretched into years, but no word ever came, not of the man, nor even of the rebellion itself, whatever sort of rebellion it was—a real one, or just a handful of runaways getting trapped, and trying to fight their way to freedom. It simply slid below the surface of the world, like a stone disappearing in a swamp.

We saw it many times in the slave South, that conjurer's trick of history: now you see it, now you don't. On Monday something happened, and by Tuesday afternoon it never happened at all. Occasionally, of course, it was the other way around. Occasionally history became retroactive, and a crime was fashioned to fit the punishment.

Slave-owners say *Uncle Tom's Cabin* was a slander, a piece of fanaticism, a pack of lies. They say the runaways were coached to make up horrible stories, so as to inflame the passions of the North. The fact is, the worst stories of slavery have never been told, and they never will be. Like the bones of John Fairfield, like the bones of hundreds and thousands of forgotten Negro people, they lie in unrecorded places; they are ashes at the feet of lynching trees, they are silt in the rivers. The guilty will never tell them, and the innocent cannot; all that is left of them is a darkness in the windows of the world.

SIX

———————✳

THE NAME AND
APPEARANCE OF A LADY

Two ladies, mother and daughter, living on Church Hill, have
lately attracted public notice by their assiduous attentions to the
Yankee prisoners . . . expending their opulent means in aiding and
giving comfort to the miscreants who have invaded our sacred soil,
bent on raping and murder. . . . Out upon all pretexts of
humanity!

Richmond Enquirer, July 1861

"If you dare to show sympathy for any of those prisoners," said a
gentleman, shaking his finger in my face. "I would shoot them as I
would blackbirds—and there is something on foot up against you
now!"

Elizabeth Van Lew

. . . The rule that everyone bearing the name and appearance of a
lady, should receive the delicate gallantry and considerate
tenderness which are due to a lady, is not absolutely without
exception.

George Frederick Holmes, Southern pro-slavery writer

It was true what I told Becky Foxe: our family lost a lot of our friends because of my abolition views. We lost more of them during the war, for being Unionists. Yet my mother never changed, never closed her heart or her door, never grew bitter. In that way, she was stronger than I was. She judged no one. She may well have saved my life with her quiet gentleness; certainly she made our work easier. We remained respectable in spite of everything. Strange and Northern bred and not to be trusted, railed at in the newspapers and pointed at in the streets, and yet, in a fashion that only rank could establish and only a certain kind of social grace preserve, we remained respectable. People still came to call. Not many, and none at all from among the Rebel firebrands, but some still came, even some with sons or brothers in the Southern army. Soldiers themselves came, occasionally, men we used to know, and strangers, too, just passing through, broke and hungry. We refused absolutely to contribute to the Southern war effort; we knitted no socks, we sewed no flags, we gave to no bazaars and bought from none. But a hungry soldier could come to Mother's door and ask for food, anytime, and he would get it. Once, I remember, two Alabama boys came late on a Sunday afternoon. They were ragged and rough-looking, both of them. One walked with a makeshift cane, and the other had his head wrapped in a dirty bandage and coughed a lot. Both of them stank. They spoke gracelessly, and didn't know enough to take their hats off in the house without Josey telling them.

Mother told Mary to cook them up a pan of grits and potatoes, and a few scraps of the leftover chicken. They ate like starving animals; they cleaned the last scraps from the plates with dirty fingers, and licked them off like little boys.

They hadn't et so good, they said, since their cousin Sarry got hitched. They reckoned we was real good folks. Officers' wives or such, but not like some. They got sent away, down the street. Lady said they looked like somethin' bad, he couldn't call to mind the word she used, but she thought they wasn't good soldiers. She thought they was just pretendin' to be hurt. Wasn't fair, her sayin' it. They killed themselves a whole passel of Yankees. They even got a Yankee colonel once, standin' up on a ledge with his spyglass, like he wasn't made of human stuff. That was at Gaines Mill. They was all over after that, raisin' hell, more hell'n you could shake a stick at. Fightin' was just like huntin', only better, you got to see the whole country. They never seen folks livin' so high like here in Richmond; such fine houses, and so many fancy things; they figured we must be just about the richest people in the whole wide world. . . .

"Them two was born in the swamps," Josey said when they were gone. "And brought up in the barnyard."

"They're just poor," my mother said. "And they never learned how to lie."

She was right, of course. My mother was right about most things. Of course I lost patience with her sometimes, as the worldly always do with those who are impossibly good. But mostly I was awed by the way she embodied the ideal of ladyhood I had never achieved. The gentleness, the impeccable discretion, the absolutely authentic good will toward everyone who happened to cross her path—all achieved without surrendering her sharp mind or her well-honed conscience.

I wasn't like her. I didn't know how to be. But I envied her mastery of that impossible identity, Lady with a capital L. I had seen enough ladies to know how many were pretending, how many hid under their fans and their perfect attire a spirit as hard as my own— yes, and harder. The Union armies discovered the same thing when they came south; they ran into a whole legion of steel magnolias, well-bred women who spat on them and called them names and slammed carriage doors on their fingers; women who hated as fiercely as men, and took the same pleasure in it. Mother and I met one we never forgot, born of the finest blood in Virginia, who kept a collection of dead Yankee bones in her garden, nicely laid out under the walnut tree, where she could smile on them first thing every morning.

But my mother's Ladyhood was absolutely real. And I'd be a howling liar if I didn't acknowledge how valuable it was. There was a great outcry when we first started visiting Libby Prison. We were denounced in the newspapers. They didn't name us, of course; they didn't have to. There was only one "widowed lady and her daughter living on Church Hill" who went to see the Union prisoners.

One of Mother's old friends, Dr. MacAllister, tried to talk us into giving the project up. He was over sixty—too old, he said, to re-arrange his whole life over politics. He was no Union man. He'd supported Secession, though he admitted he did so with misgivings. All his kin were Rebels; his grandsons were in the army. But he liked us, and he didn't see as how he could stop.

"I expect you can't change your way of looking at all this, any more than I can," he said. "But there's a lot of fools in the world, Mrs. Van Lew, and it isn't wise to be giving them an excuse. Some might read that editorial in the paper today, and figure they should come up here and burn you out."

It was late, and dinner was over. MacAllister sat back in his chair, nursing his sherry.

"I don't think anyone takes those editorials seriously," my mother said. "How could they? The newspapers are always railing at some-one. Liza and I aren't doing any harm."

"I don't want to frighten you," MacAllister said. "But I've heard some . . . some hard things. People say you're committing treason."

"Feeding the hungry? Visiting the sick? Surely no sensible person confuses kindness with treason. As for those with no sense, I think it would be hard to live one's life to please them."

"With all due respect," he said, "there are many Southern soldiers and their families who are in need of your kindness."

"Yes, indeed. And there are thousands to whom they can turn.

Who's to look after those who have nowhere to turn? Our good Lord didn't busy himself with the most admired citizens, Doctor, or the most beloved. He didn't go to those who had all of Israel behind them. He went to the despised, and the unwanted—and, yes, even the unworthy. He went to those who needed him most. We are only making a small effort to follow his example."

This response impressed me a great deal. It must have impressed Dr. MacAllister as well, for he said nothing for a time, and then he raised his glass.

"Mrs. Van Lew, say no more. I should have known better than to pit logic against virtue. It loses every time. Do be careful, though, I beg you."

"Of course. And I thank you most kindly for your concern."

Dr. MacAllister never questioned Mother's activities again. He died soon after the war. I've never met him in the afterworld. I wonder sometimes what he would think, now that everyone knows what we were really doing. I wonder if he would still be my mother's friend.

The afterworld is an uncommonly peculiar place. Mind you, when I lived in your world, I thought it was an uncommonly peculiar place, too. So perhaps nothing very much has changed. All the craziness of human living is still with us. And we can still be surprised, totally and completely surprised, left with our feet scrambling for solid ground and our mouths hanging wide as a barn door.

There is someone very odd on the street in front of us as we move up Shockoe Hill. I look, and I look again, but I simply can't tell if she's a revener, or a living person. She's young and rather pretty, and she's dressed the way the belles of Richmond longed to dress in the war years, but hardly ever could. Two Rebel soldiers accompany her, one walking at each shoulder; they are very definitely dead.

"Do you know who that is, Lucy?"

Lucy doesn't know. Neither does anyone else—which wouldn't matter at all, if the young lady were an ordinary human, or an ordinary ghost, if she didn't have such a disturbing and discordant air about her. We follow for a while, but then my curiosity gets the better of me, and we slip around them and rush ahead. Three of us spread across the sidewalk; the rest of us swing onto trees and poles and ledges. The Rebels can still get by us, of course, but only by being terribly undignified.

They stop; the young soldiers are annoyed but polite. Face-to-face now, I recognize them both as members of the Virginia Blues. A whole regiment of gentlemen, who decided to fight as common soldiers rather than use their social position to obtain commissions. I never could decide if they were truly noble or truly silly.

"Will you excuse us, ladies?" one of them murmurs. "Gentlemen? You all are blocking the path."

We don't move. The young woman is decidedly strange—more substantial than we are, somehow, and yet so much less real. I already dislike her, but I am nonetheless fascinated.

"We mean no offense, gentlemen," I tell them. "But it being such a special occasion and all, we wondered if you might introduce us to your charming guest."

The nearest Virginia Blue regards me haughtily. "We might well have done so," he says, "if you'd approached us proper. But to tell you the truth, madam, we don't much like your style. And seeing you're with Mr. Ruth here, I don't think we like your colors, either."

The young lady's eyes grow even wider. If that is possible.

"Well, I declare," she cries. "Are these here Yankees?"

"Yankees, no," Will Rowley says quietly. "Federalists, yes. A difference of considerable importance to some of us."

Meaning Sam Ruth and me, in particular. *I do love you, Will Rowley. I truly do.*

For a moment, the young lady seems puzzled by Will's answer, but her escort bends his head a shade, and offers a simple explanation.

"*Southern* Yankees," he murmurs. "The worst kind of all."

We just smile, and refuse to go away. The young men give us hard and resentful looks, and finally one of them says grimly, "Are you going to let us pass? Or do we to have to pitch you in the bushes?"

"Three uff you and eight uff us? They don't learn, Villy, do they?"

"Please. My young friends. Allow me to be of assistance, if I may?"

We all turn and look to my left, whence a newcomer is approaching. I recognize him immediately, although he never actually lived in Richmond for very long. It's Thomas Cooper DeLeon—Cooper the elegant, the man about town, the chronicler of the FFVs. He was born in South Carolina, of the most elite Spanish ancestry. (He would insist I mention this, since to Cooper nothing in the world was more important than blood.) During the war he served as a civilian attaché to the Confederate government, but what his duties actually were, none of us could ever fathom. The unkind suggested that partying, and gathering material for his books, comprised the most of it. After the war he wrote endlessly about the South. The Rebels loved him; few men did more than he to turn the Rebellion into glory, and the Old South into the best of all possible worlds.

He moves between us, smiling at the soldiers and the lady, all of whom he obviously knows. Then he turns toward me and my friends.

He was thin when he lived. He's positively wispy now, but he draws himself up to his best height and acknowledges our existence with a perfect mixture of politeness and hostility. No one can do it quite as perfectly as a well-bred Southerner.

"Miss Van Lew. Mr. Ruth."

He doesn't acknowledge the others. He looks right through them. No pun intended.

"Mr. DeLeon. How good to see you again."

"I presume, Miss Van Lew, that you've heard what they say about cats and curiosity?"

"Indeed. But you will humor the nice kitty, won't you? There are eight of us, after all, as Mrs. Lohmann pointed out, and it would be such bad taste to appear at the great convention of Southern culture with your wisps all in tatters."

"Speaking of people who never learn, I must say the Yankee resort to intimidation remains as quick and as predictable as ever."

"Who first offered to throw who in the bushes?"

"Oh, never mind. This is hardly a *casus belli*. Miss Scarlett, allow me to present to you Miss Elizabeth Van Lew, Mr. Samuel Ruth, and their assorted underlings, every one of them traitors to the Southern cause. Miss Scarlett O'Hara, of Atlanta, Georgia. Figuratively speaking."

It takes a moment for the thing to register in my mind. Will's mouth is hanging open. So is Lucy's. The Lohmanns are staring at the rest of us, wondering why. They were never interested in books.

"But . . ." Lucy looks at Cooper, at me, at Scarlett O'Hara. "But that's ridiculous. She's a character in a story. She doesn't belong here. She isn't even real."

"A hundred million people know her name," Cooper says. "How many people know yours?"

"If that's your standard of comparison, Mr. DeLeon," I say coldly, "you'd best cancel your conference and go back to wiggling grass. Southern womanhood isn't going to be impressed."

"And just what do you mean by that?" snaps the green-eyed, black-haired, foot-stamping unghost.

Rude it may be, but I stare at her nonetheless. Scarlett O'Hara. The great romantic heroine of the land. The image of the South in the eyes of half the world. "Well, I declare." "I'm never going to be hungry again." I wonder if her hunger was like Hetty Cary's starvation parties: no wine served, bring your own ham and paté. Now she's actually among us, as though she were as much a part of our history as ourselves. I truly don't know whether to laugh or to cry.

We greet her politely nonetheless. The moment we have done so, she takes both her companions' arms, very pointedly, and blinks up at one of them.

"I'd feel so dreadfully bad if we were late, Robbie."

Will Rowley bends to whisper in my ear.

"Perhaps we should just move aside, and let our erring sister go?"

Which we do then, with all the necessary polite words, and with some unnecessary, dreadfully hollow smiles. Later, I will see the charm of her coming here. The rightness, even. Perhaps there is no one more fitting for us to meet and come to terms with than this conscienceless daughter of Tara.

But just now, I am angry. Although we don't live in the world, we know something of what passes there. We know, especially, how we are remembered—ourselves, and our enemies as well. As long as the war generation was still alive, the men and women who fought to save the Union were looked upon with pride. But as they passed one by one to shadows, then began the great forgetting, the great denial. Americans wanted their heroes cut from the right cloth, and increasingly that cloth turned out to be gray.

The newly dead would come and murmur at our sides: "You won't *believe* what they're writing about you now." For a long stretch, as the decades and the other wars came and went, I was inclined to cringe and slither away. *Please. I don't want to know.*

What a foolish time it was! Chivalry dripping from the chandeliers, Yankee barbarians tramping through the cotton, and poor Miss Scarlett without a gown for the ball. Black folks in two shades only, the stupid and the bad. Slavery as just another way to hoe the garden, no problem for anyone until those crazy abolitionists started a war over it. Lee the saint, Grant the butcher, and all those beautiful magnolia-draped plantations caught in the middle. There were no issues that mattered, there was nothing at stake, nobody was really wrong except John Brown. The war itself was the great wickedness, and Sherman's March the great atrocity, the cruelest thing to ever happen in the whole history of America—and poor Miss Scarlett, wouldn't you know it, she got in *his* way, too.

Our history had turned into Rebel history, mostly: the gospel according to Old Jube. It took nigh on a century for things to begin to change again, for a worldlier generation to mature, a generation brought up hard against the clear face of evil. Not sin, which after all is only a broken rule, but evil, which thrives best when no rules need to be broken, when the rules themselves are wicked, and decent men and women carry them out without question, simply because they are the rules.

That generation, I am told, is rediscovering us.

So I watch Scarlett flaunt away, and I think maybe it's like the spring of '63. Maybe we've just begun to fight. Scarlett's silver voice drifts back to us, with a distinct note of outrage in it: "Who *are* those awful people?"

I can well imagine her companion's reply.

Cooper is about to leave, too, but I catch his attention before he can do so.

"Mr. DeLeon. May I speak with you a moment?"

He doesn't want to speak with me in the least. But whatever else, Cooper is always a gentleman. He nods his head very slightly.

"If you wish."

"How did all of this come about, bringing a fictional person here? Whoever thought of such a thing?"

"Actually, I don't remember. Somebody said it for a joke, quite a while back, in the wee hours of the morning. We had a good chuckle over it, and then we started to realize it was a smashing good idea. Don't you think so? The most famous Southern lady in all of literature, as a guest of honor for the conference?"

"I think it's rather ironic."

"Ironic? Why?"

"Well, I never read the book; it was after my time. But from what I understand, the most famous Southern lady in all of literature never cared a fig for your precious Confederacy. It made a mess of her social life. All her friends talking politics instead of parties. All those handsome young men running around chasing Yankees when they should have been chasing her. And the blockade, I've been told, simply ruined her wardrobe. It's such a pity she wasn't in Wilmington when that corset ship came in. Do you remember? 'Sixty-three I think it was. Your soldiers were short of everything God ever made except bugs, and here comes a blockade runner through all the Yankee traps and guns, with forty thousand ladies' corsets packed in his hold, pure whalebone and worth a howling fortune. He was the toast of Virginia for weeks. Now if only Miss Scarlett had met him, instead of Rhett Butler, maybe there'd have never been a book."

Cooper is not amused.

"You think we're all just impossibly silly, don't you?" he says coldly.

"Only some of you. And in this case, I think the Daughters of the Confederacy might very well agree with me."

He is only a foot or so taller than me, but just now he looks down at me from an immense height.

"Miss Scarlett was, and is, An Indomitable Lady."

That's how he says it, in capitals, the same way people talk about The Last Supper and The Golden Age of Greece. The Indomitable Lady is an icon, something raised out of ordinary history and existence into the realm of lasting symbol. And that's fair enough; I have my icons, too.

But why Scarlett? How does someone so cold, so breathtakingly selfish, so lacking in any whisper of social or moral or political understanding, get to be an icon? Would it ever happen to a man? They say even Rhett Butler had a few shreds of integrity when the chips were down; and even Attila the Hun liked his own kids.

Maybe the lady who is nothing but self is simply a reverse image, the other face of the lady who isn't supposed to have a self at all. Maybe that's how Scarlett came to be here, how they were able to summon her at all. She's an icon, perhaps, but not the sort that Cooper DeLeon imagines. She's made out of all the energies of the women whose ordinary lives were bent and snipped and shut away, energies turned icy now, like vampire blood, still feeding on the South's old, false dreams. . . .

"An Indomitable Lady? Well, if you say so, Mr. DeLeon. But you'll keep her well supplied with cavaliers, I hope? I understand she never cared much for culture, and we certainly wouldn't want her to be bored."

It's a spiteful thing to say, of course, but it has the most interesting effect on his appearance. He gets even longer and thinner, like a shaft of smoke in a cold room.

"I wish you good morning, madam. And while we're offering free advice, let me offer some to you. Don't bring your pack of riffraff too close to things. I personally wouldn't waste my time making trouble for you. Others might not be so forgiving."

"It's a strange country where the loyal need to be forgiven by the traitors."

He doesn't answer. He merely glides away with his marvelous air of untroubled superiority.

"Did you hear him?" Angelina says to me indignantly. "The man called us riffraff."

I am not indignant. I am amused—at least for the moment. It's so like Cooper and his kind. There were no disloyal or discontented Southerners in their Confederacy. The women who rioted for bread in the streets of Richmond in '63, and nearly every other Southern city afterward? They were riffraff, too. The people of East Tennessee who wanted no part of breaking up the Union? Just more riffraff. The bands of draft resisters and deserters who made northern Alabama as dangerous for wandering Rebels as a Union camp? Still more riffraff.

My friends fell into the same category, of course. Ironically, so did General Winder's Plug Uglies. Reginald Cleary might well have hanged me like he wanted to, if anyone had taken him seriously enough. But too many other people looked down on him, and Winder never trusted his judgment. I was no spy, Winder said; I wouldn't know a Parrot gun from a parrot in a cage. Besides, I lived on Church Street, and there were things you simply didn't do to people who lived on Church Street. Especially if they were ladies.

This was an attitude Reginald Cleary never understood. He thought having two sets of rules, one for the rich and another for the poor, was a pretty stupid way to run a war. And he was right; it was one of the things that did the Confederacy in.

It was also one of the things that saved my neck on a couple of occasions. Those hot dry days after Brandy Station, for example, when Grant had Vicksburg under siege and Lee was marching into Pennsylvania. . . .

JUNE, 1863 . . .

The winter's Rebel victories had rubbed off on Cleary; as the weeks passed he grew more and more aggressive. He was a continuing quiet knife of fear in my heart. But he never drove the knife to the hilt; never arrested me, never searched my person. Winder wanted evidence first. Solid evidence. Facts, not suspicions. You don't throw a lady into Castle Thunder on suspicion of anything.

At least not yet.

Every day I went out, Cleary and one of his men would follow me. Sometimes they hovered close by; more often they simply kept me in sight, and took note, I suppose, of every place I visited: the different market stalls, the apothecary shop, the bakery, the restaurant of Willy and Angelina Lohmann, where I finally sat down exhausted, to have a cup of tea. Nelson stood patient guard over my purchases outside.

I always picture Cleary having a little debate with himself while he watched us from the corner.

Should I or shouldn't I? She's been all over hell's half acre; there might be all kinds of stuff in those bags. Naw, why bother? She wouldn't go off to Lohmann's, and just leave her nigger looking after it, if she had anything to hide. Then again, maybe she would; she's as brazen as God ever made them. What better way to throw me off? Look, everybody, how harmless and innocent I am, just a footsore old biddy drinking my tea.

Cleary won the debate with himself that day—or lost it, perhaps.

He strolled over and, without a word to the black man, began to lift a bag of oranges out of the wheelbarrow.

"Them's Miss Elizabeth's belongings, sir," Nelson told him. "You oughtn't to be doing that."

"What did you say, Cuffee?"

All Negroes, under all circumstances, had to obey any white person, anywhere. That was both custom and law. On the other hand, a Negro protecting a master's property was expected to protect it diligently. My servant was in a considerable dilemma. He shifted his feet, but he didn't back away.

"Them's Miss Elizabeth's things. You take any of them, sir, we'll get the law after you."

"I am the law, you stupid black bastard!"

"Well, then, what you stealing for?"

Cleary swore, and shoved Nelson aside. He spilled the oranges out on the boardwalk. I expect it outraged him, seeing them, thinking what they must have cost. Half the children in Richmond had forgotten what an orange tasted like. And here I was buying them by the basketful for the prisoners in Libby. To Cleary, this was treason all by itself, all this food, all this aid and comfort for the enemy. There was a ham and several fresh-killed chickens. There were bags of crisp vegetables and herbs, jars of preserves and pickles for which the Confederate soldiers in the field would have traded their souls. There were dried herbs and candied ginger. There was a huge box of tea.

I still feel cold, remembering how I looked up from my table and saw him; how, for the briefest moment, I simply couldn't move. Then I stood up, pushed open the door of the restaurant, and stepped outside. The sun was deadly; the air was so heavy you had to shove it aside to walk. People were gathering from all directions. I suppose we were a sight to behold, the pair of us: a grown man hunkered down on his knees, poking his knife into a head of lettuce; and a grown woman with tangled hair picking her way down the boardwalk, carefully stepping over its cracks.

I did the only thing I could. I stared at the great mess of my carefully acquired treasures, all mangled and lying in the dirt, and I burst into tears.

"Oh, Nelson, you worthless, stupid creature, you've gone and spilt them all!"

Then I was on my knees, too, gathering things up in great frantic armfuls, shoving them at Nelson, stuffing them back into bags, snatching them right out of Cleary's hands.

"Madam! I haven't finished, madam, just stand aside now, do you hear me? I haven't finished!"

It was no use. I was utterly demented, as if I didn't hear a word the man said, as if I didn't even know he was there. He was snatching things out of the wheelbarrow and I was putting them back, everything popping up and down like vegetable jacks-in-a-box. It was funny, I suppose, but it was also dangerous, the kind of moment that could turn on you, that could go suddenly and absolutely out of control. I knew it, but I couldn't stop, didn't dare stop, hanging on to my lunacy the way you hang on to a wolf's tail.

"Madam, that's enough now! Stand aside, or by God, I'll have you dragged off! Mathieson! God damn it, Mathieson, get her out of my way!"

Something called Mathieson elbowed through the crowd, a big brute of a man taking my arms from behind and dragging me backward. *Just calm down, little lady, calm down, do you hear, this ain't going to do you no howlin' good.* . . . Nelson took a single, half-lunging step toward him and buckled as Cleary swung a nightstick full across his midsection. Before the black man could get his breath, Cleary had a pistol in his hand.

"You so much as blink, Cuffee, I'll blow your worthless black brains out! You got me?"

Neither of us blinked much after that. Perhaps I babbled a little; I don't remember. The sun hammered on my face and my eyes like a club. The man's breath and body heat came at me in waves; he stank of old tobacco and sweat. I knew it was all over. They would stick me in a rat-infested cell in Castle Thunder, and in a couple of days they'd take me down to the fairgrounds and hang me. But first they'd want to know things. Who gave me those little pieces of paper? Who was going to carry them across the lines, and how, and where? They asked Timothy Webster the same sort of questions. By the time they hanged him, he couldn't walk. But maybe they wouldn't do that to a woman. What they'd do to Nelson, though . . . no, I couldn't even let it into my mind.

The crowd was huge now, and still gathering, a great blur of faces, an equal blur of outrage and fascination. Some of them called me a traitor and a spy, the way they always did. But some were calling Cleary names instead—angry citizens fed up with every form of bullying authority, earnest young soldiers who didn't think this sort of thing was what they were fighting for. *Plug Ugly,* they yelled at him. *Baltimore scum. Thought old Winder fired all the riffraff, how come he missed you? Gawd almighty, Mister Cleary, whyn't you go down to the crazy house? You can find yourself forty spies in one go and they're already all locked up!*

I knew the last voice. Martin Lipscomb. This was New Market, after all; I had friends in the crowd. But it wouldn't help me in the least, if Cleary found the messages.

Maybe he won't find them. Maybe they're well enough hidden. Please, God, don't let him find them!

He went through everything, bag by bag. I don't know how long it took, several forevers, my body gone ice cold in the sun, as though it were already getting used to the thought of being dead. He found nothing. When he was finished, he got to his feet. He looked at me. I knew exactly what he wanted to do. What he would have done, if he had dared: arrested both of us anyway. Confiscated everything; taken it away and gone through it all again, leaf by leaf and bone by bone if need be, all by himself with nobody distracting him, nobody making him feel like a fool. He had persuaded himself before he began that there was something to find, and he would have looked and looked until he found it.

"Give it up, Cleary," somebody shouted. "Go beat up a drunk."

He had me and he knew it, the way a cat knew he had a mouse in a hole. But he'd found nothing, and without it he couldn't just drag me away. Not a lady from Church Street, a lady from a good family, who wasn't even right in the head. Winder would kill him. He made a brief, frustrated gesture to his man Mathieson, and I stumbled free. Nelson and I packed the wheelbarrow again and Nelson rolled it carefully away. Cleary didn't even bother to follow us home.

I didn't say a word to Nelson until we were safe in the house on Church Hill. I sat down in the first chair I came to and took a handkerchief from my reticule. I thought it very possible I would be sick.

"That was too close, Nelson."

"Yes'm."

"Are you all right? I didn't mean what I said, you know. About being stupid. It was purely for the Rebels' benefit."

"I know." He tried to smile, but didn't quite manage it. "I figured we was skinned rabbits, Miss Liza. That man sure enough wants your head."

I wiped my face, and called for Josey to make some tea. If I had been the drinking sort, I could have put away a pint of Tennessee whiskey right then, without even stopping for breath.

It wasn't the first time. It was merely worse than before. I wondered if it would keep getting worse.

"Josey?"

"Yes'm, Miss Liza?"

"Bring my tea to the library. And one of those chickens, too. The one that's got a toe missing."

"In the library?" She looked at Nelson, oddly, and back at me. "You want one of them chickens in the library? *Before* we cooks it?"

"Yes. Before you even wash it. Right this minute."

She brought it promptly, and watched fascinated as I probed inside its skinny neck with a pair of tweezers, and pulled out a sliver of foil.

"Lord Jesus almighty. . . ."

"Yes, indeed. Just imagine if Mr. Cleary had decided to take this home and cook it for his supper."

Inside the foil were two small pieces of paper, the second piece carefully signed: *R. L. Sanders.* The handwriting was precise and neat. Almost too much so, as if written for the approval of a difficult teacher. It was Mariel's first communication from inside the Rebel White House.

It took me almost an hour to decode it all. Mariel, still new at her task, had included too much. There were items that were already public knowledge. One or two others had no military or political relevance that I could see. And then there was another, which at first seemed only marginally important.

Gen. Lee's son still injured. Not with Stuart on northern campaign.

Then it hit me, and I almost dropped my teacup. I shoved back my chair, ran across the room, and started rifling through my newspapers. But I already knew what I was looking for, and I found it very quickly. Just a passing item in the social pages, that visit by Mrs. Robert E. Lee to her daughter-in-law in Hanover County.

This was what kept me awake until four in the morning last week. Not my handful of messages. Not even Vicksburg. This. Mary Custis Lee was practically an invalid. She never visited her husband at the front. She never went anywhere. When McClellan's cannons were all but rattling the windows last spring, and wives of high-ranking men were leaving town in all directions, Mary Lee just kept right on knitting. So why was she suddenly going off to visit the Wickhams? And especially, why *now*, with Lee's army moving out and the countryside far from safe?

Because Rooney was there. He wasn't in the hospital and he wasn't with Stuart, so he was there, and there were barely enough

Rebels left in Virginia to guard the railroad bridges and protect Richmond from the Yankees in Fort Monroe!

I took a long drink of tea and made myself relax. I laid Mariel's notes aside—rather the way a cat lays aside a dead bird while examining a live one—and opened my reticule. Inside was another small piece of paper, on which a friend had kindly written out the recipe for an excellent cake. It needed neither eggs, nor milk, nor butter—a useful recipe to have, in Richmond in 1863. I drew the heavy curtains to darken the room, placed a candle inside a glass jar, and pressed the recipe against the glass. As the paper heated, other words began to appear, printed in a different hand. The ragged, angular hand of Samuel Ruth, superintendent of the Richmond, Fredericksburg and Potomac Railroad.

As always, Sam had the latest information on the movement of troops and supplies. And this time, he had something else.

Meeting last wk. All presidents, all Reb RR's. Need 50,000 tons of track/yr to keep RR's war worthy. Can't do it. Atlanta & R'mond together don't produce enough. Tredegar unable to compensate workers for decline of CS money. Recommend placing large adverts in N. newspapers for machinists, molders, finishers, etc. for high wages; many here will desert. P.S. Tell Quaker, too.

I sent this off to Washington, of course, to Secretary of War Edwin M. Stanton. The advertisements duly appeared in several Maryland and Pennsylvania papers, and my friends made sure that copies were generously distributed among the tradesmen at the Tredegar Iron Works. A considerable number of them subsequently slipped away to the North. And, as Sam suggested, I also passed everything on to Tom McNiven. About a week later, a mysterious fire broke out at the Tredegar, and two of its huge buildings were burnt to the ground.

All in all, the shortage of track for Southern railroads got considerably worse.

"Miss Liza? Beg pardon, but your mammy wants to know if you're comin' to eat that nice chicken what nearly got away."

"Eat the chicken? Heavens above, have you cooked it already? Tell Mother I'm sorry. I can't come right now. Go on and eat without me."

"I'll bring you a nice leg, then. And some more tea. And you eat it, Miss Liza, you hear? You won't be no good to nobody if you don't eat."

I did eat. Voraciously, in fact, devouring chicken and corn bread and everything else Josey put on the tray, while my other hand carefully phrased a message, revised it, and finally enciphered it. *To Mr. James ap Jones, Yorktown, Va. Dear Uncle.* My dear uncle was probably related to me somehow, coming as we all did from Adam and Eve. He was Major General John Dix, commanding the Federal army at Fortress Monroe. He already knew about the two regiments of Carolinians brought up to guard the South Anna and other key bridges. But I sent him Sam's latest figures on Richmond's defenses, both immediately surrounding the city, and also at Drewry's Bluff. The message concluded thus:

Gen. W.H.F. Lee believed convalescing at farm home of father-in-law, John Wickham, Hanover County, Va.

I signed it with the code name I always used, *C. Babcock,* wrapped it in foil, and called Nelson.

"Have you eaten yet, Nelson?"

"Yes'm. An' it was a right tasty chicken, too."

"It was, wasn't it? Best chicken I've eaten in my life. I want you to take this to Tibo. Put it in your shoe and try and get it muddy."

"It ain't rained for weeks, Miss Liza. There ain't no mud around."

"Step in some good fresh dung, then. You don't want to get caught with this one. Tell Tibo it's urgent. And tell him to make sure he tells everybody else. I want this in General Dix's hands before breakfast."

"You want us to fly, Miss Liza, or you going to fetch the Yankee army and move it upriver a ways?"

"Before breakfast, Nelson."

"Yes'm."

He went off with a great air of dismay. But I knew he'd be at the farm by late afternoon. Each station after that was about fifteen miles apart, and by now every courier knew every twist and turn of the way. If Federal cavalry were on the prowl, as I expected, my couriers might not have to go much beyond the Chickahominy. With good speed and good luck, number four would be there by midnight.

Living in a dungeon made every moment crawl. Living under a sentence of death made hours fly by with intolerable speed. John Flinn could not reconcile the contradiction. He spent most of his time sitting by the table, with his head resting on his arms. Sawyer sat on the floor, and didn't complain. He felt bad about the letter he wrote, and he let Flinn have anything he wanted. He would even have given up some of his food, but the Indiana captain didn't want it.

The letter had no effect on the Confederate authorities, except perhaps to reassure them of how shabbily Yankees behaved. Death seemed inevitable now. Flinn no longer resisted it in his mind. He was ill and feverish, and thought he might have to be carried to the gallows, and with no shame owing to himself. He didn't know his hair had turned white. The light was so poor, Sawyer wasn't sure, and Sawyer certainly wasn't going to mention it.

Even down here, they were aware of feverish activity in Richmond. Alarm tocsins alerted them at all hours of the day and night. So did the sound of marching feet. The militias must have been drilling every day, and hurrying to one or the other edge of the city at the smallest sign of danger. Work parties, too, went tramping by, repairing old defenses and building new ones. Lee's army had gone north; everyone knew the countryside and the Rebel capital itself were vulnerable to Federal raiding parties—perhaps even to capture.

So it was the first thing Sawyer thought about, when the commotion began: banging and shouting in the upper levels, loud enough to be heard below, though muffled by layers of wood and brick. An extraordinary commotion, as if the whole of Libby had erupted into one gigantic brawl. He thought they were going to be rescued. Yankees had made it into Richmond and they were storming the prison and he was going to get out of here, oh God, they were all going to get out of here . . . !

His hope was brief. There was no shooting, neither upstairs nor in the streets. No indication of any sort of fighting at all. Just banging and shouts, and as it grew louder and louder he realized what it was.

"God in heaven."

They were cheering upstairs, cheering like drunken fools. Then a chant began. Voices, feet, pots and pans, fists against walls. And then a name, hammered out in ringing martial triumph.

"Grant! Grant! Grant!"

"Listen, Flinn," Sawyer whispered. "It must be Vicksburg! By God, can you hear them? He must have done it! He's got Vicksburg! And all the time I thought he was stuck fast between the devil and the deep blue sea."

The commotion went on. Somewhere in the midst of it were the voices of Rebel guards yelling at the prisoners to shut up. But they weren't about to listen. Defiantly they began to sing, a great roar of voices that it seemed to Flinn could almost burst the walls of Libby Prison: "Oh, say, can you see by the dawn's early light. . . ."

The Star-Spangled Banner was waving over Vicksburg, over the whole of the Mississippi River. Even Sawyer was happy, and he would be until the sun went down. But Flinn had accepted death, and he didn't want to think about the world at all. He didn't want to read the letter from Colonel Streight, which was slipped through the ceiling from the cook room, a few hours later. But the letter was addressed to him, and he had to read it.

Dear Flinn. As you must have guessed from the ruckus, Vicksburg surrendered July 4. A splendid victory, and we all have a share in it. Our little brigade kept Forrest and a whole raft of Rebel cavalry off Grant's back when he needed it most. I know it isn't much comfort, but I hope it's some. No word of Lee. There seems to have been a scrap up north, but no one seems to know how big, or who got the worst of it. We are all thinking of you, and the praying ones are praying hard. Hang on. Col. A. Streight.

He handed it to Sawyer, who read it and handed it back. "He's a damn fine man, your colonel."

"Yes," Flinn said vacantly, and laid his head on his arms again.

The crawling of minutes and the flying of hours went on. One day passed. Two. Three. On the third evening, the guard who should have brought their supper came without it.

He was a guard they liked. He was always kind. He talked to them politely, and sometimes brought news from their comrades above. Once, to their absolute astonishment and enormous gratitude, he gave them an apple.

It was hard to see his face, but his voice was cheerful.

"All right, Yanks. Pick up your duds. You all are out of here."

"Out of here . . . ?" Sawyer looked at him, at Flinn. Just for a moment, he had to lean on the table for support. "You aren't . . . ? This isn't . . . ?"

"Your hanging? Naw. The hanging's off. You're going back upstairs."

"They aren't going to kill us?" Flinn said. His voice was very calm, so calm it bewildered him.

"That's right. Your friends will tell you all about it."

Another cheer went through Libby's third level when they walked in. It was loud and deeply felt, but it had a catch in its throat. No one really expected to see these men again—including big Abel Streight, who threw his arms around Flinn and all but lifted him off the ground with his embrace.

"What's going on, Colonel?" Flinn asked desperately. "What happened?"

"We got General Lee's son. Young Rooney. Pennsylvania Cavalry went storming through Hanover County a few days back. Colonel Spear's bunch. They took out the railroad bridge on the North Anna and raised a whole lot of general damnation. And just happened to wander into a farmhouse where young Lee was recovering from that leg wound he got at Brandy Station.

"The way I heard it, King Jeff got a telegram from Washington this afternoon, from Mr. Lincoln himself. More or less to the effect that young Lee and another high-ranking officer were down in the nether regions of Fort Monroe; they're every bit as bad as the nether regions here. If you and Sawyer were returned to normal status as prisoners of war, the president said, we'd do the same for Lee. If you and Sawyer were hanged, we'd do the same for Lee.

"It's over, John."

Flinn couldn't speak. He heard Sawyer's voice, even over all the other voices in the room, whooping and hollering. But he was motionless and voiceless. By now Streight had taken note of his gaunt body, his hollow eyes, his old man's hair. The colonel's own voice was a trifle unsteady.

"You're safe, John. Leastways till you get back in the war. I don't expect we'll let young Lee go in any hurry. And while we got him, they won't be hanging anybody without a proper reason. Not anybody, by God!"

Flinn still didn't speak. Streight led him to a wooden bench, and sat down beside him, and held him like a child as he wept.

It turned out pretty much the way Abel Streight said it would. The Federal authorities hung on to Rooney Lee for an awfully long time, refusing every offer of exchange. Most of the Rebels' eagerness to hoist the black flag and hang folks from the yardarm just toned right down. I never claimed any credit for his capture. I couldn't at the time, of course. Not long afterward, Rooney's young wife fell sick, and died while he was in prison. Died, they said, of loneliness and despair, believing she'd never see her husband again. The whole affair made Virginians terribly bitter toward the North—more, I think, than many a battlefield or smoldering town.

Anyone who had a hand in it . . . well, it didn't bear thinking about. Especially as the summer wore on, and I found myself with a whole new problem on my hands. It was a pattern all through the war. Whenever things got a little better for the Union army, they got a whole lot worse for me. I suppose it was God's way of being kind, making sure I only had one crisis to deal with at a time.

Unfortunately, in the process God also made sure I was always frightened half out of my wits. And I never found a good way to deal with it. I've read accounts by soldiers who say that after the first couple of battles, the possibility of death becomes a kind of abstraction, something that can happen, of course, but only to someone else. There were other soldiers, who mostly didn't write their memoirs, for whom the possibility of death obviously became more and more unmanageable. There were hundreds of them in the hills and the backwoods—and just as many, I suppose, on the other side of the Potomac. They hid, or wandered about in a permanent state of shock and bewilderment.

I never fell into either category, but I brushed the edges of both on occasion. Sometimes I felt almost invincible, like my cat Jason, who would sit for hours on a fence and stare down every pack of stray dogs who went by. Sometimes, for the sheer damnation of it, he would pad his way slowly down to ground level and trot down the road, with his tail in the air like a battle flag, just daring them to attack. Of course they always did, and Jason would shoot back up the fence, or up a tree, and turn, and smile down at them, as only a cat can smile: *Well, hello there, fellas. Pity you can't climb, isn't it?*

Jason was a Union cat. He turned up one night in the rain, drenched and weak, missing great chunks of fur and all the flesh God intended creatures to carry between their bones and their skin. He looked like he'd escaped from a Rebel prison camp. I took him in and gave him some food, but he wouldn't even go near it until I'd backed halfway across the room.

When he was dry and had a few days' rations in him, he stopped hiding behind the coal bucket, checked the place over, and decided to stay. Of all the cats I've ever had, I liked him the best. He was half a dozen different colors, but mostly reddish ginger. I wanted to call him Sherman, but it would have brought him more enemies than even he could have handled.

My mother said Jason got to be more and more like me, and perhaps he did. Certainly there were times I was like him, climbing down from my perch and sticking my nose in the air and saying catch me if you can. And there were other times when I crawled under the furniture, and shivered, and wondered if there were any poisons in the house I could take before they dragged me off to be questioned and hanged.

Until the arrests began in '65, the worst moment was the coming of Lieutenant Bonham. Andrew Jackson Bonham. A nice-looking man, objectively speaking, although the sight of him even now would probably have me diving behind a coal bucket. He came on such a nice day, too. We were all happy. Will Rowley had brought us some New York papers the night before, filled with details of the Vicksburg campaign. We devoured every word. We were so proud of Grant, and so sure the war was nearly finished. Vicksburg had given us the Mississippi River. We knew Lee had been whipped in Pennsylvania, even though the Rebel newspapers were still trying to call it a strategic retreat. We had won. A couple of months to tie up the loose ends, and it would all be over.

Jason was the only one of us who wasn't taken in by all the glory. The whole morning, I remember, he paced from window to window and glared out at the world, twitching and twitching his straggly red tail.

"There's something wrong with that cat, Elizabeth. Are you sure he isn't sick?"

"I don't think so. Jason, come here, kitty kitty, come here. . . ."

Jason paid absolutely no attention. He sat and watched the street with the most baleful countenance imaginable.

"Probably he's spotted one of Winder's detectives," I said. "That would put any self respecting creature in a bad mood."

"You'd think they'd get tired of it," Mother murmured. "Watching us all the time for nothing. They must feel foolish."

She went on knitting for a while, her expression darkening over a thought. "Your father once told me the worst thing you could ever do was make an enemy feel foolish."

"I don't see as how I have much choice, Mother. I could make them all proud and happy by confessing, I suppose, but it does seem counter-productive."

My mother said nothing. She was proud of me, and she loved me dearly. But I knew there were times she wished she had ordinary children, manly sons and feminine daughters and piles of grand-children and no policemen pacing up and down outside her house.

There was a light tap at the door, and then it opened.

"Miss Liza?"

It was Josey, and she had a letter in her hand. "Miss Liza, this just come for you."

"Who brought it?" I asked, reaching for the folded paper.

"Just some feller. I never saw him before. But he says I's to give it to you right away."

I knew it was trouble. Before I even touched it, I knew. Yet the sight of the provost marshal's official stationery was nonetheless a surprise, a jolt of pure, unmediated fear.

The note was from General Winder's adjutant. The general would expect me in his office at three o'clock that afternoon.

"Thank you, Josey. Make sure lunch is served on time today; I'll have to go out immediately after."

"Yes'm."

"Well?" Mother demanded when the servant was gone.

"General Winder wants to see me."

"Oh, dear God."

"Mother." I walked over to her chair and placed my arm around her shoulders. "I don't much like it, either. But if he was going to throw me into Castle Thunder, I doubt he'd send an invitation."

"There's no knowing what that man will do, Liza. He's like an old cat; in the morning he purrs and sits by the fire, and in the evening he eats things alive."

"I wish you hadn't said that, Mother. I *like* cats."

"Indeed."

"It'll be all right. I don't want you worrying about it. And if John gets back before I do, for heaven's sake don't get him all upset."

Our eyes met, and it was my mother who looked away.

The provost marshal greeted me with a huge smile. He asked about my mother's health. He made polite small talk. Then he leaned back in his chair, silent for a moment. An old cat, indeed, wondering if small, blond ferrets were good to eat.

"Miss Van Lew. You know, I'm sure, that there is a good deal of, well, shall we say . . . resentment . . . against yourself and your family in Richmond. Because of your sentiments in this dreadful civil war. You are aware of it, I suppose?"

"Resentment?" I regarded him sorrowfully. "Surely not, General. Oh, some people have been terribly rude, of course, but not the *better* people. It's all so unfortunate. I know our neighbors wish we shared their feelings, but we can't help it. You've always understood us, General. You've always been such a gentleman."

"Some people," he continued blandly, "think you might be a Federal spy. My man Cleary is convinced of it."

"Mr. Cleary? That horrible creature? He's not an honest man; he actually tried to steal my groceries once."

"He's my best detective."

There was a long, unpleasant silence. Tears welled slowly in my eyes, and my mouth began to quiver. I wasn't entirely faking; I had begun to be quite afraid.

"General, you don't . . . you can't believe that . . . that I would . . . oh, you couldn't, oh God, I thought you were my friend, I trusted you completely . . . !"

"Madam, please. There's no need to be so upset. I didn't say I believe him."

His words had no effect. I let him know I was utterly devastated. I might have been a Unionist, but I was first of all a gentlewoman. I was a lady, dear heavens, and ladies didn't lie, and they didn't sneak about and look through other people's windows, and they didn't take other people's things. I could never hold my head up in his presence again, if he thought I was capable of something so ill-bred.

There now, there now. God save us, how women do cry.

"Miss Van Lew."

I wiped my eyes. "I'm sorry, General."

"I have no doubt whatever that Mr. Cleary is mistaken. However, as I said, he's my best detective. I'm obliged to pay some attention to his opinions."

"You're not going to put me in jail?"

"Certainly not." He smiled. I thought I knew the man well, but I couldn't read his smile. I couldn't tell if it was friendly, or completely diabolical.

"Lieutenant Todd has been sent to a combat unit, as he requested. His replacement arrived yesterday, and has nowhere to live. You know what Richmond is like now; even the mice can't find lodgings. I immediately thought of you."

"Me, General?"

"Yes. Your lovely big house on Church Street. You must have several empty rooms. Lieutenant Bonham will scarcely believe his luck, if you take him in. For your part, you'll be spared any more of these ugly rumors. With an officer of the provost marshal living right in your house, you can hardly be plotting dastardly deeds against the government, or hiding escaped prisoners in your closets, now can you? Mr. Cleary will be satisfied, and occupy his fine talents elsewhere. And I will have some peace. So you see, Miss Elizabeth, I've finally found a way to make everybody happy."

He was happy indeed; his eyes fairly twinkled.

"Why, General, I hardly know what to say. It does seem like the perfect solution. But . . . forgive me for asking . . . but is he a gentleman?"

"Who? Oh, Bonham. He's an angel. You won't find him a bit of trouble. Shall I send him over this evening?"

"Well, yes, that will be fine. I hope Mother will agree. Oh, I'm sure she will. You're doing this especially for us, aren't you? You're so kind, General, and so very thoughtful. Do you think perhaps . . . ?"

I let my voice falter, and my eyes fall.

"Perhaps what, Miss Van Lew?"

"Do you think people might accept us now, just a little?"

The question was so ill-considered he just stared at me, wondering perhaps how to answer it. Did I really imagine that taking in one Rebel lodger, under duress, would make the whole of Richmond forget I was a Yankee in my heart?

"Feelings run high in times of war, Miss Van Lew. We all have to live with it. As you say, the better people try to understand. Now, if you'll forgive me, I am very busy."

"Yes. Yes, of course." I got to my feet, pulled my bonnet low across my face to hide the evidence of tears. I had made a proper fool of myself, and we both knew it.

"Thank you, General. Good afternoon."

"Good afternoon, Miss Van Lew."

Andrew Jackson Bonham turned up just in time for supper. He was a decent enough fellow, I suppose, or would have been in a normal human world. But he took the war very seriously; he ate mountains of food; he thought John should be in the Confederate army; and he didn't like cats.

Moreover, he was there for a purpose, and he intended to carry it out. He wasn't even especially discreet about it. His eyes wandered

over every inch of wall and every piece of furniture, lingering sometimes on one thing or another. I could almost read the questions in
his eyes. Were there only brooms behind the closet door, or was it
the secret entrance to a secret room? What did we have hidden behind my grandfather's portrait in its old, ornate frame?

We put him in McClellan's room. We made him as comfortable
as we could. We babbled at him over supper. If all else failed, I
thought, maybe we could bore him to death. We sighed with relief
when he went to his bed, and we could go to ours.

We didn't sleep.

Fear is like any other extreme sensation. Or, I suppose, like alcohol or opiates. No matter how powerful it seems at first, you get
used to it. To a certain amount of it, or to a certain kind. When it's
changed, it's like you'd never been used to it at all.

We were scared silly after the Secession vote, but the violence of
the moment turned mostly against outsiders. We were threatened,
but nothing more, and we got used to it. Then martial law was
declared in the spring of '62, and a great many people were arrested.
Respectable people, good citizens, our own former member of Congress, John Minor Botts. If he could be thrown into a filthy unheated
cell like some ruffian they scraped off the streets, what was going
to happen to the rest of us? People fled by the scores then, Lucy
Rice's husband among them. The rest of us went on working, and
got used to it.

That's how it went. Each time I thought: *This is the most I can
bear. If it gets any worse, I'll have to get out.*

All night, the night Lieutenant Bonham came, I thought about
leaving Richmond. All three of us. My brother-in-law in Philadelphia could send us a telegram: *Anna desperately ill; please come.*
Winder would give us a pass, no question, he'd be so happy to be
rid of me.

I knew what prisons were like. I'd had a horror of them since the
first time I visited one, years before in Philadelphia. I'd visited others
since, and I knew Libby was the best of ours. Castle Godwin and

Castle Thunder were much worse. They were prisons for Negroes and common criminals—and, after the war began, for deserters, traitors, and spies. They weren't really castles, of course, though they were just as grim and dreary. Castle Godwin, named after one of the city's provost men, had once been McDaniel's slave jail. The cells were damp, unlit, and in bad weather brutally cold; some didn't even have bunks. Timothy Webster came out of his so crippled with rheumatism he could hardly walk . . . or at least the Rebels said it was rheumatism.

And there were people who never came out again at all. I thought about them a lot, tossing and turning in my bed: George Welch's three comrades, all brought to Richmond with him early in the war. They were Union soldiers, captured in western Virginia, and no reason was ever given why they shouldn't be treated as prisoners of war. They were never tried for spying, or for any other crime. The Federal government asked about them, and was told they weren't here. Cold and hunger and God knows what other brutalities did their work; they just died, one after another until only Welch was left. We managed to save him; we got his name on a prisoner exchange form "by accident," and he made it out before anyone noticed the mistake.

Would we all end up in Castle Thunder, too? Shivering in a rat-infested hole, fed on bread and water, beaten maybe, or worse? None of us were physically robust, and Mother was past sixty. And yes, we were well-known and respectable citizens; that was a measure of protection. So, for my mother and myself, was our sex. But I knew chivalry had its limits. A lady could forfeit her place on the pedestal, and when she did, she fell a long way down indeed.

Stay or go? I would not give up serving my country. If I stayed, I would go on with the work. And whether we stayed or went, it would be my decision. Since my father's death, all the decisions that mattered in the family had been mine.

I hadn't made anything resembling a decision when morning

came. We gave Lieutenant Bonham his breakfast. When he was gone I went outside to try to think.

At the back of our house were the old slave quarters, the carriage house and shed, the smoke house, and the outdoor kitchen. Beyond them, stretching downhill toward the James Valley, was the garden, lush now with flowers and shaded with trees. The entire yard was circled with a seven-foot stone fence. It had been built in our slave-owning days, and like most such fences it had an inside overhang and no gate. I would have been tempted to tear it down, but thanks to the natural sloping of the land, it was almost as though the fence wasn't there. We could sit with a full and sweeping view of the valley, and still be shut away from bands of roving dogs, casual thieves, and other uninvited guests.

Invited guests, alas, were a different matter.

I walked, brooded, plucked a weed here and a flower there. Right here in this garden, I recalled, was where I found Mariel, the day I gave her her papers. She had a great tub of green peas beside her chair, and a bowl on her lap; she could shell peas faster than anyone I ever saw. We said good afternoon, but I didn't say anything else. I handed her the folded document.

Manumission is a peculiar thing, really, when you think about it: a gift of something that was never ours to give—somebody else's self; a gift for which we expected gratitude, and always received it; yet we were never more than thieves giving back what had been stolen in the first place.

Mariel was surprised. Not terribly surprised; she liked me well enough; she respected my mother more than she would ever respect any white person, I suppose, except Abraham Lincoln. But she was surprised.

And rightly so. You could never be sure about anything a white person said, if you were black. And it wasn't that masters intentionally lied. Oh, some did, of course; but most were sincere when they made a promise to a slave . . . that is, they were sincere at the time. But it was like making a promise to yourself; no honor was involved. If later on you thought better of it and changed your mind, if you were strapped for cash or if you just grew indifferent with age, well, it was entirely your own affair. And if you died and your heirs thought better of it, it was entirely their affair. Old Mingo ran the Eagles plantation in North Carolina for nearly thirty years. He was to go on doing so, Joseph Eagles wrote in his will, as long as he felt well enough, and then be retired, with thirty dollars a year for the remainder of his life. But Mr. Eagles's widow married a tough young army captain named John Winder. He wasn't much of a planter, and in short order he sold both the land and the slaves to the railroad. He sold Old Mingo, too, without batting an eyelash.

No Negro has any rights which any white person is bound to respect. Judge Taney was talking about legal rights when he said it, but his statement covered them all, not least the right to good faith. You will honor your promises. You will treat us tomorrow as you did today. You can be trusted.

Can you be trusted, Liza Van Lew? Or are you just another speaker of fine sentiments, another one of those who's willing to do right until it costs too much? You dragged her back here all the way from Boston. Help the Union, you said. Help me. Now she's in the devil's own kitchen and you want to leave town? What are you going to tell her? Sorry, Mariel, I guess freedom isn't so important after all; forget the whole thing. Or maybe you can pawn her off on Quaker and the others; that's what people do with servants, isn't it, when they don't need them anymore? Nelson, too, and Tibo, all your couriers, who take their lives in their hands every time they step out on a Rebel turnpike. . . .

The flowers slid out of my hand, barely noticed. There was no decision to make, really. Some of us had to keep our word. That was why the Negroes sang about John Brown—because he kept his. He was a reckless man, an extremist; I probably wouldn't have liked him much if I'd met him face-to-face. But when he said black people were human beings just like himself, he meant it. When he said he'd do what he could to free them, he meant it.

Colonel Shaw, too, tramping around in the swamps of South Carolina with his black regiment, begging for a fight, any kind of fight, because there had to be one, the first one; there had to be one irreversible moment when the war and the country changed forever.

And one other man, the one my thoughts returned to so often, in sweet or troubled moments. Something of a rogue, Levi Coffin said, but the bravest of them all, perhaps; no army behind him, no God of wrath, no phantom revolution, only a promise and a dark road and a stranger waiting. John Fairfield, too, could be trusted.

I walked back into the house, trying not to remember that all three of those men who always kept their promises were dead.

Josey met me in the hallway, a smile on her face and a huge duster in her hand.

"Miss 'Lizabeth, there's something I got to show you. You remember them lions on the mantel? I was cleaning up in the library and I recalled how your pa never liked them; he said they was made so poorly. I pulled on one of them a little bit and the head came right off."

I had just been meditating on the odds of us keeping our own heads. Nothing could have interested me less at the moment than the fate of a mantel decoration.

"Well, just fix it as best you can, Josey," I said wearily. "It really doesn't matter."

"But it's hollow inside." She smiled again. "Come see, Miss Liza. You can take it apart, and put it back together, and it don't show none at all."

I stopped dead in my tracks. "Hollow inside?"

"Yes'm."

We went into the library. The two bronze ornamental lions crouched on opposite sides of the mantel above the fireplace. I had long forgotten about their existence; they were like walls and chairs, simply there. But then, I didn't dust them every day. Gently, Josey beheaded one of them and turned the head upside down. It was indeed hollow.

"We can put anything we want in there, Miss Liza," she said. "And it won't matter if that man's living here or not. Less'n he starts cleaning the furniture, he ain't going to know."

The lion heads made perfect hiding places. Messages that arrived at inconvenient moments were quietly deposited there until I had the opportunity to retrieve them. If I had something for Nelson to deliver, I would tell him we needed milk, or coal, or whatever, right in front of Lieutenant Bonham's innocent face, and off he would go to the farm or to New Market, stopping in the library on his way out.

Josey was very proud.

SEVEN

———————※

TO ELEVATE THE
FEMALE CHARACTER

... American civilization has nowhere produced a purer and loftier
type of refined and cultured womanhood than existed in the South
before the war.

William Fisk Tillett

The tendency of our institution is to elevate the female character.
... It would indeed be intolerable, when one class of society is
necessarily degraded ... if no compensation were made by the
superior elevation and purity of the other.

William Harper, Southern pro-slavery writer

Any lady is ready to tell you who is the father of all the mulatto
children in everybody's household but her own.

Mary Boykin Chestnut

The social order of the Old South was full of breath-taking contradictions. Every state in history had its share, of course, but a slave
state, especially one that claimed to be both God-fearing and democratic, had a great many more than its share. All my life I kept

finding them: stumbling over them without warning on clean, sunny streets; stepping on them in the dead of night, wondering what went squish. And finally, in the war years, seeking them out, playing on them, using them as weapons. None were worth more than my land in Locust Alley.

I don't remember what year it was—sometime in the fifties—I went down to the family solicitor's office to discuss various matters, including the manumission of a slave I had just bought for that purpose. I won't burden you with the beginnings of our conversation; Mr. Vance was a stuffy old man, and took forever to explain small, simple things; it was obvious he considered me a child.

I mentioned that I needed money for a particular undertaking I had in mind; he suggested a sum in rental earnings that I could use. Now, we had a house across from our own on Church Street, which we rented out, but the rental he mentioned was considerably richer. I corrected him, and would have thought nothing more about it. But his small mistake made him pale and flustered, and he literally began to babble. *Yes, of course, how could I have forgotten, I had the figures right here, I do apologize, something else on my mind, terrible night last night, no sleep at all* . . . and more such, until I naturally became suspicious.

"Tell me, Mr. Vance, does our family perchance have some income which I don't know about?"

"Most certainly not," he said, mauling his papers so he didn't have to look at me.

"My brother and I are joint executors of our father's will," I reminded him.

"I'm quite aware of that, Miss Elizabeth."

"Then you will understand completely if I ask to see the account books and a complete list of our assets."

There was a long silence. Finally he put his elbows on his desk and tried to look fatherly.

"Miss Elizabeth. Your brother and myself have always had your best interests at heart. Yours, and your dear mother's. Always. Surely you don't have any doubts about it?"

"I didn't say I had any doubts about you—or about my brother. I said I wanted to see the books."

"Everything is quite in order."

"Well, then there's no problem, is there? It shouldn't take more than a few minutes of your time." I smiled. I had a gift for smiling, apparently, in ways that could make people most uneasy.

He knew me. He dug into a file and pulled out a document, but he did not immediately pass it over.

"You remember David Ellard, I presume? He was a close friend of your father's—indeed, of your whole family?"

"Yes, certainly."

"This property was ceded to your father's estate in accordance with Mr. Ellard's will, in the settlement of an old, and apparently unrecorded, debt. Your brother cannot sell any estate property without your mother's consent, as you know. Because of the relationship between your families, he chose not to ask for such consent. He judged it a matter she would prefer to know nothing about. Your brother is a gentleman of flawless sensibility."

Meaning I was not a similar sort of lady. Unless of course I blushed now, and said: Oh, dear, there's no need to explain anything further. . . .

I reached and took the paper gently from his hand. It was the deed to a lot with a three-story house in a well-known part of town.

"Locust Alley?"

"Yes, Miss Elizabeth. Locust Alley."

The red light district. The very best red light district, where all the best gentlemen in Richmond, the ones with flawless sensibilities, went to buy women.

I put the deed back on his desk and walked over to the window, staring down the tree-lined grace of Clay Street. Barely in view among the trees, though I didn't know it yet, was the Rebel White House: the big, beautiful mansion they would one day present to

Jefferson Davis. There was no war yet. The streets were tranquil, at least on the surface. An old slave trudged along the sidewalk, dragging a wheelbarrow that seemed twice too heavy for his lean, bent body.

A whorehouse, I thought. *We are the proud owners of an honest-to-Beelzebub genuine whorehouse.* I was shocked, of course, though by the time Mr. Vance finished dissembling, I had seen it coming. I was something else besides shocked, however, and you may think of me what you will. I was fascinated. Fascinated by the contradiction, the pure absurdity of it. Yet another little chink had fallen out of the world's pretty white wall of pretense.

"I'm sorry, Miss Elizabeth. I would willingly have spared you such a shock."

"Mr. Vance." I turned to face him. I suddenly felt angry—so angry I could hardly keep my voice calm—but I had no idea at whom, or at what. "If you spare me any such shocks in the future, in regard to any matter whatsoever of our family's affairs, we shall be obliged to find another lawyer."

I left him to meditate on my words, and went home. I didn't talk to John. I knew exactly what he would say. *I couldn't tell her, Liza. I just couldn't. She thought the world of the Ellards. . . .*

So had I. They never came to the house without bringing me a little gift. David Ellard played the piano like a master, and sang Schubert to make a stone cry. And he owned a brothel. And yes, maybe he'd come to it by accident, like us, but probably not. Coincidence had its limits.

Later, in the burning heat of the day, when most of the respectable people in Richmond were finding ways to get out of the sun, I hired a closed carriage and drove through Locust Alley.

I knew about it, of course. Every grown-up in Richmond with a functioning brain knew about it, but I'd never been there. The area was small then; our city had only about thirty-five thousand people. We had money, though; perhaps more money per citizen than any other city in America, and it showed here as it showed everywhere else. The strip breathed of quality. A slightly tainted quality, perhaps, but quality nonetheless. The walks were lined with magnificent locust trees; the houses were elegant. Ours was perhaps the finest, tall and wide-gabled, with ornate balconies. From inside, very soft through the curtained windows and the heat, came the sound of a half-awake piano.

Does every well-bred woman in the world have a hankering to see the inside of a brothel? I peeked through the curtain of my barely moving carriage and I thought: *The house is mine. I can go in if I want. It's nobody else's business. I can go in if I want.*

I wanted to go in very much, to look at the red velvet and the bare skin, at all the sensuality and all the broken rules, to see it up close, even if only for a moment, only in passing. The right and wrong of it was quite beside the point; I wanted to see it all.

I told the driver to stop the carriage. I wrote a brief note on a small piece of paper, and asked him to take it to the person in charge. After about ten minutes he came back. Madame Clara would be very pleased to see me, he said.

Probably Madame Clara wasn't very pleased to see me at all, but she was singularly gracious. She had a talent for making people feel at ease. It was, I suspect, the most valuable talent a woman in her position could have had. She took me into a room very much like a parlor. Tucked away quietly in the corner was a desk and a cabinet, so probably the room was her office. A finely attired black man brought us tea, tiny cakes, and sherry. She made polite, casual conversation, waiting for me to explain the reason for my visit. Finally, she put her teacup down and said, "How can I be of service to you, Miss Van Lew?"

She wasn't an especially beautiful woman, but she was dressed and groomed to perfection. The perfect image of a lady, I thought. The lady who was not a lady, who was what a lady never could be. The flesh and blood contradiction who made it possible for ladies to exist.

As we made it necessary for her to exist.

"Give me," I said, "one good reason why I shouldn't cancel your lease and close this place down."

"You come right to the point, don't you?" she said. "Well, I could give you twenty reasons, but since you asked for one, I'll just give you one. I've heard you don't think much of slavery. Before you close me down, you might like to have a look at the place next door. Mr. Severn now, he thinks slavery is just about the best thing that ever happened to the business. More than half his girls are slaves. He has a buyer full-time, going all over the South, even as far as Texas, looking for likely ones. Mr. Severn makes a good deal of money, Miss Van Lew. More than I do. He wants to expand his operation. He'd like nothing better than to do business with you."

"I'm not about to do business with him," I said.

"Then with who? The Virginia Baptist Assembly? No one will rent a property in the middle of Locust Alley unless they want to run a house here. No one will buy it from you, either, except for the same reason. You see, honey," she added more softly, "I've already had this conversation with your brother. Though he was, I must tell you, a lot more uncomfortable walking in here than you were. Funny thing about men, isn't it? They're never as worldly as they think they are."

The woman had an exquisite smile, a way of tilting her face that could, for the briefest instant, make her seem playful and even innocent. Only her eyes belied the image, if you looked at them closely. Her eyes were unyielding, and belonged to someone much older, as though she had already lived several lifetimes in the same smooth, slightly plump body.

"You could have a worse tenant here than me, Miss Van Lew. If you throw me out, you probably will have. I take care of my girls. They get their money. They get a doctor when they're sick. And none of them are slaves. Nobody works for me who'd rather be someplace else."

"Wouldn't they all rather be someplace else?"

She laughed, without much amusement. "Sure, honey. In the best of all possible worlds, so would I. But suppose someplace else is a factory where your lungs are gone before you're thirty? Or a back-woods farm with seven kids and a husband who lives on rotgut? Or maybe just the dead house, because you got a baby and no husband at all, and even the sweatshops and the backwoods farmer don't want you?"

I said nothing for a time. Everything she said I had heard before, in Philadelphia, where prostitution was discussed among the radicals almost as often as slavery. There were always two sets of answers— those of the moralists, and those of the pragmatists. If you weren't careful, you could swing back and forth between them like a pendulum, and never come to rest.

I took a small sip of sherry, and changed the subject.

"Mr. Ellard," I said. "The gentleman from whom we inherited this property. Do you happen to know how long he owned it?"

"Long before my time, honey. Far's I know, he bought it years ago, when Locust Alley was just starting to fill up with sporting houses. I expect he thought it was a good investment. Of course, he was right."

"Yes, I suppose he was."

I took another sip of sherry. From beyond Clara's hardwood door I heard the sound of running steps, a young woman's protest: "Come back here with that!" A different woman's laughter. A brief scuffle. Maybe playful, maybe cruel. No way to know. An alien world. *I am a lady. David Ellard's wife was a lady. David Ellard owned this place. Now I do. A good investment.*

Did he sample the merchandise when he came to collect the rent? Does John? Would I do so, if I were a man, lonely as I am in a world full of ladies, hearing such laughter? Would a lady if she could, if young men laughed so, and waited for her in a house, beautiful and there for the choosing, for a handful of coin?

Prostitution, they said, was just another kind of slavery, and probably in some ways it was. But I was in Independence Hall one night, a night that nearly ended in a riot, when a small, consumptive woman ran up on the podium and started yelling at us. "Go out," she cried, "and ask a hundred slaves if they want slavery outlawed, and every one of them will say yes. Go out and ask a hundred whores if they want prostitution outlawed, and ninety-eight of them will say no. Doesn't that tell you something, for God's sake? And what's a prostitute, anyway? Do you really know? How many of *you* took a man in return for a house or a farm or a closet full of silk dresses?"

She would have said a lot more, probably, but she was hustled off the stage, and everyone was shouting, and the meeting collapsed in disorder. But she had made her point, at least to some of us. I knew I could live in our big house on Church Hill the way I did, thinking for myself and doing what I believed in, without a husband, only because I had money.

Suppose I'd had none? What would I have bartered for it? For there was no doubt about it, I'd have had to barter *something*.

The sherry glass, I saw to my astonishment, was empty. I got to my feet, slowly, like someone who'd been unceremoniously knocked over in the street.

"Thank you, Madame Clara. You've been very frank with me, and I appreciate it."

She rose as well, smiling very nicely, but I saw the tiniest flicker of unease in her eyes.

"If there's anything else troubling you, Miss Van Lew, I'd be obliged to discuss it with you, anytime you like."

"I don't think that will be necessary. The sherry was very nice. Thank you."

I pulled on my gloves, and she followed me into the hall. A young woman was coming slowly down the stairs in disordered hair and a bit of black silk. *Just once,* I thought. *Just once, I'd like to put on a dress like that. God in heaven, how the whole of Richmond would laugh. . . .*

I said a pleasant good-bye to Madame Clara and went home. I had a brief talk with John about it, because I wanted him to know that I knew, and to learn it from me, and not from someone else. And then we put our red velvet skeleton back in the family closet and quietly closed the door. As long as Madame Clara prostituted no slaves, broke no laws, and kept the chimneys clean, she could stay.

It was one of the wisest decisions we ever made. . . .

It's late now, and the moon is gone. So are Chris Taylor and Tom McNiven, who have wandered off without a word to the rest of us. A kind of steady yet uneven clamor is floating down from Shockoe Hill, too ghostly and too distant to identify. Whatever it is, however, it is lively.

"The Rebels," Angelina says softly, "they must be haffing vun hell of a good time."

I smile, but don't otherwise respond. *There'll be stories to tell when it's over,* I reflect. *Too bad Cooper can't write any more books. But then, if he could, he'd probably leave too many things out. Just like he did the first time around.*

"What do you think, Will?" I murmur to my old friend. "Do you suppose Cooper DeLeon ever patronized Madame Clara's establishment?"

"You ask the most amazing questions, Miss Liza."

"Well, did he, or not?"

"As regular as he could afford it, I expect."

"Yes. That's rather what I think, too."

The wind rises, and for a moment we can hear the gathering on Shockoe Hill more clearly. Shouts, and answering shouts, and then one incredible, bloodcurdling Rebel yell. This is one of those nights when the living must feel the hair stand up on the backs of their necks. Whether they actually see us, or just think they do, is a question I've never answered to my own satisfaction. But they know we're here.

"How did Tom get to know her, anyvay? He vas too poor to buy her viskey, much less anything else she vas selling."

I stare at Angelina, momentarily bewildered. "Get to know who?"

"The courtesan. Madame Clara."

"Oh. I've no idea. I never asked. Tom knew everybody."

And truly he did. All the laborers. All the hack drivers and mule-skinners and bartenders, the tradesmen, the little shopkeepers—yes, and all the low life, too, the petty thieves, the drifters, the gamblers. Tom McNiven was gregarious and outgoing, yet he knew how to guard his tongue, how to find things out without giving things away. One thing he found out was that Madame Clara felt no particular loyalty to the Confederacy. Neither did some of the prostitutes who worked for her. He also found out, or perhaps already knew, that a man enjoying himself in a brothel often drank too much. Talked too much. Liked to make a big impression on a beautiful and worldly woman.

What better way than to promise her a new dress, or quinine for a girl who couldn't shake the fever? Neither item could be found any-where in Richmond, but he would get it for her anyway, cross his heart and hope to die, there was a blockade runner due in Wilmington on the seventeenth, and he knew all the merchants who had import contracts, one of them was a very old friend. . . .

What better way than to tell her she mustn't worry her pretty head about Lincoln and his nigger army, they'd never take Richmond, not ever. They thought they had General Lee all bottled up over there at Petersburg, but they were in for one hell of a surprise. Lee's boys were breaking out; they had it all planned. He oughtn't to be telling her such things? Why the hell not, it would be all over the front page in a few more days. . . .

High-ranking men from every branch of the Confederate elite called on Madame Clara. Congressmen, senators, cabinet ministers, generals. Judah P. Benjamin, secretary of State, whose bottomless supply of Yankee greenbacks led to infinite speculation about where he was getting them. At least for a while. Until the British consul got drunk in Clara's bed and bragged about having Benjamin on the im-perial payroll. Whether it was true or not only heaven knows, but I always wondered what Colonel Sharpe did with it. I still wonder, to tell you the truth.

It was quite remarkable, really, the way some men took their wits off along with their clothes. Quite apart from the military information we got, which was considerable, we benefitted from learning all sorts of ugly little secrets about all sorts of people—secrets which at critical moments made sure a door remained unlocked, a witness remained silent, an arrest order was never given.

Oh, it was a gold mine, that house in Locust Alley.

"Miss Liza, look."

It's Willy Lohmann, trying desperately to get my attention, and wagging his head toward the west. "Someone's coming!"

Coming slowly and cautiously, pausing often, as someone might who felt unsafe, or who didn't quite remember the way. She is quite close before I recognize her.

"Mariel?"

Angelina turns, lets out a great yelp of joy, part German and part ghost, impossible to describe, and runs to wrap the newcomer in her arms. I simply stand and stare.

"Mariel! How vunderful you come! All these years—vere on earth haff you been?"

"Upriver a ways," Mariel says. She turns to me. "It's been a long time, Miss Liza."

A very long time. I'm not even sure how long, in human terms. She revened for a while, here in Richmond. We saw glimpses of her, felt her thoughts sometimes. Then she went away, as though our ghost world held too many angry memories. Or, perhaps, too many angry white men.

"It's good to see you, Mariel."

We gather in a little circle around her. Everyone is happy to see her. God knows the black people never got their share of credit for what they did in the war—not even from us, sometimes. But Mariel's twenty-one months in the Rebel White House were an achievement beyond the reach of any of us, and we all know it.

"So," Angelina says, when the greetings are properly over. "You haff heard about the big ruckus, yes? They are trying to decide who is the greatest Southern lady."

"Yes, I've heard. There's folks out nobody's seen since the war. And all the big shots, too. I think maybe they're going to talk about more than the ladies."

"Like what, for instance?" Sam asks uneasily.

"Maybe they want to secede again," Will says dryly.

We laugh a little, and move on, Mariel and I drifting side by side. You'd think we might want to catch up on what's passed since we last met; but no, we talk about the war, how we managed this, how we learned about that. So an hour passes, or more, and then she says, "I always did want to ask you, Miss Elizabeth. The nice-looking young lieutenant, I can't remember his name—"

"Jed Knight?"

There's a note of amusement in her unvoice. "You liked him real well, didn't you? That boy from Tennessee? Colonel Sharpe sure thought so. He told me Jed was always your pet."

If ghosts could blush, I would be rather pink.

"The colonel said that?"

"Oh, he meant it kindly. He was pleased about it, far as I could see. After all, the lieutenant was his pet, too. But the fellow I wanted to ask about was the other one. The Reb lieutenant. The one Old Winder sent to live in your house."

"Oh, heavens, did you have to remind me? His name was Bonham. Andrew Jackson Bonham."

It sends a chill through me, even now. Having a Rebel officer in the house was a kind of last straw, a thing I simply could not abide. I'd get up in the morning, and Bonham would be underfoot. I'd come home in the evening—exhausted perhaps, or shaken by some awful piece of news—and Bonham would be underfoot. There was nowhere I could feel safe, not even in my bed, because I didn't know what he might be up to, or where he might be sneaking about, looking for something to hang us with.

"So what happened with him?" Mariel asks. "All I ever heard was that he left. Rather suddenly, it seemed."

"Yes. He left. I think I drove him crazy. I did some pretty strange things to throw him off."

I am lying just a little. Lying by omission. I did some strange things to rattle him, it's true. But sometimes I just did them. The war was simply more than I could take, sometimes.

"One night when I couldn't sleep, I went down to the piano and started singing hymns. At the top of my voice. At three o'clock in the morning."

Broad is the road which leads to death, and thousands walk together there. . . . All the sad hymns, the dark ones, the bleak, terrible Calvinistic ones, belting them out with a driven exultation, as though I were throwing them into someone's face, maybe the Rebels', maybe God's: Do your worst, it doesn't matter, we're not going to quit. . . .

I wondered after, and I still do, what poor Bonham thought of it, if he was edified, or merely horrified. It was the middle of the night, after all.

Our relationship ended in October of '63, right around the time the Union soldiers in Chattanooga were boiling mule hoofs five times over, trying to stay alive; and General Rosecrans, the man in charge, was walking around like a duck who'd been hit on the head. I wasn't in much better shape myself, some nights, prowling the house for something harmless to do. I'd sit in the kitchen and feed Jason milk out of a spoon, scratching his ears and wishing he was big enough to eat Lieutenant Bonham.

Oh, I can talk brightly about it now, as I can about so many dark things. But the truth is, it was a desperate time, and through it all the war kept right on going. It didn't end after Vicksburg and Gettysburg, like we'd expected. The Rebels licked their wounds and backed off a ways, and circled around, and knocked the living daylights out of us along a tangled riverbank called Chickamauga.

We couldn't believe it. It was the worst defeat of the war, after we'd imagined there wouldn't be any more big defeats at all. After we'd imagined it was almost over.

Chickamauga broke my heart. I didn't know it then, but I suppose I had begun to crack a little at the edges, the way people do in a war. You have a name for those things now; we didn't. All I know is that through the whole of August and September, after young Bonham moved into our house, I would cry at the drop of a pin, and I couldn't sleep, and I saw things sometimes, strange things I couldn't explain. And then came the September afternoon I still hate to remember, people running up the streets, and down the streets, and every which way, waving their hats and their newspapers and anything they could find, shouting to their neighbors: "Did you hear? Did you hear? We whipped the Yanks to pieces in Georgia? Did you hear? . . ."

AUTUMN, 1863. . . .

Chickamauga. The River of Blood. A brutal, ghastly slaughter, the dead lying everywhere like last year's flowers, and worse was likely still to come. The beaten Army of the Cumberland had fled back into Chattanooga, and now it was trapped there, the river on one side, Braxton Bragg's Rebels on the other. One little dirt road the only way in, the newspapers boasted, and hell the only way out.

I don't remember how long I cried. Probably for hours. It was dark when Josey finally persuaded me to come down and have a little tea. At the parlor door I stopped utterly still, staring with my hand across my mouth. Lieutenant Bonham was sitting in the old cane chair opposite my mother, his face like a death's head, with all the bones showing through; he was twirling a hangman's noose lightly in his hand.

The room tilted, and my knees turned to water. I have never fainted, never in my life, I refuse to faint, I don't believe in it. But I came very close to it, just then. Josey held me up on one side, and Mother ran to support me on the other. When I steadied myself and looked up, Lieutenant Bonham had risen and taken a couple of steps toward us, concerned and ready to help. Lying on the chair was a harmless little curtain cord, which, I learned later, my mother had asked him to fix for her. He was very good with his hands.

But I knew. I knew already, and when I looked into his eyes, I knew for absolutely sure. He'd made up his mind about me. All he had to do was spring the trap.

It's strange, that other sight. Knowing the apparently unknowable, without evidence. Knowing it instantly, without process. Men have the gift, too, but they always pretend it's something else. Chamberlain on Little Round Top. *We're out of ammunition? Well then, all we can do is attack.* Pure intuition, straight out of the bones of the earth. But nobody admits it. You can't give a man a medal for being irrational, after all. Even if he was right. Even if he saved the whole Union line, and maybe Gettysburg itself, in a single improbable act of knowing.

But a woman can admit to any amount of witchery, especially a spinster. It's practically expected of us. And I believed what my intuition told me: This pleasant-faced young man was about to destroy me, if I didn't find a way to stop him.

I spent the whole night standing by my window. The next morning I sent Josey's boy out early to fetch the papers, hoping against hope there might be some good news. There wasn't. There was only more grief. Tomorrow at the stroke of noon, the citizens of Richmond could witness the hanging of yet another Yankee spy.

His name was Spencer Kellogg Brown. He had been a scout for the Union navy in the west, and did all manner of marvelous things inside the enemy's lines. He returned to regular service, and was captured near Port Hudson—captured in Federal uniform, as an ordinary prisoner of war. While his superiors hastily tried to arrange his exchange, he was recognized by a Rebel engineer whose defenses he had scouted. He was charged as a spy and sent to prison in the east, where, after a year of futile protests and appeals from Union leaders, he was condemned to death.

They hanged him at the fairgrounds on the edge of town. I should have stayed away, I suppose, heartsick as I was from the shock of Chickamauga. I could do nothing for him, after all, standing alone at the farthest edges of the crowd. I could only grieve, and frighten my own self half to death. He was so young, and just recently married, and by strict military law they had no right to hang him, not anymore, but it didn't matter. Somebody pulled a lever and the poor, ragged form fell and tossed, and most of Richmond applauded. I looked at the ground and at the sky; when I looked at him again he was almost still, just turning a little, like a rag doll on a wire. How many of us would follow him, I wondered, to the same wooden steps and the same vile death, our last sight on earth a ring of faces filled with hate, wishing us Godspeed to hell?

I turned away, shaking, so sick I feared I might retch in front of my neighbors, and half expecting to see Lieutenant Bonham smiling down at me with a curtain cord in his hands.

It's hard now remembering him. Sometimes I can't even see his face, only his form, a presence moving in the dark places of my mind, as he moved in the darkened places of my house. He never went to bed early; sometimes he never went to bed at all. He had taken to sleeping in a storeroom behind Winder's office, so he could stay awake all night in the house on Church Hill.

He was a man who wanted very much to do his duty. He felt buffeted and bewildered by the whole situation, I suppose, not knowing what to believe, what to think of the family he was living with. . . .

OCTOBER, 1863. . . .

Everyone kept telling Lieutenant Bonham something different.

The neighbor lady thought the entire Van Lew household should be hauled off to jail. He had barely moved in before she got to chatting with him on the street, and inviting him to tea. She marveled at what he must be putting up with, living in that house. "They're from the North, you know," she said. "And they're up to no good."

She saw a man one night, she told him, all ragged and dirty, sneaking toward the side door like a thief, and they took him in. The next day it was all over town that a prisoner had escaped from Libby. She went to the provost marshal, and the house was searched from top to bottom. Of course, it was too late; the bird was flown. That was in '61, she said. She'd seen it a dozen times since. She'd seen other things, too. People coming late at night, in ones and twos, and staying for hours, with barely a light on in the house. Decent people didn't behave like that. Did she tell the authorities? he asked. No. She was tired of telling the authorities. General Winder was too busy mollycoddling the Yankee prisoners to pay attention to anything that really mattered.

General Winder, on the other hand, assured him the family was perfectly harmless. The mother was a lovely old lady, he said, and the daughter was just soft-headed and hopelessly emotional, the way women got when they had no children and didn't have enough to do. And Winder's detective Cleary was absolutely certain she was a spy.

Bonham didn't trust Winder's judgment; he didn't trust Cleary's. And he didn't especially trust the lady next door, either. Anyone who thought the prisoners in Libby were eating better than the guests in the Spotswood Hotel did not have a terribly solid grasp of reality.

At first, when Liza started wandering around at night, he was convinced she was up to something, though he could never discover what it might be, other than fetching a book from the library or talking to her cat. Then she sang hymns in the middle of the night, and he was no longer sure of anything. He wished he was at the front. He hadn't joined the army for this, really he hadn't.

Finally, around the middle of October, Cleary told him something useful. There was a Yankee courier in town. A *known* Yankee courier.

"He came in last night," Cleary said, "real quiet, but we spotted him. Thought we'd give him some rope. Ten will get you fifty Miss Liza's got something for him."

Bonham would have raised the stakes even higher by the time the household went to bed. The blacks didn't know in which direction to look. Long silences at the table were broken by sudden bursts of mindless conversation. Miss Liza was so on edge she spilled her tea.

He was not at all surprised when she got up in the night. She was very quiet. Much more quiet than usual. Had he been asleep, or even seriously engrossed in his own thoughts, he might never have noticed.

He followed her very carefully. He knew where to step on the stairs so they didn't creak, and how to turn all the doorknobs so they didn't rattle. He watched her pad down the long hallway, pause once at the library door to look back uneasily, and then disappear inside.

He waited for several minutes just outside the door. He wanted her to get well started on whatever she was doing. He wanted to be absolutely sure, to have something that would convince everyone, including himself. He wanted this to be over. It wasn't triumph that he felt, having finally caught her; it was relief.

He heard a key rattling in a lock, a drawer opening, papers being moved. Then it got very quiet, except for an occasional rustle of paper. He shoved open the door, saw the woman turn her head, saw her mouth open in a great "Oh!" of dismay. She sprang to her feet, shoving things back into the drawer, trying to block his view with her body. Her eyes were wide with surprise and fear. Nonetheless she made a valiant attempt to be calm.

"Lieutenant Bonham, what on earth are you doing here? Are you ill?"

"No, madam. Stand aside, please."

"I certainly will not." The words were strong, but the voice wasn't. Her mouth quivered ever so little.

"Madam, I am an officer of the provost marshal, and I mean to look in that drawer. Stand aside."

"There's nothing in there to interest you, Lieutenant. And you have no right to go through my private things."

He moved toward her, and she began to cry.

"Please," she said, "don't tell John and Mother. Please. I just can't abide living like we do. I just can't. Please don't tell them."

The words were meaningless until he opened the drawer. It was full of sweets. Cookies, some of them crumbling and covered with mold. Pieces of candied fruit, with bits of dust clinging to them. Lumps of sugar in several small, ratty bags.

"I try to do without," she went on. "I try so hard but I can't. I feel so awfully weak when I don't eat sugar, it's like I can barely stand up. There's something wrong with my blood. Josey told them years ago but nobody believed her. And soon we won't be able to get any more at all, I just know we won't. So I have to save it, don't you see, but they wouldn't understand. Oh, please, don't tell them. . . ."

He stared at her. There were crumbs on the front of her dress. There was a smear of chocolate on the side of her mouth.

My God. I've gone sleepless for three weeks to catch a March hare who steals the family sweets, and sneaks out of bed to stuff herself in the middle of the night. No wonder Dave Todd couldn't wait to trade Richmond for the front lines. Any man in his right mind would rather be shot at.

He went through the drawer anyway, because he knew he should. He went through the entire desk. He made her empty her pockets, but all that fell out of them was candy. Her thin face was pale; even tears failed her as the enormity of her humiliation sank in. What would her family think if they knew? What would her Yankee pets in Libby think?

If she'd been a very young woman, or a really old one, he might have felt sorry for her. But as it was, nothing softened his distaste. She was a horrid, pathetic creature, and all he wanted was to get out of this house as quickly as he could.

He didn't tell her family about it, though. He only told General Winder, when he was able to get his attention, which wasn't easy anymore. Winder didn't comment; he just sat for a while behind his desk, smiling a little, like any man would who'd finally been proven right.

Shortly afterward, Lieutenant Bonham was quietly transferred somewhere else. Liza Van Lew never asked where. She never had the smallest wish to know.

EIGHT

———————※

MAN'S DESTINY
IN THIS WORLD

General Grant . . . contained no spark of military genius . . . He . . . had such a low idea of the contest, such little appreciation of the higher aims and intellectual exercises of war that he proposed to decide it by a mere competition in the sacrifice of human life.

Edward A. Pollard, Associate Editor, *Richmond Examiner*

. . . From Shiloh to Appomattox, he never made one combination stamped by mark of any soldiership, higher than courage and bull-dog tenacity.

Thomas Cooper DeLeon

It seems that man's destiny in this world is quite as much a mystery as it is likely to be in the next.

Ulysses S. Grant

As I've told you before, I never planned to be a spy. When the war began I simply wanted to help the Union cause, and the most obvious way to do it was to help the prisoners who came to Richmond. It didn't occur to me that newly captured prisoners of war, having just seen the enemy army close up, could be excellent sources of useful information. They'd had a firsthand look at numbers, arms, supplies, and morale. They might know if the army had detached some of its troops, or if it had received reinforcements. Sometimes, they could even guess the enemy's plans.

It was the prisoners themselves who brought this fact to my attention. I was known in Libby by then, and trusted; I still had permission to visit the hospital wing. A wounded officer asked me to write a letter to his father. As he dictated it, he interspersed, very softly, a single question to me: "If I give you something, can you get it to Fort Monroe?"

I must confess, I thought the idea was very exciting. Maybe, just for a moment, I thought I would put on some kind of disguise, jump on a horse, and gallop all the way to Fort Monroe myself—the same sort of thing Belle Boyd did for the Rebels. Or at least, they say she did it, racing hither and yon on a beautiful bay horse, hair flying in the wind, precious military secrets tucked inside her bosom.

I told him yes. Of course, when I got back to Church Street with my little scrap of paper, I realized I had no idea whatever how to get it through the lines. But I had friends, and they had friends, and I still remembered how the Underground Railroad worked. Disguises occasionally, but very little fuss. A headlong ride now and then, perhaps, but mostly just quiet planning and quiet, cold nerve. You put a sack of something you were selling into a wagon and drove it to a neighbor's house. They had a sick cousin down the valley, and went to visit him. The sick cousin's wife went across the county to buy some hay . . . and eventually somebody got to Canada. Or to Fort Monroe.

I remembered one other thing about the Railroad. Everything that could be done openly was done openly. I went down to the provost marshal's office and got myself and all my servants passes to go in and out of Richmond.

That's how it began. At the time, though, I didn't think of it as the beginning of anything. It was simply something I did, because I had to. A couple of months later I found myself with an escaped prisoner in my garret. He was not the first. Two others had stayed with me briefly. I gave them food, John gave them some of his clothing, and Nelson sneaked them through the picket lines in the dead of night.

This man, however, had injured his leg while escaping, and was barely able to walk. And while I could go through the pickets easily enough with a piece of paper sewn into the hem of my skirt, I couldn't do it with a Yankee soldier curled up in my wagon. I spoke to a couple of friends, but they weren't able to help. Then one of them asked me if I knew Mr. Ruth.

"Samuel Ruth? The railroad superintendent? I've met him, but I don't know him well. Why?"

"He's a good Union man, Miss Liza. Maybe he can think of something. Go and see him. Tell him I sent you."

I admit I was skeptical. Union man or not, Samuel Ruth held a high-ranking job and counted many important people among his friends. Would he really be willing to risk it all, and his personal safety as well? I had several arguments prepared, including, if all else failed, a tearful plea for a ragged, wounded boy who would surely die if we abandoned him to the miseries of Belle Isle.

I didn't need any of my arguments. I merely had to explain the situation.

"Keep him under wraps," Sam said calmly. "I'll send someone to get him when I'm ready."

All unbeknownst to me, Sam Ruth had been using his very convenient, aboveground railroad for Union work for some time. Escaped prisoners, deserters, and reluctant conscripts were carried to the rail end at Aquia, a mere few hundred yards from the Potomac River, and rowed across to the Union side at night. If the Rebel army was campaigning anywhere near Fredericksburg, Federal scouts found Sam's trains a fast way to get deep into enemy territory, and out again. And of course, since the railroad was itself a major means of transporting troops and supplies, there was a lot

Sam could tell the scouts himself, not only about activity on his own line, but often on other lines as well.

He didn't tell me any of this at the time, of course. But he took my fugitive off my hands with such competent ease, it was obvious he had done such things before, and would probably do them again.

So it all just grew, like Topsy. Through Sam, I was put in touch with the Lohmanns, who were related by marriage to Robert Orrick, who kept a safe house along the R.F. & P. line. I'd known the Lohmanns before the war, but only as the keepers of a nice restaurant in New Market, where you could get the best apple strudel in Virginia. Through them I recruited Martin Lipscomb, who liked strudel a great deal, and money even better. Another Union friend introduced me to Tom McNiven. He had been involved with the Underground Railroad for several years before the war and, like Sam, was already doing Union work on his own. Still another confided to me that Richard Walker, a city councilman and a major in the Home Guard, had never been in favor of Secession, and could probably be won over. In time he was.

By Christmas of '62, I had a loosely connected network of some thirty or forty people. We all chose code names for ourselves. I was Babcock, as I've mentioned. (I thought it a nice, ordinary name when I picked it. Later, when Grant came to Virginia, he brought along a staff officer named Babcock. If the Rebels ever found my alias on any messages, they must have been wonderfully confused.) Tom McNiven called himself Quaker; Sam Ruth was Mr. Hills; Will Rowley was John Phillips. We sent out military communications from time to time—various facts that one person or another noticed and considered important. But except for Sam's firsthand information on troop movements, I truly don't know if anything we sent out, during the first year and a half of the war, was of any use at all. I don't know if anyone important even saw it. There was no organized intelligence service in the Union army at the time, only a few individual spymasters running about, telling the generals pretty much what they wanted to hear.

But I learned a lot in those early months of floundering. I learned that if you pricked a raw egg on both ends with a pin, you could carefully suck out the inside, let the shell dry out, and then slip a rolled-up paper inside. I learned that even honest men might have difficulty telling the difference between a favor and a bribe. I learned to look around my house and spot all the good places where I could hide something—and then not to use any of them, because somebody else could look around and spot them just as easily as I had. I learned that sabotage and subversion were also part of war, and therefore a lot of information didn't have to go across the lines at all; it merely had to go to Tom McNiven.

Finally, in January of '63, after the disastrous Union defeat at Fredericksburg, Joseph Hooker took over the Army of the Potomac, created the Bureau of Military Information, and put George Sharpe in charge. That's when things began to change.

Hooker was a brilliant organizer and administrator. Better than any other general in the Army of the Potomac, he understood how much a commander's success depended on reliable information. And he knew that if such information was to be obtained regularly and accurately, and passed on to him quickly enough to be of use, it had to be handled in an organized fashion—not by the commander himself, who had too many other things to worry about, nor by his equally busy and sometimes inexperienced staff. He needed men trained for the job, men with nothing else to do. He needed, in short, an information service.

Hooker had a book on this very subject, but it was written in French—presumably for the armies of Napoleon. The general couldn't read French, but he knew of someone who could, a young colonel from New York, George H. Sharpe.

Sharpe was one of those men who, back in ancient times, they would have called a favorite of the gods. He was strikingly handsome, with dark hair, a dark handlebar mustache, and an air of elegant worldliness that was, I discovered, entirely authentic. Good food, good wine, and good company were things he took for granted in life, and fortune always provided them. When the war began, he was thirty-three, with a wife and three children, a thriving law practice in Kingston, and a history of succeeding at most anything he tried to do. He joined the war as colonel of the 120th New York, and at that point, he had no more notion of getting involved with spies and spying than I did. He was fond of his regiment of New York volunteers. He didn't want a staff job. He didn't even want a promotion. He wanted to stay with the men who had followed him to war.

Fortunately for all of us, he knew French. Hooker summoned him to headquarters, and put him to work translating his book on military information. He also, I must assume, talked with the young colonel, evaluated him, and liked what he saw. A gifted man, this linguist. Graduated from Rutgers University at the age of nineteen. Served with the diplomatic corps in Rome and Vienna. Spoke four languages. Raised his own regiment in twenty-two days, on the strength of his own charisma, and with his own funds. All this and a lawyer to boot, professionally trained to sift and evaluate evidence, to ask searching questions, and elicit information even from those who didn't want to give it.

Yes, indeed. This was precisely the sort of man to put together an intelligence service out of just about nothing.

To George Sharpe's complete dismay, he was relieved of command of the 120th New York, and placed in charge of the newly created Bureau of Military Information. At the time, it was the last thing in the world he wanted; he even begged General Hooker to reconsider. But, compelled to accept it, he set about to do his best. He was not ambitious for fame or high command, but he was proud; he wanted to do something important in the war, and do it well. He must have realized very quickly that the Bureau was a singular opportunity.

Though General Hooker didn't stay in command of the army, the Bureau of Military Information stayed in place, making a significant contribution to the Union victory at Gettysburg. But it was the next year, when Grant came east and made the fur fly, that George Sharpe really found his spymaster's feet. And we found ours.

"We were the best, Miss Liza."

Neither of us was alive anymore, when Tom McNiven said it; we were just wraiths drifting over the water out by Belle Isle, more aware of the dead men who brooded there, than of the living children who played.

"Union or Reb," he went on, "we were the best by a mile."

A man can say such things, of course. A lady isn't supposed to. But Tom was absolutely right. We were the best by a mile. In the spring of '65 I could send a Richmond paper and a bouquet of pretty flowers out every night at dusk, and both would turn up on Grant's breakfast table by morning, as predictable as his pickles and black coffee.

But there. I've got ahead of myself again, probably on purpose. I don't like remembering the fall of '63—those terrible, sorrowful weeks after Chickamauga. Prisoners came into Richmond by the trainload, turning Libby into a human sardine can and Belle Isle into a deadly warren of ragged tents and despair. There weren't enough blankets; there was hardly any medicine. Food was a mouthful of this and a spoonful of that, and on a good day they got wood to cook it. And still the prison trains kept coming in.

Then Colonel Streight decided to buy his way free.

I never asked him about it, after, so I don't know precisely how or why he tried. Maybe it was happenchance; the opportunity merely turned up and he took it. But I think he went looking for it. I think he couldn't bear it anymore, the crowding, the awful food, the hopelessness. He'd imagined the war was almost over, as we all had. He thought he would get out soon, and instead there were only more and more men coming in, not one of them ready for it, their uniforms still bright blue, the spring still in their walk, and the sass still in their eyes. One or two would get themselves killed outright, just for walking near the window to have a look at the street. Others would succumb to typhus or scurvy or dysentery. Some would learn how to cheat and rob and betray their comrades. Some would die inside, slowly, and never be whole men again.

He wanted out, and he didn't much care about the risk. Maybe the guard made an offer, or maybe Streight asked. But one quiet, foggy night a deal was made. One gold watch for a certain door left unlocked, a sentry looking quietly the other way. He made it ten feet or so into the street, and found himself surrounded. Richard Turner was there. And three guards, all holding pistols, one of them the man who had taken his watch. And Little Ross, coming up with the lantern, the familiar, scornful, twisted smile on his face.

"Well, Colonel." Turner stood, looking him up and down, exactly as he might have looked at a fox in a snare. "Well, well, well."

Streight's big hands knotted into fists, but there was nothing he could do. The watch was gone, and he was going back to Libby.

"You miserable thieving son of a bitch," he said to the guard.

Turner hit him. Hard, in the face.

"You're a brave man with three guns backing you up," Streight said bitterly. "Why don't you send them inside and try it again?"

"I think we'll all go inside," Turner said. "Move."

But inside, when they came to the stairwell, and Ross started up with the lantern, Turner called him back.

"The other way, Ross. This one needs to stew in his own juice for a while."

Ross grinned, and turned, and trotted past them, heading for the door that led to the cellar stairs and the hole.

Streight didn't move. "You have no right to put me down there," he said. "There are conventions of war, Captain Turner. A prisoner can't be punished merely for trying to escape."

"Is that a fact? Well, then, I guess I'll have to punish you for being a town-burning, cattle-stealing, nigger-loving piece of Yankee shit. What would you say to that, Colonel Streight?"

"I guess I'd say that's why I'm wearing this uniform, and you're wearing that one."

You've got to learn to keep your mouth shut, Abel. His father said it a hundred times, or maybe a thousand. His father was probably right, but he didn't care. He'd call a rat a rat until the day he died. And Richard Turner was a rat.

The jailer smashed him against the wall, and when he tried to hit back the guards took hold of his arms. They ate regularly and he didn't, but it still took two of them. Turner hit him again, and again, and again, cursing, calling him names. The guard who had taken his watch turned away, ashamed. Even Ross looked like he was going to be sick. The little clerk had a mean tongue, but not much stomach for the sight of blood.

There was a good deal of blood to look at by the time Captain Turner finished.

They put Colonel Streight in the vilest hole in Libby Prison. Without light, without a blanket, without the sound of another human voice or another human footstep, except for the guard who, once a day, brought him a pitcher of water and a single piece of bread.

There were objections, of course, even from some Confederates. But objections were becoming the order of the day, and most of them were ignored. There was too much to object to. A hanging here, a quiet backwoods massacre there. Broken paroles, and broken promises, and all manner of lies. The war was turning dirty. Not entirely, not everywhere, but more than anyone expected, more than we wanted to believe.

More than most of you believe, even now.

October became November. The days grew cool, the nights damp and cold. Above his cell, in the cook room, his comrades pried loose a floorboard, as they always did when someone was in the dungeon. They dropped him food, a candle and some matches, a wooden whistle to play with, brief letters on tiny scraps of paper. *Seems all the thuggery in town has finally come home to roost; they broke into Gen. Winder's house last night and stole everything; Richmond's laughing itself silly. . . . Captain Jessop of Ohio got out; no-*

body knows how.... We got a Baltimore paper; says they're sending Grant to Chattanooga; hope to God it's true....

For the first time in his life, Abel Streight was scared. Not sensibly scared, the way any sane man was in combat, but scared inside, quietly and coldly, in a manner that never went away. He could die here. Just die and be carried out one morning and left in the shed for the grave digger, like all the others. He was tough as a prairie wolf and he thought he could survive anything except a minié ball, but maybe it wasn't so.

Sometimes, when the guard came with his bread and water, he actually thought about begging. *Please. Talk to Captain Turner. There's no need for this. Hell, maybe I did push him too far; it wouldn't be the first time....*

He thought about it, sometimes, but he knew he wouldn't do it. Not yet, and please God not ever. He wanted no truck with the Rebels. None.

The guard who had taken his watch and then betrayed him never came down to the dungeon. Never except once—one particularly cold, gray, and bitter morning. He put the water pitcher down carefully, and the piece of bread beside it. He looked at Streight, and then away, and then back again. He chewed on his lip a little before he spoke.

"Look, Colonel. I want you to know something. I didn't . . . I never thought it would turn out like this. I mean, it was just a watch. You weren't going to miss it. You got money; everybody knows it. Only . . . I had no idea Captain Turner would do something like this. I thought he'd just put you back where you was."

Streight said nothing.

"I got a family," the guard went on, desperately. "I got five kids, and they're hungry most of the time. I just thought—" He faltered, and stopped.

"You could have let me go. If you wanted the watch."

"No." The guard shook his head. "I couldn't do that. Not in a war. Neither could you, I figure."

He dug into his pocket, and pulled something out. "We ain't all like Turner. Those Yanks who came in from Chickamauga, they can tell you. Our boys gave them their own food, when they hardly had none themselves. Gave the sick ones their blankets. Carried them when they couldn't walk. You ask them." He took a small step forward. "Here."

He held out a bread roll. Streight reached for it eagerly. Even before he brought it to his mouth he could smell the maddening, heavenly scent of mustard and ham.

"We ain't all like Turner," the guard said again. And then, before Streight could even thank him properly, he turned away, unable perhaps, with his five hungry children, to bear to watch him eat it. . . .

In mid-October of '63, after the Union disaster at Chickamauga, President Lincoln reorganized three of the western armies into a single command under Ulysses S. Grant. Ten days later Grant and his small staff took the wilderness road out of Bridgeport to join the besieged Union army in Chattanooga. The Bridgeport road was the only route into Chattanooga not held by the Confederates, and it was scarcely a road at all, just sixty-five miles of mud and rock and desolation, so narrow that two wagons, traveling in opposite directions, could hardly ever pass. In the lowlands muck came up to the horses' bellies; on Walden's ridge the trail was so steep the animals fell and sometimes died from exhaustion. It would have been difficult to supply a village over such a road; to supply an army was impossible. Unless the siege was broken, the Army of the Cumberland would be starved into surrender.

So we watched the events in Tennessee with great anxiety. Then, in the midst of them, my family was plunged into a serious crisis of its own. My brother was conscripted into the Confederate army.

The draft law had been on the books for some time, but in the early months it was easy to evade. Only poor and uneducated men were actually taken to fight against their will. Slave-owning families could exempt one white male for every twenty slaves they owned. Hundreds of trades and professions were exempt. If all else failed, and you had money, you could get out of it by hiring a substitute or paying a bribe.

But then General Lee lost a third of his army in Pennsylvania, and Pemberton's entire force surrendered to Grant at Vicksburg. The Rebels needed men. The list of lawful exemptions grew smaller, and John was caught up in the newly tightened net. Substitution was out of the question; we were not about to pay some dirt-poor, hungry farm boy to go shooting at our flag. And General Winder, corrupt though he was in his own inimitable way, was not a man who could be openly bribed.

I must have waited three hours to see him. I know he was hoping I'd go away. He was tired of me, no doubt, and tired of most everything else. According to the street talk he was growing more and more ill-tempered as the weeks went on, more impatient, more unwilling to listen to anything he didn't want to hear.

It didn't look good for me. It didn't look any better when Philip Cashmeyer, his top aide, came out and said to me, wearily, "You may as well go home, Miss Van Lew. The general simply cannot see you today."

"I have to see him, Captain."

"It is not possible."

"It's absolutely necessary."

Cashmeyer was of German background, a pale, slightly stooped man with receding hair. He spoke perfect English, but slowly, as though he never wanted to make a mistake. He was quiet, unobtrusive, and efficient. He was Winder's right hand man.

He also worked for me.

"He will not see you, Miss Van Lew. Believe me, I know when he is serious. Please go home."

"Then perhaps you can help me."

"Perhaps another day. Most certainly not today. I have no time."

Suffice it to say that we shared several more such exchanges, while some of the other people waiting shook their heads in frustration or amusement. But in the end, of course, Crazy Bet had her way. He took me into one of the little offices down the hall, and said, before I could even sit down, "Really, Miss Van Lew, I must impress on you, this must stop! You simply cannot keep coming here asking for things. He will get so tired of it he will have you shot."

"Yes, Captain. He very well might. In the meantime, my brother has been conscripted."

"So let him desert. Please, Miss Van Lew. There is a war going on. There is nothing I can do. Please. Go home."

"Well, if I must I shall. But there's a matter of some seriousness I wanted to pass on to General Winder, since we've been friends for so long. Perhaps you can do it for me. I heard it from a neighbor, so of course I can't be certain if it's true—"

Cashmeyer already had a glazed look in his eyes. "Miss Van Lew, please, I am a very busy man."

"What I'd like, Captain, is for you to draw General Winder's attention, with all the care and good sense I know you possess, to the fact that he might be victimized by a terrible scandal. I know there's nothing to the story, of course, and I said as much to the woman who told me. I made her promise she'd never say another word about it, ever, to anyone. I know the officers of the provost marshal would never do such a thing."

"And what sort of thing is this, which they would never do?"

I looked down at my hands, and I wasn't pretending. Captain Cashmeyer always seemed a very . . . well, a very *proper* man.

"Taking city property, and using it to pay for . . . favors. In Locust Alley."

Suddenly he was very wide awake. He leaned forward in his chair. "What sort of city property?"

"Things for the hospital, she said, and blankets they bought for the refugees."

"Were the men seen?"

"Apparently."

"They were seen, doing this which they would never do?"

"So I have been told."

"If this is true, Miss Van Lew, it is most valuable information. Perhaps it should be preserved for a more critical moment—"

"My brother won't raise his hand against his country," I said. "And I won't see him killed for it. I think this moment is quite critical enough."

"Very well. I will tell General Winder of your concern."

"And of my friendship as well, Captain. You must stress our friendship. Tell him it's the least I can do, to try and protect him, after everything he's done for our family."

"And everything he will do," Cashmeyer added, without a hint of irony. "Well, I shall try my best."

I got to my feet. "Thank you, Captain."

I knew it was dangerous, what I was doing. Dangerous to threaten a man like Winder, no matter how indirectly. Dangerous to ever make him wonder if I might be someone other than the old, familiar, addlepated Crazy Bet.

On the other hand, it was said the feebleminded did possess a peculiar, unpredictable cunning. It made them very hard to deal with, since, after all, they could not be expected to listen to reason. . . .

No exemption turned up for John, and no medical discharge. He went to Camp Lee with all the other recruits, and drilled and marched and got yelled at, just like they did.

I waited, sick with dread. Maybe after two and a half years of being raked over the coals, Winder didn't care anymore what anyone said about himself or his men. Maybe Cashmeyer hadn't even talked to him. Maybe . . . well, the rest didn't bear thinking about.

Training finished, finally, and the men were marched off, willing or not, to join the Army of Northern Virginia. All except three. Two, obviously in poor health, were made guards at Castle Thunder. And my brother was assigned to a unit under the direct command of the provost marshal, Richmond.

I suppose it surprised you to learn that General Winder's top aide was working for the Union. The fact is, I had several people working, as you might say, on the inside. Mariel, of course, and Cashmeyer, and a man in the Engineering Department who made us maps of all the Rebel defenses around Richmond. I had a clerk in the office of the adjutant-general, and another in the War Department. And I had Kiley, too, who was perhaps the strangest and most unlikely of them all. But Kiley's work is another story, and it must be left for later. As for Philip Cashmeyer, I recruited him myself, yet he was the one whose motives I least understood. Perhaps, being such a precise, orderly man, he simply couldn't abide the *messiness* of a rebellion.

There were hundreds of other people in the Union camp as well—people who weren't spies or saboteurs in any formal sense, but who would, at least occasionally, do something to help the Federal cause or to undermine the Confederacy. It was Thomas McNiven, in particular, who made it known among the ordinary people the many small, ordinary things they could do. Lose something, break something, forget something. Leave a window open for the rain, or a gate for the thieves. Neglect to notice a rotting timber or a chain nearly rusted in half. And grumble, of course. Grumble loudly, grumble often, and then grumble some more. We played havoc with Rebel morale. And sometimes, I must confess, we enjoyed it.

There was always food in Richmond. The prisoners were half starving, the army was half starving, the poor in the streets were half starving, but the elites ate very well. So Tom paid a couple of youngsters to catch some mice for him, and some rats, and three or four skunks for good measure. He pried loose a window of Seabrooke's warehouse and dumped all the animals inside. The mess, when it was discovered, was ghastly.

"Well," he said, when he told us about it, "if all the food is for the skunks, the little skunks might as well eat along with the big ones."

For a long time after, all anybody had to do was say the word "skunk," and we'd smile. Even after Chickamauga. Perhaps especially after Chickamauga. You can scarcely imagine, I think, how defiant the Rebels became. How confident. They knew Lee would never be beaten in the east—not on his own ground—and now they had the Yankees all bottled up in the west. Burnside was stuck fast in Knoxville, running out of food. Grant was trapped in Chattanooga. And yes, he'd punched a nice, big hole in their siege line almost the day he arrived, and had supplies coming in, but it wasn't going to matter a fig. Bragg had all the high ground. Impregnable high ground. Missionary Ridge. Lookout Mountain. Nobody was getting up there except a legion of angels, and they'd probably have to say please. It was the beginning of a magnificent Southern comeback.

Then, one cold, damp day in November, as I recall, I went uptown with Nelson to buy groceries. There was an air of flamboyant optimism everywhere. People would hail old friends with a smile, and gather on the street in little clusters to talk about the war. At the corner of Fourteenth and Franklin we had to stop as a company of cavalry ambled by. The horses were as thin as fence rails, and the men were as scruffy as thieves. But they doffed their hats to the ladies who waved and blew them kisses, and picked up a boy who was shouting "Hurrah for Jeb Stuart!" at the top of his thin, little voice, and let him ride along for a block or two.

It was easy, on a day such as this, to forget how battered and vulnerable the Confederacy actually was. You could see it everywhere on the streets, if you looked past the smiles and the guns. Those cavalrymen were hungry, and cavalrymen could, and did, help themselves pretty freely to whatever pigs and chickens and garden plots they found. I knew Lee's men were a good deal hungrier.

There were signs in Richmond, too: storefronts boarded up, fine old houses with their paint peeling, and their wrought-iron palings beginning to rust. One day there was no meal in the markets, the next day no milk. Women of rank were beginning to sell their silver and their jewelry, slipping into the Broad Street stores with discreetly wrapped bundles, or sending their servants to do it, hoping no one would know. Those with nothing to sell lived on turnips and grits; meat had become a luxury for salaried workers, a mere memory for the widows and the poor.

Yet you could not go abroad in Richmond without seeing well-dressed people, men in fine broadcloth and linen, with gold watch fobs and gold rings. Come evening, they would fill the streets outside the Varieties Theatre and the Exchange Hotel. Beautiful young women in Paris gowns hung on their arms, or flirted with proud young officers who bought them oysters and champagne.

On this particular November day, I remember, Nelson and I walked past the house of John Daniel, on Broad Street. He was the editor of the *Richmond Examiner*. There wasn't much in the world Mr. Daniel seemed to like, and a great many things he hated—most of all Yankees, uppity niggers, Jeff Davis, and Jews, usually but not always in that order.

Daniel raged against corruption and profiteers in his editorials. He despised the predators in their gold watch fobs, the fancy women in their blockade-run silks. But today, like every other time, I noticed how fine his own house was, how immaculate. No rusted palings here, no chipped paint, no sign at all that he was living in the middle of a war. Sam had dinner at his house once, and told me after it was the richest, most exotic meal he'd eaten since Fort Sumter.

It took forever to find the things we needed, and we didn't find all of them. By then the sun was low, fading in a red glare behind the Tredegar's chimneys. We went to Broad Street to find a hack, just as a train was pulling in at the R.F. & P. depot. It came chugging and clattering, spewing out impossible amounts of smoke and cinders and noise, disgorging Rebel soldiers in all directions, then a few passengers, and finally, inevitably, a handful of Union prisoners. Enlisted men, all of them, bound for Belle Isle.

I didn't think about what I did; I just reacted. I had baskets full of food beside me, and the men were barely a stone's throw away. I would never get this close to them again. I snatched a few things and ran, through the astonished crowd and the prisoners' guards. Someone shouted at me: "Here! What the devil do you think you're doing, madam?" Someone else grabbed at my arm, but it was too late; by then I was shoving muffins into the captives' hands, bundles of carrots, a huge loaf of bread.

"You want to give us some of that, ma'am?" said a tired voice at my shoulder.

I glanced up at a Rebel guard. He looked exhausted, and he was thin and dirty, with an empty sleeve pinned up to his shoulder.

"We been on the road for two days with these'uns," he said. "I had but one piece of hardtack, and I gave it to the kid."

The kid he spoke of was a wounded Yankee, wrapped in bloody bandages and not looking a day past fifteen. He couldn't speak; his mouth was bulging with muffin. But he nodded when I looked at him, acknowledging the gift.

There were two muffins left in the bag. I handed it to the Rebel. "Thank you," I said.

He just stared. "You on their side?" he asked.

I didn't answer. In that moment, it seemed to me both armies were on the same side, and something quite different and horrible was on the other.

The hack took us home very slowly, the driver allowing right of way to most anything that happened by. There was a lot of movement on the streets, and most of it seemed to be in the same direction.

"Where's everybody going?" I asked him. "Do you know?"

"Telegraph office, I reckon. There's been a crowd building there for most of an hour."

It took all the strength I had to ask if he knew why. He replied with a small shrug.

"The usual. They say Bragg's pulling out of Chattanooga—"

"Pulling out?"

"That's what I hear. But I don't believe it. There isn't a day goes by when somebody doesn't tell me we've whipped the Yankees to pieces somewhere, or they've whipped us. Last week somebody told me the president had shot himself. Washington had burned down. The Yankees were invading Canada. If we could live on rumors, ma'am, we'd all be rich and fat."

"Go by there, please," I said. "By the telegraph."

"Cost you more."

I didn't care. I had to know. There was indeed a crowd gathered outside, milling and dazed. There was no cheering. Nobody shouted, "Did you hear?" at the newcomers. I had to ask them. Some cursed, not caring about the presence of ladies. Others said maybe it wasn't really so; we should wait for more news. They said there had to be some kind of explanation. But what they all said was that Lookout Mountain was gone. Missionary Ridge was gone. And Braxton Bragg's army was gone, out of Tennessee and pouring hellbent into Georgia. Withdrawing, he called it, but we all knew what *that* meant.

The magnificent Southern comeback had run headfirst into General Grant.

Of course you all know how it happened: Union troops going up Missionary Ridge to take a few rifle pits near the bottom, and not stopping till they hit the top. Nobody planned it that way, nobody ordered it. They just went. People said it was the soldiers' victory, after, not the general's, and of course they were right. But I always wondered if the soldiers would have done it for anybody else.

I still wonder, all these years later. Those men trusted Grant. They knew if they won something there, they'd get to keep it. He wouldn't bungle it away with some mindless blunder on the field, and he wouldn't fritter it away afterward by doing nothing. And maybe they didn't think about it on Missionary Ridge; they didn't have time to think about it. But they knew. . . .

Something—probably the Rebel gathering on Shockoe Hill—startles me out of my memories. It's so easy to get lost in them. I know Chattanooga isn't Grant's most famous campaign, the one he's most remembered for, but from the start of it to the end, I always thought it showed a lot about him—not least that he could think: fast, clearly, and on his feet. And that's what the Rebel mythmakers always tried to deny, especially Jubal Early and our good friend Cooper DeLeon. Grant wasn't much of a general, they said; not much of anything, just a sledgehammer in shoulder straps, a heads-down bull in a military china shop, who only won because the other boys ran out of china before he did. Jubal Early said comparing Lee to Grant was like comparing a great pyramid to a pygmy standing on a mountain. I wanted to strangle Old Jube when he said it, but after I thought about it for a while I decided he might be right. What's a pyramid, after all, except a tomb, a monument to some bully's gigantic ego, with the bones of innumerable slaves crushed in its very walls? Not a bad symbol for the Confederacy, though I'm sure Old Jube didn't notice. I much prefer a mountain, green and flourishing, and a man who climbed to the top of it on his own two feet.

I smile to myself a little, and tug lightly on Will Rowley's arm.

"Where do you suppose he is right now?" I ask him. "General Grant?"

"Missouri, most like. Sitting on a riverbank with Julia. Fishing."

I don't say anything to disagree. Wherever Grant may be, Julia isn't far away. But I wouldn't bet he's fishing. That's Will's picture of the man, the one he drew in his farmhouse long ago, the night we made our bet—the picture of a plain, ordinary man, who rose heroically to an extraordinary occasion. It's attractive, and so very American, but it's a man's picture: too neat, too sensible, and much too untroubled.

Taking a nation's vast armies into fire and blood and butchery, and winning there, is one thing. Going to the Saturday auction mart to rescue a neighbor's mule is quite another. They're not different in degree, they're different in kind. Both may demonstrate a man's talent for solving problems, but they don't come from the same place in his heart.

Will was right about the outcome; Grant got to Richmond first. But as for the general himself, well, he isn't so easily accounted for. I'm no closer to it than I was the first time I met him, when he sat on my veranda wreathed in smoke, holding as always his ritual cigar. It was his metaphor, I think, so deceptively plain, so plainly deceptive. A universal image of domestic contentment. A piece of imprisoned fire. A source of strange and always changing apparitions. A symbol of power turning relentlessly to ash.

A comforting and well-meant gift, which killed him in the end.

Such a simple thing, that cigar. Kind of stubby and weathered-looking, scarcely worth mentioning beside a lightning bolt or a crystal chandelier. But you will have written quite a bit about the world, by the time you've finished properly explaining it.

NINE

———————— ✳

WHAT TO ME
WAS MOST SACRED

I recall days in the fall of 1863 when we got nothing but a chip of
corn bread and half a potato, medium sized.

Bernhard Domschke, Libby prisoner

The guards . . . used to gun for prisoners' heads . . . [like] . . . boys
after squirrels; and the whiz of a bullet through the windows
became too common an occurrence to occasion remark unless
someone was shot.

Frank Moran, Libby prisoner

. . . The Van Lews marketed as regularly for Libby Prison as they
did for their own house. They put their hands on whatever of
their patrimony they could realize and expended it in what was
substantially the service of the U.S. government.

George H. Sharpe

. . . What to me was most sacred—Federal soldiers in prison and
in distress.

Elizabeth Van Lew

I told you at one point that Libby was the best prison in Richmond. It's true, but I wouldn't want you to get the wrong idea. Libby was nasty enough. Long after the war, a former prisoner told me Libby was where he got his first real glimpse of what it might be like to be a slave. Not for the hunger, he said, or even for the loss of freedom, terrible as both of those things were.

"It was the caprice, Miss Liza," he said. "It was knowing that somebody could just take it into his head to do anything he wanted, and you had to stomach it. And it might be the same man who'd been perfectly decent to you the day before. Or because you'd done something you'd done a dozen times already, without anybody minding."

Quite often, he told me, if the ground-floor cook room was free, the men would go down in small groups to exercise. The prison had no enclosed yard. They were never allowed outside, except on the rare occasions when a work detail might be assembled to carry in supplies. The cook room was hot and smoky. It wasn't a good place for wrestling or running; it was simply the only place they had. Sometimes they sang Union songs, tramping back and forth along the blackened walls. One day, a day just like any other, Richard Turner stormed in with his guards.

What the devil did they think they were doing? he demanded. There were decent people walking by on the streets, women and children, having to listen to all this miserable caterwauling. It was going to stop, did they understand? He would not have the citizens of Richmond subjected to any more of their disgusting Yankee insults.

Turner's lecture went on for some time, all of it peppered with the vilest of obscenities, none of which, presumably, the decent people heard. When he was done shouting, he left them standing at attention, under armed guard. Four hours, five, maybe six; the man who told me the story could not remember. Shoot anyone who moves, Turner said.

"The guards would have done it, too, probably. I told myself they wouldn't. All the time I stood there in the sweltering heat I thought, no, this is a civilized country; they couldn't possibly, not for something as stupid as this. But I knew they might. The rules were gone. It was all arbitrary, all just a matter of somebody's will. And some of them really liked the idea of shooting a Yankee."

Some of them really did. And if there was one thing that made Libby truly ugly, beyond the bad food and the insults and the punishment cells crawling with rats, it was the casual ease with which some guards used their guns. Libby was not in a compound, with walls and watchtowers. It was right on the street, and every foot of its perimeter was patrolled by armed guards, twenty-four hours of the day. Those guards were bored, no doubt, and sometimes angry, and had standing orders to shoot at anything that came near the windows.

The prisoners knew about these orders, of course; but sometimes they forgot. There might be a commotion in the street, or gunfire, or a child might scream. And one of them just reacted, and ran to look, and died. Or remembered in time, and flung himself to the floor, and the bullet slammed into a ceiling or a wall, or sent a canteen spinning across a table . . . or killed another man who sat harmlessly reading his newspaper. Sometimes nobody went near the windows, and random bullets came whizzing through them anyway, just to remind the captives, I suppose; to remind them where they were, and who had the guns.

Libby was in a rough part of town, near the juncture of the James River and the Kanawha Canal. Downriver a ways was the Tredegar, its black chimneys eternally fouling the air. Mills and tobacco factories puffed and belched in all directions; at times a pall of smoke and mist settled all along the valley, till the sun was sickly and yellow, and the whole world stank. There was always rubbish on the streets, and a good many ruffians to go with it; the navy yards were just across the bridge, and Locust Alley was a few blocks up the canal. It was certainly no place for a lady.

Yet I went there every few days, taking food and books for the prisoners, bringing back small, stealthy messages. This one, like so many others, scratched out in a novel—John's book, actually, *The Mill on the Floss*, which ended up in Libby just like all the others.

Digging. Out. Thirty. Men. Plus. In. Two. Weeks. Need. Everything. Straight.

You may think me a fool, but I almost cried for excitement and hope. Nothing in the war, except ultimate victory for the Union itself, mattered to me more than the captives in Richmond. And so, even now, I remember it all, how they lived, and how they died, and how some of them dug a tunnel under Libby Prison. And I remember how the whole thing got blamed on Abel Streight, even though he didn't have a thing to do with planning it. . . .

WINTER, 1863 . . .

Streight walked down the stairs into the cook room with some care, that cold, windy December evening. He had been out of the cellar for three days. Light didn't hurt his eyes anymore. He could eat a normal meal—normal by Libby standards—without getting sick. But he still felt weak; and sometimes, for no reason at all, the room would tip, and he would have to grab hold of something for a few seconds, quickly and discreetly, so no one would see him weaving on his feet.

He had lost fifteen pounds in the cellar, and acquired a severe cough. But he supposed he was lucky, all things considered. Still alive, and still on his feet, thanks to his own vitality, and to the bits of food and comfort the men had slipped to him through the floor. They gave him a hero's welcome, too, when he came back, and different prison messes vied with each other for the privilege of having him to dinner.

Tonight he had received yet another invitation, from Colonel Rose of the Seventy-seventh Pennsylvania, one of the men who had been captured at Chickamauga. Streight was very flattered by the invitation, since this group, unlike the others who had welcomed him so warmly, were men he did not know—men he had never met, until he came coughing and filthy from his dungeon.

The mess cook for the day was a ragged but cheerful Kentucky captain named Isaac Johnson—Zack to everyone in the world except his mother. He stood at the bottom of the stairs like a head waiter, pressed one lean blue arm formally across his belt, and bowed ridiculously low.

"Gentlemen, your table is waiting."

The only cooking he'd ever done before the war, he said, was maybe roast a rabbit over a campfire, when he was out hunting. He was obviously a young man who learned fast. The dinner, by Libby standards, was decidedly tasty. It was generously enriched with food purchased in the market, with the prisoners' own money. The day's beans were made into some kind of stew, laced with tiny pieces of real bacon. There was a bit of carrot as well as a bit of onion floating in the soup. Streight felt grateful to have been asked to share it, but he could not escape the feeling that it was leading up to something. From time to time, discreetly, he studied his host. Physically, Thomas Rose was a lot like Streight himself: big, bearded, and exceptionally blessed with pure animal strength and endurance.

The talk was casual, though. A lot of joshing, a lot of speculation about the war.

"What do you think about all this talk in the newspapers? Them wanting to make Grant lieutenant general? Give him the whole damn kit and caboodle to run?"

"I think they should stop talking and do it. After Chattanooga, what's there to talk about?"

"You know what a lot of the eastern fellows say, don't you? They say everybody's making too much fuss altogether about Ulysses Grant. They say he just looks so good because he's had it so easy. Because he's never met up with Bobby Lee."

"Vicksburg was easy, was it? River on one side, swamps on two more, and the whole damn Confederacy on the fourth?"

"Sounds perfectly easy to me."

"Maybe you should ask the eastern boys why they make such a fuss over Lee. He just looks good because *he's* had it easy, never meeting up with Grant. Or Sherman. Or George Thomas."

"Or Zack Johnson."

"With all due respect, sir, eat your stew."

"Well, something's got to be done, that's certain. It's six months now since Gettysburg, and all General Meade seems able to do is follow the Rebs around the countryside like a God damn chaperone. . . ."

They talked, and they laughed, and they complained. And sometime in the course of the evening, or perhaps at the end of it, Rose found an opportunity to draw Abel Streight aside, and offer him a second invitation: "Come down here tomorrow night. After lights out. I have something you might like even better than Captain Johnson's stew."

The cook room of Libby Prison was on the ground floor. The door opened right onto Cary Street, where two heavily armed sentinels paced, never moving more than ten or fifteen feet away. Any light inside would be seen; any voice above a whisper might be heard. The gathering the next night was, of necessity, extremely discreet.

Four men waited for Streight in a huddle near the stoves, barely visible in the bit of gaslight that came in through the windows. Rose greeted Streight with a brief handshake, and introduced the others. Major Bedan MacDonald from Ohio. Captain Andrew Hamilton from Kentucky. Zack Johnson he knew.

"As I said," Rose went on, "I have something which might interest you. First, however, there are two things we have to settle. We've all taken an oath of secrecy, and I have to ask the same of you. What we discuss here tonight, or anything which follows from it, must remain between ourselves. Your word of honor, Colonel?"

"You have it."

"The other thing is, I remain in charge. No offense, sir, believe me. You may well rank me; I don't know. But I'm the expert for the project in hand. We're all agreed the final decisions and the final responsibility rest with me. Can you live with that?"

"Easily, if you know what you're doing."

"He does," Andrew Hamilton said. "Count on it. He does. He's the best damn mining engineer in the whole of Pennsylvania."

"Mining engineer?"

"Yes," Rose said. There was the tiniest trace of a smile in his voice. "We're digging our way out of this rat cage, Colonel. We thought perhaps you'd like to help."

The cook room took up the entire middle of the building on the ground level. Solid brick walls separated it from the section to the east, which contained the prison hospital, and from the section to the west, which contained the administrative offices and the sleeping quarters of the guards.

The basement was similarly divided into three completely self-contained areas. Under the offices was the main supply room. Under the cook room were the punishment cells where Streight had been confined. Under the hospital was nothing at all.

"Except rats," Zack Johnson said. "Lots and lots of rats."

"When we first came in from Chickamauga," Rose went on, "Captain Turner was like the old woman who lived in the shoe. He had so many of us he truly didn't know what to do. So he made another kitchen for us down there, in one corner. It struck me at the time it might be a good place to dig out of. It must have struck Turner the same way, because he closed it up again right quick. He even nailed the stairwell shut."

"Which was really a blessing in disguise," Hamilton said, "since nobody goes in there now."

"Except you, I presume," Streight murmured. "So the tunnel starts there, right? Where's it going to come out?"

"There's a sewer running right alongside the building. It's a big one. I had a pretty good look at the workmen going in one day—

as good a look as I could, without getting my head blown off. And the Kanawha Canal runs right alongside of us, too, just a bit farther south. So the sewer will lead into the canal. It has to. Nothing else would make sense." He straightened. The trace of a smile was back in his voice. "So, Colonel Streight. Would you like a guided tour of Rat Hell?"

Behind the stove where they gathered was a huge chimney, running from the basement to the roof, along the cook room's east wall. Several slop barrels were stacked around it, in which the mess cooks dumped whatever pitiful bits of waste their lives in Libby allowed them—mostly dirty water. Since no Rebel guard was ever going to demean himself by carrying out Yankee slop, the barrels were never moved except by the prisoners themselves.

Rose moved a couple of them, carefully, and knelt, spreading out a rubber sheet on the floor, covering the area all around the fireplace. Streight heard a soft scraping sound; then Rose's hand reached out, holding a brick.

"You're going down through the chimney?" Streight asked him. "Won't that just land you in the dungeon?"

"It would have," Hamilton said. "So I had to cut an 'S' through the damn thing—down to get under the hospital wall, and then east to get to the other side of the dividing wall, and then down again. Without breaking through anywhere, or the guards would have seen it."

"The captain did a hell of a job," Bedan MacDonald said cheerfully. "But he thinks we're all made like snakes. Rosey got stuck in there and damn near suffocated."

Hamilton didn't bother to answer. He had done the only thing possible, and they all knew it.

"How long have you been at this?" Streight asked.

"Oh, weeks, I guess. The chimney was the worst. It took forever. The tunnel's going faster. In fact, Colonel Rose thinks we might hit the sewer in as little as ten days."

"When do you sleep?"

"We didn't, for a while," Hamilton said. "Now we've got three teams, so we only dig one night out of three. We lost a man a week ago; he got sick. We weren't going to bother replacing him. It's too hard to know who you can trust. But when you came back, we figured we'd like to have you along."

"Thanks."

"Wait till you're down there awhile, Colonel," Johnson said wryly. "You might change your mind."

You forget, Captain, I was down there awhile. Rather a long while. Hell's going to freeze over before I change my mind.

Rose backed out of the chimney and got to his feet.

"All right, let's go."

Hamilton rolled the rubber sheet into a funnel, carefully shaking the accumulated soot into a pail. He dug inside his blouse, and pulled out what looked like a mass of tangled rope. He tied one end to a kitchen pillar; the rest of it had been knotted into a sturdy ladder.

"You boys are good," Streight said. "Are you going to tell me where the devil you got that?"

"Sanitary Commission. They sent in a whole raft of blankets for the boys on Belle Isle. All tied up in nice long ropes just like this. Colonel White took one and snuck it back. He didn't even know about the tunnel at the time. He just thought a good rope was a good thing to have; if all else failed he could use it to hang himself."

"Watch it, Zack. The whole damn Rebel army can hear you."

"Sorry, sir."

They threw the rope into the opening and climbed down. Johnson, the lightest of them, remained last. He untied the ladder so it could be pulled down and out of sight, and crawled backward into the opening, pulling slop barrels after himself to cover the hole in the chimney. MacDonald waited to catch him as he slid down the ten-foot wall into the place they called Rat Hell.

It was well named. Squeaks and scratching claws and rustling straw erupted all around them. The darkness was absolute—not a dimness to which the eye would gradually adjust, but a permanent, utterly impenetrable black murk. Carefully, Rose led the way, and the others followed him, holding hands like schoolboys in a pit.

They'd begun digging six days before, in the southeast corner, near the back of the abandoned cooking area. They had made good time, Streight thought, considering what they were using: a chisel, a wooden spittoon to put the dirt in, a clothesline to pull the spittoon back and forth, a candle for the digger, and the rubber blanket for fanning air. One man dug, one was responsible for receiving, emptying, and returning the spittoon, one fanned, one kept watch, and one served as relief for the others.

It was sickening work. The ground was soggy. The air was a thousand years old and impossibly vile, reeking of rats and death and decay. It was worst of all for the digger, whose body filled much of the tunnel and who therefore got barely enough of what wretched air there was. Yet Rose had done from the start, and would continue to do, far more than his share of the digging.

Once started on the work, they did not talk, except for the briefest whispers. A tug on the clothesline indicated that the spittoon was full, or empty. A tap on the shoulder offered relief. The darkness and the dead air numbed everyone's senses. After a while everything became fuzzy—one's sense of time, one's sense of direction. It should have been an easy thing to walk to the north end of the room, empty the spittoon under the straw, and walk back again, but more than once a man would find himself stumbling into a wall, without the slightest idea of which wall it was, and then into another, and then find himself back in the straw, hopelessly lost and impossibly frustrated. It didn't help that the rats were constantly squealing and running over his feet. He couldn't call out to his friends to find out where they were. He couldn't even kick at the abominable things around him, lest he kick into something that would make noise.

As desperately as they wanted the tunnel finished, every man was thankful to the point of tears when the four o'clock watch was called, and they had to quit. Light-bodied Zack Johnson scurried up the chimney from the shoulders of his comrades and threw the ladder down for the others. They piled the bricks back into place; tossed the soot by hand all over the rebuilt masonry, working it here and there into the cracks as necessary; shoved the slop barrels back into place; rolled up the rubber sheet and stuffed it into somebody's blouse, the rope ladder into somebody else's.

Exhausted and filthy, their lungs full of pestilence, their eyes burning, they crept back up the stairs to their respective quarters and collapsed on the floor, where the most restless of their comrades were just about to begin getting up.

That, more or less, was how Abel Streight became part of the tunnel team. In return, he told them he had a link to the Richmond underground, to people who might be able to help them after they got out. Streight's prestige in Libby was by this time enormous; no honest man there doubted either his loyalty or his judgment. He said we should be told, and Rose agreed, and George Eliot's novel was returned to me with thanks, ever so slightly and imperceptibly defaced.

As for myself, I must say my sanity improved remarkably after Lieutenant Bonham left the house. So did my confidence. There's nothing quite as good for one's morale as getting into a bad pickle and getting out again intact. It happened at the right time, too. I was going to need every ounce of morale I could find to get through the year ahead of me.

The bloody summer of '64, they would call it afterward. I don't know why they picked on the summer; the whole howling year was bloody, and frightening, and cruel. On New Year's Day the battlefront from the Atlantic Coast to Arkansas was buried under snow, and men found the water frozen in their canteens as far south as Memphis. Here in Richmond, in the prison camp of Belle Isle, the bodies piled up faster than Martin Lipscomb and his crew could bury them. The starving prisoners ate any ghastly thing they could find, plant or animal, living or dead. A stray dog wandered onto the island one day, and was lured close with a scrap of food, and killed. A lot of jokes went around the city afterward: *Keep your pets on a leash, boys; it's dog eat dog among the Yankees.*

"The devil's come upstairs," my mother said to me once. "And he's planning to stay for a spell."

The Union victory at Chattanooga had changed the face of the war. And the change wasn't simply in the military situation. It was in the soul of the Confederacy, too. A kind of splitting happened. A lot of people gave up. And in many who didn't, we saw a growing recklessness. The newspapers poured out venomous editorials in a steady, putrid stream. Lincoln the orangutan and his depraved hordes were going to reduce the South to the vilest subjugation imaginable; bestial black savages would be set loose upon a defenseless citizenry; every city, every village, every sacred homestead, would be torn apart with rape and butchery and fire, and the whole of Christian civilization would vanish into ash and desolation.

I am not exaggerating. We read these phantasmagorias, in one paper or the other, nearly every day. We were told of hideous atrocities committed by the Northern troops, but there never were any details. The precise town, the precise date, the names of the victims—none of this ever appeared. Only the hate.

Perhaps that hate bewilders you now, but there was a reason for it. There was more at stake for the slave-owners than eight hundred million dollars invested in human property. There was a sense of rank and power whose loss would be irreplaceable. Through every waking moment of his life, a slave-owner was reminded of his own superiority. The reminders were real, tangible, made of living flesh and blood. Lowered eyes and quick, ingratiating smiles. Hands within a whisper's reach, barely needing the whisper, anticipating: "There's a draft, sir, shall I close the window?" Carriages at the door, men existing for no reason in the world except to sit there, holding the reins. Everything a slave-owner looked on paid him honor, not least the ignorance of untaught minds, the timidness of fettered wills—sometimes real and sometimes feigned, but always real to him. *Look at them, how weak they are, how childlike. What on earth would they do without me?*

That paid him honor, too. That perhaps most of all.

Now the mudsills of the North were tearing his honor and his superiority to pieces. Coming into his states, his cities, perhaps his house, telling him it was a myth, telling him his slaves weren't his and they sure as hell didn't need him, nobody needed him, not in that sense, he wasn't Massa anymore, he was just a man like everybody else—which was the same thing as saying he wasn't a man at all, since "everybody else" meant niggers and white trash and foreigners and all the scrapings from the gutters and the jails and the lunatic asylums.

No one would do this to him unless they were evil. No one would so overturn the natural order of the world unless they were themselves beyond reason or redemption.

That's how it was, by '64, in the hard center of the Rebellion, among the radicals. Slave-owning destroyed men's sense of limits. And it was going to be a deadly business indeed, trying to put some sense of limits back.

There was a particularly nasty editorial in the *Examiner,* the day Clarinda came. I read it at Lohmann's restaurant, with my tea, and I promised myself, for the seven hundred and seventy-seventh time, that I wasn't going to read another one, ever.

When I got home, Josey met me at the door. She took my coat and parcel, leaning near and speaking in a stage whisper.

"We got company, Miss Liza."

She saw my troubled reaction and said quickly, "Oh, no, Miss Liza. I mean *real* company. It's Miss Clarinda from Devon Hill. She just come a while ago. She's in the parlor with your mammy and Mr. John, and they're talking right serious about something."

"Just Clarinda? By herself? Miss Catherine didn't come?"

"No, ma'am."

"Do you have any idea what they're talking about? Why she's here?"

"None at all. But your mammy asked me to give you a message before you go in. No matter what Clarinda says, she begs you to let it pass. To not let on your feelings about the war. You know how Miss Clarinda is, she says."

Oh, yes, indeed, I knew. "Maybe I'll go hide in the cellar."

"Just eat a mint, Miss Liza. I put out a whole tray full."

I gave the black woman a wan smile and walked toward the parlor with something close to dread. I hadn't seen Clarinda since John and Catherine separated, and I didn't want to see her—not as long as I lived, I thought, and well into the hereafter.

Clarinda was the widow of Compton St. Clair, Catherine's eldest brother. The St. Clairs were highborn planter folk from South Carolina, who moved west, as so many other Carolinians did, to take advantage of the rich new soils of virgin land. Also, like so many other Carolinians, they moved west because they were broke, although that part of the family history never got mentioned anymore. The previous generation of St. Clairs had four sons, all of them with an appetite for gambling and good times, all of them spending every dollar the plantation made and more. As cotton drained the life from the eastern fields and their incomes declined, they borrowed. They sold off land and slaves to pay their debts, but somehow there were always new debts, and less and less property to sell. Eventually they sold their home itself, took what money and what slaves they had left, went to Mississippi, and started over. In one generation they were rich again, richer than ever and prouder, too, on a sprawling plantation they named Devon Hill.

Good blood, the St. Clairs had, to prosper the way they did. Good Norman blood, not a drop of lowly Anglo-Saxon in it anywhere. But alas, they were westerners now, and by that fact alone they'd come down in the world. It was probably the only reason Catherine was allowed to marry someone like John Van Lew. Clarinda had not approved. Rich Virginians his family might have been, but they were still only shopkeepers, after all. They had that funny, foreign-sounding name, too, and they had a mouthy spinster daughter who wanted to turn all the niggers loose and ruin the whole country. The marriage would be a disaster, Clarinda said.

She was right, of course, and I saw the disaster coming as readily as she did. Catherine St. Clair was bright, charming, and extremely pretty, but she and John didn't have a thing in common, as far as I could tell. I said nothing about it, however. It was one of the few times in my life when I kept my mouth shut. I knew John wouldn't listen; he would only be angry at me. I also knew that, once in a while, the most unlikely people married, against all common sense and against all the advice of their peers, and proceeded to be ridiculously happy together for the rest of their lives. Most important of all, perhaps, I knew that a single woman over thirty, objecting to someone else's marriage, was by definition just being nasty.

John married, in a great splendiferous celebration on the St. Clair estate. People spoke about it afterward for years, but I was never so bored in my life. We got up every morning, piled into half a dozen carriages, and went to one place. We met several thousand relatives of impossibly complicated degrees, chattered politely about nothing for an hour, piled back into the carriages, and trotted off to another place to meet some more. This went on for two weeks. I had never before seen so much idle glitter, so much endless, purposeless running about. But I bit my tongue repeatedly and sailed through it, for John's sake. I never said a word about slavery or abolition. As for other political issues, when I brought any of them up, when I made any comment or asked any question concerning the issues of the day, the result was at best a collective shrug: *Oh, that? We don't know anything about that.* At worst there was silence, and embarrassed looks flying around the room like splatter from an overturned punch bowl.

I could not believe so many women were so totally uninterested in the world. Surely it was just a performance; surely they were playing out a role. Unfortunately, in time the role could shape the woman, just like bondage sometimes shaped the slave. There, on the St. Clair estate, it first crossed my mind how much good women and good slaves might have in common.

It took about four years for my brother and his wife to realize the enormity of their mutual mistake. Catherine didn't like Richmond. The lower sort were mostly foreigners, and the rest of us were impossibly bookish and artsy, forever looking down our three-hundred-year-old noses at everything west of the tidewater. She grew lonely for her family, and bored without the endless visiting and socializing which had so bored me. Worse, she discovered that John was inclined to be frugal—an infuriating and miserable and totally *Yankee* trait. He thought one house, one carriage, and one closet full of clothing were all anyone could use, and therefore all they should bother to acquire. He saw no need for employing an army of servants. There was nothing for them to do, he said. Which missed the point, of course. Poor John went through his entire marriage with Catherine missing the point. She didn't care if there was a practical reason for doing certain things; she did them simply because they were done. She wanted lavish possessions, a lavish social life, a great circle of important friends. She had been born to these things, and reckoned them as a measure of her own worth. John hadn't the means for such a lifestyle? Well, that also missed the point. A proper man did everything possible to acquire the means. He cultivated the right people. He embraced the right ideas. He kept, if necessary, a lid on the loose mouths of his dependents. He became Massa.

Even love couldn't make John into any sort of Massa. She left him late one December, as though she literally couldn't face the thought of starting another year in Richmond. It was a holiday, she said, to visit her family. Perhaps she intended it so. Perhaps she thought he would come after her. He never did, and her visit home became a permanent, informal separation.

Was she perhaps coming back?

I paused with my hand on the doorknob, numbed by the thought.

Devon Hill was in a war zone now. Perhaps Richmond, by comparison, had become a lot more attractive?

I shoved open the door, and heard Clarinda's voice. It was low and delicate, as any lady's should be; but it held a deep, melancholy bitterness.

". . . Every last thing. Every chicken, every hog, every sack of corn. They took it all. They pulled the vegetables right up out of the garden. They cleaned out the smokehouse. And do you know what their captain said to me when I protested? He said it was all General Van Dorn's fault, and I should complain to him! Can you believe it? He told me I should go and complain to our own leaders about the villainy of the Yankees!"

Clarinda was dressed entirely in black. Compton St. Clair, a colonel in the Confederate army, had been killed at Stone's River, one of many things for which the Union would never be forgiven.

"Hello, Clari," I said.

Before Clarinda could respond at all, John was on his feet. "Oh, Elizabeth. My heavens, you came in like a cat."

I walked over to Clarinda's chair, gave my sister-in-law a polite peck on the cheek. "It's good to see you again, Clari. Are you well? And the family?"

"We're keeping body and soul together, my dear, though I swear sometimes I don't know how. What can we possibly do, just three poor women all alone, and Catherine failing like she is? But the Yankees don't care. We could fall down starving in the road, and they'd tramp right over us. And you know, I used to think they meant well. Before the war, I mean. All those horrible things they were always saying about the South, I just thought they didn't know any better. But they're just savages, and it's all they ever will be. I've never wished evil on anyone, Eliza, never in my life, but I know they'll pay for it in the end. God has a long memory."

I helped myself to some tea, and sat down. I knew things were difficult on the St. Clair plantation. One brief, cold letter from Catherine early in the summer had made it very clear. Devon Hill was going all to wrack and ruin. Grant's army had been there.

Why it had been there, of course, she never mentioned. Back in December, Earl Van Dorn's cavalry had destroyed the huge Union supply depot at Holly Springs, and Bedford Forrest tore up the railroad over which new supplies might have been brought. Many another general, in Grant's place, would have pulled his forces out. An army couldn't survive without a base and a supply line. Everybody knew as much. Grant looked around, saw the whole Mississippi Valley full of food, and said "Piffle." He stayed, and fed his army off the land, and so discovered how easily the thing could be done.

Useful knowledge, a few months later, when he struck out without base or supply line again, this time on purpose: a lightning sweep down one side of the Mississippi and up the other, to Vicksburg— a campaign for which no supply line could have been established or maintained. With thirty thousand Rebels captive, and the great river finally free, he may well have sat down, lit himself a cigar, and silently thanked Earl Van Dorn for the lesson.

I knew I ought to feel sorry for the St. Clairs, and I did, in a distant, detached kind of way. On the other hand, it was the planters' war, more than it was anyone else's; I couldn't quite see why they should escape its teeth.

Besides, there was another reason they were all so upset.

"All our Negroes are gone," Clarinda was saying. "Every last one, except old Cato, and Jezzie, who's too lame to do anything, and just wants us to feed her, and Jezzie's little granddaughter. That's all we have left. The others all ran off when the Yankees came. Right in the middle of whatever they were doing. Young Joe was halfway through milking the cow, and he just put the pail down and left it there, and went sashaying down the road. Mother St. Clair is absolutely heartbroken. They were like family to us, and they just ran off and left us to starve. I couldn't believe it. I just couldn't. They were laughing and singing, most of them, like it made them happy to see us robbed and abandoned."

"Maybe it wasn't that," I said. "Maybe they were just happy to be free."

My small remark immediately drew a warning look from John, and a frown from my mother.

"Free?" Clari said scornfully. "Free for what? To dig ditches for the bluebellies, and be their sluts? They were just stupid running off, and they'll wish they hadn't in the end. Even Jezzie says so. The Yankees have to move on sooner or later. Old Cabe Lyons says the first thing he'll do is get up a patrol and fetch all of his back he can find, and they'll be the sorriest niggers in the whole of Mississippi when he's finished with them. I can't really say I blame him. Between the Yankees coming and them going there isn't a planter in fifty miles could get his crop in this spring. With Catherine sick, it was all I could manage to put in a garden. Now poor Mother's over sixty and has to drag in firewood and scrub clothes every day, after she took care of those people all her life? It's enough to make you cry, to see her brought down to that."

"Catherine is sick?" I said. "I didn't know."

"Yes," John said. "That's why Clarinda is here. Catherine and the family want me to go to Devon Hill."

"Go to Devon Hill?" I groped like a drowning person for the first piece of wreckage I saw. "But. . . . but how can you? You're in the army now."

Clarinda looked sharply at me, revealing just a hint of surprise. Had Miss Lizzie actually said something even remotely patriotic?

"There will be no difficulty in getting a discharge," she said coolly.

She didn't elaborate. She didn't have to. The St. Clairs had many powerful friends—in South Carolina, in Mississippi, and of course, now in Richmond. They must have had half a regiment in the Confederate army, if you added up all the cousins and the in-laws. If they wanted one slender, bookish, decidedly unmilitary and uncommitted brother-in-law back, to keep their plantation from falling into absolute ruin, and to protect their womenfolk, somebody would pull the necessary strings.

"I see."

This I was not ready for. I sipped my tea, so I did not have to look too carefully at anyone.

"I'll have to give it some thought, Clari," John said. "You must understand, I have responsibilities here, too. Mother and Elizabeth."

"Why, they must come with you, of course. We'd never expect you to leave them behind."

"Then we shall all have to give it some thought," John said. "But tell me, you said so little about Catherine's illness. What does the doctor say? Surely it isn't serious, is it?"

"She's coughing all the time, and losing weight. The doctor thinks it might be consumption."

"Oh. Dear God."

"It's the hardship making her sick," Clarinda said bitterly. "She was fine before the war. The family's always been healthy. But the Yankees won't quit until they've wiped every one of us out." She picked up her teacup, but did not drink. "I know you're from the North, Eliza, and your husband was, too, and you must understand I'm not saying this to be unkind. But I'll never forgive them as long as I live. I'd starve first, and I'd watch my children starve, too, if it came to that—"

"Oh, Clari . . ." Mother whispered.

"How can I forgive them? My husband's dead. I've got four brothers in the war. Two of them dead, and one half dead in that horrible Elmira Prison, and nobody knows where Calvin is. . . ."

She went on. A quiet, heartrending litany of names. Cousins, cousins-in-law, friends. I stopped listening. It was cowardly of me, I suppose, but I couldn't afford the strength to deal with her grief. Sometimes it was harder for me to think about the Rebel dead than to think about our own. Ours had meaning. A terrible, desolate kind of meaning, perhaps, but meaning nonetheless. But to die for the Confederacy, it seemed, was to die for nothing. Even if they won the war. Even if they built an empire. It was still for nothing. A life wasted for the empty privilege of owning other lives. Most of them understanding so little of it, riding to the flag and the drum with all the buoyant courage youth can possess. . . . No. If I had listened to Clarinda I would have wept like a beaten child, or screamed at her: *Then why did you ever begin? Lincoln's government was the first in fifty years you didn't control, the very first, and you bolted, and started a war. He wasn't going to take your slaves away. He couldn't have. All he could do was try and stop the thing from spreading. And yes, it would have died eventually; it had to grow or die, like all monstrosities, but it would have taken years. Decades, probably. You could have been waited on right into your graves, the whole howling lot of you. So why didn't you just let it be?*

I put a mint in my mouth, and thought about other things. About my meeting with Martin Lipscomb, earlier in the day; he'd hired two more grave diggers, he said, trying to keep pace with the bodies piling up on Belle Isle. I thought about the Libby tunnel. They might be surfacing in a matter of days, and if nothing went wrong now it would be the biggest breakout of the war. We had to have hiding places ready. Clothing, money, guides. . . .

I caught snatches of the conversation. Mother had quietly and gently steered the talk away from the war, to matters of family. How was Grandfather St. Clair's back? And the children? Madison was nine now, wasn't he?

"Yes, and a real little Rebel," Clarinda said proudly. "You should just see him. I made him the finest gray jacket you'd ever want to see, and his grandpa made him a wooden gun. All he wants to do now is march up and down the road, popping away at Yankee birds and Yankee squirrels. When he's ten, Grandpa's going to give him a real gun."

God help us. Just what he needs. I stopped listening again. Martin Lipscomb wanted money. Quite a lot of it. I knew he was taking far too much for himself, but there was little I could do. How long, I wondered, was our money going to hold out? I'd raised Madame

Clara's rent substantially, and even persuaded her that it was for her own good. After all, rents were going up everywhere. If her sporting house went on paying a pre-war pittance to a known houseful of Yankee sympathizers, somebody was certainly going to wonder why.

Clara sighed, and paid. A couple of weeks later, Tom McNiven came asking for funds, grumbling bitterly that the cost of information in Locust Alley had quite suddenly gone up.

Sometimes you couldn't win.

I sighed mentally, sipped some tea, and turned my attention to my kin. Clarinda had finally got around to the gossip. Who was mad at who, and why. Who was courting who, and whether or not she approved. Who had done the unimaginable or the unforgivable. Cousin Liddie's husband, the Dennison boy, did we remember him, he was in the cavalry when the war broke out, and Liddie begged him and begged him to resign, but he wouldn't listen. He was an officer of the United States Army, he said, and there was a war on; he would do his duty. Southern born and bred, the apple of his father's eye, and he walked out on them. Went over to the Yankees. Well, he wasn't a Dennison anymore. They cut his name out of the family Bible. Took his picture off the mantel. Even papered over his room, where he'd lived as a boy, and threw out everything he'd owned.

"Liddie can hardly bear to talk to anybody now, she's so ashamed."

The war, Clarinda went on, was ruining more than soldiers' lives and planters' crops. It was destroying families, marriages, morals. People were doing things now they'd never have dreamt of in the fifties. It was so sad, what the country was coming to; it was enough to break your heart. Miranda Wyatt, she was Nathan Wyatt's girl, did we remember, we'd met them at John's wedding; she picked up a soldier in her buggy, going home on leave, he had a train ticket but the track was torn up for thirty miles, and he had to walk. He hadn't eaten in three days, he said, so she took him home and fed him, even though she knew no one else was there, and with one thing and another it got late, and the weather turned bad, it was just pouring rain, and he asked if he could stay the night, he was so tired, he said, and the silly girl let him. Afterward she swore up and down that nothing happened, nothing at all, but they were all alone in the house, and the whole countryside was talking about it, and her mother was heartsick because Zeb Leland wouldn't marry her now, and how could you blame him, he'd never live it down. Even if she was telling the truth, and probably she was, he had to consider how it *looked.* . . .

Well, it looked like poor Miranda maybe had some sense, more than you and Zeb Leland and the rest of Devon Hill put together. . . .

I almost said it. I had my mouth open. I even made a tiny sound, but the others weren't sure they'd heard it and I grabbed a mint and drowned the words in sugar. Wise Josey, to put out a whole tray full. A lady couldn't talk with food in her mouth. She could only think about what had been said, and what it really meant, and how crazy it all was.

The way things look. Honor, in other words. The central pillar of the whole genteel slave state, with its moneyed patriarchs and its sainted ladies and its slave cabins full of paler and paler children. A woman's honor was the most precious thing on earth, and she didn't ask what made such honor possible, or why it was so fragile she could scarcely sneeze without blowing it to pieces. She didn't ask why it led so easily to the dueling field or the battlefield. She preserved it at any cost, not only the fact of it, but the name, and if need be the name rather than the fact. Honor was a public thing by definition; if she lost it, she might as well be dead.

If she kept it well enough, of course, there were rewards.

Was it worth it, Clari? Your miles and miles of cotton, your miles and miles of silk? Your easy life, your terribly prestigious marriage? What's it like, I wonder, sleeping with prestige? You mourn him now, but even Catherine said you never loved him, and he never loved you. It was all horse breeding and high finance, and everyone approved. Especially you. Was it worth it? If the Yankees hadn't come, if you could have kept it all, was it worth what you paid for it—your soul?

Do you think as little of me as I do of you? You would if you knew me well enough. Given half a chance once, I would have bedded down in the woods with a slave stealer, and given half a chance now, I'd send your honorable Confederacy to the devil. You and I are farther apart than the North and the South, and likely to be longer in finding a peace.

Somewhere, in the background, Mother was asking yet another question. I put another mint in my mouth, and pulled a shawl around my shoulders. For the rest of the evening I said almost nothing, only answering when I was spoken to, answering with few words and less energy. When I thought a sufficient amount of time had passed, I told them I was dreadfully tired, and went to my room.

By then I really was tired; tired and knotted up inside, like an overwound clock. Clarinda had brought it all with her, all the silence, all the rage, all the miserable rules, brought them in her soft gloved hands like a fresh basket of Mississippi clay.

People are doing things now they never would have dreamt of in the fifties. As if my sister-in-law ever knew what other people dreamt of in the fifties. Or ever wanted to know.

Why don't you ask Wade Hampton's violated daughters what they dreamt of, down in Carolina, four pretty maidens all in a row? Old maidens now, just like me, wondering what happened to their lives. I, at least, have a fair idea what happened to mine. The scarlet letter on my breast stands for Abolitionist.

Did they dream of redemption, or revenge, or just escape? Of heroes riding out of the mist to carry them off somewhere safe, where nobody remembered that Uncle touched them? Uncle James Henry Hammond, Uncle James the mudsill man, planter, patriarch, politician, defender of the Southern way of life, of all those God-given institutions that keep us honorable. . . .

I walked to the window. I was exhausted, but I knew I would not sleep. It was all around me again, like a house full of evil spirits, and I didn't want to deal with it. There were so many things I didn't want to deal with, didn't even want to think about, at least till the war was over, and first among them was my place in the world. That place so carefully circumscribed, so carefully defined. Woman. Lady. Spinster. Concentric circles, around each of them a wall of loneliness, and in their bone-dry heart a stifled will and an empty bed.

Poor Miranda Wyatt. Or maybe not. Maybe lucky Miranda Wyatt, to have it all thrown in her face at once. Do what I never did, Miranda. Climb on a westbound train and sing them all a long good-bye. I played by the rules too well, for way too many years. Be nice, Elizabeth. Be good. Forty-five howling years of it, and still no end in sight, remember you're a lady, Elizabeth, you mustn't challenge people, you mustn't make them feel bad. You're a lady, Elizabeth, you don't think about men, not that way, and you don't think about freedom, either, not that kind. Think of your future, Elizabeth, a man may be loved for many things, but a woman is loved only for her virtues. Womanly virtues, of course. Unimpeachable modesty. Gracious submission. Each enlisted in the service of the other, twin angels beckoning us from the walls of a high, doomed fortress—the offspring of honor, perhaps, or its unnatural parents—but we climbed for all we were worth, and the best of us, I think, climbed the hardest. For a while.

Idealism did that to you, when you were very young. You wanted to be good. Only it became clearer and clearer as the years passed that you weren't cut out to be a real lady, it just wasn't in you, you kept running headlong into your own self like a brick wall, your willfulness, your hard, analytical mind, and yes, your idealism, too, the same idealism as before, telling you half of it was pollywoggle, anyway; there were more important things in the world than wearing all the right clothes and saying all the right things to people you didn't even like. And then you were trapped, caught between one way and the other. You couldn't live the role, but you couldn't really throw it over, either, because they'd done too good a job on you when you were young; and besides, when you looked hard and honest at the world, you didn't much like what else it had to offer for a woman.

So you had a choice. You could die inside, or you could go away. To some place, however strange, however tiny, where they wouldn't come—or at least, where they wouldn't come very often, and where they wouldn't stay. A sickbed. A garden. A room full of books. And if all else failed, an empty house and an attic window.

I sat down at my dresser, stared at my face in the mirror. I was surprised by the hardness in my eyes. I was over-reacting to Clarinda's presence, and I knew it. I also knew why. It frightened me to remember Clarinda's world. It had been designed for me as well, and it wounded me even to brush past its sharp and perfumed edges. I'd had a taste of freedom. A real taste, strong and sweet and sprinkled with danger; it wasn't a dream anymore; I'd had it in my hands, and in my belly. I would have killed for it now.

I can hear the catch in your breath as you read, and see the uneasiness in your eyes. Some things haven't changed much at all, I've been told, from my generation to yours. Women are still supposed to keep the rules. We're still presumed to be loving and motherly, and not much troubled by sensuality or pride. A woman shouldn't be as comfortable in the world of warfare and violence as I was. And if she is, well then, she should certainly never admit it.

But I'm dead now. I can admit to anything I please. I never wanted the war to begin, and a day never passed when I didn't long for it to end. Yet those four years were the richest of my life, the most alive, the most passionate. It was then, and only then, that I tapped the wellsprings of my own gifts. I tasted courage I never knew I possessed. I found cunning in my soul, and quickness, and resolve. Those are the years I remember eagerly, even now, while most everything else recedes into blankness.

And that goes against everything we know about my sex. The

hearts of men may be touched with fire, but the hearts of women are touched only with love. Everyone knows it. That's why Grant was the general, and I was the one who sent him flowers.

I did it on impulse, the first time. Jed had been in Richmond, talking about the camp at City Point, how it was all mud and gray tents, scarcely a tree left, or a piece of grass. The biggest working port in the world right now, he said, and exciting as anything to a Tennessee mountain boy. Boats all over the harbor; trains coming in one after the other, all day and all night, and big shots, too, with their staffs and their pennants; wagon trains and horsemen splattering mud on you everywhere you turned. It was exciting, he said, but desolate, too, in a way. You got to hankering for the sight of something pretty.

I was in my garden a couple of evenings later, waiting for my courier, and I walked around and picked a few weeds and stopped beside a patch of particularly exquisite sweet williams. We were well into the bloody summer of '64 by then; the Union army was at Petersburg, and had gone through no end of dying and misery to get there. Some people were criticizing Grant for the high casualties, even though he'd done in three months what nobody else could do in three years: he'd backed Bobby Lee into a corner.

I looked at the flowers and I thought: *I should send him these.* Something pretty for City Point. Something from a lady to a knight in plain, muddy armor.

My way of paying honor . . . and paying honor back.

TEN

———————— ✳

PROPER RELATIONS

How fortunate for the South that she has this inferior race, which enables her to make the whites a privileged class, and to exempt them from all servile, menial, and debasing employments.

George Fitzhugh, Southern pro-slavery writer

Expansion is the peculiar necessity of the Southern people . . . slavery will expand . . . till stopped by snow.

Augusta Constitutionalist

We have now three and a half million slaves, and in thirty years we shall have seven or eight million. When they have become profitless or troublesome, we want a South to which we can send them. We want it . . . and we mean to have it.

Albert Gallatin Brown, Governor of Mississippi, 1853

Compelled by a long series of tyrannical acts . . . these States withdrew from the former Union, and formed a new Confederate alliance . . . based on the proper relations of labor and capital.

Confederate Congress, Address to the Southern people, February, 1864

I was the earliest riser in the family, as a rule, but when I went downstairs the morning after Clarinda's arrival, Josey was already clearing away the dishes from somebody's breakfast.

"Is Mother up already?" I asked. It was still dark, and the house was chilly.

"No, Miss Liza. Nor Miss Clarinda neither. But Mr. John's out back. Mary can fix you something right quick now, if you like."

"No. I'll wait for the others."

I wrapped a coat around myself and went out into the yard. I found John in the shed, quietly currying our only remaining horse. The Army of Northern Virginia had all the others—without payment or permission, needless to say.

Even in the lantern light I could see how troubled he was. But he gave me a wan smile, and said good morning.

"Good morning," I said.

"I don't have to report in till noon, so I thought I'd go out to the farm for a bit. See about some things."

"You mean think about some things."

The curry comb rested on the horse's shoulder, no longer moving.

"She brought me a letter from Catherine, you know," he said. "I'm going to feel awfully guilty if I don't go."

"If it'll help any," I said, "I can write another letter, and make you feel even guiltier if you do."

He laughed, without much amusement. "I'm sure you could. But it won't be necessary. I'm not going anywhere. I even have a reason. Three reasons: a mother, a sister, and a war. A man does need some halfway decent reasons for turning down the pleas of a dying wife, doesn't he?"

"She isn't dying, John."

"She might be. Don't be so infernally cold-blooded, Elizabeth. She might be."

"I'm sorry. That wasn't . . . I meant . . . oh, be hanged to it, John. I'm no good at dividing up my loyalties. I never was. You're in danger, too."

"Quite beside the point, my dear. I'm a man." He combed the

horse slowly, without attention, and then stopped again. "I loved her, Liza . . . a long time ago. All this . . . it makes me remember how much I loved her. How much I wanted to make her happy, and didn't."

"Do you *want* to go to Devon Hill?"

"No. I don't want to. Maybe it would be easier if I did. Then staying here might feel like a sacrifice. This way I just feel like I'm a coward."

A sacrifice? Yes, of course. Duty is always supposed to be painful, isn't it?

"Well, you aren't," I said. "And what's so wonderful about sacrifice, anyway? The way I see it, when your heart and your mind and everything inside you rebels against doing something, maybe there's a good reason."

"An interesting idea," he said. "Did you ever consider discussing it with the passel of Rebels we have all around us?"

I laughed. "You're incorrigible, John."

"Yes. My only saving grace, I'm afraid." He tossed a blanket over the horse's back, and then his saddle. When he had done, he turned back to me.

"Don't worry about me, Liza. If guilt could do us in, I'd have hanged myself long ago. So would have you."

"Me? What on earth do you mean?"

"I mean that you, my dear, are the most incorrigible, unredeemable, unreconstructable rebel who ever lived. And you've got to feel guilty about it sometimes, no matter how well you hide it."

"Really?"

"Really. Give Clarinda my apologies. I'll see you when I get off duty tonight. If anybody's still up."

"I'll be up."

He smiled. For the briefest moment, we were very close. Then he took the horse's reins and led it outside, jumped on its back, and rode away.

* * *

Perhaps the hardest thing John ever did in his life was to try to explain to the St. Clair women why he wasn't going to Devon Hill. I have no idea what he wrote to Catherine, or what he said to Clarinda, who must have given him a considerable argument. They were closeted in the library for almost two hours.

"I pleaded my honor, what else?" he said when I asked him, and then he said nothing more.

A few days later, Clarinda left us, and went back to Mississippi alone. Our farewells were courteous enough. Mother plied her with gifts to take back for the children and for Catherine, including two huge baskets of food. I know John gave her a considerable amount of money.

What he had said to me was true, of course. I felt guilty over the whole howling business—guilty because it seemed I owed the St. Clair women something, and I couldn't give it; I didn't even really know what it was. Guilty because everything I knew how to give was committed elsewhere, to strangers instead of my own kin, to an army these women hated, to ragged prisoners I didn't even know.

Maybe that was why I wondered, afterward, if Clarinda was responsible for what happened. Maybe it was my own guilt. Or maybe it was just the war, just living surrounded all the time by enemies. You get so you can believe anything. For a long time I wondered if Clarinda might have had something to do with it. And I felt guilty, of course, for wondering. I felt like I'd sunk so low a cottonmouth could have gone over me without noticing a bump.

Then again, maybe I was right.

Within a fortnight of Clarinda's visit, John was transferred to active duty at the northern Virginia front.

As if that wasn't trouble enough, things had gone wrong in Libby, too. When Rose's men dug past the prison's brick wall, they found that the whole side of the warehouse nearest to the canal, built on low, wet ground, had been placed on a foundation of massive timbers. They would have to cut through this foundation to reach the sewer. Hardly anyone in the group believed they could do it with the meager tools they had. Even Abel Streight didn't think so, but he agreed with Rose when the Pennsylvanian said they had to try.

So they chipped the blades of their two penknives to make them into crude saws, and went to work. It was an impossible task, but they kept at it. Hours and hours of desperate work produced only a tiny groove. Hours and hours more did not make it noticeably bigger. When a man crawled out of the tunnel, his neck felt half broken and his fingers were too numb to move.

Days passed, and they kept at it. They made jokes now and then. *Catch us one of those rats, Colonel, why don't you, and let him scratch at the damn thing for a while. You should learn how to cook sawdust, Zack, then there'd be some point in all this.* The best knife broke. They used the other one. It broke. They used the pieces.

The whole howling thing was impossible, and they knew it, but they did it anyway. A day finally came when the timber was cut clear through on one side, and cut deeply enough on the other side that Captain Hamilton could tug on it and twist it until it snapped off. He dragged it out with him inch by inch, and finally emerged triumphant, like a cat backing out of a hollow with a rat four times its size.

Triumphant, but not entirely. "It's gone wet as hell down there, Rosey," he said. "I don't like it."

Rose snatched the candle from him and dove in, crawling as fast as he could. The ground wasn't damp anymore, the way it used to be; it was soggy as a garden in the rain, soaking his clothing, sucking at his hands as he crawled. He was halfway across perhaps, when he stopped absolutely still. Stopped and listened, hearing what he knew he might hear and what he could not bear to hear. Water whispering. Not running, not yet, just whispering up through the gash in the timber. Even in the small time he lay there, the whisper grew louder, more insistent, and the mud below his bracing right hand began to dissolve like melting gelatine.

He didn't have time to grieve for the tunnel, not then. It took all his strength simply to get out, to scrabble backward as the water came more and more quickly and the ground went treacherous beneath him, sliding away as he shoved, dragging at his arms and his legs. It took all the strength the others had to obey his one half-strangled command.

"Close it up! Fast!"

They rammed the timber piece back as far as they could, flung dirt on top of it, rubbish, anything they could find; they ran back to the north end of Rat Hell and filled their jackets with the earth they had dug, and emptied it down the hole, over and over till the opening was full and pounded hard and there finally wasn't any more water oozing out.

Then they faced it. Or tried to. Zack Johnson put his head on his arms and cried. Someone's hand closed gently on his shoulder. He didn't know whose, but it helped.

"Sorry," he said, after a bit.

"Don't worry about it," Rose told him. "I'd probably do the same thing myself, except I'm too damn mad."

"So what now?" Streight wondered. "Is there some other way out? Besides the sewer?"

"You want to dig another tunnel?" MacDonald asked wearily.

"No. But I don't much want to stay here, either."

Nobody said anything for a long time. Then Rose slowly got to his feet. "It's late," he said. "I think we should call it a night. I want all three teams in the cook room tomorrow. We'll talk about it then."

They talked about it. But what could they do, being the men they were, except try again? They aimed a second tunnel toward a smaller, secondary sewer . . . and, all unwittingly, ran it right under a brick furnace hung with huge, cast-iron pots. The tunnel roof buckled. The guards, blaming rats, did not investigate. But this one, too, had to be closed and abandoned. They tried for the cook room sewer. By now even the strongest were weary, and some were sick, worn down by lack of sleep and contaminated air. They coughed constantly; they had sores that no longer healed; they kept going purely on will, on the dream of freedom lying always just in sight, like a mirage.

A mirage it proved to be again. After digging their way painfully to the cook room sewer, they found it lined with heavy planks, solid oak and three inches thick, the opening too narrow for any grown person to slip through. They couldn't cut through the planks; the wood had hardened through the years into something much like rock. Their worn-out tools didn't even make a dent.

Nobody cried that time. They were beyond it. They had been digging for five weeks and had nothing to show for it. No one was in any condition to start again. Even Abel Streight was defeated; he had been weeks in the cellar before he began; he had nothing left. Still, he wouldn't be the first man to say quit.

A shivering young lieutenant, who in any sane world would have been tucked under a quilt with somebody feeding him chicken broth, spoke for them all: "Begging your pardon, Colonel, but there ain't no use. We're killing ourselves down here."

A murmur of agreement passed around the gathering.

"Andy?" Rose murmured.

They'd begun it together, he and Hamilton. They had met in this cellar, strangers, both of them prowling after lights out looking for a possible escape, armed with makeshift weapons, ready to club the other senseless if he turned out to be a Rebel. They found no escape that night, but each man found an extraordinary friend.

"I think we should disband," Hamilton said. "I don't think we can ask any more of anyone."

Except ourselves.

Alone, Rose and Hamilton began again. I don't know how they did it, how they found the strength. Sometimes, when I look back on the war, and all the impossible things people did, and all the desperately brave ones, Grierson's raid, and Little Round Top, and those blind, headlong assaults against cannon and stone walls, I think the Libby tunnel should be ranked right up there with the best. Not in numbers, no, and not in military importance; it didn't change the course of the war, as far as anybody knows. But for sheer grit in the face of misery and defeat, it was as astonishing as any.

So it came about that, some eight or nine days later, Rose called yet another meeting of the disbanded party. There was no way left to the sewers, he said, but there still was a way out. They could dig from the northeast corner of the cellar. The ground was higher there; they would avoid both the timbers and the risk of flooding. The digging itself would be easier than any they had done before. Trouble was, he said, there was only one way for the tunnel to go—east—and only one place it could come out. In the yard. In plain view of the guards.

The building nearest to the prison on the east side was the storage shed. The prisoners knew all about that particular shed; it was the place where their parcels from home, and the relief supplies sent by the U.S. Sanitary Commission, piled up to gather cobwebs and dust, until the guards had time to search them thoroughly, and help themselves to everything they wanted.

"Fortunately for us," Rose said, "the shed has a fenced yard with a covered gate. Properly directed, the tunnel could surface under the shadow of the gate. The sentinel's beat there is about fifty feet long. If you watch, and come out just as he's turning away, you should be some distance gone before he turns back and sees you. Far enough that he won't see the color of your uniform. Far enough so's you could be anybody, a civilian, another guard, anybody. You walk calmly, and you keep walking. And the man behind you does the same."

"Won't they wonder, after a bit? Why so many people are walking there, late at night?"

"Probably. It's a chance we have to take, I guess."

No one could see Johnson's grin in the darkness, but they could hear it in his voice. "Who knows?" he said. "Maybe they'll just think we been rifling the Yankees' parcels."

"God knows they might," Rose said. "Well, gentlemen, what do you say? Are you up to trying it one more time?"

"When do you want to start?" Streight demanded.

"We have started. We've already breached the wall. We need help to finish it, though. We got forty, maybe fifty feet to go."

"Hallelujah," Zack Johnson murmured. "Just give me the spittoon!"

Poor Captain Johnson. He was a brave young man, and full of that mellow, unshakable resilience that only the young seem to have. He would need all of it, and more, in the weeks to come.

Little Ross was useless with numbers. How he ever got hired as the prison clerk was a mystery to everyone, but then, Rebeldom was full of such mysteries. He made no end of simple errors, especially if he was angry or distracted; and though he usually got things right eventually, it could take a great deal of his and everybody else's time.

Twice a day, around nine in the morning and four in the afternoon, the prisoners of Libby were counted. The inmates had to gather in one room, and line up in five or six long rows. While bored guards stood by, waiting for the tiresome ritual to be over, Little Ross walked slowly down the rows and counted: one, two, three, four, pointing to each man with his finger as he took due and careful note of his existence. At the end of the row he would stop, pick up his little notepad, and painstakingly write the number down.

It didn't take the Yankees long to discover this system had some flaws. If an officer had escaped overnight, or was absent from the roll call for some other reason, one of his friends could usually wait until he himself had been counted, and then slip over to another row while the clerk's back was turned, and so be counted again.

Rose's tunnel teams got very good at this. They had to. Several things were conspiring to make the prison administration edgy. There were ongoing rumors of a Yankee raid being planned to free the prisoners. There had been two separate small escapes. The Rebels seemed to know that something was afoot. They did unexpected searches of the prisoners' quarters, of the cook room, even of Rat Hell. They didn't like the cellar much, though, and did nothing more than walk about briefly, and shine their lanterns at the corners. They didn't go into the straw-filled area where the rats lived, and where the tunnel began. Not yet.

Rose and his men knew they were running out of time. One better-than-usual search, one small lapse of caution among their fellows, and they would be discovered or betrayed. They started leaving one man in the cellar every morning, to hide all the signs of their work. One day they failed to cover for him, and Zack Johnson got trapped in Rat Hell. . . .

A slow drizzle is falling over Richmond, and there is fog tonight, mixed with the rain. The streets have a cold black sheen, like mirrors; the muted lamps could pass for gaslights, if you weren't paying close attention. Sometimes, lost in my thoughts, I truly expect to hear the sounds of carriages and horses, to see soldiers marching, living soldiers, and women in hoop skirts with little velvet reticules on their arms.

There are more than thirty of us now, and we're feeling considerably bolder. We make jokes. Why, we ask, are the Rebels looking for the quintessential Southern lady? Why not the quintessential Southern gentleman?

We know why, of course, just as you do. General Lee has already been chosen, raised up as the enduring symbol of the Confederacy— indeed, of the war itself. But for myself, here in Virginia, I always thought the quintessential Rebel men were rather different ones. Edmund Ruffin, for one, the aging fire-eater with long white hair hanging to his shoulders. He wanted a war so badly he rushed off to Charleston to lobby for it, and was rewarded by being allowed to pull the first lanyard on the first cannon at Fort Sumter. When Lee surrendered at

Appomattox, old Ruffin took his trusty squirrel gun and blew his own brains out. More than one person, hearing of it, wondered why the devil he hadn't done it four years sooner.

The other man who symbolized everything the Confederacy thought, and dreamed, and did—and ultimately couldn't do—was the Rebel president, Jefferson Davis. It was so in the war, and it is still so, here in the afterworld. He revens a lot, and mostly we steer a wide circle around him. Or, if we come upon him unexpectedly, we whistle down through a grate or scuttle into a hedge. It drives him crazy. Richmond, he complains bitterly, is full of Yankee spies. Which of course Richmond was.

Sometimes, though, we stand our ground, and face him down. It makes us uneasy, every time; we draw together, wanting to pull our ghost collars up around our ghost necks, as though a sudden, chilly wind had come up through the valley. So we feel now, as we notice the men approaching slowly along Grace Street. They pick their way with dignity among the rain puddles, keeping their unfeet carefully on the ground. All four have their heads bent close, as if their thoughts were words, and the perilous world around them could still hear.

Three of them are performing, just as they did in life. The fourth is absolutely sincere, also as in life. He's still an impressive figure, tall and severe, eternally presidential: Jefferson Davis, supreme leader of the one-time Confederate States of America.

Beside me, Mariel has drawn herself into a thin, unmoving wisp of bitterness.

"Lord, now I remember why I never wanted to come back here. He hasn't changed much, has he?"

"Not a bit," I said.

"Do you ever speak to him?"

"Sometimes," McNiven replies. "But you maun be mighty careful what you say."

"You always did."

"It's considerably worse now," I tell her. "He doesn't know he's dead."

There's nothing quite like a ghost's giggle: a kind of high, shivery, uneven growl.

"You're going to have to tell me that again, Miss Liza."

So I tell her. Jefferson Davis simply refuses to believe he's dead. For a while, a long time ago, various friends and one or two enemies tried to enlighten him on the matter. One by one, they all gave up. Since the day he was born, in June of 1807, or perhaps it was 1808, Jefferson Davis has never been mistaken about anything. He isn't about to start now.

They tell all manner of stories about him. They always did. In the gloomiest days of the war a Jefferson Davis story was always good for a laugh, and it didn't much matter which side you were on.

Nobody likes to tell them better than Martin Lipscomb.

"He met up with God himself one day," he says to Mariel. "Over on Chimborazo hill. Did you hear about that? God knows which of them was more surprised. But they said good morning like the finest of gentlemen, and walked together for a bit. Of course, old Jeff's staff went tiptoeing right up close behind, listening to everything they said. Well, you can imagine what they thought, when God kept telling the president he was wrong. The thing Davis was talking about never even happened. Or the reason for it was altogether different. And more such, I don't remember anymore; God knows God had a lot to choose from. Well, old Jeffie being a Christian man and all, he wasn't about to argue with the Lord. But his staff were on pins and needles wondering what he'd do about it after. Would he change his mind now?—now that he had the truth from God himself?"

Mr. Lipscomb draws himself erect, and strikes a most exaggerated authoritarian pose. For a moment, he almost resembles the Rebel leader. "Why ever should I do so, gentlemen?" he intones. "God knows perfectly well I'm right. He's only testing me to see if I'll stick to my guns."

Mariel smiles, and shakes her head a little, quietly. "I never thought a man like that could get any crazier by dying."

"You thought he was crazy?"

"I don't know, Miss Liza. Not in the usual sense, I reckon. He wasn't one of them what talks to the furniture, or goes running down the street in his underwear, waving an ax. He was real smart and well-bred and all, like they say. But inside . . . I don't know . . . inside something was broken down. He'd be up till three and four in the morning, working, and most of it was stuff any secretary could have done. It was like he had to do every single thing in the world himself. And suffer everything himself, too. It was always Thursday night in the garden in that house. I got to thinking there must be some awful, ugly secret in his life."

"Like what?"

"Don't suppose we're ever going to know. But there's something. Any man who's trying that hard to be God has seen the devil up close someplace."

I don't know what to think of this idea. Some people say he was changed by his first wife's death, back in 1835. But he was almost thirty by then, and the striking flaws of his character—the touchiness, the arrogance, the absolute inability to yield control or ever admit to being wrong—all these traits had shown themselves long before. Yet his childhood seemed ordinary, his parents responsible and kind, and when he went off to St. Thomas boarding school in Springfield, one of the priests thought so well of the little boy that he put a small bed for him in his own room.

No, to me Jeff Davis is a puzzle, a man of extraordinary gifts, still as severed from reality in death as he had once been in life.

The president's party is less than a hundred feet away now, and a large body of tramping reveners swings onto Grace from a side street to join him.

"The king's escort," McNiven murmurs.

Three do not join the bodyguard, but angle over in our direction instead. One of them is Cooper DeLeon.

"You again," he says.

"We again." I smile at him. "My, you are looking elegant, Mr. DeLeon. But then you always did."

"Would you please tell me what all these people are doing here, Miss Van Lew?"

"Doing here?" I look around, vacantly. "We live here, Mr. DeLeon. Figuratively speaking, of course."

"This is a *Confederate* gathering."

"Ve couldn't sleep," Angelina tells him. "All that howling up there on the hill—I tell you, is enuff to vake the dead."

No one can ignore you better than Cooper. He does it beautifully, with a tiny shift of mood, a tiny flicker of irritation or distaste, as if he's seen a bug he detests but can't be bothered swatting—in this case, a rawboned female tavern-keeper with an appalling foreign accent. He turns to Sam, whom he probably considers the only other real person there.

"Mr. Ruth. Since Miss Van Lew will not discuss this matter sensibly, I must ask you, as one gentleman to another, to take your party elsewhere."

"Where is elsewhere?" Sam wonders, sensibly enough.

"The other side would be suitable," Cooper tells him.

"North or below?" I ask.

"Is there much difference?"

"Oh, dear. Hard words from a gentleman, don't you think, Will?"

"Listen," Cooper says wearily. "All I'm asking is that you let us be. That really isn't a lot to ask, under the circumstances."

I want to ask him what circumstances he's referring to, but Mc-Niven speaks first.

"Let you be, laddie? There was nae a passel of rebels in the history of the world was let be like the lot of you. We sent you all home and hanged nary a one of you. So just what is it you're asking us now? To crawl back in the ground and pull our tombstones round about our heads?"

"No. Just leave us alone. What's so complicated about it, anyway? What was ever complicated about it? We had our own ways, and you had yours. But you never could abide it, could you?"

"Suppose we had?" Will says quietly. "Where do you reckon it would have ended? Your ways, and ours, in the same country?"

"There were two countries."

"Well, that's a matter of opinion," I tell him tartly. "But even if there had been, the question still stands. Where would it all have ended?"

"It didn't have to end in a war. We didn't want the North; you didn't need the South. We could have gone our separate ways."

"And who was going to get the west?"

Sam Ruth, seeing the drift of the conversation, moves back into the shadows, and several others follow him. For some of us, the question is still too painful to face. For others, it's too settled to bother discussing.

"Some of it would have gone to the Union, I suppose," Cooper says, "and some to the Confederacy."

"Decided how?" I demand. "Like it was in Kansas? Midnight raids with fire and butchery? Rigged elections, and every man and woman sleeping with a pistol by the bed? How many variations of Kansas would we have had, do you think, with pro-slavery settlers pouring into each new territory from one side, and free-soilers pouring in from the other?"

He makes a small, dismissive gesture.

"Slavery was never the issue. You wanted to subjugate us; you just used it for an excuse. And I dare say it was a pretty shabby excuse, Miss Van Lew. Slavery wasn't worth fighting over. It was ending all over the world. It would have ended here, too, quietly and peacefully, and all by itself."

This, of course, is what all the Rebels started saying after the war. They hadn't been fighting for slavery at all. They'd been fighting for independence. Of course, what they wanted their independence *for* was never very clear. Tariffs got mentioned a lot. Wrangles over the Constitution. The Southern way of life. But the preservation of slavery? Dear heavens, no; slavery was dead and done for.

And perhaps, in the moral consciousness of the western world, it was. But it was still here. It still *worked*. It worked extremely well.

Therein lay the great Southern dilemma. There was a corpse in the mansion, and half the neighborhood was holding its nose. But every summer the coffin was filled to bursting with sugar and cotton and tobacco and rice; every day it spilled out favors and comforts and reassuring whispers of submission. And the whole west was waiting to be taken, maybe the whole continent, fortunes stretching to the last horizon for men with such a pool of unpaid labor. What was a gentleman to do then, or a lady? Sigh a little, and fetch a shovel, and give it all up?

Or did one scatter more and always stranger perfumes? Build walls and altars all around the smelly thing? Tell us it was sacred, it was the cornerstone and heart of Southern life? Treat criticism the same as blasphemy, and pass laws against the very sense of smell?

And afterward, when blood and fire took the temple down, tell us all: *Oh, that old thing? We were just about to get rid of it ourselves.*

"When?"

"I guess we'll never know now, will we?" Cooper retorts. "But I don't expect you care much. You got what you wanted. You got the South on its knees. We could have lived with the Yankees, if they would have lived with us. I know the South, Miss Van Lew, and I know the Southern people."

"Piffle. You know the Southern cafés. The Southern hunting parties. The Southern riverboats racing each other down the Mississippi, all for a boast and a drink of brandy afterward. That's the only South you know."

His graceful unbody goes absolutely rigid. I have finally made him truly and completely furious. And I'm not finished.

"You see, I read your books, Mr. DeLeon. Both of them. Though I thought I was reading the Bible sometimes, all that genealogy, all those pages and pages of marryings and begats. *Belles, Beaux, and Brains of the Sixties,* wasn't it? And nary a word about us. *Four Years in Rebel Capitals,* too. That one was better, but still nary a word about us. Look at my companions over there, Mr. DeLeon. Do you think there might be a brain among them? Something of importance to a

Rebel capital? Samuel Ruth, superintendent of the Richmond, Fredericksburg and Potomac Railroad. Union agent. Mary Elizabeth Bowser, domestic servant in the Confederate White House. Union agent. Martin Lipscomb, official undertaker of Union and Confederate dead, employed by the provost marshal of Richmond. Union agent. Et cetera, et cetera. The South wasn't all rich, Mr. DeLeon. It wasn't all white. *And by God, it wasn't all Rebel!"*

"There are traitors in every country on earth, madam. That is a painful and a sorry fact. There are, I suppose, spies in every war. At the risk of offending whatever may be left of your sensibilities, I'll tell you frankly: I don't consider such people worthy of my interest—or, indeed, of anyone else's. A man has to step in mud occasionally; he doesn't have to track it into his house. I chose to write about the best, Miss Van Lew. That is what we value in the South. The best. The ones who are worth remembering, who were governed by ideals instead of greed. They were the last of their kind, the purest and most generous of women, the most impossibly valiant young men—"

"Whose valiant ranks you never troubled yourself to join, as I recall."

I shouldn't have said that, I suppose. But I'm tired of being called a traitor. And I'm tired of the Walter Scott Confederacy, too. I lived in the real one.

"I don't think we have anything more to say to each other," Cooper tells me stiffly. "Except one thing, perhaps: Be grateful you're not a man. Good evening."

He turns away with all the dignity he possesses, which is a great deal, and joins the group around the president. They all move on together, keeping the same worldly, measured pace as before, pretending Jeff Davis is living flesh and blood, and can't even float across a puddle. It's astonishing, really, the way they treat him, the way so many people treated him, even Yankees, especially during those two years he was in prison, after the war. It was as though everyone forgot. During the war he was hated by half the Confederacy, and by most of the Union. He was blamed—and rightly, I think—for many of the

South's military disasters. But put a single Federal manacle on one of his lean shins, and all his faults vanished, poof. Just like Lee's would, a few years later.

Miraculous, it was. We all stood back and watched in amazement, like youngsters in a magic tent, wondering what was coming next. Southern churchmen acclaimed him as a Christian martyr, and made sermons about his brimming chalice and his chains of gold. They put stained-glass windows in the churches in his honor. Then the pope in Rome sent him an honest to Gethsemane handmade crown of thorns, and the whole Union doubled over in howls of unbelieving laughter.

When we were done laughing, though, some of us wanted to cry.

ELEVEN

———————— ✳

THEY FELL
OUT THE WINDOW

The cellar was now my home. . . . I had plenty of company—little
of it, however, agreeable, as it consisted of rebels, rats, and other
vermin. With the former I had no communication whatever;
whenever they made their appearance I leaped quickly into a hole
I had prepared in the straw, and pulled the hole in after me. . . .

Isaac Johnson, Libby prisoner

We began asking at the crack of dawn: How many got away? The
number, we learned, exceeded a hundred. . . . Ross, the imp, asked:
Where are they all? We answered: They fell out the window.

Bernhard Domschcke, Libby prisoner

[Colonel Rose] told us of his wife and child he had not seen for so
long, and begged us for God's sake to let him go. There were
those among us who felt the eloquence of his appeal far more than
he ever knew, but war is—war. . . . So we took him back to
Richmond.

Thomas Polk Sanders, C.S. Army

The word came late on a chilly afternoon, in February of 1864. I
wasn't at the house. I had been out on an errand—I no longer re-

member where—and Mother met me at the door when I returned. She was pale, and I could see she had been crying.

"There was a boy here," she said. "He said his name was Hayden Bates. Joshua Bates's boy. Do you know him?"

"Yes. The family is friends of Tom McNiven."

"Then it's true," she whispered, and put her hands to her face.

"What's true? God in heaven, Mother, what is it?"

"John is at their house. He's deserted, Liza. He got new orders yesterday. They transferred most of General Winder's men to another unit. To go up to Culpeper. To join Lee."

"Oh."

"They'll kill him," she said. "If he gets caught. They shoot deserters."

"He won't be caught," I said. "I know the Bateses. They'll never give him away. We'll get him out, Mother. It'll be all right. Please. It'll be all right."

I tried to believe it. I kept saying, *It'll be all right*. I must have said it to my mother twenty times. I said it to myself, too, over and over as I went to my room and dug about in my closet. It didn't help at all, saying it. Telling myself my brother wouldn't be caught, wouldn't be marched out in front of his regiment and shot down like a dog. Even in the very act of denying it, I was acknowledging it. And so I put it out of my mind altogether, and thought only about what I had to do, and who I had to see, the same as if he were a stranger out of Libby.

First of all I had to get to the Bates house. I had played around with disguises before, not very seriously. After all, my real disguise was a tangle of wild hair, a stain on my bodice, and a sharp, old maid's tongue. A disguise for the soul, and far more efficient than disguises for the body. But it wouldn't help me now. Feebleminded or not, I was still John's sister, and anywhere I was seen to go, they would go looking for him.

I found an old dress that I wore sometimes on the farm, when I worked in the garden. I took all the trimming off. I pinned every scrap of my hair back, and pulled on one of Josey's work bonnets. And then I looked at myself in the mirror.

I looked strange to myself. Severe, without my hair, like an aging, tired nun. I looked worn and poor. But I still looked myself, and that was the strangest thing of all. Almost as if . . . No. I put that thought out of my head, too. I didn't have time to worry about the future.

Josey, standing behind me, adjusted the bonnet a bit, and said, "You still too much a lady, Miss Liza. You got to darken your face, like you been out in the sun. And your hands, too. Just wait now. I'll try and fix you something."

She came back about fifteen minutes later with a mix of what looked like browned flour and berry juice. It wasn't very good makeup; it colored me rather unevenly, and she warned me it would probably streak.

"You dasn't cry now, less'n you want to look like one of them there tabby cats."

"I won't cry."

But I did, as it happened. I cried a good deal before I came home again, and I had cause.

The Bateses were poor. Their house was in one of the most down-trodden parts of town, an ill-shaped wooden structure that kept the rain away, and not much else. Molly Bates was originally from western Virginia, and like a lot of mountain women, she could shoot a gun as well as any man, and cuss better than most. She tried not to cuss in front of me, my being a lady and all, but she forgot fairly often.

John had been staying out of sight in an upstairs bedroom. He stared at me when he came down. Looked at Molly, and then back at me.

"Liza? God in heaven, is that you?"

Well, I thought, maybe the disguise wasn't too bad.

Molly left us alone, and we talked for a while, quietly. The decision to transfer the men had come quickly, John said. He had no time to plan. It was go with them, or bolt.

"You're missed already, then?"

"Probably. By dawn for sure. They're leaving at dawn, poor devils. Hardly any of them want to go. The Confederacy's dead, one of them said to me; why the hell don't we just bury it?"

I gave him what I'd brought: a change of clothing, some extra socks against the cold; his Colt handgun from the house, loaded, with some extra shells; three gold dollars, and twenty Confederate.

"Keep the pistol," he said. "I have one. I stole the lieutenant's. God knows you might need it yourself."

I took it willingly. "Three years back," I said, "you would've shuddered to see me holding one of these."

"Yes, well, three years back I thought the world was sane. Did you bring any food?"

"Yes." I opened another bag, containing bread, a small chunk of carefully wrapped ham, and some dried fruit.

"For the road," I reminded him.

"Or maybe the pickets," he said dryly. "It's worth more than money, you know."

"If we do this right, you won't have to worry about pickets."

Suddenly, he could not meet my eyes. Under all the sensible, ordinary talk, we both knew nothing about this was sensible or ordinary. Desertion was a journey into darkness. Freedom at the end of it, maybe, laughter and bright fires in a camp full of friends. Or a circled field and the Rogues' March, and a volley, and an unmarked grave. . . .

It was dark by then. Molly and John both advised me to stay the night, because the streets were so unsafe. There was no gas in the house, and the Bates family had little money to spend on kerosene or candles, so we bedded down early. John shared the couple's upstairs bed with Joshua. Molly and I slept below, on a narrow, lumpy bunk commandeered from one of her children. She pulled on a heavy, shapeless nightgown. Then, sitting against the wall with the blankets pulled up to her chest, she began, with the greatest solemnity and care, to fill her clay pipe.

"You smoke?" she asked.

"No. But I don't mind it in the least."

"Don't have my smoke," she said, "I can't sleep."

She lit up, and puffed for a while in weary contentment.

"You never got yourself hitched with a man, did you?" she asked, after a bit.

"No."

"It's a lotta damn nonsense, marrying," she said. Puff. "Living in cities. Never wanted any part of it."

"But you did—" I faltered, realizing my words were indiscreet. But she answered me anyway.

"Got caught. Damn fool preacher said I had to." Puff. "Never liked preachers none. Army men neither." Puff, puff. "Always telling people what to do."

Seeing that I was abed, she leaned over and blew out the light, and sat back again. She said nothing more after that, thinking perhaps that I wanted to sleep. The coals of her pipe glowed and faded as she drew on it. The smoke burned my eyes. The bed was warmer than the floor would have been, but scarcely more comfortable. Outside, dogs barked and quarreled endlessly; drunken soldiers laughed and sang as they came and went from the taverns.

I did not sleep for a very long time.

I ate a humble breakfast with the Bates family. I tried to give Molly some money for John's care, but she refused it.

"We ain't doing much," she said. "I told Quaker more than once. We ain't stealing nothing and we ain't carrying no messages. But we'll put folks up as needs it, and we'll feed them. So you just put that away now, Miss Liza."

"Thank you. You're very kind."

I felt a strong temptation to embrace her, but I wasn't sure. Our difference in rank seemed in some ways so immense, and in other ways, completely irrelevant.

"If you ever have need of anything," I said, "ever, as long as you live, please call on me, or any of our family. Please."

"That's real decent of you, Miss Liza, but I reckon we'll be fine."

I had told Nelson if I wasn't home by morning he should come for me with the carriage, around eleven. I told him to make sure he wasn't followed, and to do a few errands and go home without me, if he had to.

He came, but very, very late. I could see right away that something was amiss. He stood in Molly Bates's hallway with his hat in his hand, looking at the walls and the floor and everywhere else except at me.

"Something I got to tell you, Miss Liza," he said. "They got out last night. At Libby. Nobody knows how many, over a hundred maybe. They got out and we . . ."

He stopped. Joy was leaping into my heart, my throat, my eyes, and fear was running hard behind it.

Nelson's head fell even lower. "We . . . we sent them away."

"*You what?*"

"We didn't know. . . ." He paused again, and looked up. Never in my life had I seen such misery in his face. "God help me, Miss Liza, none of us knew. It was just this fellow, scruffy as anything, come to the door, and the first thing he said was he was 'scaped from Libby and he was looking for Colonel Streight. And there was some other ones with him, skulking back out of sight. I didn't like the look of any of them, and we know them detectives is always trying to trap you, one way and another, and you wasn't home—"

"So you didn't take them in?"

"I swear to God, Miss Liza, I thought they was Rebs. I said I didn't know nothing about no Colonel Streight, and I sent them away. And then this morning we heard about what happened. They dug a big tunnel and got out. They was ours, and I sent them away."

"Oh, God! Oh, God, Nelson, how could you?"

"I'm mighty sorry, Miss Liza," Nelson said. "I'm sorry enough to die. But we was thinking about you, me and Josey, how they're always after you. And how you wouldn't be no good to nobody in Castle Thunder. We just didn't know."

No, you didn't. Because I didn't tell you. Because I wasn't there for those poor men when they needed me most. God forgive me, where are they now, cold and starving and with nowhere to turn . . . God, why wasn't I there, why didn't I go home in the dark, damn the ruffians, damn the police, damn the Confederacy to howling bloody hell . . . !

I didn't know tears were pouring down my face until they ran into my mouth, tasting of salt and stale berries.

"You're right, Nelson. You couldn't know. I should have been there."

I wiped my face. This was not the time to cry. "What's happening now?"

"Richmond's gone all topsy-turvy and inside out. There's soldiers everywhere, searching everything. That's why I was so late, and I went a mighty way around, making sure they wasn't watching me."

"We have to get word to Fort Monroe."

I turned to Molly Bates, who had listened to all of this in grim silence.

"They might come here," I said uneasily. "Searching for the prisoners."

"I reckon," she said. "But your brother can stay. We ain't the sort who turns tail when it rains."

"Tell him to stay out of sight. I'll take him off your hands as fast as I can. And God bless you, Molly Bates. I won't forget."

I rode in the carriage for half a mile or so. Richmond was, as Nelson had said, all topsy-turvy and inside out. Bands of uniformed men were everywhere in the streets, militia and regulars alike, hammering on the doors of homes, pouring pell-mell into business establishments, pouring out again with curses of frustration. After I was far enough away from Molly's house to feel she was safe, I told Nelson to stop, and climbed down before he could help me.

"Take the carriage and go, Nelson," I said. "I'll make my own way home. Get to Tibo as fast as you can, and tell him to get a relay to Fort Monroe. No, two relays, in case one doesn't get through. They have to get there fast, Nelson. Make sure they understand. *Fast!* The Rebels will be hunting those poor prisoners down like dogs."

"You going to write me something?"

"No need. Just tell them what happened. There's a hundred Federal prisoners on the run and they need help. General Butler will know what to do. Now go!"

"Yes'm," he said, and was gone.

On the night of February 9, 1864, Colonel Rose and his fourteen companions met for the last time in the cook room of Libby Prison. They shook hands and wished each other fortune. Then they slipped down into Rat Hell and crawled one by one into the tunnel.

Fortune rode on their shoulders that night. There was no unexpected search. There was no alarm. There was no moon. They stepped out into their dark, wintry freedom and walked away, and no one followed them. Zack Johnson was mostly joking when he said it, but he was right. The storage shed was heaped high with a raft of new parcels from the North, and all the activity in the shadows there was taken for just the sort of activity it usually was.

Each of the fifteen had chosen one man to tell about the tunnel, and the second set of fifteen was supposed to do the same. They got away in the same quiet fashion, but then the word got out, somehow, among the prisoners. After that it was a stampede, with every man for himself. Those who didn't make it closed the tunnel up and went back to their quarters, hoping against hope that it might escape detection, that they might have their own chance at freedom when night came again.

Roll call was late for some reason, and Little Ross, as usual, was slow. The prisoners did everything possible to confuse him, jumping lines everywhere. He counted six times. Each time there were prisoners missing, but never the same number. By then he was beside himself. He cursed them royally and ordered a personal roll call, by name, with each man coming forward when his name was called, and then leaving the room. It was almost noon by then; three precious hours had been added to the fugitives' head start.

A hundred and nine men were gone, and no one knew how. Furious, Richard Turner tossed the entire night staff into Castle Thunder. The Home Guard was called out in force, and couriers hurried off to alert the countryside and the prowling Rebel cavalry.

I went home in despair. The joy I should have felt at the prisoners' successful flight was all but overwhelmed with dread for what might become of them, and worry for my brother, and shame at my own failure. All I could do was hope that other members of the underground had been on the job. Maybe someone else took some of them in, or gave them papers and clothing and food. And maybe someone got word to Fort Monroe right away, in the middle of the night. Sam Spear's cavalrymen were still there, and they were daring and experienced. They knew the Chickahominy countryside like they knew their own Pennsylvania fields. Maybe things would turn out all right.

Still fighting tears, I flung off my bonnet and gloves, and climbed to the uppermost level of the house. The attic was, as attics usually are, full of unused and half-forgotten things. We kept it intentionally messy, but we never allowed the dust or cobwebs to accumulate to such a degree that disturbing them would leave any sign.

There was a small alcove in the back, not especially noticeable from the yard and not visible at all from the street. As a young girl, with my head full of romantic novels, I noticed how readily it could have been walled away from the attic proper, and made into a secret room, where I could hide pirate gold or a secret lover. I grew up, became an abolitionist, and thought about using it to hide runaway slaves. But since neither pirates nor lover nor runaway slaves ever came to my house, the secret room did not get built until the spring of '62. Then the Lohmann brothers, who were both fine carpenters, put in a solid oak wall with a narrow sliding panel, which opened just enough for a man to slip through. When it was closed, a casual eye would never have noticed it. We assumed the provost marshal's eyes would be somewhat more than casual, however, so we hid the opening behind an old, discarded wardrobe. Every time Winder's men searched my house, they always looked in the wardrobe, but they never tried to move it. It was big, ugly, and full of junk; given the apparent layout of the room, there was no earthly reason to move it.

I moved it now, and looked inside my secret room. Everything was where I had placed it more than a month ago, when the tunnel plan was first made known to us. Blankets and mats, a basin, a chamber pot, a water pitcher and some tin cups. The room could hold five or six men, if need be, warm and dry and safe.

And it was sitting here wasted. Mocking me with its horrible emptiness, while Union officers dragged themselves through ravines and swamps and freezing rivers, horsemen hard on their track, and maybe dogs, too, as if they were runaway slaves. . . .

If only I had known. If only they could have told me when they were ready. We knew it was coming, but it had been coming for so long. *Any day now,* they said, three separate times, and then they didn't make it. I didn't blame them. I didn't suppose the completion of a tunnel was something they could predict with great precision, and once it was completed, they certainly weren't going to hang about. No, I should have been home. Or I should have told Nelson and Josey about it. But I never told people anything, not my mother, not anybody, unless I had to. Unless it was immediate. That was how I worked, and all my instincts told me it was a good way. The best way, probably . . . nearly all of the time.

I never stopped wondering about the men who were sent away from our house that night, wondering who they were, and if they ever made it home. I tried repeatedly to find out, but I never could. It was a sadness I carried with me till the ending of my life.

Abel Streight was a natural leader, and a man of great personal integrity. He was also—as I understand you would call it in your own day—a continual disturber of barnyard muck. He made trouble for his Rebel jailers whenever, wherever, and however he could. He smuggled out to the North a bitter denunciation of the treatment of Libby's prisoners, especially their rations. He made a great fuss over the money that had been confiscated from him when he was captured. He used both his rank and his personal popularity to undermine the so-called Royal Family, the cabal of prisoners who snuggled up to the Rebels, and cheated and betrayed their comrades for their own personal advantage.

So it was not surprising that every Confederate in Richmond, civilian and military alike, simply assumed that the great Libby tunnel was Colonel Streight's doing. As it turned out, this would prove a blessing for Thomas Rose. But it also meant things would go hard for Streight if he was captured.

"He'll nae leave Libby alive if they get him," was McNiven's considered opinion.

A harsh judgment perhaps, and perhaps not. Day after day the Rebel patrols came back with small groups of recaptured prisoners. All of them were thrown in the dungeon. It was not supposed to be a crime, escaping, but they paid for it anyway. Streight was not among them. Then, unexpectedly, I received another note from Lucy Rice. She had relatives visiting, who wanted very much to meet me.

Lucy had an extraordinary number of relatives. We all did. We had so many cousins and uncles we could have peopled a whole new territory, though, as Will Rowley said once, it was the strangest famdamily in America. Be that as it may, I went to Lucy's house that night, and thus, finally, I got to meet Colonel Abel Streight.

I suppose the first thing I noticed about him was how big he was. And I suspect the first thing he noticed about me was the opposite.

"Well. Miss Liza. What a pleasure to meet you at last." He held out his hand, a great huge bear's paw, with a huge, shaggy smile to go with it. I had the feeling he could have lifted me up with one hand and tossed me across the room like a toothpick.

Bedan MacDonald was with him, and two other men whose names I no longer remember. Rugged westerners they may have been, but they were wonderfully gracious and polite; they treated me like a queen. I was eager to know about the tunnel, so they told me about their three failed attempts, and about how young Zack Johnson got trapped in Rat Hell.

"The Rebs were getting edgy," MacDonald said. "They were doing more searches, and looking closer at things when they did search. So we started leaving one man in the cellar every morning, when the others went up. His job was to hide every trace of the work we'd done the night before. We covered for him by jumping lines at roll call. One morning when it was Zack's turn to stay down, we weren't able to cover for him. It had happened a couple of times before, and the boys had to think up some pretty ingenious excuses as to why they'd missed roll call. We thought our good excuses were pretty well used up. Zack didn't want to take any chances, in case they threw him into solitary. So he said he'd stay down there till the tunnel was finished."

"And of course," Streight added, "once he began, he had to stick it out, no matter how long it took. The Rebs thought he'd escaped; he couldn't very well turn up again." Streight shook his head. "Poor lad. He was down there thirty-seven days. I don't know how he did it."

"But you were in the cellar nearly as long yourself, weren't you?" I said.

"Not as long. And Rat Hell is worse than the punishment cells. A lot wetter. Less air. More rats. He'd have died, I think, but we made him come upstairs for a few hours every night, and at least get warm and get a little sleep. I sure hope he makes it out safe. I hope they all do, but him and Rosey, they're the ones who really deserve it."

"Rosey?"

They both chuckled.

"Colonel Rose," MacDonald said. "The man who planned it all."

"It wasn't you?" I said to Streight. "The whole of Richmond's ready to hang you for the ringleader."

"Well, that's very flattering," Streight said. "But no. I wouldn't know how to dig anything more complicated than a potato patch."

"The Rebels want to catch you just the same," Lucy Rice said. "You more than anybody. They're turning the city inside out."

I was silent for a little time, looking at the officers, one after another. MacDonald was the handsome one, and yes, I noticed, as I always did. He seemed worn out, and very thin, but he was beautiful. Even while I noticed, though, and knew I'd be remembering his finely sculpted face for quite a few days, my mind was quietly fondling a different idea.

"If the Rebels thought you were safely gone, Colonel," I said, "they might stop looking quite so hard."

I had their instant attention.

"If you like," I said, "we can send word to Fort Monroe, and ask General Butler to announce your safe arrival. He can make a big fuss about it. After all, it *is* the sort of thing that would get in the papers. Everybody wants to know who got away. You could even send along a comment or two for publication."

"That's good," MacDonald said softly. "That's dandy. Don't you think so, Abel?"

Streight was looking at me intently. "Yes," he said.

"You'd have to stay put for a few more days," I went on, "till the news got back to Richmond. But that shouldn't be a problem, Lucy, should it?"

"Not at all," Lucy agreed.

"Shall we do it?" I asked Streight.

253

"Absolutely." He was grinning like a rogue. "You enjoy tweaking their tails almost as much as I do, don't you, Miss Liza?"

You should have seen the outrage in the Richmond papers a few days later, when Colonel Streight's unflattering comments about Rebeldom in general, and Libby prison in particular, were reprinted from the *Washington Post*. He was still in Lucy's house at the time, himself and his three comrades. The poor men ate like wolves, Lucy said, and soon Chris Taylor was smuggling food to her house at night, since a lonely grass widow couldn't suddenly be noticed buying groceries for a platoon. Finally, clean-shaven and almost healthy, dressed in civilian clothing, with perfectly forged papers and passes, they climbed on one of Sam Ruth's evening trains and rode to Fredericksburg, where, like so many others, they were rowed across the Potomac in the dead of night.

My brother had to take a harder route, on foot and mostly by darkness, all the way to Fort Monroe. Andrew Hamilton and Thomas Rose, friends through so much, became separated almost immediately after the escape. Hamilton made it. Colonel Rose was captured within sight of Union lines, and brought back to Libby. And you can well understand how thankful we were, then, that the Rebels blamed everything on Abel Streight.

Altogether, more than half of them got away, through the swamps and the rivers and the Rebel cavalry, through hunger and winter winds and all imaginable damnation. It was the original Great Escape, greater than all of them, and almost forgotten now, a musty tale in old, musty books, untold and unremembered, while poor old Longstreet ruins everything at Gettysburg, over and over again, one book after another; and Custer gets himself martyred on the Little Big Horn, and Wyatt Earp does them in at the OK Corral, over and over and over again, as if all of American history only ever had three stories in it, and none of them more than halfways true.

✳   ✳   ✳

While we sat that night in Lucy's quiet house, planning how we'd tweak the Rebels' tails, Zack Johnson and John Fislar were huddled in a thicket along the Chickahominy. Behind them was a swamp as old as the world; ahead was black countryside, wooded and icy with winter; in the distance, just a glow northeasterly above the trees, was the faint light of picket fires.

The pickets, they thought, might well be the last of the Rebel line. Get past them before daylight, and somewhere beyond, not very far away now, was freedom. Butler's men. Dry tents, and warm fires, and food.

"You all right?" Fislar asked.

"Yes," Zack answered, but he wasn't. He was shivering with cold and exhaustion, wrapped in mud to his waist. Mud clung to his hands and his face and his hair. He stank of it; he could taste it in his mouth. Old mud, sticky and rotten, vile as the depths of Libby Prison. The swamp had almost got him.

"You're going to dry out stiff as a statue, you know," Fislar said. "They'll be able to paint you and put you in a church."

Zack laughed, just a little. He put his head back and tried not to remember how it felt when the log slipped and there was no bottom under his feet, no bottom in the world, just the mud pulling him down and the black trees lifting away with pitiless indifference, everything cold, cold and ancient and alien. . . . Men did not belong in these swamps, and sane ones did not come.

Fislar sat down at Zack's shoulder. He was a young lieutenant of the Indiana artillery, tall and sturdy. He was ready to move on, but he knew his companion was not.

"You've brought serious deprivation and hardship into my life, Captain Johnson. I want you to know that."

"I have?" It was too dark to see Fislar's face. Zack could only hope his friend was joshing.

"I made a whole raft of promises to God while I was pulling you out of that quicksand. And now, being an honorable man, I suppose I'm going to have to keep them."

"Oh. What sort of promises?"

"That I won't ever say Jesus Christ or God damn again, as long as I live."

"Well, a man can get by without cussing, I guess. They say Grant doesn't cuss. The whole world could be coming down around his ears, and all he'd say would be shucks."

"I'm not General Grant."

"That's true."

"I said I wouldn't have any more doings with fancy women, either."

"Get yourself a pretty lady of your own," Zack said, "and you won't even miss them." Then, remembering who it was he spoke to, he added: "Much."

"I said I'd never touch a deck of cards."

"You didn't swear off liquor or dancing, did you? Or take some vow like the priests do? To never get married?"

"No. I wouldn't've done that till you were sunk to your ears."

"Well, it's all right, then. You can find a nice girl to marry, go dancing every Saturday, get drunk twice a year. Hell, John, what more does a man need?"

They laughed together, softly. There was a lot more, probably, but just now a safe, simple life sounded like a miracle from God.

Fislar lay down on his back and put his hands under his head. "I sure did like those fancy girls in Louisville, though. They were as daring as anything, and so damned pretty, too. It was like one big candy shop, Louisville town. Or didn't you notice?"

"I noticed."

"But you didn't buy?"

"Nope."

"Not anything?"

"Nope."

"Why the hell not?"

Zack thought a bit before he answered, wondering if he'd sound like a fool. But John Fislar was his friend, and he always figured he should tell a friend the truth.

"I thought about it. Especially when I met them on the street, and they'd smile and flirt and treat me like a hero, even though I hadn't so much as seen a Rebel from a mile off. But somehow or t'other I always ended up thinking about Annie, and how she wouldn't like it none. And I always walked away."

"Hell's bells, Zack, there was no reason Annie'd ever have to know!"

"No, there wasn't. But I'd know. And I wouldn't like knowing something she wouldn't like knowing, somehow."

"Well, if that's what it's like falling in love with some girl, I'm not ever going to do it."

"There's another side to it, John. All that time in Libby, being hungry, being cold, digging that tunnel, it was Annie kept me going. Especially in the cellar. Do you know what it was like, thirty-seven days down there, never a speck of daylight, nobody to talk to? Scared pure silly sometimes, and of the damnedest things. The rats, the silence, the smell. I couldn't stand the smell after a while; I thought my whole body must be rotting, from the filth and the wet. I know it doesn't make any sense, but your mind goes funny in a place like that. I can't tell you how many times I just wanted to go screaming out of there, not caring a damn if it wrecked my hope of freedom, and yours, and everybody else's.

"I hung on because of Annie. Because of you and Streight and Rosey and the others, and the country, too, of course. I couldn't let you all down. But sometimes it was just Annie I couldn't let down. She was my last line of defense. If all the others had broken, she'd have still been there."

"But the other lines didn't break."

"I don't know, John. I wouldn't want to say. I'd never have gone to pieces willingly, but sometimes maybe willing isn't quite enough. Sometimes . . . hell, I just wouldn't want to say. I only know when I needed my last possible scrap of courage, that's where I found it.

Loving a good woman real hard makes you strong, my friend. Stronger than anything else ever can, maybe."

"Well. Coming from you, that's a considerable statement. I will, as my old man would say, take it under advisement."

"You do that."

There was a long but comfortable silence.

"John?"

"Yeah."

"I want to thank you. For what you did back there."

"You already thanked me. Seven or eight times."

"Well, I'm thanking you again."

"You're welcome." Lying down had been a mistake, Fislar thought. He was getting sleepy. He got to his feet, stiffly. "Now, although you may be a superior officer, may I suggest that you get up off your duff, and we get ourselves the hell out of here? Sir?"

Even as he spoke he reached down to help Zack to his feet. They moved on, slowly, cutting eastward to avoid the Rebel fires. After twenty minutes or so they came out on a rough wagon track. It was chewed up by a recent supply train, and full of mud holes, but it was a track, and they followed it thankfully. By now, Zack was on the edge of collapse, and would have fallen twice except for his companion's steadying arm.

One more day, he thought. Maybe he could make it one more day. . . .

The cavalry came from nowhere. Afterward, Zack realized they must have been stalking the wagon track, because even weary as he was, he would have heard horsemen coming from any distance. These just exploded out of the darkness. One moment he was walking, half asleep, aware of nothing but the wet road and Lieutenant Fislar holding him up. The next moment horsemen were bearing down on them, black centaur shapes pouring out of the night. He heard a shout, the voice rough and challenging; he dove for the woods, and Fislar didn't have to help him. But it was already too late. Horsemen crashed into the woods behind them, around them.

They ran on, and heard a rider tearing the underbrush directly ahead.

"Wait!" Zack hissed. They stood very still. Their pursuers were everywhere, one so close he could smell the hot sweat from his horse.

"Come on out!" a voice shouted. A decidedly Southern-sounding voice. "You're surrounded."

It was overcast, too dark for the cavalrymen to see them. He thought about trying to break through. A quick dash between them, a bit of luck. . . . But he thought perhaps he'd used up all his luck in the swamp. And God knew a man didn't have to be seen to be shot.

While he was thinking about it, he heard the hammer drawn back on a rifle, perilously close. "Identify yourselves, or we'll blow you to hell!"

"John?" he whispered.

Fislar's voice was lifeless with defeat. "I guess we're gone up, Zack."

"Well, we made them work to catch us, didn't we?"

Fislar said nothing. Zack turned toward the challenging voice, slowly. "Don't shoot," he said. "We're unarmed."

"Identify yourselves!"

"Federal prisoners, escaped from Richmond."

"Just the fellows we've been looking for." The cavalryman sounded pleased, and no doubt he had cause. Johnson wondered how many others they had rounded up, chasing exhausted men on foot, with guns and good horses. The man dismounted lightly, stepping closer in the darkness. "We're the Eleventh Pennsylvania Cavalry," he added.

It took a moment for the words to register, or for Zack to realize that the Southern-sounding accent was all gone from his voice.

"*Pennsylvania* Cavalry?"

"That's right. Pennsylvania. And as long as we're standing on it, this is Union territory. Welcome home, boys."

"They're ours," Fislar yelped, gone witless with joy. "Holy God damn Moses, they're ours! Oh, shit, I just swore."

Then they were laughing and getting slapped and hugged and having pieces of food stuffed into their hands and thinking it was good that it was pitch dark and nobody there could see the tears running down their faces.

TWELVE

———— ✳

RICHMOND COULD BE TAKEN

I met everywhere the rough, unplaned coffins of the wretched prisoners.

Elizabeth Van Lew

. . . Richmond could be taken easier now than at any time since the war began.

Unidentified Richmond agent, quoted by General Benjamin Butler

. . . These Dahlgren papers will destroy, during the rest of this war, all rose-water chivalry . . . Confederate armies will make war after and upon the rules selected by their enemies.

Richmond Dispatch

As I've told you before, time in the afterworld is a very loose affair, vague and open-ended, lacking most of the urgency it had when we lived. We know the Rebel gathering will go on for a long while—for weeks of human time, probably, filling the autumn nights with a strangeness most of you won't even notice. So, as the stars begin to burn softly out, and traces of pink appear in the eastern sky, we leave the gray ghosts to their own devices and look for a murky, quiet place to spend the day. We're not vampires; don't misunderstand me. We aren't hurt by light, or by living people, either. But we hate noise, and clamor, and fuss; and we tire easily. We prefer to keep to our own world, most times, and leave you to yours.

We all have our favorite haunts, of course. I used to spend a lot of time in my old house on Church Street, before they tore it down. Scared the stuffing out of more than one little Rebel—sometimes on purpose; I was an angry ghost back then. Martin Lipscomb likes to hang around the Confederate Museum, heaven knows why; but then, Mr. Lipscomb always was a little odd.

We all like Belle Isle, of course. And sometimes, when we're in a fighting mood, we go to the monument—the one they built to Ambrose Powell Hill, north of Richmond. He was one of Lee's top generals. Tom McNiven and his friends used to gather there for years after the war, every second of April, the day when Hill died. I went a couple of times myself. It was a marvelous bitter irony, going there; everyone thought we were paying tribute to the general and his cause.

But we went to remember. To remember who we were, and what we had accomplished. To remember things that were already slipping through the cracks of history. We erased them ourselves, sometimes, out of our own grim necessity. There was no Grand Review in Washington for the loyalists, no reunions, no parades. We began in shadows and we ended so; they hated us more after the war than during it, and we were more alone.

So we went to Hill's monument and remembered. The end of March, 1865. The Rebel army, pinned down by Grant at Petersburg, was preparing a last-ditch effort to break out. Everyone expected it. A drunken officer bragged of it in Madame Clara's bed. But the Rebels had thirty-five miles of Grant's trench lines to choose from; if they chose well, and struck quickly, a full-scale attack might yet break through.

I still remember the night Sam came to our house, looking for a courier. It was pouring rain, and he was drenched even in his slicker; he looked like a ruffian—the real kind, not Cooper DeLeon's variety—the kind you could find on the streets of Richmond every night back then: drunken brutes who smashed strangers into the cobblestones for sport; thieves with garrotes in their pockets and bloody knives on their belts. Crime had become so common it was no longer news.

So it was doubly dangerous for my people, being abroad in the dead of night. Yet Sam came anyway, alone, to the house on Church Hill. He never told me how he learned it—that the Rebel attack would be centered on Fort Stedman. Military men were always in his office and around the depots, arriving, departing, arranging supply. I expect he overheard a conversation he shouldn't have—or, perhaps, several conversations, from which he plucked all the right details, like choice raisins from a pudding.

I think back on it as Sam Ruth's finest moment, that rainy night in March. Through the whole war, he gave the Federal army God knows how many pieces of valuable information, but this was the piece that mattered most, and I knew it even then. I roused Mary to make him some hot coffee; before he had a chance to taste it, Nelson was already heading out. We had a man in City Point by morning. And the rest, well, you know the rest. The Rebel strike force was gobbled up at Fort Stedman, and the dust was barely settled before Grant ordered a counterattack. When it was over, Lee's lines were shattered in three different places, General Hill was dead, and the road to Richmond was clear. We ran up the flag here the following day.

But we had to hang on to our victories with both hands, after the war, when the old Rebels began to ride again. They rode in white instead of gray, with no faces and no names, and nothing was sacred in the South then, neither law nor ballot box nor flag. They turned polling stations into slaughterhouses, and killed black people for no crime except their freedom. It was as though the war had happened, in all its savagery, but not the victory; as though Appomattox had fallen through a fault line in the world. So we went to Hill's monument every second day of April, and drank blood-red wine and remembered how it really was. Remembered what we had achieved—all of us together, soldiers and citizens, slave and free, we had changed our country forever. We cupped the truth in our hands like a last bit of water in a desert, and held on.

No one is surprised when McNiven suggests we go to the monument again. The cloud cover is heavy, keeping the morning twilight at bay. So we almost brush against the wanderer before we see him. He is delicate even as ghosts are reckoned, carrying into the afterworld the fragility of human age. But he stands erect when he sees us; every wisp of his uniform is trim and bright.

We stand at attention and exchange salutes. That's the kind of ghost he is.

"Miss Van Lew. Mr. Rowley."

Ours are the only names he remembers. He nods toward the others. "Good morning."

"Good morning, Admiral. How are you?"

"I am well, thank you."

But he isn't. He hasn't been well for a very long time. He wanders constantly, all over King and Queen Counties, down the peninsula, back sometimes into Richmond, west again even to the Piedmont. We meet up with him occasionally, and hear of him often. He is looking for his son. Ulli Dahlgren was buried in three different graves, and rests peacefully in none of them.

The admiral always asks the same questions, in the same way.

"Have you seen anything? Have you had any word?"

"No, sir. I am sorry."

He looks away, into the ragged trees and the gray morning light.

"He won't ever come back, will he? Because of his name. My name."

He frames the words as a question, but they are not a question anymore; they are a fact. The admiral has been searching for a long time, and grieving even longer. His son was his idol, a cavalry colonel at the age of twenty, the youngest in the war. Hot-tempered, daring to the point of folly, Ulli Dahlgren was the stuff legends are made of. Only the legend took a dark and bitter turn; all that's left of it now is ugly memories, and a hopeless dream of vindication.

"You'll tell me, won't you? If you hear?"

"Yes, sir. Of course we will."

"I'm grateful for what you did," he goes on. "I haven't forgotten." He touches his cap again, very slightly, and fades into the morning twilight. If I had human eyes, they would be drowning in water.

"Where is he, do you think?" Mariel asks me, after a bit. "The admiral's son?"

I shake my head for answer. I don't want to speculate. He's an angry revener, I'm sure, like those in nightmare tales, tormented and driven from place to place. But where he is . . . no; I don't want to speculate.

"Maybe the Rebels got him," Mr. Lipscomb says. "Again."

Trust a grave digger to be morbid.

"He is lost, I think," Angelina says. "He vent off like the reckless boy he vas, and now he cannot find his vay back."

Only McNiven is untroubled by the sadness of the moment. He was always resilient, always ready to find a laugh in something, or at least a quiet stab of mockery.

"He's got scores to settle, that one," he says. "He'll be back when he's finished, with a fine ring of ghost scalps hanging from his belt."

It's true enough, I think. Ulli Dahlgren has scores to settle. With his superiors. With his enemies. Perhaps even with us.

You see, it all began with us. Oh, not entirely, of course; we didn't make decisions for the Federal army, not on that occasion or any other. But we nudged, once or twice. We saw what Richmond was like, at the start of '64. Hunger everywhere, except in the houses of the rich. Ten thousand Federal prisoners in the city, most of them living in tents in the snow. Hunger there, too, and sickness; prisoners carried from Belle Isle to the hospitals, and from the hospitals to their graves, day after day, two hundred and more every month, and the numbers going up. Lee's army in winter quarters on the Rapidan, whole units of Rebel cavalry disbanded for lack of horses, and Richmond's defenses down to skin and bones. I couldn't tell you now, even with hindsight, when or where we first started talking about a raid against Richmond—McNiven and Will Rowley and I. No doubt the Federal generals were talking about it, too, and the politicians in Washington. It was an idea whose time had come. . . .

FEBRUARY, 1864. . . .

Our point of contact with Union forces at the time was Fort Monroe, where General Benjamin Butler was in command. Sharpe and his men were at Culpeper, a long ways distant, across territory through which we had never established a loyalist line. More importantly, General Hooker was gone, and Sharpe's new commander was George Gordon Meade, who wasn't much interested in spies, or in Sharpe's Bureau, or in anything else that wasn't spit and polish traditional.

So we were left with Butler. At first we were optimistic, since he showed a keen interest in our work, and sent one of his scouts into Richmond with instructions for us, and money, and supplies. He put Will Rowley on the Federal payroll, and gave me enough invisible ink to write him letters for the rest of my life.

We were rapidly disillusioned. Butler was what they called a political general back then, raised to his high rank by opportunism and powerful connections. He was a lawyer before the war, a self-made man with a huckster's eye for possibilities and a shrewd grasp of other people's weaknesses. He could make the Rebels mad quicker than any man alive. By the time he was placed in General Dix's old command at Fort Monroe, he had been declared an outlaw by the Richmond government, and actually had a price on his head.

Maybe that's how the whole thing began—with the price on Butler's head; with his huge sense of self-importance; with his eagerness to fashion grandiose schemes which had often worked in the civilian world he understood, but which he could never adapt to the world of armies and war.

Unfortunately, the information we sent encouraged his schemes. For weeks we'd been telling him how bad things were for the prisoners. Then, in January, when the Rebels began to make plans to move most of them to Georgia, I sent him both a letter and a man to carry it, someone who could answer his questions, who could tell him precisely what the situation was.

Richmond could be taken easier now than at any time since the war began.

Those were my words. It was my dream, I suppose. I got caught up in it. We all did. We assembled a small, select group of friends and made plans to support the raid we knew had to come. We copied maps of the city to distribute to whomever might need them. We hid away discreet piles of weaponry—small arms, shells, knives, even clubs—anything that might give a loyalist or a prisoner an advantage in the streets. We went carefully through our lists of rural allies and identified the ones who would be the most capable guides; we even warned a couple of them to be ready to leave on a moment's notice, since we expected Butler or his cavalry commander to ask us for such assistance. We warned a few carefully selected prisoners also, so they could alert their fellows, and organize them when the hour came. We planned diversions to create confusion and draw the Home Guard into scattered sections of the city.

God, how pitiful it all looks now, as I remember it. All the work. All the *care.* We were so desperately, so impossibly responsible. We worked into the long blinding hours of the night, rather than increase our numbers, rather than share the load with one single person whom we didn't absolutely and completely trust.

Then we greeted the morning sun, not once but twice that winter, and read about it all in the newspapers.

The first raiding party set out in early February, even while Colonel Rose and his friends were digging their way out of Libby Prison. They were stopped at Bottom's Bridge, their way blocked by four regiments of regulars and four batteries of artillery. The whole howling Rebel army knew they were coming. They learned it from a deserter, who learned it from a private on picket duty, who learned it from . . . well, you see how things worked, in Butler's army.

Of course, it didn't end there. There was another raid. The one you all know about, and quarrel over even to this day. Kilpatrick's raid. It was planned in Washington, and you may as well know the truth: Security wasn't any better there than it was at Fort Monroe. Junior officers had wind of it. Their wives and their girlfriends and their bootblacks had wind of it. Newspapermen sent confidential messages to their papers in Chicago and New York: *Big Raid Planned on Richmond. Don't print this yet.* Even the commanding general, young Judson Kilpatrick, went to a ball and couldn't resist hinting that great things were under way. Great things were important to Kilpatrick; after the war he meant to be governor of New Jersey, and maybe even president.

Nobody, however, bothered to get in touch with us.

Oh, we heard rumors, of course, like everybody else. And then we heard the alarm bell clamoring at the Capitol, heard militias tramping through the streets, heard guns for a time in the northwest, late on a warm March afternoon.

I rushed uptown. Except for the war sounds, mostly in the distance, the city was deathly quiet. Richmonders knew how weak the city was; fear was as cold in the air as a mist. I spoke to some of my people, and sent messages to others. Nobody knew what was happening. None of us knew what the guns meant, any more than the Rebel citizens did. We alerted everyone we could, told them to be ready, and we waited for something promising to develop. Then the sound of guns died away.

It was another failure we could read about in the papers.

Days passed before we knew the whole story. General Kilpatrick's force, about four thousand strong, had separated above the North Anna River. Kilpatrick led the main body to attack Richmond from the north. His second in command, young Colonel Dahlgren, took a small detachment that was supposed to cross the James River and attack simultaneously from the south. But Dahlgren's guide couldn't find a crossing, and Kilpatrick, running into more resistance than he expected, didn't wait for him. I suppose he realized he'd never get to be president if he was dead. He made a bit of loud noise and hightailed it back to Union lines. Dahlgren, arriving after he was gone, had little choice but to try to fight his way home.

He didn't make it.

I watched them bring the prisoners in. Over a hundred and fifty of them, almost half of Dahlgren's little force, to add to the ten thousand who hadn't been freed. They sent his body in by train, and put it on view at the York River Railroad Depot. The despair among the Union party in the city, and even more among the prisoners, was almost bottomless.

But there was more to come, a couple of days later.

I was in Lohmann's restaurant when the first papers reached the streets. I heard the newsboy shouting some distance away, "Awful Yankee Doings Here, Read All About It!" I remember smiling to myself a little, because I knew the boy. He was always talking about how awful the Yankees were, and how scared of them he was. He was thin and cute and entirely convincing, but his name was Roe Rowley.

So I didn't think much about the "Awful Yankee Doings" until a shadow fell across my table. I looked up and saw my old nemesis, Millie Franklin. She had an *Examiner* in her hand, and the sort of look on her face I suppose the angel Gabriel will have, when he finally confronts the damned, flings out a long white arm, and points them the road to hell.

"Well," she said bitterly, "do you believe it now?"

Believe it? I was completely at a loss. "I'm sorry, Millie. Do I believe what?"

"How evil they are! He was going to burn the city! Slaughter the president, the cabinet, everybody, just shoot them down like animals! Oh, they're savages, Liza, they're worse than wild Indians, and you can't deny it anymore! Not anymore! We've got proof this time!"

She flung the newspaper onto my table.

I didn't even glance at it for a moment. I kept staring at her, realizing there was more than condemnation and anger in her face. There was fear. The kind of fear that went right down into your bones, and stayed there, keeping you awake nights, spoiling every peaceful moment with sudden, unexpected whispers of doom.

I read the lead headlines. RICHMOND SPARED A CRUEL FATE. DAHLGREN'S ORDERS CAPTURED. YANKEES HOIST THE BLACK FLAG. I read the story. Papers had been found on Colonel Dahlgren's body. They were brought to Richmond, examined, and were now being published, so the people of the Confederacy and the entire world should know the merciless and unconscionable designs of the invading army.

This was followed by the full text of Dahlgren's address to his men. It was the sort of address you might expect from a twenty-year-old, full of talk about danger and glory and selling one's life dearly. The relevant lines were just a few. I know them by heart, even now, the several lines from his address, the one line from his accompanying notebook. *We hope to release the prisoners from Belle Island first, and having seen them fairly started, we will cross the James River into Richmond, destroying the bridges after us and exhorting the released prisoners to destroy and burn the hateful city; and do not allow the Rebel leader Davis and his traitorous crew to escape.*

Jeff Davis and cabinet must be killed on the spot.

"Well, do you see what they are now?" Millie demanded. "Can you imagine what it would have been like? The city so dreadfully crowded like it is, and full of refugees, with everything on fire and the bridges gone? Can you just *imagine?*"

"Yes, I can, Millie. And I dare say I wonder how they ever expected to get out again themselves."

My hands were almost trembling, but I folded her *Examiner* neatly and gave it back.

"Where are these papers, do you know?"

"You mean Dahlgren's papers? The government has them, I suppose. What's the difference?"

"I think they should exhibit them, don't you? In a nice glass window, like General Pope's captured coat."

"What on earth for?"

"Well, I think people ought to see them. Right there in plain view, on U.S. army letterhead, in the man's own handwriting. I mean, that really would be proof of their evil designs, wouldn't it?"

She tapped the *Examiner* grimly on the tabletop. "It's all here, Liza. We have the proof."

"That's not proof, Millie. That's a newspaper."

Her eyes went very cold. "Do you think our leaders are making this up?"

"Well, it would hardly be the first time they made something up."

"I hope the Yankees burn you in your bed," she said, and walked away like a queen.

I was calm, facing Millie Franklin. It's easy to be calm when someone else is talking nonsense. But I bought a newspaper myself after, and took it home, and read every word of it, and I wasn't calm anymore.

The war was savage enough sometimes, but this, if it was true, was savagery of a whole other kind. This was warfare Kansas-Missouri style; this was Bloody Bill Anderson and William Quantrill.

No. I did not believe it for a moment. No commanding general in the Union army would have ordered this atrocity, or stood behind a subordinate who carried it out on his own. Some bloodthirsty citizens would surely have approved, but few would have said so in public. Foreign opinion, if nothing else, would compel *any* government to repudiate it.

And Colonel Dahlgren had to know as much. He was an admiral's son, proud and ambitious, yes, and even reckless, but he had grown up in high military circles. He, more than many others, had to know. *A man could not build a career on something like this.*

It was pure fabrication, I thought, a desperate attempt to stiffen the Confederacy's faltering morale. This was an election year, after all. The Rebels had to hold their own till November. They needed every possible effort from every Southerner alive; they needed passion and rage, they needed a commitment that would yield to nothing: *Don't tire, don't quit, don't measure the sacrifices, the Yankees will cut us down like dogs, and burn our children in their beds. Everything and anything till November, and then God willing the Northern people will boot Lincoln out and we can negotiate a settlement and an independent Confederacy. . . .*

It was a strategy of war. Ugly, I thought, but effective; I had seen the black fear in Millie Franklin's eyes.

But was it something more?

So many secret meetings, Mariel kept telling us, meetings no one was allowed near, not even servants with food and drink. So many unknown men, coming to the White House at unlikely hours. And that little piece of paper my War Department clerk had found on the floor a couple of weeks ago. It was in General Rains's handwriting, he said, so maybe it meant something, and maybe it didn't. Rains was important, the head of the Torpedo Bureau—the unit that had, among other things, mined the James River.

I'd sent the note on and forgotten about it . . . until now. Now I could almost see it, just a ragged scrap with a boot print on it, and a few scrawled words: *TC. 20 men. Not enough.*

Who or what was TC? And what, precisely, were twenty men not enough for?

They could justify anything now, with Dahlgren's papers to fly from their standard. Anything. Washington in flames. Murderers in the streets, and in the camps of our generals. . . .

No. I shut my eyes hard against the pale spring light. The trees in my yard looked like gallows trees; even the sun was befouled. I felt cold all through. Cold from things I couldn't name, and didn't want to think about.

Just like Millie Franklin.

We're all going crazy, I thought, *and I am, too. The dark has got to me, the secrets, the lies. God forgive me, I'll soon be dragging assassins out from under my bed.*

Then again, maybe. . . .

Of course, there was more to the affair than a story in the press. There were the papers themselves. On U.S. Army letterhead. In what appeared to be the colonel's handwriting, over what appeared to be his signature. U. Dahlgren. Only he never signed anything else that way. He always signed his full name. And as far as we know, he always remembered how to spell it. . . .

"You believed those papers were forgeries all along, didn't you?" Sam's question is soft and meditative as he settles down into a small curl beside me.

"They were tampered with somehow, yes. Don't you think so?"

"I've been back and forth on it. God knows I had enough people around me arguing they were real. Only too many things about them just didn't make sense."

"If they wasna tampered with," McNiven says, "then why did none but a handful of Rebels ever see them? Photographs is all anyone else ever saw. Anyway, if I had it in my head to kill a lot of important folks and burn down a city, I'd be a sorry damn fool to write it all down."

"Look at General Sherman," Martin Lipscomb says. "He didn't exactly pussyfoot around in Georgia. But he only burned Atlanta after the civilian population was moved out. And maybe he lied about it, but he always said Columbia was burned by accident. And he was a top general; he could do pretty much what he pleased. Now we're supposed to believe some twenty-year-old *colonel* took a thing like this upon himself? Bah, it makes my head ache."

"And what about all those instructions for his men?" I add. "Seize the ferry boats. Spike the guns. Destroy the bridges, the supply depots, the mills—but not the hospitals. Why did he bother, I wonder, if the whole city was to be gutted from end to end anyway? The mills and the depots would go along with everything else. And how did he imagine the hospitals would be spared?"

"That was one of the things I wondered about," Sam said. "All those instructions, and not a word about finding Davis and the cabinet. No strike force detailed to the Capitol, or to the White House. No hint on what to do if Davis wasn't there. But there's something even stranger. Twice in those orders he talks about General Custer coming up behind them. Well, the fact is, General Custer wasn't coming up behind them. His part in the campaign was strictly a diversion—to draw the Rebels' attention *away* from the raid. Custer wasn't headed anywhere near Richmond, and Dahlgren knew it."

"But the Rebs didn't."

"Precisely."

"But vat about the talk?" Angelina wonders. "Even on our side, people shook their heads, and said maybe there vas something to it; they said he vanted Davis."

"Wanted him, hell." Will Rowley is an easygoing man, most times, but he doesn't have a lot of patience on this particular subject. "Of course he wanted him. It would've been a marvelous feather in his cap. You run a cavalry raid into the enemy capital, you pick up any of their leaders you find lying around; that's only common sense. You pick them up and you pack them off the same way we packed off Rooney Lee—bedclothes and all if need be. That's a far cry different from murdering the lot of them and burning the city to the ground."

"Aye." McNiven drapes his small, wiry unbody against a tree, and wraps his arms behind his head. "It was all a big load of horse leavings. And the poor laddie's still carrying it on his back. The whole thing a failure, and his name disgraced, and his bones tossed about like they wasna even human. And all the ugly names they called him—gad, it's nae wonder he's gone missing from the world. . . ."

MARCH, 1864 . . .

Life in Richmond was hell for the loyalists, after the Dahlgren affair. People stopped me on the sidewalk and berated me; one man shook his fist in my face, and told me to take my worthless carcass off to Washington, or I might find it hanging from a tree. People stopped calling. Some who had been friendly even until now would duck into business establishments when they saw me coming, or suddenly cross the street, so as not to encounter me at all.

About three days after the story became public, I came outside in the morning and found a paper tacked to a pillar of my veranda. A rough, childish drawing of a hooded skull stared at me from above a Rebel battle flag. Across most of the page was a scrawl of uneven, handprinted letters: *Old maid, is your house insured? Yours truly, White Caps.*

The worst thing of all, then, was wondering if the person who brought the note was still in my yard. Waiting for me. Watching. I made my eyes search the garden, the shadows by the carriage house, the clusters of trees. Then, with all the indifference I could manage, I shoved the note into my pocket and went back into the house. I never told anyone about it.

It was the first such paper I found; it was not to be the last.

Others paid for the "Awful Yankee Doings" with more than simply threats. Libby Prison was mined, and the prisoners told bluntly they'd be blown to hell if there was another attempt at a mass escape, or another Yankee raid. All of Dahlgren's men were tossed into the cellars, without exception, even those who were seriously wounded. For a while there was open talk about hanging them, not merely in the newspapers and in the streets, but at the highest levels of government. The Federal authorities still held Rooney Lee, however, and his father wisely counseled Mr. Davis against it.

Colonel Dahlgren's body had been stripped in the field of everything valuable—most of his clothing, his weapons, his gold watch. They cut off one of his fingers to get the ring it held, and took his wooden leg from its stump. After the publication of the papers, the body was taken by darkness from the railway depot and flung into an unmarked and unremembered grave.

Or so the Rebels imagined.

It was a dog's burial, the *Examiner* boasted, without coffin, winding sheet, or service. But they were seen by a black workman who made a note of the place, and told us. So we took him from his vile grave, and let him lie in honor for a day at Will Rowley's house, and then we took him out of Richmond, through the Rebel pickets to Robert Orrick's farm, and buried him again, in a sealed metal coffin, in a quiet orchard, where he might rest in peace until the war was over and his family could come and take him home.

It was, I suppose, one of the strangest missions any cabal of spies ever undertook. I still remember the night at Orrick's farm. The dark all around, crowding us, as if it meant to drive our feeble circle of light back into the lantern and snuff it out. The thud and scrape of the shovels, rhythmic and pitiless as a chant. The smell, which always seemed to me the smell of time itself, a miasmic thing, formless, ancient, and utterly amoral. I could have believed in many strange gods that night—and just as easily in none at all.

We did not speak. Calm and serious we had been when we started, honorable people performing an honorable duty. But there is something about a *secret* burial that makes even honorable people unduly conscious of the cold and the shadows. And it came upon me, slowly, that we were trying to do an act of magic. Trying to rescue the whole wretched enterprise along with his bones. As though it could be rescued. As though it weren't over, failed, finished. As though an honorable grave could shut away forever the lost possibilities, the unanswered questions. *Our* questions. Why didn't anybody come to us? *Why?*

It must have taken an awfully long time. I grew cold, standing by, and the night seemed to thicken like dead blood. I would not have been surprised to see vampires abroad, or Ulli Dahlgren's ghost, one-legged and angry at his graveside, glaring at us: "Who the devil are *you*?"

We, Colonel Dahlgren, are the friends no one told you you had. We did our best. This is all we can do for you now. . . .

More than thirty people had a hand in his burying, from the beginning to the end. It went together like a puzzle, every piece in its place, smooth, seamless, we know where he is, we know what we need, a metal coffin, sealer, men to dig, a hiding place, a burying place, a way through the lines, someone to do it, someone as calm as the dead, how do you hide something as big as a coffin in something as small as a wagon, easy, peach trees and idle talk, Will Rowley can talk pickets to death, he's done it before. . . . It went smooth as clockwork, not a misstep, not a trace. The Rebs never knew what happened. They buried him and then they went to fetch him and he was gone, poof, right out of the ground; maybe they thought it was witchcraft, or maybe they thought the devil came and fetched him personally to hell for his innumerable Yankee sins. But they had a devil of a time of it themselves, after, when they told his father they'd behave like civilized people and send the body home, and then had to tell him they lost it. . . .

It was mad, what we did. Mad and magnificent and so very Southern. No Yankee would have done it; they had far too much sense. I never regretted it for a minute. But there was a hard irony to all of it, in the end. People remembered what we did, but they remembered for all the wrong reasons. Not for the skill or the planning, or for the proof of how complex and far-reaching our network had become, or how it was ignored. Though we never intended it so, at least not consciously, burying Dahlgren was a rebuke to General Butler, and to Kilpatrick, and even to Meade. *You could have had this, you gold-braided martinets—all of it, working with you, every step of the way. We could have been ears for you, eyes for you, lies for you; we could have given you Richmond, instead of burying you there.*

But no one read it so, not then, and not afterward. They remembered the gothic strangeness of it. The melodrama. The risks we took—took, as they saw it, for nothing. They remembered very little else. Partly I suppose it was my own fault. There were so many things we did I never wrote about. Some things I wrote about, and then I burned the papers afterward, even when the war was over. And a lot of my papers just . . . got lost. But the Dahlgren story endured, and moved finally to front and center, and stayed there, as though our small gesture of courtesy and defiance were the only action we'd ever carried out. As though all the competence we showed there had fallen from heaven, hadn't been practiced, hadn't been used elsewhere, hadn't saved any living Federals or sent any Rebels to their own dark graves.

We became, like the rest of the South, romantic. A society can thrive on that. So can an army, especially if it's been beaten in the field. But a spy? A romantic spy is just entertainment, just military meringue, Belle Boyd fluttering her eyelashes, Crazy Bet digging up corpses.

We still encounter it, even in your own day. Some of the newly dead go to a great deal of trouble to find us, and then they say the most amazing things. "You people were sure naive," one of them told me, without a hint of a blush. "Brave enough, I suppose, but you didn't know much about espionage or warfare, did you?" He learned it from some kind of talking picture box. They tell stories about us there, apparently. About Belle Boyd being just *so* irresistible, and Rose Greenhow winning the battle of Bull Run single-handed, and Timothy Webster getting all crippled just from sleeping in the cold, and me with a basket on my arm, talking to myself and digging up corpses. My young questioner didn't know a thing about Sam Ruth or Will Rowley or Spencer Kellog Brown. He didn't know why Lee's supply train never got to Amelia Court House, or why the Rebels got mauled to bits at Fort Stedman. He'd never, God save us, even *heard* of George Sharpe.

But he was absolutely fascinated by Civil War spies.

Well. Never mind. That was how the bloody year of '64 began.

But there is one thing more I should tell you about it—something none of us knew until the war was over.

Jefferson Davis had an interesting black paperweight on the desk in his study. Mariel saw it more than once, and never imagined it was anything different from what it seemed to be—a piece of varnished coal. It was, in fact, a model of a time bomb, designed by a naval captain named Thomas Courtney—the TC of my boot-printed note, I suppose.

In February, the Rebel Congress passed in secret session a bill drafted by the same Thomas Courtney, creating a special secret service corps with a special mission—to plant these and similar explosive devices on Union targets in the occupied Confederacy, in the North, and abroad. Courtney had something of a mercenary mind; his agents were to be paid, in Rebel bonds, up to fifty percent of the value of whatever they destroyed. I always wondered, afterward, what William Sherman would have thought of such a notion, when he was marching through Georgia.

Courtney's bombs would show a long reach and a remarkable ambition. Ships blew up with no credible explanation in New York harbor, on the Mississippi, and especially on the James. Only twice was sabotage ever proven; only once were the saboteurs ever named. But the string of mangled ships and mangled bodies stretched from the gunboat *Chenango* in April of '64 to, quite possibly, the *Sultana* in May of '65, carrying a thousand prisoners liberated from Andersonville, most of whom never made it home.

It was, of course, all just retaliation for those "Awful Yankee Doings" Dahlgren didn't actually do. So was the attempt to burn down New York City. So was the murder of Abraham Lincoln. All poor Ulli Dahlgren's fault.

But, for what it's worth to you to know it, Courtney's bill was passed on February 17, 1864. Ten days *before* Colonel Dahlgren began his doomed ride to Richmond.

THIRTEEN

———————— ✳

THE FUR WILL FLY
IN THESE DIGGINS

[General Grant] talked less and thought more than any man in the service.

Horace Porter, Staff of General Grant

. . . The ordinary, scrubby-looking man, with a slightly seedy look, as if he was out of office and on half pay . . . had a clear blue eye, and a look of resolution, as if he could not be trifled with. . . .

Richard Henry Dana

Ulysses don't scare worth a damn.

Union soldier, Virginia, 1864

We suppose that after his return the fur will fly in these diggins.

George H. Sharpe

Mary Custis was the great-granddaughter of Martha Washington. From the day Robert E. Lee married her, and took possession of the revolutionary hero's Arlington estate, he considered himself, if not precisely Washington's heir, certainly the custodian of Washington's legacy. He had the family bond—by marriage rather than by blood, but he had it, and in Virginia it was a precious thing to have. He had Washington's books, and the magnificent sword presented to him by the Continental Congress. He had Washington's lantern and his china and his splendid silver tea service.

But Washington's mantle of command he never got. On March 2, 1864, that mantle, untouched by any intervening hand, fell gracefully upon the slender shoulders of Ulysses S. Grant.

Walter Scott should have been there to see it. It was, after all, his kind of story—a story of mortal peril in the land, of usurper and lawful heir. But it changed, crossing the Atlantic to the New World. The legacy wasn't a crown anymore, or a grand estate, or a better kind of blood. It wasn't a house full of famous possessions. It was a government, a dream of freedom, a hope for a better way to live. That's what Washington left to us to inherit, and to Grant to defend.

I wonder if the usurper ever understood.

Will Rowley and his family and I drank a toast together, the day we learned that Grant was coming to Virginia. He'd been named lieutenant general a week or so before, and given command of all the Federal armies in the field. He could have stayed in Washington, as many expected; or in the west, where all of his great victories had been won. But no. He was coming east, where it all began, to finish it. He would design the strategy for the entire war, set all the forces in motion, but he would lead the Virginia campaign himself. And I can scarcely tell you how glad we were, how recklessly hopeful. God knows we needed something to celebrate, with Kilpatrick's failure still heavy on our minds, and the whole of Richmond simmering around us, talking nothing but hatred and blood. So we toasted our new commander with a bit of sherry I had bought for the occasion, and made jokes about our bet.

"I think we should renegotiate it," I said. "Your shinplaster isn't worth much anymore."

"Neither is your picture of General McClellan."

"It is, too. He's going to run for president."

"Well, he ran for Richmond once, as I recall. He never arrived."

"Do you think the war will be over by then, Pa?" Roe asked. "Before the election?"

"God willing, son." Will looked at Kitty and smiled—rather feebly, I thought. The end of the war seemed more and more like the horizon—something we could tramp toward forever, and never reach.

"Grant has to win a big victory, doesn't he?" Merritt said. "Or Mr. Lincoln won't be elected again. Leastways, that's what everybody says."

"I reckon so. And I reckon he will."

"The Rebels don't think so," Roe said. "I heard a couple of ladies talking to each other, yesterday, after they bought my paper. One of them said the Yankees must be awfully hard up for leaders, having to put a man like that in charge. He doesn't have a *scrap* of breeding, she said, and everybody knows he drinks. And the other one said Lee was going to pick him up by the scruff of the neck and throw him in the Potomac, just like all the others. And that would be the end of it. They don't have any more after this, she said; they've scraped the bottom of the barrel."

Kitty eyed him skeptically. "They really said all that, Roe? You remembered every word?"

"Pretty much, Ma."

"Well." Will took his pipe out of his mouth and rearranged the tobacco. "The bottom of the barrel. They aren't paying attention, are they?"

Moods are strange things. I was so happy, sitting with Will and Kitty, talking about Grant, about how everything was going to be done right this time. No more sitting in camp waiting for the army to grow big enough to scare Bobby Lee to death. No more eyeing him across some river or some patch of no-man's-land, like old cats growling at each other from opposite roofs. It would be down in the dirt now, fight it out and finish it; the fur was going to fly indeed.

Then I drove across Richmond to go home again, and all my happiness dissolved. There was so much energy in the streets, so much fire. Defiant headlines graced every newspaper, and a lot of Rebels believed every word of it, just like young Roe had told us. Their cause was sacred. Lee was unbeatable on his own ground. Grant would fail like the others. Eight months was all it would take. Eight months till November. Lincoln would be turfed out and the new government would finally accept what the South had always known—they could never be conquered.

What if they were right? What if Grant didn't win the one big fight we needed? Even the best of generals could be beaten, once, somewhere.

Just then I understood, at least a tiny bit, what it might mean to get down in the dirt and fight it out. To take such a risk. How hard it must be, and why some men maybe just couldn't do it, why they waited and waited, why they circled and growled from the rooftops, and forgot they could lose there, too—lose slowly, so it would seem to be no one's fault, but lose just the same. Looking down from those rooftops was looking down at forever. For the army, and for the nation. Especially now, I thought, eight months from an election, with three years of futility behind us, and the whole country weary to death of the killing.

It would be the hardest thing imaginable, maybe, taking the Army of the Potomac across the Rapidan this one last time. . . .

No one slept in Richmond for days when it began. By the fifth of May, Grant was on the move, and Butler's gunboats were coming up the James. That much we knew, but from then on, we heard nothing except wild rumors. One day Grant was trapped in the Wilderness, and the Army of the Potomac was cut to pieces. The next day the Rebels had lost the Petersburg Railroad, and Federal cavalry were within five miles of the city. From hour to hour, loyalist or Rebel alike, it didn't matter, we were tumbled from triumph to black terror, and back again. Ladies paced their verandas long into the night, or walked the streets as though it were day. Children climbed onto rooftops to watch the glow of Butler's cannon, booming endlessly down the river. Some days, all day long, we could hear the alarm bells clanging. The secretary of War himself had called out every man capable of bearing arms. You could not walk a block in Richmond without colliding with a company of militia, or a half-dozen citizens with rifles on their shoulders. Trains from the North spilled out Federal prisoners in a steady stream, and half-grown boys in homespun marched them through the streets to Libby and Belle Isle.

I was not allowed to see any of them. General Winder was gone, shipped off to the Deep South to take charge of all the military prisons in the Confederacy; and Philip Cashmeyer went with him. But I still had other people in the Rebel ranks, and everything the prisoners knew got back to us anyway, bit by bit. How Grant tried to get through the Wilderness before Lee caught him, and didn't quite make it. How they fought for three days—like cats indeed, cats in a hemp sack, tearing each other to pieces in a tanglewood where a man could hardly move and hardly see. How the Union lines almost broke, poor Sedgwick hanging on for dear life in the dead of night. It was the darkest place they had ever imagined, hell come to earth, blind men shooting their own comrades without knowing it, the dead and the wounded burning together as musket fire severed the tree trunks and set the thickets ablaze. Yet when they stumbled out, half blind from smoke and half dead from exhaustion, and saw their road led south—not back across the river to safety and recovery, but on to another fight, and another, and another, until it would be done—oh, how they cheered Grant then!

They had never cheered him before, not here in the east, the way they used to cheer McClellan and other dashing officers, the way the Rebels cheered Lee—never but that once. On that most improbable moment, on the heels of what was surely more a disaster than a victory, when every sane man among them might have longed to stumble back into camp and lick his wounds—then they flung their hats into the befouled sky, and called out their bands, and sang down the darkness on the road to Spotsylvania.

The road to Cold Harbor.

The road to Appomattox.

By the eleventh of May, we'd been living one full week in the middle of a whirlwind, and two full days expecting imminent attack. The rumors were true for once, and Secretary Seddon's desperate call to arms was justified. Philip Sheridan's Union cavalry was literally at our gates. He'd come storming in from the northwest, twelve thousand strong and backed by horse artillery, and collided with Jeb Stuart at a crossroads, a bare six miles from the city, near a quiet country inn called Yellow Tavern.

I was at the home of a loyalist friend for most of the afternoon. Everyone could hear the fighting now, even in their houses. The armory was open all day, and the Rebel authorities were giving out guns to anybody who would take them.

We were so hopeful, I remember, wondering if Sheridan could take the city, wondering if tomorrow or the next day the war might be over for us. Such naiveté. We had nearly eleven months of war left to endure.

The black lad came into the house very quietly, just around sunset. His name was Chip, and he worked for the Cross family, who lived near Yellow Tavern. Miz Cross had sent him into town, he said, to find me or Mister Tom. She thought we'd want to know.

"General Stuart was shot in the fighting," he said. "Real bad. They say he's going to die."

My friend and I exchanged looks. "How do you know?" I asked.

"They took him right past our place, to Dr. Brewer's. Miz Cross talked to some of the soldiers. They say he's gut shot; they say there ain't no way he can live."

That night Sheridan pulled back. He had what he came for—not Richmond, but Stuart. The once proud Rebel cavalry was chewed to pieces at Yellow Tavern, and Jeb Stuart was dead.

Would you believe me if I told you even I was sorry? I never thought I would pity any of the Rebel leaders. The men, yes, the thousands of brave and decent men marched off to die in what was surely one of the most uncalled-for wars in the history of human-kind. But the leaders were another matter. If the Yankees really had hung Jeff Davis from a sour apple tree, instead of just singing about it, I would have thought it little more than he deserved.

Then Stuart was killed, and Richmond draped itself in black. Richmond wept in the streets. Jackson's death had destroyed their faith in the Confederacy's invincibility. Lee's death, if it had ever chanced to happen, might well have destroyed their faith in God. But Stuart's dying broke their hearts. He was the knight from the storybooks, the *chevalier sans peur et sans reproche,* the knight without fear and without dishonor, who rode daring circles all the way around McClellan's army . . . twice. He was, more than any of them, what the whole South imagined itself to be, colorful and care-free, a splendid hero on a golden horse, riding to war with music at his sword arm and feathers in his hat.

It rained the day of his funeral, a black, slow, heavy rain that just kept coming from a black, unrelenting sky. I still remember it, how dark it was, and how people looked at me on the street. It was worse than the days after Dahlgren's raid. They had been angry then, and I could be angry back, because the whole howling thing was a lie, whether they knew anything about it or not. Now they grieved, and for their grief I had no answer, neither anger nor any other. It met me everywhere I turned. On Broad Street a small crowd had gath-ered around an old man with an old guitar. He sat barely sheltered from the rain, against the wall of Harrington's tailor shop. His voice broke sometimes as he sang. *The flowers of the forest, The bravest, the foremost, The pride of our country lies cold in the clay. . . .*

Some turned as I went by, and every eye that knew me called me murderer, simply for existing, for being who I was. I went home again with half my tasks undone, defeated, for the first time in my life, by the hatred of my neighbors. And by something else . . . something very much like guilt.

It is hot in the grove where we shelter for the day. One by one my companions slip down under old logs or clumps of dark moss, until only Will Rowley is left.

"Can I ask you something, Will? Something rather . . . personal?"

"I reckon. Might not answer, though."

"Did you ever wonder if what we were doing was wrong? In the war?"

"You mean us personally? Or the Union?"

"Either. Both. All of us, I guess."

It grows very quiet suddenly, except for the living things.

"Sometimes," he says at last. "And are you going to tell me now, after all these years, that you did, too?"

"I didn't at first. Not for a long time."

"Yes, we noticed. Sam told me once you'd cut the word 'doubt' right out of your dictionary. Said you probably didn't even know how to spell it."

"Oh, I knew. Sometimes I felt . . . what my sister-in-law called me, before she went away. She said I was . . . unnatural."

Will makes a small, dry sound, rather like a cat's cough.

"Who decides, Miss Liza? What's natural and what isn't? Once that cannon went off at Sumter, we all had to betray something. Only question was what.

"Something happened to me in '64, when I was out by the Chickahominy," he went on, a bit later. "I never told you about it. Never told anyone but Kitty. I came upon a wounded Rebel in a shed, on an old abandoned farm. Hell knows how he got there; it was a long way from any fighting at the time. He thought I was just a local farmer, and friendly. He asked me for food. I gave him what I had, and we talked a little. He was a town kid from Mobile. When he got home

287

again, he said, he was taking over his father's barbershop. He'd have made a good barber; he liked to talk.

"I was dog-tired, Miss Liza. I'd been dodging Reb patrols all day. So I didn't even notice, at first, when he reached in his pack. All that happened was I looked up and I saw his hand moving and it held a gun. I shot him. And then I stood there, while this sorry little pistol slid out of his hand, and he held himself with blood coming through his fingers, and said, 'Why?' He said, 'I wanted to give you something for the food, and it's the only thing I got that I don't need anymore.'

"He was quitting the war, he said. He was going home, and he wasn't planning to come back. And I killed him. For a long time afterward, for years, I couldn't get him out of my head. He never should have died, and there were how many thousands more just like him. And I told Kitty once, maybe we should have let them go. I said maybe no country, no government, no fine words or ambitions or ideals or any other howling thing men use as excuses were worth a tragedy like this. All she said was this: And if we had let them go? What other tragedy was lying in wait for us, instead of this one?

"I figure she was right, Miss Liza. It's a question that has to be asked. Can't be answered, I reckon, but it has to be asked. It isn't enough just to grieve. . . ."

SUMMER, 1864 . . .

The summer dragged on, and the quick, decisive Union victory we longed for never came. Lee and Grant fought again at Spotsylvania, to another stalemate. General Butler, true to form, bungled his way up the James so badly that he put his army in a box, and spent the whole summer there, capturing nothing but battalions of mosquitoes.

Spirits in Richmond changed like the wind. The Rebels saw Grant's mighty army stopped at every turn, its passage through Virginia a long, unending dead march, and they knew they had won.

He was paying a terrible price for his invasion, they said, one bloody battlefield after another, and he had nothing to show for it.

But some of them, once in a while, took a long hard look at the price General Lee was paying for Grant's handful of nothing, and they found it harder to smile. Lee's casualties were also high, and his marvelously mobile army was finally pinned down. Holding its ground, yes, but holding it the same way Grant was contesting it—with blood.

Except Grant could do what Lee no longer could. He could maneuver. On the twelfth of June, in the dead of night, the Union army moved out of its trenches at Cold Harbor, and headed across the Virginia countryside toward the strategic rail center at Petersburg.

It was one of those things about the war that I cannot remember without blind pride and blinding regret. Grant's move was dazzling, difficult almost to believe, when you think about the numbers: nearly a hundred thousand men, a supply train thirty-five miles long, a journey across fifty miles of enemy land, across the wide James River without a bridge . . . all unnoticed. They were unseen by Lee's army, most of it within yelling distance when he left; undetected by Rebel scouts; unreported by Rebel spies. All Lee got was rumors and warnings, talk of empty trenches, hints of movement, but no direction; then finally, desperate appeals for help from Petersburg: *Do something, for God's sake, the whole damn Union army is in our face!*

Unfortunately, the whole damn Union army didn't attack. The men wanted to; they knew they'd stolen a march on Bobby Lee. They knew there was nothing between them and the biggest, sweetest, most unexpected triumph of the war except skeleton defenses and handfuls of men. They'd been shot to pieces in the Wilderness, at Spotsylvania, at Cold Harbor, and they still wanted to go in; that's how obvious it was.

The corps commanders thought they knew better. They waited. They made certain of everything. By the time they were ready to give the order, Lee's reinforcements had arrived, and they were beaten back.

We grieved over Petersburg. For weeks. Had Petersburg been taken, Richmond would have followed. The war would have been over for us, over for everyone, maybe. What could Lee have done, with his supply line gone and the whole Federal army closing in, except what he did ten months later when Petersburg *did* fall—surrender?

"Two thousand men in the city." Angelina cupped her hands around her coffee, and shook her head. "Is enough to make you cry. Vat is wrong with those generals? To vait like that, when they could have taken the city in an hour?"

"God knows, Angelina. There's leadership problems in that army; there always was. I guess even Grant couldn't solve them all."

"You vant some more coffee?"

"No, thank you."

"I don't blame you. Willy says ve should stop pretending this stuff is coffee, and call it . . . vell, never mind. You know, ven the Yankees come, I think the first thing I do is ask someone for coffee. The first vun I see. I vill say, do you haff some coffee, please? And then after I vill say hello, and velcome, and God bless America."

I had to smile a little. I was a tea drinker myself, so I didn't grieve so much over the horrid rubbish that passed for coffee in the Confederacy these days. It was made of chicory and bark and browned flour—and usually some other things, best not investigated.

"It is good they are across the river," she went on quietly. "Ve must look at the bright side, Liza. Not at vat they didn't accomplish, but vat they did. The Rebels can do nothing now but dig in, and hope ve lose the election. That's all. They are in a box."

In a box. Well, maybe. Trouble was, we'd said it before. They'd said it before, too. Both sides kept on saying it. *Aha! We've got you now!* And then we didn't.

Through the window we could see the McNiven's Bakery wagon pulling up outside. Angelina got to her feet with a sigh.

"There is Chris. I must take the day's orders. You vill excuse me, please."

"Of course."

I leaned back in my chair and waited, wondering if Chris might have something for me. He did, but it wasn't quite what I'd hoped for.

Chris Taylor was a stocky, quiet black man of twenty-five or so; he was Tom McNiven's right hand. He was freeborn, shrewd, and very brave. Like Will Rowley, he seemed able to get through picket lines with anything.

He came into the living quarters behind the restaurant about five minutes later.

"Morning, Miss Liza."

I greeted him in return, and offered him a cup of what Willy Lohmann thought we shouldn't call coffee. He accepted with thanks, and sat down.

"So is anything happening?" I asked. "Any news?"

"Nothing much. Another train of prisoners came through last night. It didn't even stop, except to drop off some Rebel wounded. They're shipping the Yankees straight through to Andersonville. Oh, and Mister Tom needs money."

"Any *good* news?"

"The Richmond Theatre's got itself a brand new silver water cooler."

"Really."

I didn't care much about a water cooler, one way or the other. But mention of the theatre made me remember how long it had been since I'd seen a play. Or bought a new novel, or a new piece of music, or anything else that I wanted. I used to have money to spend. I used to buy things purely for pleasure. The war swallowed every-thing. Like a monster, I thought, a beast out of nightmare that you just kept feeding, until it ate the whole world. . . .

"Is Mariel all right?" I asked.

"Fine, as far's I can tell. I saw her yesterday. She says the Davises are in pretty bad shape, both of them, what with their boy dying like he did. But she says it ain't going to matter. Old Jeff just sets his jaw and keeps on living in his own storybook. She says he wouldn't recognize reality iffen he fell over it on the street."

Chris drained his coffee cup; he seemed to find the brew quite acceptable.

"There's something I been meaning to tell you, Miss Liza, except I don't quite know how."

"Well, unless it's something very rude, straight out is usually as good a way as any."

"Well, then. Mister Tom broke your cipher code."

"*What?*"

"Yes'm. He didn't mean any harm. I think he just wanted to know if . . . if it would be hard to break or not. In case the Rebels ever got our stuff."

"And was it hard?"

The young man bit his lip, just a little. "It took him 'bout half an hour."

"I see."

"I told him he should tell you, but he thought you'd take it bad, so he didn't want to."

"Well." I hardly knew what to say. Half an hour, he said. The Federal army had trained men, professionals, whose whole business was designing and breaking codes. The Confederates probably did, too. How long would it take a professional to break my code? All of five minutes? And I had been so proud of it. . . .

"I'm sorry," Chris said. "I reckon Mister Tom was right; I shouldn't've said anything."

"No, I'm glad you did. It's better that I know. I'll . . . I'll have to think of something else, that's all. And don't worry. I won't let on you ever said a word."

Some days, I thought, a person should never get out of bed. It had rained overnight, and crossing a side street I stepped in a mud pud-

dle halfway up to my knee. The message drop I visited was empty—
for the third worrisome day in a row. Everywhere I turned, news-
boys screamed Confederate heroics in my ear. By the time I got
home I was exhausted, dirty, and my head hurt. The last thing in
the world I wanted to hear was Josey's whispered warning as I came
in the door.

"There's a Reb in the parlor," she said. "All busted up. He come
asking for food, and we took him in, just like the others. And then
he wouldn't leave. Says he wants to thank you in person." She
paused, standing in the middle of the hallway as though she wanted
to stop me from passing. "I don't know what to make of him, Miss
Liza. It's like he's . . . he's just too blamed interested in you, somehow."

"Well. I expect he won't go away until I've talked to him."

Any number of dark possibilities flitted through my mind as I
walked down the hall. A Rebel deserter, perhaps, wanting to get
smuggled out. Or someone from Devon Hill, with some awful news
or some impossible demand. Or, God help us, maybe another Andrew Jackson Bonham. Our new provost marshal was forever promising to crack down on disloyalists and spies. Whoever this Rebel
was, he was trouble, that was certain. Nothing but more trouble.

I stood for a long time with my hand on the doorjamb. Leaning
on it, really. Maybe if I stood there long enough he'd go away.
Maybe it would all go away, the war, the danger, the lonely, fruitless
work.

I wanted to quit. You might as well know it. Sometimes I just
wanted to sit down and quit, because it never ended. One more big
battle, we told ourselves; and then there was another, and another.
One more winter, we told ourselves; and then there was another,
and nothing was any different except there were more dead, and
more prisoners, and less to eat and less to believe in. All we'd been
doing back in May was whistling in the graveyard, I thought, drinking fools' toasts and talking about how things would be fine now.
Just whistling in the graveyard. . . .

Do it, Liza. He isn't going to go away. Just go in and face him.

I opened the parlor door and stepped inside. He must have started to get up even as he heard the doorknob turn, for he was on his feet before I was fully through the door. A young man, as they all seemed to be. Dirty and bedraggled, his shirt in tatters, one of his arms in a filthy sling. One foot bare, the other wrapped in bloody rags, almost to the knee.

Afternoon sun was pouring through the parlor window, sharpening every detail. I remember exactly how he looked: spent and vulnerable, like a young, wounded animal. Someone you wanted to feed and shelter and brush the hair from his eyes. Someone who couldn't quite—even when you knew better—seem in any way dishonest, or dangerous.

Even I, who should certainly have known better, was taken in, and felt my guard go down.

"Good afternoon," I said. "I'm Liza Van Lew. I understand you've been waiting to see me?"

"Miss Liza." He smiled, inclined his head. "Or should I say Mr. Babcock?"

Needless to say, my guard went back up in a heartbeat. I stood absolutely still, pasting as bland and bewildered a look upon my face as I could manage. "I beg your pardon, sir?"

"And I beg yours." He sat down again, and bending forward, began to unwrap the bandage from his foot, peeling off strip after strip of bloodstained, filthy cotton, and scattering about in the process a distressing quantity of grass, dirt, and dead insects.

"I apologize, ma'am," he said. "It isn't pretty, but it works."

Inside one of the folded rags was a piece of foil, and inside the foil was a piece of paper. An enemy might have captured him, searched him, even ripped off the bandages to search them, and never found it, unless they carefully pried apart a tattered strip, folded over upon itself and caked solidly together with dried blood.

He stood again, and handed me the paper.

"With Colonel Sharpe's compliments, Miss Liza," he said.

I took it, but I did not immediately look at it. I looked at him. The sweetest, most innocent face you'd ever want to see. The most candid brown eyes. This one could talk his way past the gatekeeper of heaven in two minutes flat. Or, perhaps even faster, the gate-keeper of the other place.

I opened the paper. It was official stationery. Office of the Provost Marshal, Army of the Potomac.

Dear Mr. Babcock. The bearer of this letter has my fullest confidence. He will explain the reason for his visit. Col. George H. Sharpe, Assistant Provost Marshal.

I knew the hand. I knew the signature. It was genuine. This clever young man with the angelic brown eyes was one of ours.

"Welcome to Richmond," I said. "What should I call you?"

"Oh. I did forget that, didn't I? Lieutenant Jedediah Malachi Knight, at your service, ma'am. Folks mostly call me Jed."

"Please, sit down and make yourself comfortable, Lieutenant. I'll have Josey bring us some tea and cakes, and we can talk. Forgive me for asking, but your wounds . . . that is, is there anything we can do for you, or . . . ?" I faltered. Even under the circumstances, I couldn't quite bring myself to ask if they were fake.

"Thanks, Miss Liza, but no. They're purely decorative. But tea and cake sounds real nice."

He looked tired, I thought. I told Josey to bring the brandy, too, and said we were not to be disturbed thereafter. By anyone, not even Mother.

He drank his tea with obvious appreciation, took a small glass of brandy and two large pieces of cake, and told me what was happening at City Point.

Well, actually, he didn't tell me half of it—not at the time. Grant was changing things in the Bureau of Military Information. In June, just around the time Grant was heading for Petersburg, Jubal Early had taken a small Rebel army into the Shenandoah Valley, and was practically knocking at the gates of Washington before the Federal commander knew for certain where he was. This, in his opinion, was completely unacceptable; it was precisely the sort of thing the Bureau of Military Information was supposed to prevent.

The Bureau was part of the Army of the Potomac, and since Hooker's day, it had been under the direction of Hooker's replacement, General George Gordon Meade. The goggle-eyed old snapping turtle, they called him. A career officer of twenty-odd years, with a temper like a lit fuse and an ego like an open wound. He had little use for Sharpe's Bureau, and sometimes assigned its experienced scouts to trifling tasks like guarding wagon trains and escorting civilians around the camp. At one point he said the unit was good for absolutely nothing, and ought to be disbanded. (This was one of the things Jed did *not* tell me. Nor did anyone else, for quite some time.)

What Jed did tell me was that the Bureau had been moved. It wasn't in Meade's camp anymore; it was with Grant at City Point, and in everything important it was answering directly to him. George Sharpe was just about living at the general's headquarters now—untethered finally, and just itching to run. They had liked each other since the first time they met, back at Culpeper in March.

"They're different in a lot of ways, I guess," Jed said, "but they're the same in one. They come to a wall, they find a way to the other side. Under it, over it, around it, and if all else fails right through it. But they go. They don't whine about it being there, and they don't sit down and wait for it to go away. The colonel says Grant is one considerable of a man."

"I'll have to pass that on to Mr. Phillips. He's been saying the same thing since Donelson."

"I'll tell him myself. Actually, that's mostly why I'm here. To meet with everybody. Yourself, the colonel said. Quaker. Phillips. Mr. Hills. And to get to know my way around. It seems I'll be coming here again from time to time."

He smiled when he said it, like a boy going fishing.

"The general wants regular lines set up to City Point. From here, from Fredericksburg, and from the Valley. I'm supposed to look after this one. Colonel Sharpe figures if you all can get your couriers to the Chickahominy on a regular basis, we can have scouts there to meet them, day or night. What do you think?"

"I think my life has suddenly got a whole lot easier," I said.

Jed stayed more than a week in Richmond on his first visit. Most of it was spent meeting with the Richmond loyalists, sometimes at my house, sometimes elsewhere. He slept in my garret, though, most nights, and we found time occasionally to speak of other things. He was from East Tennessee, one of more than a hundred thousand men from the Confederate states who fought in the Union army. He had served in the west for a time, scouting for Grenville Dodge's command.

"I kind of wore out my welcome there," he told me. "I got caught three times, joined the Rebel army so many times I don't even re-member, and escaped hanging once by all of ten minutes. General Dodge figured my days with him were numbered, so he gave me to Burnside, and Burnside gave me to Sharpe. Lent me, actually, but then Sharpe wouldn't give me back."

"He must think very highly of you," I said.

"He thinks highly of Dodge. He figures anybody who scouted for Dodge for two years—and survived it—is a man who knows what he's doing."

"Your family are all Union people? In Tennessee?"

"My folks are, and all of us young'uns. Some of our kin went Reb, but not many. My pa said the whole thing was crazy. Secession, the war, all of it, just the wild doings of crazy people. He didn't want any of us in the army, and we weren't much interested in going. We figured it would all blow over. Like a cat with the dis-temper, my pa said. You shut the barn door and stay out of its way till it comes to its senses. Then the militias starting coming around, taking stuff, and saying we all had to join the Rebel army."

"Yes," I said. "I heard about some of that."

"I reckon you didn't hear the worst. More'n half the valley was

Union folks, so the Rebs decided they'd put the fear of God into us right quick. They took a few young men off at rifle point, but pretty soon they couldn't find us anymore; we'd know they were coming and head for the woods. Then they took most everybody's livestock and corn, and left a list of names; the men on it had one week to turn up at the recruiting center, or they'd start clearing out the valley.

"We weren't rich by any means, but we had a real nice house. My pa was always adding things, making it nicer for my ma. I think he could've borne it, seeing it burned by accident, or maybe even by some foreign army. But the men who did it were his neighbors. They'd drunk whiskey together. Helped each other out in bad years. Celebrated each other's birthings and weddings. And then one day they just came riding in demanding his three boys for their rotten little war, and when he said we weren't there, they torched everything. The crops, the barn, the house. They shot the dog. They poured salt down the well. There was nothing left when they rode away. Absolutely nothing, except two old people and a yard full of ashes. It took all my father's faith. He wasn't a fighting man. He didn't believe in it; said it never settled anything. He thought we could stay out of the war. He couldn't believe his own neighbors would treat him so."

"And that's what you found, when you came home? You and your brothers?"

"That's what we found. We got them food and a wagon, so they could get to Knoxville; half of East Tennessee was refugees by then. And then we went to the recruiting center . . . but not the one they had in mind for us."

Jed shook his head thoughtfully. "You know, the first thing when we heard about Sumter, my brother Lije said we'd be fighting. He said there wasn't going to be any way around it. And Pa said he didn't want to hear that kind of nonsense in his house."

"Did he know? I mean, when you joined up? Did he . . . accept it?"

"He cried. He said maybe we should go west instead, or just get jobs somewhere across the line, till it was over. And we said there wasn't any way on God's green earth we were going to do that. Lije said the cat didn't have the distemper, it had the rabies, and the only thing to do with it was shoot it. And then Pa said maybe we were right; he didn't know. He didn't know anything anymore, he said."

"Poor man," I said. "And your mother? It must have been terrible for her, too."

"She took it better than he did. It was her I worried about the most, and yet when the time came, she was the one who stayed strong. . . .

"Anyway. . . ." He smiled at me, putting it all out of sight in a breath—a gesture I readily understood. "That's how three Tennessee mountain boys ended up wearing blue. What about you? Born and bred in Virginia, I understand, and working for the Union; I reckon there's a story here, too."

"I detest slavery," I said, "and I love my country. The rest followed."

He was silent a moment. Speculative. "As easily as that?" he murmured. "I don't think so. But I'll drink to it, anyway." He raised his sherry glass. "To the bravest lady in Virginia."

I went pink right to my toes. Fortunately, it was evening, and we never lit the lights until we had to, so perhaps he didn't notice. It was a long time since a young man drank me a toast, least of all one as cool and gallant and graceful as this.

"Thank you, Lieutenant." I picked up my own glass. "To the daringest scout in the whole Union army."

He laughed. "Wait until you meet Harry Young. That man could brew his coffee at the devil's own fire, and walk out of hell again with the devil's own tail in his pocket. And Old Nick wouldn't even notice till his backside started getting cold. I'm afraid the daringest scout in the whole Union army isn't me. But I'm flattered just the same, Miss Liza."

We touched glasses. That's how it began for me. A night breeze drunk with summer flowers. A sound of distant guns. A mouthful of sherry. It could take so little, sometimes.

Long years after, almost in your own time, someone wrote a story about me. Or so I have been told. They made me fifteen years younger than I actually was, so they could put a man in the story. As though there were some hour, some magical or diabolical moment when the bell tower chimed our irrevocable midnight, and we all turned into pumpkins. As though the time ever came, or ever would come, when all men would be the same to me, when one could no longer be suddenly and magically different, when I would no longer notice that he laughed like a schoolboy and moved like a cat, when I would no longer find him as hopelessly beautiful as I might have done at twenty.

As though the time ever came, or ever would come, when I'd forget how high a price I had paid for my freedom.

FOURTEEN

──────────※

SPIES ARE CONTINUALLY COMING AND GOING

When the armies reached the positions below Richmond, I established communication with Union people . . . from whom I received regular and frequent advices, both oral and written, containing all the information that could be collected from various sources.

George H. Sharpe

Miss Van Lew had a friend in the Adjutant-General's department at Richmond, where he had access to the returns showing the strength of rebel regiments, brigades, divisions, and corps, their movements, and where they were stationed . . . which were regularly delivered to General Grant. . . .

Colonel D. B. Parker, Staff of General Grant

I have satisfactory reasons for believing that spies are continually coming and going in our midst. . . .

Jefferson Davis

I was to learn many things about the war from Jed Knight. He saw a lot, for he was constantly on the move, keeping in touch with all of our agents along the Richmond-Fredericksburg line: the Orricks, and Isaac Silver, and at least a dozen others. His work also brought him into personal contact with many of the highest officers. He told me much of what he saw, and what he thought about, throughout the bloody summer of '64—not least the clear, scorching summer day when General Grant was almost killed. . . .

AUGUST 9, 1864 . . .

The Union camp at City Point wasn't quiet when Jed Knight rode in, merely, in the burning heat of the noonday sun, somewhat quieter than usual. The harbor was churning with gunboats and transports; huge barges filled with supplies for Grant's army stretched along a wharf nearly a full mile long. At the near end, a passenger boat slowly drew apart from the cluster of military ships, and began to puff its way down the river.

Jed was dog-tired. The sun glinting on the water hurt his eyes; so did the dazzling glare of two great ironclads lying at anchor. They were painted white to repel the sun. And maybe, he thought wryly, to blind any poor damn Rebel who looked at one of them long enough to try to shoot it.

There was something awesome about City Point. Rebel prisoners had been known to sit down and cry after they had seen it—seen the size of it, the wealth it represented, the expertise, the sheer material power of the Union army. *No, they said, there's no way on God's green earth we can fight this and win.*

Jed liked what he saw here, most of the time. He was glad City Point was Grant's camp, not Bobby Lee's. But there were moments, all unexpected, when he felt uneasy; when he wondered where it would lead—all the power, all the guns, all the grim, unyielding will to win. It was safe enough in Grant's hands; when the war was over he wanted to go home and pave the sidewalks in Galena. But after he went home it would all still be there; everything he'd learned about war and taught to his countrymen would all still be there. . . .

Jed took a handkerchief from his pocket and wiped away the sweat that was running into his eyes. He couldn't afford to think about it now. Whatever any of it led to, a Rebel victory would lead to something worse.

He rode on to Colonel Sharpe's headquarters, where he found two junior staff officers sitting at a rough wooden table under a makeshift awning. Each had at his elbow a pile of papers weighted down with a rock.

"Hello, Lieutenant. We were wondering when you'd be getting back."

"Is the colonel around?" Jed asked.

The staff officer cocked his head toward a log cabin and a cluster of tents a few hundred feet away.

"He's with the general. Tom brought us a tub of lemonade. Do you want some?"

"Sounds like heaven." Jed swung down from his horse and helped himself to the dipper. The lemonade was wonderfully cool and refreshing.

"Reckon Old Baxter's making himself a fortune today," he said.

"Couple more days of weather like this, he'll be so popular he could run for president. There's grub in the tent if you need some."

"Later. I have to see the colonel."

Jed thought briefly about walking to Grant's headquarters, and decided to ride. Downriver, the Baltimore passenger boat was picking up speed; the small crowd that had gathered on the wharf to see it off was almost dispersed.

Grant's headquarters, like everything else about the man, was unpretentious. He had a two-room cabin for his personal quarters, and a large headquarters tent where meetings and other business was conducted. As usual, a few orderlies and guards were on duty, and the general-in-chief's pennant was flying from a high pole. Otherwise, it looked much like the rest of City Point, muddy in the rain and dirt-bare in the sun.

The headquarters tent was open in front, for a bit of air, but Jed could see no one of high rank outside. Which meant they were talking about something serious. Which meant maybe he couldn't interrupt. Which meant he'd probably die before he got any sleep. . . .

The explosion seemed to blow earth and sky apart. His horse screamed, but he did not hear it; a roar like a thousand cannons going off at once swallowed every other sound, swallowed his own yelp of pain and astonishment as the ground slammed into his face. He tried once to get up, wanting to dive like an ambushed soldier into some kind of cover, but there was no cover; bullets were flying all around him, bullets and pieces of metal and chunks of splintered wood; he put his arms over his head and waited for one of them to kill him.

Sweet holy God, not here. . . .

The unimaginable thundering went on, *boom, boom, boom,* explosion tumbling into explosion, sometimes a heartbeat between them, and then he could hear other sounds, screams, the pounding hoofs of horses gone mad with fright, rifle fire, except there weren't enough rifles in the world to account for it. For the tiniest moment he turned his head and moved his arm a little from his face. A huge cone of water and debris had risen over the harbor, spreading into a mushroom-shaped cloud; everything beneath it seemed to be blowing apart. Even the earth beneath his body was shaking from the force of it.

The barges, he thought. *All those damn barges loaded with arms and ammunition . . . !*

Something small and soft thudded into the dirt beside him, splattering dust and blood into his face. It was a piece of human flesh, dark-skinned, with a bit of blue cloth still clinging to it. He covered his head again. Seconds later, a twelve-pound artillery shell exploded somewhere between himself and General Grant's cabin.

For a time, when it seemed to be over, he lay still. His shoulder throbbed painfully, but otherwise he thought he was unhurt. He got up very tentatively, shaking off the debris with an eerie sense of unreality. The danger wasn't entirely past. Shells were still bursting here and there around the wharf, set off by the heat of earlier explosions. All the buildings along the near end of it had vanished, leaving only smoke and ruins in their place. Jed remembered where he had been going, and looked up the hill, instead of down. One of Grant's orderlies lay in a pool of blood beside the headquarters tent, wreckage and dead horses scattered around him.

He started to run. He saw men emerge from the tent, spotted Sharpe among them, then Grant. Both alive, then, thanks be to God. Someone knelt beside the orderly, opening his coat and feeling for a pulse. A moment later he stood up, shaking his head.

A pistol barked, silencing the struggles of a dying horse, and Jed almost dove to the ground again. The whole camp was in chaos, but for a moment this small knoll held all his attention. It could have been any of them lying in a pool of blood, he thought. All of them. So easily. George Sharpe was a cool man, most times, but he was shaken now, and sweat was spilling down his tanned cheeks like tears. Only Grant showed no emotion, but he was biting down on his cigar as though he intended to eat it.

"Are you all right, sir?" Jed asked. "Are the others all right?"

"Yes," Sharpe said. "Except for the orderly. Colonel Babcock was hit in the hand, that's all." He wiped his face. "Take a look in there, Jed. I don't know how any of us are still alive."

The tent roof was hanging in shreds; everything imaginable had come through it. Bullets, broken metal, pieces of trees, the twisted cover of somebody's trunk. Something bloody Jed could not identify and did not want to.

"Do you want to know what we were meeting about?" Sharpe went on wearily. "I came to tell him I thought there were Rebel agents here, and what we should be doing about them."

"Your timing was impeccable, Colonel. If you don't mind my saying so."

"Perhaps it was," Sharpe said. "God knows where we all might have been, if we hadn't been here. Did you see anything?"

"No, sir. I was blown right off my horse. All I know is that something blew up in the harbor."

"Yes. *Something* certainly did. Were you coming to see me?"

"Yes, sir, I was."

"Is it urgent?"

"Under the circumstances, no."

"Then go to my headquarters, will you, and gather up everyone you can find. Send someone over to the provost marshal; we'll need Patrick's boys, too. Then get down to the harbor and start asking questions. I'll be there myself in a few minutes."

"Sir."

Jed had seen more death on the battlefield, but never in his life had he seen such destruction. Shock waves had toppled buildings, wrenched ships from their moorings, and sent a landslide roaring down the bluffs. The rifle of a sentry flew half a mile across the camp, and was found in the woods the next day, with its bayonet sunk to the hilt in the ground. Men and animals alike had been thrown about like leaves in a windstorm, and lay now in bizarre places and twisted shapes. Mangled horses hung in the ruins of their wagons. A dead cow dangled in the crotch of a tree.

Closer to the wharf, rescue workers carried past him the body of a woman, and laid her gently on a bit of grass. Two others lay there already, in drenched and blood-soaked finery. One of the soldiers made the sign of the cross, and laid a blanket over them, covering their faces.

"Who are they?" Jed asked, dismayed.

"Don't know. They got off the Baltimore boat. I guess they had friends here."

"Sweet holy God."

He walked on. The injured and the dazed seemed to be everywhere, picking their way out of the wreckage, weeping, or staring in bewilderment at the bit of splinters and broken metal that moments before had been a sutler's wagon or a warehouse full of goods. Many were dead. The barber, who simply vanished, along with his tent and his customers. The lemonade man, crushed by a flying saddle. Of some there remained only a hand or a bloodied shoe. Of those on board the barges, there remained nothing at all.

Jed discovered no information of use to his superiors. No one knew anything. No one had seen anything . . . at least, no one did who was still alive. Everyone told him the same thing; told Marsena Patrick and his stubborn investigators the same thing; told Grant the same thing.

It just blew.

A mile or so away, two Confederate secret service officers, John Maxwell and R. K. Dillard, rode quietly into the Virginia countryside and disappeared.

At Petersburg, the roar of the explosion drowned out the sound of two armies' guns. At Richmond, twenty miles away, we thought the arsenal had gone up. We didn't find out what happened until our own papers reprinted the story from the *Washington Post.*

No one ever knew for certain how many people died at City Point. It was judged an accident by everyone, at least in public. Something, it was assumed, had struck a shell on one of the ordnance barges, and set off a chain reaction. But I went cold all over when I read the story. Crawly cold and faintly sick, as though I'd stepped on something dead. I was with McNiven, I remember, and he looked at me, as grim as I'd ever seen him, and put the newspaper down.

"Something struck a shell, did it? Well, that's as good a piece of blather as any other, I suppose."

Suspicion comes to you naturally, I suppose, living as we did. McNiven knew a good deal about sabotage himself; nothing could blow up anywhere without him wondering.

But we weren't alone in our suspicions. Colonel Sharpe never accepted the accidental explanation. And Grant's staff officers quietly held a meeting the same evening in the absence of their commander; thereafter, all unbeknownst to the general, one or another of them stayed up every night, with a pot of half-lethal coffee and Spencer rifle, and stood guard.

Maybe it sounds like I'm just spinning you a tale. I know a lot of you, out there in the living world, don't want to picture Civil War officers going about making bombs and blowing people up. Especially *Confederate* officers. They were the aristocrats, after all, the men in silk shirts and silver-plated pistols, who'd meet you at the crack of dawn to redress the tiniest slight upon their honor. A coal bomb hardly belongs in the same hand as a mint julep.

But there. What can I tell you, except that it happened? City Point was neither the first time nor the last; it was merely the one for which a written record survived: the report submitted by Maxwell and Dillard to their own commanding officer.

The bloody summer of '64 dragged on, and the bright hopes of the spring seemed to be crumbling all around us. Grant and Lee were dug in at Petersburg, and were likely to stay there for a while. Sherman had made it to the gates of Atlanta, but no farther. Jubal Early and his Rebels were still in the Shenandoah, too weak to invade the North again, but too strong to drive out.

Nothing seemed to change, and yet the dying went on. Every few days some other town, some other cornfield, some other patch of broken railroad, unknown names made immortal in a black geography of death. Kennesaw Mountain. Morris Island. Kernstown. The Crater. Globe Tavern. It was all I could manage, sometimes, to read the newspapers.

For the first time, demoralization began to show in the ranks of the Union army. Most of the early three-year enlistments were expiring, and a lot of men were choosing to go home. The war could not be won, they said. The Confederacy could not be defeated.

It was a strange, frightening time for us in Richmond. We knew, better perhaps than most any Union soldier, that our cause might be lost. We also knew, better than most any Union soldier, that the Confederacy could be defeated; was almost defeated; was a hollow shell breaking apart in a dozen places. We were on the inside; we saw the cracks.

The sense of urgency we felt in those months, I can scarcely communicate. Our network had never been more active, or better organized. Sharpe's men were a joy to work with; they gave us tools, money, a great bag of theatre wigs and makeup, a new cipher code; they shared their years of accumulated experience as scouts; and best of all, they told us precisely what they wanted. We were all amateurs in Richmond. We could only guess what might be useful to a general in the field. Sometimes we guessed well. Sometimes, I suppose, we had risked our necks for things that were totally useless, things the officers must have chuckled at, or sighed and shaken their heads. "Damn fool civilians. . . ."

At the end of August, George McClellan won the nomination as presidential candidate for the Democratic Party. In Richmond, you would have thought the Rebel army had won a massive victory; everyone was so happy. McClellan would negotiate, they said. McClellan was a gentleman and a soldier, adored by the soldiers of the Union armies. They would support him to a man. They would write eager letters home, telling their families to vote for him, so the war could be ended and they could come home. Encouraged, General Lee called for the drafting of slaves to work for the Confederate armies, so that every able-bodied white man could fight.

It was too late. The very same day, Sherman's army marched into Atlanta.

"I happened to be at Petersburg when the word came through," Jed told me. "They went crazy in the trenches. Hats went flying, knapsacks, everything. Men hugged each other, and danced, and laughed, and cried. A whole lot of them risked getting shot at, but the Rebels didn't fire. They thought we were celebrating McClellan's nomination.

"It was like a light going on in a dark room. Finally they could see there was a plan. All the blood and the misery—it hadn't been for nothing. They had tied up the whole northern Confederacy— every man, every bullet, every moment of conscious thought. Everything the Rebels had was expended here, holding the front door, while Sherman was coming around the back. One of them said to me a bit later, he said . . . well, he cussed, and said he'd been mad as anything when they brought Grant in from the west, and put him over their own generals. But now he thought maybe Mr. Lincoln knew what he was doing. And maybe Grant did, too."

Jed laid his head back against his chair. It was very late at night.

"How are they taking it, here in Richmond?" he wondered.

"It depends who you ask," I said. "A lot of ordinary folks are afraid it's a death blow. Some are still banking on the elections. And Mr. Davis says Sherman will never get out of Georgia alive."

"Well, heaven knows in a war something can always go wrong. But if I was laying bets, Miss Liza, I'd put my money on Sherman."

"So would I."

Just a single candle was burning in the room, and the curtains were heavy and carefully drawn. To the neighbors, or anyone else who might be watching, the house would have seemed respectably asleep.

There was a soft scratching at the hall door. Jason, I thought, wanting to come in. Just as well. A reason to get up, to focus my eyes and my thoughts on something else. But at the door I looked back anyway. Jed Knight was . . . no, not beautiful, not really. Something else, something less powerful and yet more enduring. There was a marvelous vitality about him, animal and carefree, and it had nothing much to do with his youth. I don't suppose I ever put it into conscious thought, not back then, but I knew this man knew how to live; he would approach every part of his life as he would a laden table, and feast on it all. He could teach me things, things I had only ever halfway dreamt of in my walled and girdled world . . . or he could have taught me, in some other time and place. Now? No, it was too late now.

I let Jason in. He trotted over to his favorite chair and curled up in it, washing himself lazily.

I didn't want Jed to leave. I also didn't want to make an idiot of myself. The cat was a safe topic of conversation. I told him how Jason had turned up starving in the rain; how we'd taken to each other right from the start. I told him about the homeless young woman I brought home with me one day, a milliner out of work who asked me for food in the street. She seemed so lost, so vulnerable—or perhaps it was myself who was vulnerable, when I met her. In any case, I brought her back to the house. To have a good meal, I told her, and a good night's sleep, but she stayed for almost a week.

"Jason hated her," I said. "He avoided her whenever he could, and growled at her if she even looked at him. He'd pout and glare at me whenever I talked with her. Mother and I thought he was jealous, and we smiled at it. Then the young woman left. She was all gratitude and tears, blessing us and saying such lovely things, and as soon as she was out of sight she went straight to the provost marshal's office, with enough lies about us to fill a wagon train. We had detectives climbing all over the house for half a day."

"They found nothing, I take it?"

"Nothing at all, except a couple of Jason's dead mice. I think he left them on purpose. Needless to say, he's been the king of Church Hill ever since."

"And acts like it, I expect."

"He does indeed. Twenty-four hours a day."

"Everyone in our line of work should have a pet like that," he said. "All the times you have to gamble, and wonder who you can trust, and who you can't. . . . Maybe I'll tell the colonel to forget about my pay raise and get me a nice cat."

"And how would you explain it to the pickets?"

"*Anything* can be explained to a picket," he said, and then added dryly, "Once." He shook his head a little. He was being flippant, but not entirely. "My poor parents. I wonder what they'd think if they knew I was earning my daily bread lying, stealing, and sleeping in strange women's beds."

"They don't know?"

"They know I'm in the army, that's all. I haven't even told Lije. They worry enough as it is."

"So how did you ever get into it?" I asked. "Lying and stealing and sleeping in strange women's beds?"

He did not answer, and I hastened to apologize, realizing I must have touched a wound. A terrible grief, perhaps, which he was trying to drown in danger or in revenge.

"I'm very sorry, Lieutenant. I didn't mean to intrude—"

"No." He shook his head. "It's all right. It's just . . . I never talked about it before." He was silent yet another long moment, and then he said, bluntly, "I had to get off the firing line. I couldn't take it."

It was just about the last thing in the world I expected him to say.

"But what you're doing must be a hundred times more dangerous," I said.

"It is, I reckon. In every way but one. There's not much danger of me having to kill anybody. And if I do, it's likely to be quick and in the dark."

He looked at me squarely, openly. "I've surprised you some, I see."

"Yes, a little."

"Well, I surprised myself. I was so mad at the Rebels when I joined up I thought I could shoot them easy. It didn't turn out like that. At first I thought it was nerves. Then I thought worse things. One day I ran into one of them in the woods, by myself. We must have both been exhausted, because we weren't more'n fifteen feet apart when we saw each other. He said, 'Hello, Yank.' I didn't say anything. Maybe I nodded, I don't remember. He said, 'I'm going this way,' and made a little motion with his head, off to the side. I said, 'I'm going that way.' And we walked away, the both of us, in opposite directions. And I realized after, he could have killed me if he'd wanted to, and I wouldn't have been able to stop him. I couldn't shoot somebody who stood in front of me in broad daylight and said hello.

"After that . . ." He made a small, melancholy gesture with his hands. "It all sunk in too well, you see. All my folks' teaching. Don't hurt people if you don't want them to hurt you. Don't put anybody down; they're no different inside; they're just like you. I wasn't any howling good at killing people, and I wasn't ever going to be any good at it. That's when I got scared. Scared that maybe one day soon I would just stand there and let some Reb blow me to kingdom come. But a whole lot more scared that I'd just stand there and let him blow *somebody else* to kingdom come. Maybe one of my friends. Maybe a whole bunch of my friends. Maybe the whole line would end up with a big hole in it and I'd still be standing there like a stump, doing nothing. . . . When I got down low enough, I figured I could lose the whole war, all by myself."

This was a face of the matter I had never seen before. Never even thought about.

The little bit of smile was back on his face, suddenly. "When Colonel Kilbourn asked for a couple of volunteers to go scouting, I asked him what a scout was expected to do. He said, 'You ride like the devil, you tell lies like the devil, and you order your headstone before you start.' I told him that didn't sound too bad, where did he want me to go?" Jed laughed. "He gave me a big lecture, after. He thought I didn't understand the risks."

I didn't say anything for a time, trying to absorb what I had heard. Since the war began I'd thought a good deal about what it might be like to be a soldier: thought about the long marches, and the poor food, and the muddy, dreary camps; thought about the camaraderie and the pride; thought about how awful a battle must be. It seemed perfectly reasonable to me that someone in a battle might be scared to death, just like I was sometimes, doing what I did: scared of dying, of pain, of other people's hatred, of being torn and maimed and blown apart; scared of the bottomless unknown. But scared of your own decency, your own reluctance to destroy? I had never imagined that. But then, I'd never been asked to do it.

He misread my silence.

"Does it bother you, Miss Liza? What I just said?"

"You mean, do I think any less of you for it? No, Lieutenant. I most certainly do not. Quite the opposite."

He believed me, I think, but perhaps not entirely. He got to his feet, and fished in the dim light for his hat. He drew my attention back to the reason he had come. The Shenandoah Valley. It was General Grant's top priority right now, except for Bobby Lee himself. If anything bigger than a crow was moving between Richmond and the Valley, he said, the general wanted to know about it. Then he asked if there was anything I needed. There wasn't. I walked him to the door.

None of us, as a rule, went about telling each other to be careful; it seemed rather superfluous, after all. This time, however, I touched his arm beside the door, just for the briefest moment, trying hard not to think about how warm it was, or how it might feel wrapped around my back.

"Good luck, Lieutenant. And do take care."

Feeble words. Poor, pale ghosts of what I wanted to say. But for a long time after, I thought about him, and wondered if maybe, in spite of everything, in spite of all the thousand reasons why I shouldn't, I might yet tell him the truth, and see where it would take me.

Jed didn't come into Richmond very often. It was dangerous for him, of course, and it was rarely necessary. For most things, our courier lines were perfectly adequate. But I worried a good deal about my easily broken cipher code. Sharpe had sent us his own, of course, and I used it most of the time. But there were, quite frankly, some things I didn't want anybody reading except Sharpe himself: Mariel's communications, for one, which came from a source so obviously close to Mr. Davis. Messages passed through half a dozen hands sometimes, before they got to City Point. It wasn't that I didn't trust my people; it was, I suppose, that I didn't trust fate. I knew things could just . . . happen. To anybody, including myself.

It was Jason who found a solution for me. And if you want to think I was a witch, like some people said, and he was my familiar, just go ahead and think so. It happened on a wildly stormy day—a perfect day for witching, I suppose. Mother was making herself a new dress—her first in years, perhaps her first since the war began. We couldn't afford it, of course. Few people could, by the summer of '64, except fancy women and the wives of profiteers. Fabrics were selling at two hundred dollars a yard, when you could get them at all.

Josey found the cloth stored away in the bottom of an old trunk. It was of indifferent quality, and a very dull green color—which was probably why it had been put away and forgotten, years before. Of course I was going to sell it; I was already thinking of what I could do with the money. Then I saw my mother's face when I carried it down the stairs.

"Oh, Liza, it's so lovely, wherever did you find it?" She took it from my arms, unrolled it, held it up. "Look, it's enough for a dress!"

I opened my mouth to object, and then I shut it again. We had already sold half of Mother's jewelry. (We would have sold all of mine, except having no husband, I had never acquired any.) We had sold furniture. John's room was as bare as a monk's cell. The silver candleholders were gone from the table, the crystal from the dining room buffet, the mahogany table from beside my bed. It had all gone down to the auction houses, bit by bit—usually for money to spend on our war work, but lately, sometimes, just to spend on food.

I knew Mother would sell a dozen other things, rather than give up that piece of cloth. So I said nothing, and she made herself a dress. She commandeered the dining room table, and by late afternoon she had all the pieces cut and laid out.

Now I may as well tell you, I hate sewing. My fingers are long and slender, and can do just about anything around a piano, but they all turn into thumbs at the mere approach of a piece of fabric and a needle. So I have nothing whatever to do with making clothes, and I never will have. God, I presume, created seamstresses for a reason, and I would be the last person alive to interfere with his arrangements.

That afternoon, I recall, I walked into the dining room with Jason trotting at my heels. Mother, for some reason, wasn't there. Then a lot of things happened very fast. Thunder cracked right overhead, like a twelve-pounder going off in the attic. Jason bolted—right through my feet, where he was accidentally stepped on. He yowled and was gone, across the floor and over a chair and onto the window ledge and back down on the table, right on top of Mother's carefully laid-out dress pieces. The table was polished hardwood, and he slid as he landed; cat and cotton went flying over the edge together. Of course, my mother picked precisely the same moment to return. She let out a wail of outrage, whereupon Jason reversed himself in midair, cycloned back through the mess he'd just made, and went headlong up the stairs to hide under my bed, the one place he knew he was safe from absolutely anything except, I suppose, the provost marshal and the Army of Northern Virginia.

"Oh, Elizabeth!" Mother stood for a moment, looking at the scatters of cloth in total dismay. "Oh, that wretched cat!"

"He didn't mean it, Mother," I said. "He just got scared."

"Of a little thunder? What kind of an animal is scared to death of a little bit of thunder? I don't know, Liza. I think he's strange. Oh, Lord, this is such a mess. I didn't have a single piece of it pinned."

I knelt and helped her gather it up. I couldn't help her sort it. I didn't know what anything was. Just puzzling shapes, squares and ovals, and long, skinny strips. This one was probably a piece of skirt and that was probably a collar. No, it looked too small, maybe it was a cuff. And this piece? If it hadn't been my mother's work, I would have thought someone had been playing with the scissors.

And I *knew* this was all supposed to be a dress.

What if I didn't know? What if I just found these pieces lying in the street, and didn't know what they were part of? What if I only found some of them?

"Liza, dear, if you're not going to help, just give me the pieces. Don't sit there staring at them."

"What?"

"Liza? Are you all right?"

"What is this, Mother?"

She took it from my hands, turned it a couple of times, compared it with another similar piece, and said, "It's the left front yoke."

"What else could it be?"

"Nothing else. Whatever are you on about?"

"If you found it on the street, what could it be? Part of a baby's gown, maybe? A quilting piece? A leftover? A back *right* yoke?"

"Yes, I suppose so. If I didn't know what it belonged to, I suppose it could be anything."

"*Exactly!*" I stood up. "Oh, Mother, I adore that cat!"

"Well, I don't, at the moment. Are you going to tell me what on earth you're talking about?"

I went to fetch a small scrap of paper, and wrote on it: "jason is the best cat in the world." Then I tore it into four pieces, and handed her one.

"What does it say?"

She looked at it, and then at me. "It says 'at in the w.' "

I handed her the other pieces, one at a time: "orld." "s the best c." "jason i."

When she had the last one, and put them together, she smiled.

I knelt beside her. "See, Mother. They're just like pieces of a pattern. You have to know what they're part of before you can tell what they mean, and you can't know unless you have them all."

"Well," she said, "you can make a fair guess with the first three. Jason is the best cat in the w. I'd guess the rest was world."

"Maybe it's wintertime. Jason is the best cat in the wintertime. Or the west, or the woods, or the war, or the White House. You have to have them all!"

"All right. But this isn't really about cats, is it?"

"No, Mother." I kissed her cheek, and stood up. "It's not about cats at all. But he *is* the best cat in the whole wide world, just the same."

It took near half an hour to coax Jason out from under the bed. For a long time he crouched just where he could see me, but he wouldn't come a whisker farther. He'd been knocked about, obviously, at some time in his young life.

Finally, though, he crept out, very cautiously. I picked him up and petted him for a long time, and told him what an extraordinarily marvelous creature he was. Then I went to see Will Rowley.

There wasn't a trace of formality between us anymore. He still called me Miss Liza, but otherwise I might have been his sister. Sometimes, if he was really busy, he wouldn't even stop working when I came. We'd talk, and maybe Kitty would bring me a glass of water flavored with fruit juice, or a cup of sassafras tea; and maybe I'd hand him a wrench he needed, or a handful of nails, one at a time. He was always behind with the farm work, during the war.

"What do you think, Will?" I asked him. "If we wanted to double our number of couriers, or even triple them, could we do it?"

"Now why would we want to do that?" he asked, noncommittally.

"So we can send Sharpe everything in pieces. So if somebody gets picked up, the Rebs will only have part of the message."

I handed him two pieces of paper. Just two, not four. But it was ciphered, and half of it probably wouldn't give anyone enough text to figure out the cipher.

He examined them for a bit, and gave them back. "That's a good idea, Miss Liza. Have you talked to Mr. Ruth? Or Quaker?"

"Not yet. I wanted to get your impression first."

He smiled, just a tiny bit. He understood perfectly. I was both paying him a compliment, and angling for his support. I wanted this method adopted by everybody, not just myself.

"Sam will like it," Will said. He put his wrench down, and tugged on his beard. "I'm worried about Sam, you know. It's wearing him down, all of this. He won't let on about it, but he's completely exhausted, and I'm not the only one who's noticed. Kitty says he looks ten years older every time she sees him."

"I know," I said. "I've noticed, too." Noticed the black hollows under his eyes, and the way his hands would knot sometimes, over nothing. Noticed how he stood at my darkened doorway, the last time he was there, paralyzed for a moment by the night, the unknown shadows in the street. Turning to me, hat in hand, and soul as well, vulnerable as a boy. *Do you think I'm being watched?*

"We can all come home and take our masks off," Will said. "My wife, my kids, we're all on the same side. How does a man like Sam Ruth sit by his fire every night, while his wife makes gifts and clothing for his enemies?"

"I've no idea," I said. "If I was married to a Reb—"

I was about to say something flippant, and then I stopped. Suppose I had been married, and my husband had chosen to support the Rebellion? Suppose I really cared for him? Suppose we had children, as Sam Ruth did?

"If you were married to a Reb," Will said wryly, "he'd be long gone to Texas."

Probably, I thought. As I told John, I wasn't any howling good at dividing up my loyalties. We would have separated. Maybe Sam should have, too. But it was such a scandalous thing, to break up a marriage. We had more respect for the people who broke up a country.

FIFTEEN

———————✳

ACCUSTOMED TO COMMAND FROM OUR CRADLE

All true power, whether in speaking, writing, or fighting, proceeds quite as much from strength of will as from power of mind or body; and no men have half the strength of will that Southerners possess. We are accustomed to command from our cradle.

George Fitzhugh, Southern pro-slavery writer

There are gay parties given . . . where the most elegant suppers are served—cakes, jellies, ices in profusion, and meats of the finest kinds in abundance, such as might furnish a meal for a regiment of General Lee's army.

Judith McGuire, Refugee in Richmond, 1864

Damn patriotism if it don't pay.

James Henry Hammond, 1864

All through the bloody summer of '64, Southerners were told to hang on until November. We probably couldn't beat the Yankees in the field, it was admitted—not anymore. But then, we didn't have to. We only had to survive till the elections, till Lincoln was turfed out and the new Northern government sat down with us, and made peace, and let us go.

Only November came, and Lincoln wasn't turfed out. Whereupon the moribund Confederacy was propped up in its chair, and scrubbed and combed and polished, and dressed in its best boots, and presented to the world not merely as breathing and alive, but as downright formidable. The year's events, Jeff Davis said, had resulted in no disadvantage to the cause. Grant's campaign was a total failure. Atlanta would become Sherman's Moscow, the lack of snow and winter notwithstanding. Hood would march into Tennessee and sweep everything before him. France was about to go to war with the United States.

And the Angel Gabriel, Martin Lipscomb said, was down at the Spotswood Hotel, eating oysters and champagne.

The leaders of the Confederacy were no longer living in the same world as the rest of us. Accustomed to command from the cradle, just as their admirers said, they never adapted to a world where Massa's word wasn't law. They just kept on believing if they said something often enough it would turn out to be true.

Sometimes, during that long, terrible winter, I had trouble believing what I saw. Homeless women held out their hands to me on the street, begging for food, yet there were flamboyant parties in the great houses, night after night. We knew from our own scouts that Lee's soldiers were slipping into Federal lines by tens and twenties every day, and just as many more were melting away to their homes in the South. Their families were desperate, and they themselves were half starving. They had no coats, they had no blankets, they had no shoes. So when I read the little piece of paper Martin Lipscomb handed me, I couldn't quite believe it. According to a report made by President Davis to the Rebel Congress, since the first of October—in other words, in less than four months—some five hundred thousand pairs of shoes and eight million pounds of bacon had been brought in through the blockade.

I read the paper again, and looked at Mr. Lipscomb, wondering if he was engaged in playing me a bad joke.

"Is this genuine?"

"Genuine? I wouldn't stick my neck out on it, Miss Liza, but it was in the same spot as all the other stuff Cotter's been sending."

"Half a million pairs of shoes? And Lee's men are walking barefoot in the snow?"

"I reckon."

"God help us, Mr. Lipscomb, they'd need five pairs of feet apiece to use all those shoes."

"Well, there are some other Rebel armies, though I dare say nobody in Richmond seems to notice."

"Well, they don't have five pairs of feet, either. Davis is lying to the Congress, or else most of it's been sold somewhere for profit."

"Would that surprise you?" he asked quietly.

"No," I said.

But in a way it did. It surprised me over and over, the way self-interest walked hand in hand with all the rhetoric of heroism. Desperately needed grain was hidden away in sheds and barns for those who could pay what the owners wanted, and every season they wanted more. Plantations untroubled by the Yankee army let their fields lie fallow because they couldn't sell cotton, and if they grew food or forage, it might be impressed at government-set prices. Many among the Southern elite seemed far more willing to spill their blood than their treasure, and some were rather obviously willing to spill neither. When Lee came to Richmond begging for soldiers, they swept teenaged boys off the streets, and consumptives, and the mad, and sent them to the trenches, while rich men and their sons were made into magistrates, and commissary inspectors, and even ministers of God, so they wouldn't have to fight.

I reached up and shoved a bit of loose hair back inside my bonnet, and tucked Mr. Lipscomb's scrap of paper into a slightly opened seam. It was a cold, foggy January morning; there wasn't a living person in the graveyard where we stood, except ourselves, but caution was second nature to me now. I hid everything, immediately, without even thinking about it.

"So what did you want to see me about?" he asked.

"I need somebody to go out tonight."

"What's wrong with Nelson?"

"He's sick. He can't even get out of bed. Quaker can't go; they took his permit away a couple of weeks ago."

"I'm no courier, Miss Liza. Besides, didn't you hear? The order went out today: nobody's allowed to leave the city."

"Nobody?" I whispered.

"No civilians. Black or white. Less'n they got a pass from the War Department, or from King Jeff himself."

"We have to get somebody out."

"Well, you know who to ask, don't you?" he said. "He's getting scout's pay; I reckon he can do scout's duty."

Oh, yes, I know who to ask. I looked away, past the gravestones spattered with hoarfrost and snow. Will's farm was a considerable distance away, on the Mechanicsburg Road. I had the grippe, and all I'd been able to hire was a broken-down buggy pulled by a horse with three days to live. And the Rebels were obviously on edge, if they weren't letting anybody out.

What a small man you are, Mr. Lipscomb. No wonder Will calls you Marty the Shovel.

I needed to cough. I pulled a handkerchief from my pocket and did so, as pitifully as I could.

"Gracious, Miss Liza, are you all right? I thought you were looking awfully peaked."

He helped me to a large monument and sat me down till I recovered. He pulled a brandy flask from inside his coat and was about to offer it; then he remembered I was a lady, and drank from it himself.

"Look, Miss Liza," he said. "I'm not going through those pickets for anything. But I'll go to the Rowley place for you, if you want."

"That would be a great help, thank you. Ask them if someone can come by tonight, after dark. Tell them to be careful—even more than usual."

He went away then, quietly, and I did what I had come to do. What I always did, one Sunday in every month, ever since my father died. I cleaned the dead leaves from his grave, and took away the old flowers, and placed new ones, beautifully dried from the Church Hill garden. I didn't know much about ghosts back then, but I wondered sometimes if he could see me. If he knew what I was doing, and what I had become. If he would think well of me for it, or shake his head in dismay. He always wanted me to be responsible, to do things well, to think for myself. And he always wanted me to be a genuine lady. He was, I suppose, a man who believed in miracles.

I was weary and feverish; maybe that's why it happened. I straightened up from the grave and I looked down the valley and Richmond was gone. All I could see were graveyards, hundreds of them, stretching in all directions, to the farthest corners of the sky. No monuments, no names, just places of the dead, gray and cold, wrapped in eternal lostness, half a million broken lives, forever irreplaceable. I closed my eyes, shutting away the image and my own exploding tears.

I tremble for my country, when I remember that God is just. . . .

Was it God's work, I wondered, as Jefferson feared it would be? Or was it something far less conscious, something quite elemental, really: a poison tree planted by our own hands, nurtured year after brutal year, by men and women alike, by government and clergy and law, now, finally, bringing forth the last of its fruit? Not divine justice, though we chose to call it such, but nature itself, unfolding a pattern we could have changed once, perhaps even quite recently, had we chosen to, but which we had no hope of changing now, no more than we could stop a flooded river from plunging through a broken levee.

It was long past lunch when I got home. The hack driver saw I had been crying, and dawdled, trying to cheer me with idle talk. The streets were slick with fresh snow and freezing rain, and the horse stumbled frequently. He was old, and worn right out—the only kind of horse you saw in Richmond anymore. The Rebels had all the others. They took them right out of people's yards. They unhitched them off the bakery wagons and the coal wagons in the middle of the street, and dragged them away to pull wagon trains and Bobby Lee's artillery. We still had our one horse, but only because I hid him in the library when the impressment officers came. Needless to say, I used him very sparingly.

Mother took one look at me and told me to go to bed, but instead I went to the library. I took yesterday's messages from the lions' heads, and drew three more out of my bonnet and my newspaper. I asked Josey for tea and a muffin, wishing to God it were proper English tea instead of this green stuff from the woods, which was all we could get now, and which we called tea merely to console ourselves. Then I wrote a long letter to Colonel Sharpe.

> We have word from a friend on the Danville RR. They have 8 trains running every day; 45 engines plus cars taken from Petersburg RR. Transport has been provided for 16,000 men from Lee's army. Kershaw's division and Hoke's division will be sent to Wilmington. This from a good source and reliable.
>
> The Danville and Greensborough line has been damaged by flood; Hills says it will take fifteen days minimum to repair. The army has been put on half rations. Everyone in Richmond talks of evacuation, and it seems to be in earnest. There is the most dreadful misery in the city. Flour is $800 per barrel, meal $80 per bushel, coal and wood $100 per load. City council has raised the price of gas to $50 per 1000 feet. The majority of ordinary people no longer have any

confidence in the president, the Congress, the cabinet, the commissary, or most of the generals.

Some railroad companies in the South have arranged to get tin, zinc, and other necessaries, from a firm in Philadelphia. They will be paid for in cotton, to be shipped down the Blackwater in small boats.

Mr. Davis appears to have recovered from his illness. Talk in the streets is that he tried to poison himself. Three more of his slaves have run away; one apparently started a fire in the basement of the White House before he decamped.

What are the chances of smuggling us a flag?

Your ob't servant, C. Babcock.

Darkness fell as I worked. My head ached, and I couldn't stay warm. Josey brought me a bowl of hot soup, but it didn't help much. When I heard the door open below, and voices in the hall, I thought Will Rowley had come. But it was Chris Taylor who hurried through the library door, with Josey at his heels.

"Hello, Mr. Taylor," I said. "I'm glad to see you. The letter is almost ready."

"Letter?" He looked at me blankly, more troubled than I'd ever seen him.

"Weren't you sent to take my letter out?"

"No, I come on my own. Something terrible's happened, Miss Liza. They took Mr. Tom."

"Took him? Who took him? Where?"

"The provost marshal's men. They came in just as we was closing shop, and put a gun to his head, and called him a rotten Yankee spy, and took him away."

God help us. I sat down. I had to.

"Do you know where they took him?"

"No, ma'am. Castle Thunder, I reckon. I'm scared for him, Miss Liza. I think they mean it this time."

"This time?" I whispered.

"They arrested him before. A couple of weeks ago. They'd heard rumors he was doing more than buying tobacco when he traveled out of Richmond."

"He never said anything about it."

"He didn't think it meant anything. They pick up just about everybody, one time or another."

It was true. Will Rowley had been taken in and questioned; so had the Lohmanns. Even my poor, aging mother was hauled down to Winder's office once, on the strength of some harpy's accusations.

"They were polite, the first time. He said he knew howling well they didn't have anything; they were just fishing. This time . . ." Chris shook his head. "This time I think they mean it."

They meant it. All damnation was about to come down on the heads of the Richmond loyalists. The same night they took McNiven, the Rebel authorities raided the house of a man named Duke, who worked with the Lohmanns. They hauled off Duke and his sons, the eight conscripts he was about to smuggle out, two other Union men, and Angelina's husband, William. They picked up John Timberlake in Fredericksburg, and Isaac Silver at his farm. A few days later, they arrested Samuel Ruth.

In a single black sweep, more than half of the Richmond-Fredericksburg loyalist line was gone. We could hardly believe it. And we couldn't, at the time, begin to guess why. Only later—many months later—would we learn how important that small patch of Virginia happened to be, how carefully the Rebels were watching it, and talking to the locals, and taking note of everything they heard and saw. It was the precise patch of Virginia through which John Wilkes Booth and his companions were supposed to come galloping, just about any day now, with the desperate Confederacy's last, mad, desperate ace in the hole: a kidnapped Abraham Lincoln.

How do you talk about fear? Terror, yes. Nightmare things, monsters and demons; they are easy to describe. But the quiet fear that wakes you in the dead of night, and turns your food to ash; the fear that turns you cold at the sight of a shadow on the street, or the small, unexpected rustling of a mouse . . . no. Sometimes I can't even remember just how bad it was. And yet, if you had met me on the street, I truly believe you would have thought me unconcerned, untroubled, unafraid. And that was part of the awfulness—having to hide it all, and being so afraid I couldn't.

Jed came to Richmond in the middle of it, very quietly. There wasn't much Sharpe and his men could do for us, he said, but if there were people in danger we needed smuggled out, they would try to help.

"And the colonel thought you could probably use this." He handed me an envelope. "There's twenty thousand Confederate here. Use it any way you see fit, to help your friends."

"Thank you. And please tell the colonel I appreciate it more than I can say."

"I will. Are you going to be all right? I mean you, yourself?"

"I'll be fine."

"He says he'll get you a flag, too, but he didn't think right now was a good time. Is Phillips all right?"

"Yes, as far as I know."

"He had a dreadful time his last trip, did he tell you? There was no way open out of Richmond except the Brooke Turnpike; I guess he walked about thirty miles to get to us, and rowed himself across the Chickahominy on the worst broken-down old boat I ever saw. He made a joke of it, but the poor man was dead on his feet."

That, I thought, was so typical of Will: he never quit. "He's as true as they come, our Mr. Phillips."

"So are most of you, I think. Colonel Sharpe is very pleased with the quality of material you're sending out. He said to tell you so."

"Well, you must thank him for me."

"If you think it wise to keep your heads down for a while," he said, "do it. We'll be needing you more when the spring campaign begins than now."

"We'll be as careful as we can," I told him.

He went off then, into the foggy January night. I had felt safe for the little time he was there. It wasn't rational, of course. The presence of a Yankee scout in my house was no protection against anything more perilous than a burglar. And he had, God knows, other things to do. But I wanted him with me, and no amount of common sense was going to change it. For a long time I sat and played the piano, trying to drown out my black mood with sentimental songs. Nothing helped. Even Jason did not come to comfort me; he was off somewhere on his own, chasing mice or lady cats or phantoms. I felt utterly alone, deserted by the whole world.

Morning dawned overcast and gray. Nelson was still sickly, so I went out myself to feed the horse and bring in a slab of bacon from the smokehouse. Everything was colorless, as things become in winter, and so my eyes were immediately caught by the sight of something orange in the trees.

It took a moment for the image to resolve itself, and another for me to realize what it probably was. I hurried across the yard, and found what I knew I would find and what I could scarcely bear to look upon: the long, rigid body of a hanging cat.

"Jason. . . ."

He'd been dead for a long time. Wisps of frost clung to his fur. One paw was raised, the claws caught in the rope as he'd made his last wild fight for life. A ragged piece of paper was tacked to the tree where the rope was tied. Written, like the first one, in a rough hand, with the same flag and the same signature: White Caps.

The message was simple. *Yure next.*

I had no knife with me. I tugged savagely at the rope, but it was knotted tight and rigid with cold. I went to the shed and got a hatchet to cut him down. I laid him on a bench and wiped the snow from his body, and cried like a small, beaten child.

Oh, Jason, you poor thing, you poor dear thing, you never did anything to anybody, how could they do this, how could they . . . ?

Jason was a smart cat, and a wary one; even I couldn't catch him sometimes. A great deal of effort had gone into this small piece of savagery.

I hid away the piece of paper from the White Caps. Nelson wasn't well enough to dig a grave, so I hired a destitute black laborer off the streets to bury Jason, and to cut him a small wooden headboard: Jason. A Good Cat, Murdered by Traitors.

"You sure, ma'am? You want me to write that?"

"Yes."

"Don't, Elizabeth," Mother said. "It's foolish."

I looked at neither of them. I stood at the window and looked out at the city and the hills, desolate with winter and with war. Somewhere out there was Grant's army, so close and so unbearably far away. Coming, dear God, always coming, and never getting here.

"Elizabeth, did you hear me?"

Foolish, that headboard? For most anyone, yes. But crazy old maids were different . . . as the world kept reminding us, over and over and over again.

"Carve what I told you, Clem. I want those rats to see it."

Mother shook her head and walked out of the room. I didn't follow her. I never tried to explain. My small war, like the great one, had taken on its own life, its own direction, and it would unfold as it began.

Strangely, Jason's death and the threat from the White Caps did not make me more afraid, but less so. Perhaps it struck down into the bottom of my soul, and found there a last reserve of strength and defiance. And though we all were more careful after the arrests, we never stopped working. Messages found their way to Church Hill inside the cores of wizened winter apples, in the fingertips of gloves, between the hilt and the handle of a mended hoe. I still fetched them from under a certain chair in Angelina's restaurant, and from under the flowers on my father's grave.

Mariel sent me the terms the Rebels were taking to the Hampton Roads peace conference. The negotiations were merely a sop to the disheartened population, and so their terms weren't peace terms at all, just blunt demands which the Federal authorities were rather obviously not going to meet. We scrawled them on walls and fences all over Richmond, to the absolute horror of the Rebel government. We did the same with the menu from one of Secretary Trenholm's extravagant dinner parties—right before an official day of prayer and fasting. When Jefferson Davis started selling off some of his valuable personal property at auction, we sent Colonel Sharpe an itemized list.

We didn't neglect military things. In January, at Colonel Sharpe's request, we sent out a detailed report, with maps, on all the obstructions the Rebels had placed in the James River. As in the summer, we kept watch on the railroad stations and the bridges; nothing passed through Richmond without somebody taking note, even in the dead of night. Between ourselves and his own scouts along the Virginia Central Railroad, Grant must have known almost to the hour and the man the step by step withdrawal of the Rebels from the Shenandoah Valley.

It would take a miracle now, I think, to retrace the path Colonel Sharpe's money traveled, or where most of it finally ended up. Suffice it to say I passed it to friends who were less suspect than myself, with instructions to use it on behalf of our imprisoned comrades. I also supplied them with certain bits of nasty information garnered in Locust Alley.

I can't prove it, of course, but I suspect the whispers out of Locust Alley served us even better than the money. For a lot of Rebels now, even dedicated ones, the war was all but lost, and so was much of the world as they had known it. Their good names were about all they had left.

So, a week or so after the arrests, I received a terse note from Lucy Rice: *Quaker here. Can you come?*

I dressed very carefully in my old farm clothes. It was an effective disguise, provided I left my own house undetected. There were so many refugees in the city; a bent farm woman in old clothes, with a bonnet pulled low across her face to shield it from the wind, attracted about as much attention as an old crow on a fence.

Lucy slipped me inside quickly.

"I'm glad you could come, Miss Liza," she said. "He wanted to see you before he leaves."

"How did he get out?"

"They gave up and let him go. They had nothing. Not a scrap of evidence, just suspicion. Somebody's accusation, probably, that's all."

She led me to a back room and opened the door. For a moment I thought she had made some absurd mistake, because the man I saw there did not resemble Tom McNiven.

He got to his feet very slowly, holding on to the heavy arm of the chair. His face was swollen and cut; one eye was closed altogether. When he made it upright, he was reeling on his feet.

"Miss Liza."

"God in heaven, Quaker, what happened?"

"I was sair uncooperative, it seems. And they wanted to know the damnedest things. Sorry. Didn't mean to cuss."

He gave up trying to be a gentleman, and sank back into the chair. "I'm a mite weak, ladies. It's been a time I nae want to live through again."

"Who did this to you?"

"Provost men. They got it in their heads the city's full of spies. Hanged if I know why. They asked me what I knew about Mr. Ruth. And about you. I nae told them anything, Miss Liza. Nary a word." He looked at me for the briefest moment, and then looked away. "Can you get me out?"

"Of course," I said. "It may take a few days to set up."

"I feel bad about leaving you," he said. "But they'll be back. They promised me as much. 'We're nae done with you yet,' they said. 'We'll be watching every move you make.' And I know they talk bigger than they walk, but . . ." He paused, whether to find words or to find courage, I wasn't sure. "I nae want to hurt the rest of you. I think it's better I go."

"You don't need to explain, Quaker," I said. "Nobody's going to blame you for a moment."

"Excepting me myself," he said.

"No," I said. "Not even yourself. It's a wise man who can put good sense ahead of pride. A wise man and a rare one."

"Well, thank you for that, Miss Liza."

"How badly are you hurt?" I asked.

"Oh, I'll mend. There's nae call for worrying."

"I meant now. To cross the lines."

"I dinna care to walk it," he said. "Not for a while. One other thing, Miss Liza. I'm thinking I should tell Chris and the others that you're in charge now. That they should come to you with anything they know, and for instructions. Are you willing?"

"How many people do you have, besides the ones I know about already?"

"Maybe twenty who are serious. Another hundred or so who can be trusted in a pinch."

"Well." I drew one of Lucy's chairs over, and sat down. "I guess you'd better start telling me about them. . . ."

According to the newspaper accounts after Samuel Ruth's arrest, the government's case depended upon "circumstantial evidence," and the testimony of a certain Miss Elizabeth Dade. She was a young lady from King George County, of excellent family and impeccable Rebel credentials. Both of her brothers had served in the Confederate army; one later died of his wounds.

At the beginning of February, Miss Dade was brought to Richmond to testify at Sam's hearing, and was lodged at the Spotswood Hotel. It was a grand old place, the Spotswood. If it hadn't burned down in '70, I suppose it would be full of ghosts. Most of the Rebel government lived there for a time, when they first came to Richmond. After the powerful men and their wives moved out into fine

rented houses, the place filled up with functionaries. Even little Erasmus Ross had a room there—a tiny one, I suppose, tucked into a
corner somewhere above the bar. The building was six stories high,
and looked magnificent from the outside. Cooper DeLeon always
said the food was awful, but Cooper had spent all his life among
the very rich, and he was used to eating like a king.

Lots of times during the war, I wished I could be a bug on the
wall in the Spotswood. I always wondered what sorts of things were
said in the sanctity of those rooms, what the officers on leave and
the cabinet aides and the congressmen and the speculators all talked
about when the doors were shut and they could be themselves.

I wondered about Elizabeth Dade, too, when she came there. I
wondered what sort of person she was, what moved her, a woman
young and single, to go out of her way to target a powerful man
like Samuel Ruth. I wondered if she was uneasy about it now, and
afraid—or if perhaps she was entirely comfortable, proud to be doing her bit for the cause. I felt a certain affinity toward her, and at
the same time a truly mortal enmity.

I still see her sometimes, on the stage of my memories, in her
room the day before the trial. It was a dismal morning, gray and
cloudy. Perhaps she stood by her window, wishing the time would
pass more quickly, desolated by everything she saw: buildings with
broken windows papered over against the cold; red auction flags in
the store windows, and refugees endlessly wandering the streets,
searching for food; half-grown boys in ragged uniforms, slogging
toward some newly identified point of danger. No fine carriages
anymore; no pertly dressed slaves out to do the morning shopping;
no great clouds of smoke pouring out of the Tredegar. Everything
dirty, crumbling, abandoned, or shipped south. All that was left for
Richmond, she thought, was for the Yankees to burn it. . . .

FEBRUARY, 1865 . . .

Miss Dade was thankful when the chambermaid knocked on her door. It was a white woman, not at all young, pale and somewhat haggard-looking. Perhaps Miss Dade's surprise showed a bit too much, for the woman stopped, part of the way across the room, and looked back at her uneasily.

"What you all staring at?"

"Oh, nothing. I just never saw anyone but darkies cleaning rooms before, that's all."

"They run off. Anyways, white folks got to eat, too. I got four kids, and my man's dead fighting the Yankees at Sharpsburg."

"I'm sorry."

The woman went about her work efficiently, but she was painfully talkative. She complained about her backache. She wondered if the weather would clear soon. She admired one of Miss Dade's combs, lying on the bureau.

"My husband give me a real nice comb once, when we was still courting. Course it wasn't quality like this, but it was real purty. You got an awful lot of purty things. You're the lady who's going to court, ain't you? Against that railroad man? Mr. Ruth."

"How do you know about that?"

"I can read some. It's been in all the papers. I sure wouldn't want to have to do it. Go and stand up in front of all those men and all."

"I don't mind doing it in the least," Miss Dade said. "He's a traitor, and he deserves to be hanged."

"Higher'n a housetop, I reckon. Iffen he done it. There's a whole lot of folks saying he couldn't have, though. Being such an upright Christian man and all. Sure would bother me, wondering about it."

"I don't have to wonder about it. I know what I saw."

"I reckon you do, miss, and you got to do your duty. We all got to do our duty sure enough. But I feel awful sorry for you. It's sort of like you're between the devil and the deep blue sea, ain't it, what with him being a leading citizen and all? I mean, if he's got so many folks standing by him here, well, you sure got to figure if he's working for the Yankees, they'll be standing by him, too. They're likely to be madder'n a plowed-over hornet's nest if anything happens to him."

"They can be as mad as they like," Miss Dade said, lifting her chin.

"People say they're right mean when they're mad. Or maybe they're just born mean, like that fellow Dahlgren, all those awful things he was going to do, and he didn't even have a reason." The chambermaid shook her head, sadly. "It don't look good for our boys, you know. I keep hoping, and I pray like anything, but it don't look good. And if the Yankees come here . . ."

She picked up the buckets, and moved slowly toward the door, pausing there to look back at Miss Dade. "They got a fella in Georgia, I heard. Seems he put a couple of Union men away. They burned everything he owned, till there wasn't nothing left but a little pile of ashes and a chimney. They beat him awful bad, too, till he couldn't even crawl. And then they locked him away in a little bitty hole in the bottom of one of them big forts."

"This isn't Georgia," Miss Dade said. "And anyway, I don't want to hear about it."

"Can't say as I blame you. It's a hard thing you're doing, miss. I sure wouldn't want to be in your shoes. Specially now, with the war nearly over, and them as likes the Yankees getting so uppity. They don't even wait for the army to turn up, some places; they do the paying back themselves. Kind of seems like there ain't much point, don't it? You taking such an awful risk, when it ain't likely to matter none anyway."

She paused, and opened the door. "I sure wish you good luck, miss. I'll be thinking of you every day, till it's all over."

"That's very kind of you, but I'll be perfectly all right."

Now for heaven's sake get out of here, you miserable, whining old crow. . . .

The woman shuffled away. The door closed. Elizabeth Dade sat down, bitter and angry. The Confederacy, she reflected, was being carried on the backs of a handful of heroes. Everybody else was giving up. Maybe everybody else had given up a long time ago.

She brooded so for quite some time, until someone else tapped gently on her door. A black woman stood there, hair in a kerchief, basket in her hand, mechanical smile pasted on her face.

"Chambermaid, miss."

"The chambermaid's been here."

"Begging your pardon, miss, but I ain't. I ain't been down this side at all."

"I know you weren't, for heaven's sake. The other one was."

"Other one? What other one, miss? I do everything on this floor myself. Been doing it for seven years, and they ain't never got me any help yet."

All the blood drained from Elizabeth Dade's face, and much of the steadiness from her voice.

"The room is fine. Go away."

"Yes, miss."

Badly shaken, she walked back to her chair and sat down, burying her face in her hands. God in heaven. They could just walk in here, in broad daylight. And walk out again, just like they owned the place.

It don't look good for our boys . . . they got a fella in Georgia . . . sure wouldn't want to be in your shoes . . . some places, they do the paying back themselves. . . .

I'll be thinking about you every day, till it's over.

Thinking about you. Every day.

I did not, of course, attend Sam Ruth's hearing. As a known Unionist, I could hardly be seen to show any particular interest in his fate. But the outcome was all over Richmond before the sun was high, and the details were public knowledge by suppertime.

Miss Dade went to court very finely and modestly attired. She made an excellent impression on everyone present. She confirmed, under questioning, that yes, she had seen a gentleman meeting with two others in Federal uniform, seen them shake hands and talk, apparently on the best of terms, seen him pass to the Yankees an envelope, which one of them opened, examining the contents and placing it in his pocket. She had then seen the gentleman ride away, without haste, having clearly no intention of informing anyone that enemy soldiers were nearby.

"And was this gentleman Mr. Ruth, the defendant here present?"

"I thought so at the time, sir."

"You thought so at the time? Do you no longer think so?"

"I don't know, sir. I was told the gentleman was Mr. Ruth. I may have been misinformed."

"You were *told* the gentleman was Mr. Ruth?"

"Yes, sir."

"But are you not personally acquainted with Mr. Ruth yourself?"

"No, sir. Before this incident, I never so much as heard of the man."

Now she was laying it on with a trowel. There probably wasn't a mentally competent adult in northern Virginia who hadn't *heard* of Samuel Ruth.

"Look carefully at the defendant, Miss Dade. Is this the man you saw meeting with the enemy?"

"I don't know, sir. It was evening. There wasn't much light."

At this point, apparently, Sam's attorney jumped to his feet and demanded a dismissal. It was granted without much fuss. Sam went home, to the general satisfaction of nearly everyone—except, I suppose, the Rebel spycatchers, and young Miss Elizabeth Dade.

Afterward, many Unionists believed Miss Dade had been suborned, and then, in the courtroom, could not bring herself to lie under oath. But later, when I asked Sam if she'd actually seen him meeting Federals, he could only shrug.

"She might have. I took chances sometimes. I had to. . . ."

✳   ✳   ✳

All the time, while the war was going on, we seemed to live in constant peril. And certainly, any one of us, caught with sufficient evidence to convict, would have paid a bitter price. For those without rank or name, like Tom McNiven, even evidence wasn't necessary.

Yet now, looking back with the calmness of time and death, it's clear the Richmond underground, collectively, was never in as much danger from the Rebel authorities as it should have been. There was never any concerted, organized attempt to root us out. The Confederates spent vast amounts of money and effort on clandestine activity—far more than the Union did—but all of it was aimed against the North.

It was another one of those amazing contradictions that ran everywhere through Rebeldom like fault lines through rock. Despite the public clamor about spies and saboteurs, despite the occasional savage attack on a particular individual, deep down inside a lot of Confederates could never quite bring themselves to believe in us. So many of us, of so many ranks, in so many places, doing so much damage. Our existence called into question not merely the unity of the South, but its virtue as well.

Believing in the Union underground was rather like believing in slave rebellion. On the one hand, a pervasive dread, echoed in laws and night patrols and rifles and hounds. On the other hand, a blinding but absolutely necessary illusion of security. Slaves were family. Slaves were happy. Slaves were stupid. *They'll turn on us the first chance they get? Don't be ridiculous. The Confederacy is laced through with Unionists, spies, the purely indifferent, and quite a few people who'll sell it down the river for a handful of greenbacks? Don't be ridiculous.*

It couldn't be. The Rebellion was a vast, national birth, rooted in blood and race and history. It gave shape to a unique identity that every Southerner shared; it ran in the veins of every man and woman who walked its sacred ground. It had to be thus. Otherwise it was just treason.

SIXTEEN

———————— ✳

THERE SHOULD BE NO REAL NEGLECT OF THE DEAD

The negroes are no more free than they were forty years ago, and if one goes about the country telling them they are free, shoot him. . . .

Emerson Etheridge, 1867

No nation rose so white and fair
Or fell so pure of crimes.

Masthead text of "The Land We Love"

Our literature has become not only Southern in type, but distinctly Confederate in sympathy.

Albion Tourgee, Southern writer, 1888

There should be no real neglect of the dead, because it has a bad effect on the living.

William T. Sherman

The moon is high and brilliant, almost full. I don't remember it waxing. This sort of thing happens to us all the time; we tend to lose track of the ordinary living world. Several days have passed, obviously,

since we gathered at Hill's monument. More loyalists are out, including Charles Palmer, the aging merchant from Cary Street who spent
huge amounts of his own money on the Union cause. Rebel numbers
seem to be growing, too, and Martin Lipscomb, joining us late, tells
us he's just seen General Lee—talking to some soldier boys, he says,
and doing his best to stay away from Jefferson Davis.

"He's been avoiding Old Jeff for an awful long time," Mr. Lipscomb
says, partly to Mariel, and partly to no one in particular. "Ever since
that night they went walking together by the river. Did anyone tell
you about it?"

"No," Mariel says. "But I think someone's about to."

"It was years and years ago. Lee had barely come out before the
president collared him, and said they had to talk—plan the campaign
in Texas, I suppose. Anyhow, they got to talking real serious, and Old
Jeff got so interested in the conversation he didn't notice where they
were going. After a while the general stopped, and said to him: 'Forgive me for mentioning it, Mr. President, but I'm afraid we've wandered from the path. We seem to be walking straight down the middle
of the James River.' He thought for certain this would make Davis
realize they were ghosts. But Davis only faltered for a moment. 'My
God,' he said, and turned a little pale. Then, without the smallest
hesitation, he threw his arms around Lee. 'Don't be alarmed, General,' he said. 'I'm sure I can hold you up.' "

"Do any of these stories ever get back to him?" Mariel wonders.

"Who knows? Who cares? Listen, why don't we go down to the
White House? It's likely to be empty now, with all the Rebels off
speechifying."

We look from one to the other. Sam Ruth shrugs. It's a museum
now, and Martin's favorite haunt, but the rest of us haven't been there
for a long time. I don't like the place much, and neither does Will.
Like Davis himself, it has a sense of something dark about it. Something dark and mortally cold, which only a few of us notice, and the
living don't seem to notice at all. It's a lovely place to look at, of
course, with its tapestried walls and tiffany furniture, all refurbished

to its antebellum splendor, and draped in just about as much Lost Cause romanticism as one house can hold. But too much happened there to deceive the dead. Too many desperate men came and went, leaving tiny traces of themselves; there is a presence there, a memory of violence. Thomas Courtney climbed those elegant steps. Secretary Seddon, who said the best solution to the problem of black prisoners of war was not to have any. Jacob Thompson, off to burn down the city of New York. And yes, let us never forget, John Wilkes Booth.

Too many such men, too often and too willingly received. Even when the ghosts are all away, something else lingers, unpleasant, like the smell of old ashes. But on this night, despite the great convention, the ghosts aren't all away. There is a party in the garden, and right in the heart of it is The Indomitable Lady herself, Scarlett O'Hara, fanning her bosom and telling stories, surrounded by four handsome colonels and a brigadier. We shouldn't be surprised by it, of course; military pageantry and long-winded speeches were never much to Scarlett's taste.

It takes considerable time and effort for a few of us to get inside. We come over the wall with a gust of wind and dead leaves, and slither along thereafter in a manner you would probably consider disgusting, if I described it to you, so I won't.

We shouldn't be getting away with it at all, of course; ghosts are normally quite alert. But Scarlett is now the absolute center of everyone's attention, including her own. She's talking about how hard she had it, after the war; and how awful the carpetbaggers were; and how most of the Negroes were ruined by them—except of course her own, who were faithful as the twelve apostles, even if they were *so* silly. She talks about how desperately she held on to her land. Whatever it cost, whatever she had to do, she was keeping her land and making it pay; she was never going to be hungry again.

And after a while, I stop listening to her. I'm not a man, after all; those flashing green eyes don't do a thing for me, and her story reminds me of another one. It was a story Jed might have told me, since it came from Tennessee, but I heard it instead from a Libby prisoner who was hiding in my garret, back in the spring of '64.

He was a staff officer, and had served with one of Sherman's brigadiers in Chattanooga. After the fighting was over, they headed straight for Knoxville. Burnside's small army was trapped there, pinned down by the Rebels and running out of food. "Facing imminent starvation," the last wire said. Then the lines were cut. That had been three weeks before.

The president was worried sick about it, my prisoner friend told me, and Grant wasn't exactly unconcerned, either. As soon as Chattanooga was secure, he sent Sherman off east, and told him to hoof it.

Well—so the story went—Sherman hoofed it. Through rain and mud and rocks and mountains, forced marches all the way. By the time they hit Knoxville they were about the weariest, wobbliest, hungriest passel of Yankees anyone ever saw. But they thought at least they'd get a hero's welcome. Some of them had their knapsacks already open, ready to hand out hardtack to their poor, famished, half dead comrades. Imagine their surprise at seeing Burnside's men looking about twice as good as they did, and asking for news and tobacco, instead of food. Sherman found General Burnside himself just sitting down to dinner, with a tablecloth, and roast quail, and apple cake, and I don't know what else. Sherman, it seems, was considerably miffed, and ate most of it.

I feel a blinding urge to tell the story to Scarlett O'Hara, to climb out from under this pile of dead leaves and ask her how hungry she thought the people of East Tennessee might have been. Sherman marched through Georgia without pity, but he kept on going. The Home Guards and the militias in the mountain country were always somewhere nearby, resident pillagers who came back, and came back again, ready not merely to plunder but to kill, to attack their neighbors for the merest hint of collaboration, to hunt down any man of fighting age who wasn't in the army and didn't have a furlough paper in his hand. Burned fields and empty tables and grief were as familiar as sunrise to the Tennessee people, long before Sherman ever got to Georgia.

But when they learned a Union army was starving at Knoxville, they were willing to get even hungrier. My friend never told me what all they did—hunted and fished, I suppose; dug roots and picked berries; emptied their own corn cribs and smokehouses, too, what little was left in them now. Burnside's men built a rope boom across the river, just like a big fishing net, and all along the valley, every night, the people went down to the riverbank with whatever food they'd been able to collect. They strapped it onto little homemade rafts, or anything else that would stay above the water, and floated it down to Knoxville. They fed the whole Army of the Tennessee for two weeks.

I always thought it one of the best stories to come out of the entire war, and I heard a lot of them, from both the living and the dead. But it's a forgotten story now. They were only poor people, after all, on the French Broad River, only backwoods farmers and mountaineers. Cooper DeLeon would call them riffraff, and Miss Scarlett would call them poor white trash.

A silver unlaugh floats across Jefferson Davis's yard, followed by the murmurs of approving men. "A hundred million people know her name," Cooper said once. "How many people know yours?"

Or theirs?

How was it allowed to happen? So much of our history disappearing, so quickly and so cunningly, and all the disappearing wrapped up in golden words like reconciliation and respect? We never saw it coming. We never imagined that reconciliation would be purchased at the price of memory. We never thought Americans would come to see the war as nothing but a tragic accident, a quarrel over vague identities in which everyone was gallant and everyone was somehow right; or worse, a quarrel in which everyone was wrong, but the North so much more wrong, since they were the ones who made a fuss over nothing, they were the ones who invaded. We never thought Lincoln's dreams would one day be indistinguishable from those of his mortal enemy. We never, God help us, thought our story would come to be told by Scarlett O'Hara and Bobby Lee's horse.

I slip quietly away from my friends, away from this museum of misremembered stories. They will worry about me when they notice, but I can't afford to care. I need to think, and I think best alone; heaven knows I've had plenty of practice. I don't consciously choose to go back to Church Hill, yet that is where I go, drifting right over what used to be Locust Alley. I think about Madame Clara then, and how much she helped us. She should have a monument, McNiven said once. Of course, she never will; how on earth would we explain it to the tourists?

I smile to myself. For a little while, without really noticing it, I forget about Scarlett, and return, as I always do, to the living world of the past. . . .

SPRING, 1865 . . .

The arrests of January '65 knocked a considerable hole in our Richmond-to-Fredericksburg line. Although Sam Ruth and Jacob Timberlake were freed, Isaac Silver was not, nor were any of the people who'd been taken at the Duke home. Mr. Silver and Will Lohmann were locked up in Castle Thunder, along with John Hancock, who'd been serving as one of Sam's chief couriers. So, with Tom McNiven gone and Sam's line crippled, the house on Church Hill became the depot for nearly everything moving in and out of Richmond.

We got very bold in those last months of the war, and no one more than Sam. Like a troubled soldier who'd finally seen the elephant and survived it, he came out of jail and threw himself headlong into the fight. Sometime early in February the Confederate quartermaster turned up at the head office of the R.F. & P. The quartermaster needed to arrange some transportation. He had four hundred thousand pounds of tobacco to ship to Hamilton's Crossing, near Fredericksburg. He would also, from time to time, have large amounts of Northern bacon to bring back. The tobacco, obviously, would be ferried across the Potomac by night, to purchase those desperately needed supplies for Lee's army.

General Grant was not much given to personal hostilities and malice, but he thoroughly detested war profiteers—of which the North, regrettably, had as many as the South. From the time he took over the Bureau of Military Information, such exchanges were high on our list of things to watch for.

Needless to say, a remarkable little piece of paper soon turned up at Angelina's restaurant, wrapped in a shinplaster, payment for strudel and that which we didn't call coffee, from Samuel Ruth. A couple of weeks later still, several thousand Northern raiders swooped down on Fredericksburg, carried off as much of the tobacco as they could carry, burned the rest, and took four hundred prisoners into the bargain. They made a ghastly mess of Sam's railroad, tearing up miles of track and putting a torch to the station house and two bridges.

It was all in the newspapers, and it all redounded to our benefit. Sam got sympathy instead of suspicion. The Rebels judged it treachery, of course, but like so many other times, they saw the enemy without, rather than within. They assumed the Yankee traders had double-crossed them; those lickpenny scoundrels weren't content to get their tobacco cheap; they wanted it for nothing.

It was one of those mornings—and there were more of them of late—when I could read the Richmond papers with complete satisfaction. It was a fine spring day; Mother and I were having tea on the veranda. I put the paper aside and laid my head back against the chair.

Mother was aging, I noticed. She was paler than ever, and she'd lost some weight she couldn't really afford. I knew she missed John terribly. So did I, of course, but a lot of times I was too busy to notice. Now, quite suddenly, I felt his absence like a wound. I wanted him sitting by the table, having tea with us, sitting there for hours and telling us about the wonderful new book he was reading.

Josey came out so quietly I barely heard her.

"Young Master Merritt's here, Miss Liza. Shall I send him out, or do you want to come in?"

I went in. Will Rowley's boy was in the parlor—not a boy at all anymore, but a sturdy young man who'd inherited all his father's talent for crossing picket lines. The note he gave me was brief and direct: "Our knight taken. Dead if recognized. Can you do anything? Sharpe."

Sweet holy God. . . .

For a time, five or ten minutes, perhaps, I did nothing at all. I didn't even finish decoding the signature. I sat numb, thinking about Spencer Kellogg Brown. The fairgrounds filled with people, the thin body twisting slowly against a burning noonday sun. Dead if recognized. . . .

Not Jed. Please God, no.

I could not face it. You may think of me what you will, but of all the deaths that bloodied our land for four pitiless years, this was a death I simply could not face.

I went to my room and took my farm clothes out of the closet, and put them in a bag. I had Nelson hitch up the buggy and drive me to Lucy Rice's house, and then wait there, like a good and faithful servant. I changed clothing in Lucy's house, slipped out her back door, and went to see Martin Lipscomb at his scruffy undertaker's office.

He was not pleased. He whisked me into the back, bolted the door, and whipped the CLOSED sign into the window. Then he stood glowering at me.

"What the devil do you think you're doing, Miss Van Lew? Coming here in broad daylight? Are you trying to get me hanged?"

"May I sit down?" I said.

What could he say? He waved distractedly at a chair. "Yes, of course."

The tiny place was piled with plain, wooden coffins. Not a good thing for me to be looking at, just now. Not the right man for me to be talking with, either, but I had no choice. Martin Lipscomb was my only direct link to the man I needed.

"Lieutenant Knight has been captured," I said. "Colonel Sharpe wants to know if we can do anything."

"What can we possibly do? They hang spies, Miss Liza. If he's captured, he's dead."

"No. If they'd caught him out of uniform, they'd have hanged him on the spot. He'd be dead already, and Colonel Sharpe wouldn't know anything about it. He must have been taken riding courier, or in a skirmish somewhere, and they'll send him to Libby. Somebody will recognize him in Richmond, Mr. Lipscomb, sooner or later, and sooner more likely than later. We have to get him out."

"Well, if he can arrange to get sick and die, I'll go fetch him for you."

"No." It was a good escape method, and a fairly safe one now, since we hadn't used it for a long time. But Jed was young and hopelessly healthy. It would take some time to fake a credible mortal illness, time we might not have. Worse, an illness would attract attention, and that was the last thing we wanted.

"No," I said again. "It will take too long. You have to find a quicker way. Kiley might be able to help. I want you to go and see him today."

On several occasions, I knew, Mr. Lipscomb thought I was driving my buggy with two wheels off the road. Now he was sure of it. His mouth opened, and closed again very quickly, probably swallowing an oath.

"A quicker way? Do you think it's *easy* to get a man out of Libby? And what's the use talking to Kiley? The man is scared of his own shadow. He's never done anything that wasn't twenty-four-karat solid gold safe."

That, I thought grimly, was a matter of opinion.

"Well, I want you to ask him. One way or another, you have to get Lieutenant Knight out. As fast as you possibly can." I stood up. "He knows everything about this network, Mr. Lipscomb. He knows a lot of things even Quaker didn't know."

It was wicked of me to say it, of course. I knew Jed wouldn't tell the Rebels anything, no matter how roughly they questioned him. But Martin Lipscomb didn't know it.

I opened my reticule and pulled out five hundred Confederate dollars. "Give Kiley half," I said. "Tell him. . . ." I paused, and looked hard at the undertaker. The money was primarily for him. Kiley had other motives. "Tell him this one really matters."

He took the money idly. A cold, dry smile played around the edges of his mouth.

"And why, precisely, does one young lieutenant matter so much? Or should I say to whom?"

I hadn't been raised a lady for nothing. I showed no reaction at all, I believe, except to cast on him a look of infinite, withering disdain.

"The lieutenant is head scout for Colonel Sharpe, who is chief of Military Information for General Grant, who is commander of the armies of the United States. Does that answer your question, Mr. Lipscomb?"

"Yes, ma'am."

I wanted to storm out with my nose in the air, but I needed this man; I would need him as long as the war went on.

"Talk to Kiley today. Whatever you decide to do, I'll try to supply anything you need."

He flipped the Rebel bills with his hand, lightly. "This won't even buy a barrel of flour, you know."

"It'll buy a talk with Kiley, I think."

"Yes, I expect it will."

I made myself smile. "Thank you, Mr. Lipscomb. I'll contact you tomorrow."

"For heaven's sake, don't come here again! I'll send you word."

"By tomorrow night," I said. "Or I will come here again. I'll be so worried I won't be able to help myself."

I smiled at him again, and walked out the door.

For the first time since its takeover as a prisoner of war facility, the Libby warehouse was relatively uncrowded. Most of the Federal officers had been exchanged, or sent south to Georgia or the Carolinas. Among those who remained was Captain Edward Schenk, of the Eleventh Pennsylvania Cavalry.

The Eleventh was Sam Spear's regiment, the horsemen who captured Rooney Lee, and went storming out to rescue the Libby fugitives, and generally spent their time raising hell along the Chickahominy from Fort Monroe. On one occasion, late in the fall, Jed Knight had carried a message from General Meade's headquarters to the prowling Colonel Spear, and was sheltered for the night in the tent of Captain Schenk. It was the briefest of acquaintances, but now, in a place full of strangers and enemies, it was quite enough for Jed to consider Edward Schenk an old friend.

Schenk was more than willing to be friendly. He remembered the young courier as a cheerful fellow who loved to tell stories. But this time, the courier seemed more inclined to listen than to talk. He wanted to know everything Schenk could tell him about Libby. Most especially, he wanted to know how to get out.

"Out?" Schenk shrugged. The new ones were all the same, he thought. They always imagined there was some easy, obvious way to get out.

"A lot of ways have been tried," he said. "Except for the big tunnel, most of them depended on chance. And nobody's likely to try a tunnel again; there's a couple of tons of explosives spread underneath the building."

"Can the guards be bribed?"

"Well, I've heard Colonel Streight tried it once, and got a whole long stretch in the cellar for his trouble. On the other hand, some boys do get out from time to time, and nobody knows how; they don't come back and tell us. So maybe there are guards who take bribes. I'd go about it real careful, though, if I was you."

"Tell me about them."

"The guards?"

"Everybody."

So Schenk told him, as best he could. Richard Turner was mean clean through; he wouldn't help a Yankee if God was standing right beside him, offering heaven itself for a reward. Little Ross wasn't much better.

"He's the prison clerk. If you want to buy food from outside, or anything else, you have to go through Ross or Harkins. It's a real shell game they've got, buying stuff for the prisoners. Harkins isn't too bad, but Ross is a damned thief. Among other things."

"And the guard who set Colonel Streight up? Which one is he?"

"His name's Sobol. Tell you the truth, I think he's sorry he did it. He's been pretty decent to everybody ever since."

Captain Schenk took a long hard look at his companion. Jed Knight was an awfully nice-looking kid. He had the kind of face that would make young women want to kiss him, and old women want to brush his hair out of his eyes. But much of the cheerfulness Schenk remembered was gone; he seemed a man with something heavy on his mind. And Schenk had a fair idea what it was. The men sent out on courier missions were often scouts, and scouts usually doubled as spies.

While he was reflecting on it, there was a stir at the door. The prison clerk came in, accompanied by several guards and the adjutant, who bellowed for attention.

Schenk got to his feet. "Roll call," he said.

They lined up, as always, in five rows, and Little Ross made his painstaking way down each line. He counted Lieutenant Knight without attention, passed him, and then, as if something had suddenly caught his eye, he stopped and turned back to him.

"I don't remember seeing you before, Lieutenant."

"I was brought in last night."

"Your name?"

"Jedediah Knight. Ninth Tennessee Volunteers."

Ross's thin mouth twisted with distaste. It always bothered him, seeing Southerners in blue.

"Well, well," he said. "One of us. We'll have to make you especially comfortable then, won't we?"

He's evil. . . . Schenk said it bluntly, coldly, over last night's small offering of watery beans in the cook room. *Some men here have a heart,* he said; *they'd like to treat us better. Ross wishes he could treat us worse.*

Jed was hungry. Breakfast had been about three bites big, and there would be nothing more till supper. It was the Yankees' fault, Ross told them. If they didn't burn crops and wreck railroads, there would be plenty to eat.

The man made Jed uneasy—uneasy deep down inside, where his instincts lived. He thought perhaps Ross had seen him before, somewhere on a Richmond street, but wasn't quite sure, couldn't quite remember. Several times, when Ross was in the room, he would find the clerk's eyes on him, dark and speculative. Schenk said Ross was always watching people; it didn't necessarily mean anything. The man was like a snake, Schenk said. He never blinked.

Jed worried nonetheless. He knew he had been in Richmond too often; he'd ridden halfway around the inner defenses once, escorted by a militia officer; he'd been all over the harbor. But the more often he went to Richmond, the more he knew about it; and the more he knew, the more reasonable it seemed that he, rather than someone else, should go again.

A scout's life, he reflected, was something of a trap.

From time to time there was work to do in Libby, and prisoners would be selected by the Rebel officers to do it. Usually it amounted to nothing more than carrying in a few wagon loads of supplies. But of late, because the prison was relatively empty, some maintenance work was also being done.

It was the evening of his third day in Libby when Ross and several guards came to fetch a work detail. A shipment of rice and beans had come for them, evidence of the Confederacy's continuing and heroic efforts to keep them fed. If they wanted to eat breakfast tomorrow, he said, they would have to unload it tonight.

It was a fine, warm night, with patches of cloud and a sliver of moon. The mere fact of darkness made Jed think about escape, but he knew there was little hope of it.

The prisoners carried the supply crates into the commissary room one by one. They didn't hurry. This was the only fresh air and exercise they were going to get.

Jed got very little. He put down his first crate, only to see Ross standing directly beside him.

"You. Come with me."

Jed glanced about. The other prisoners and guards were all outside. If this ended bad, he thought, there wouldn't be any witnesses.

He had no choice. He went where Ross pointed him, down a long hallway, through a door, and into a cramped office with a small desk and two chairs. The room had a window to the street, but the curtains were carefully drawn. It had a door, too, heavy oak, with an iron bolt rammed securely shut. The door drew his gaze instinctively, but he knew it was of no use to him. The cook room had a door, too; the prisoners walked past it every day. With gaslights illuminating every inch of the prison's circumference, and guards with rifles patrolling every foot, a door so close at hand was just something to grieve over.

In the center of the room, he turned to face whatever might be coming.

Ross was watching him with the same quiet, veiled interest as before.

"What part of Tennessee you from?" he asked.

"Hawkins County."

"You got a wife there? Kids?"

"No."

"Got a farm?"

"My folks do. Or did. I don't know how much of it's left now."

Where, Jed wondered, was this leading? One on one, Ross seemed a different sort of person altogether. The vindictive little gnome had turned into a quiet, watchful creature, possibly quite harmless. Possibly, also, quite deadly.

"What'll you do then, when the war's over?" Ross asked.

"I don't know. Whatever it is, it'll be something I never did before. Open a school, I guess, or maybe even a theatre."

"A theatre?"

Something wistful flickered over Ross's face, something wistful and innocent and painfully brief—so brief Jed wasn't sure he'd actually seen it. Then the clerk turned to business, harshly, like a boss caught napping in his chair.

"That cupboard in there's a hell of a mess. I want you to clean it up. Top to bottom." He paused, for just a second. "That means now, Lieutenant."

Jed looked about, spotted the closet, and strode toward it. He expected the clerk to follow him, so as to explain precisely what he wanted done. Before he got there, however, he heard a door open and close, very quietly. Ross had left the room.

Well, don't give me any duff then, Mr. Ross, if I don't do all of this to your highfaluting expectations . . . !

The cupboard did not look especially disordered. The shelves were neatly stacked. A pile of boxes sat in one corner. Jed opened the door wider, so as to get more light, and his breath caught in his throat. Lying neatly across the boxes was a Confederate uniform. It was still in good shape, but somewhat worn, somewhat dirty—in short, entirely perfect. The pocket contained a jackknife, matches, hardtack, and ten Confederate dollars.

His hands clenched on it in a moment of bitter indecision. It was all too perfect. It had to be a trap—the very worst kind of trap. The moment he put on an enemy uniform he was a spy.

The Rebs knew, he thought. They knew, but they weren't sure, and this would resolve the matter, quietly, simply. No questions before, and no sympathy after.

But oh, the thought of walking out of here and going free!

Colonel Streight walked out of here a while back, through that same damn door, probably, and they were waiting for him with guns in their hands. . . .

Well, what of it? Maybe it was a trap, but there was only one way he was going to find out. He'd been carrying a noose in his back pocket for a long time now; he ought to be used to it. . . .

He put the uniform on. It didn't fit especially well, but then, except for officers who could afford to have them tailored, nobody's did. He blew out the lamp, and stood for a moment before the outer door. He wasn't a praying man, generally, but he prayed then, just a little. *Lord, into thy hands I commend one very fragile Tennessee neck, amen.*

The light from the gas lamp seemed painfully bright. He stepped into the street without hesitation, walking calmly, without hurrying and without paying any attention to the sentries. They saw him, stiffened a little, noted the uniform, and lost interest.

He reached the end of the street and turned the corner. A figure stepped out of the shadows, dark, barely discernible, moving onto the sidewalk beside him. He reached for his knife, but the other was already speaking, very softly:

"Don't be alarmed, sir; it's only Nelson. Mr. Babcock sent me to meet you."

Relief drenched his body like cool rain. Only then did he realize how ready he had been to die.

When the prisoners finished unloading the commissary supplies, they found Little Ross in an ugly mood. They also found a puddle of distinctive appearance and odor lying in the adjoining hall, which Ross promptly ordered them to clean up.

"What is it?" one of them asked uneasily, though he had a fair idea.

"Lieutenant Knight's supper. It seems work doesn't agree with him. He had to go upstairs and lie down. Oh, take good care of that, by the way. He might want it back."

One of the prisoners cursed, softly. Another glared at Ross with bottomless contempt.

"If we ever get out of this place, Reb, you'd better find yourself a good place to hide."

"I'll be so old when you get out of here, Yankee, it won't matter."

The men finished their unpleasant duties and were allowed to retire. They were understandably worried about their companion, and the first thing they did when they returned to their quarters was look for him. They couldn't find him anywhere. They checked with Captain Schenk, and with their own friends. No one had seen him. As far as anyone knew, he had never returned from the work party.

The explanation was obvious. He had come up with some ingenious escape plan, faked sickness to escape Ross's attention, and bolted.

At morning roll call, they covered for him. It was easy. Ross, as usual, couldn't count worth a fig. Jed Knight was two days gone from Libby before the Rebels missed him.

Nelson brought him in very quietly, through a side door into an unlit hallway, and we took him straight to the garret room. I was so happy to see him I found it hard to speak.

Nelson, too, was extraordinarily pleased. "It all went off just perfect, Miss Liza," he said.

"I don't know how to thank you," Jed said. "Did you plan this whole thing?"

"No," I said. "Mr. Ross chose his own means to free you. I merely insisted that it had to be done."

Jed grinned wryly. "What did you threaten him with, if you don't mind my asking?"

"Nothing. Mr. Ross is one of us."

"One of us?"

"Yes. He's always been a Union man. That's why he hired on at Libby."

Given his line of work, I don't suppose Jed Knight was easily dumbfounded. But he looked dumbfounded now. I turned to Nelson for a moment.

"Go to Mary, will you, and ask her to fix a nice plate for our guest. You must be famished, Lieutenant."

"I hadn't thought about it until now, but yes, I am. Thank you."

"You can stay here, of course, as long as you need to. Mr. Ross will try to cover your escape; you probably won't be missed till morning."

"All the more reason to keep going, then. I appreciate the offer, Miss Liza. But I think perhaps a bit of food, and a minute to catch my breath, and I should hoof it on out of here."

He was right, of course. We had assumed as much ourselves. I heard Nelson's steps receding down the stairs. There were no chairs in the room, but I had piled some of the blankets against the wall. I put the lamp down carefully on the wooden table, beside the water pitcher. The wick was low, and I didn't turn it up. The dark walls swallowed most of the light. It felt a very secret place, my secret room.

We could lie together here, before he goes away. . . .

The thought flashed quietly across my mind—absurd, of course, but nonetheless real, and powerful. All at once I couldn't breathe very well.

"Make yourself comfortable, Lieutenant," I said. "I'll see about your supper."

I went to my bedroom, drew the curtains closed, put on the light. Looked at myself in the mirror above my dressing table. I didn't look my years; I never had. My face had been judged pleasing when I was young. I could pass for a woman in her thirties, I thought . . .

well, late thirties, perhaps, with evening light, and my hair shaken loose, pale as it was, and long. . . .

I took the tray of food right out of Mary's hands. "I'll take it up myself," I said. "Thank you."

He was famished, as he said. He sat on the blankets with his plate on his knees, and for a time few words passed between us, except for him saying how grateful he was, and how it was the best food he'd tasted in weeks. And because he was mostly looking at his supper, I mostly looked at him. He was rangy, as you'd expect a young mountain man to be; everything about him was long—his limbs, his fingers, his hair. No perfection there, but gracefulness and animal vitality and more courage than any ten men in the trenches. I wanted him so very much, just then; I could have reached out and touched any part of his body, as innocently as a breath of wind, and melted from the pleasure of it.

I watched him, and thought about what I might say, or do; how I might approach him without seeming a fool, and more and more it seemed to me that no way existed; that we would not lie together in this perfect, secret place, not tonight and probably not ever. He would never make the smallest gesture toward it, and I could not; I did not know how, not with our difference in years, and my lady-hood so well learned, and the risk of humiliation so great. In your world, perhaps, it would be different. Perhaps even in mine . . . for someone else. Perhaps in one quiet mansion or another across the South, some other lonely woman no younger than I took some lonely, passing soldier in her arms, a soldier no older than he, and no one ever knew, and the world went on exactly as before.

But I was afraid. That was the whole thing, I was afraid. All my life my courage had gone for other things, for surviving and resisting, for study and politics and finally for war. I had no courage left now for love, for its unpredictable follies or its terrible wounds. To be despised by this man, or laughed at, or pitied . . . no, I could not even contemplate it. My womanhood was the only thing left of myself that no one had ever been allowed to find amusing. And so I would keep it to myself, unimagined, unsuspected, safe.

The last, cold gift of honor.

There was nothing to do then but say good-bye. I gave him John's pistol and plenty of food—enough to feed him in the woods for a couple of days, or to make friends with several pickets or passing strangers. He asked me if I expected to see Mr. Ross at any time.

"I might," I said.

"Then would you thank him for me? Between the two of you, you've probably saved my life."

"I'll tell him," I said.

"I still have trouble believing it, you know. Little Ross on our side. The whole of Libby hates him. When you think about it, it's been a mighty strange war."

"Yes," I said.

We went down to the same side doorway, and I put out the light. It was hard not to cry. I knew he dared not come to Richmond again, at least while the Rebels held it. And then, because I knew I would never do more, I took his arm, and kissed him lightly on the mouth. It was a tiny thing, but exquisite. He could think it mere kindness, if he wished. You may be very sure I did not.

"A mighty strange war indeed, Jedediah Knight. Will you send me word when you are safe?"

He said he would, and he did. As it turned out, he was in City Point by morning, sharing Colonel Sharpe's breakfast—and telling him, I suppose, about the remarkable double life of Erasmus Ross.

Ross was Mr. Kiley, of course, the most secret of all my secret agents. The man no one suspected, ever. The man no one understood, not even me. All the Unionists in Richmond paid, one way or another, for their loyalty to the flag. But except for those who died, I think perhaps no one paid more bitterly than Little Ross.

The night before it ended, he came to my house. You cannot imagine the chaos: no law at all, the government gone and all its hirelings with it, the skies red with fire in nearly every direction, and the Federal army still ten miles away. Rich men rushed about the streets with fistfuls of money, desperate, like the hunchbacked king at Bosworth Field, offering kingdoms for a horse. Looters and thugs roamed the uptown streets, taking what they pleased, smashing what they pleased, settling old scores. On Church Hill, we were up all night, wondering if the fires would reach us before the army did. Or if the mobs would.

We were already sheltering nearly twenty people. The Rebels had tried to take most of their prisoners along, and several got away, John Hancock and William Lohmann among them. They were in my parlor, eating like starved men, and drowning themselves in tea, still scarcely able to believe they had actually escaped. Josey came and bent close to my chair.

"There's another gentleman at the door, Miss Liza. Says his name's Ross, and he's begging you to take him in. I don't think I ever saw a man so scared in my life."

I went to the door. Ross was indeed scared. He was turning his hat around and around in his hand.

"I'm sorry, ma'am," he said. "I'm right sorry to bother you like this. But I got nowhere to go. They're going to kill me for sure."

"It's all right, Mr. Ross. I'm glad you came. Please come in."

He followed me into the house, but when he saw who was in the parlor, he stopped, and backed away. That's when it hit me. *They're going to kill me for sure. . . .*

It was the Union men he was afraid of.

I had never known him well. In fact, there were really only two things I knew about him for sure. He was loyal to the flag, and he was lonely. He was the one person in the world I thought might be as lonely as myself—by that I mean lonely for no apparent reason. Lonely not because he was crazy or stupid or refused to wash, but because he simply couldn't find a place where he belonged.

Perhaps he hoped to find a place at Libby. It must have nearly killed him to be hated by the men he wanted so very much to help. He talked to me about it once, very briefly, a long time afterward.

"I never wanted to be cruel to them," he said. "I thought the world of them, Miss Liza. Every last one. But I was so scared when I started, I didn't know what else to do. It was like they just had to know. The Rebs, I mean. All they'd have to do was look at me, and they'd know. So I made a big show of being mean, right off. And then I couldn't stop. How could I stop? They'd get suspicious for sure then, worse than if I'd never been mean in the first place."

He was silent for a long time. And then he said, very bitterly: "God, it was such a trap."

Little Ross lived quietly in Richmond after the war, more isolated than ever in the shambles. He burned to death in '70, when the Spotswood Hotel went up in flames. He doesn't reven. Perhaps he's found his quiet grave less lonely and less fearful than the world he used to live in.

As for Colonel Sharpe's favorite, and mine, he made it home again, married one of his cousins, and became a schoolteacher. I lost track of him after a while, but there were rumors he was still carrying a noose in his back pocket, having run afoul of the Tennessee Klan. He came to see me before he was mustered out, riding proud into Richmond in his Federal uniform.

"Still new," he said, grinning a little, and fingering the sleeve. "They must have issued me a dozen of these through the war, and I hardly ever got to wear them."

There were a dozen people in the house that day, and we didn't have so much as a single private word. And so I have always thought of his escape from Libby as our real farewell. A meager farewell, you might think: a few kind words in a darkened hallway, a kiss such as you might give your own brother. But I saw it differently. I loved him too late, and perhaps too prudently, but I loved him very well.

Sometimes, when the mists are heavy, and I am alone in this world without end, I still do.

SEVENTEEN

———— ✳

HOW GLORIOUS
WAS YOUR WELCOME

My lines are broken in three places. Richmond must be evacuated
this evening.

> Robert E. Lee, April 2, 1865

All over, good-bye; blow her to hell.

> General Martin Gary, C.S. Army, Richmond, April 3, 1865

Say, darkies, have you seen the massa
    with the mustache on his face,
Gone down the road some time this morning
    like he's gonna leave the place?
He's seen the smoke way up the river
    where the Lincoln gunboats lay,
He took his hat and he left very sudden,
    and I 'spect he's run away.

> Henry C. Work

Oh, army of my country, how glorious was your welcome.

> Elizabeth Van Lew

The advance units of the Federal army approached Richmond at
daybreak on the third of April, 1865. I spoke to some of them after
the war, and they told me different stories, but one thing they told

me was always the same. Not one of them, cresting the last hill and catching his first full view of the city below, could quite believe what he saw. Some cursed, and some were reduced to absolute silence; one told me he truly wondered if he might be dead, looking down upon the kingdom of the damned.

Richmond was literally a sea of flame; only a church spire could be seen here and there above the inferno, and great clouds of black smoke rolled away from it, swallowing the morning sun. The departing Confederates had fired the arsenal, the tobacco warehouses, sundry supply depots, and most of the city's bridges. All the fires spread, but it was the arsenal that did the most damage, seven hundred and fifty thousand shells exploding in every direction, crashing into homes and businesses, killing people where they milled on the streets, sending burning debris high and wide on the wind, to start new fires wherever it fell.

One of those who stopped his horse for a moment, and looked on in wonderment and horror, was Colonel Ely Parker. He was a senior member of General Grant's staff, a civil engineer who had caught the general's attention with his fine work at Vicksburg. He was also Donehogawa, great nephew of the reigning chieftain of the Six Nations in New York. I have often wondered what he thought that morning, riding into Richmond; if he reflected in any way upon the bewildering lunacies of white men. Probably he didn't. The Union army had been fighting for days, ever since Fort Stedman, turning Lee's futile breakout attempt back on itself, and pouring down on his lines again and again, until finally, yesterday, they collapsed. Colonel Parker had been up all night; and like everyone else, he must have been hungry, dirty, and exhausted.

So I suppose he only shook his head, and rode on down the New Market Road. As the soldiers swung past the navy yards and the wharves at Rockett's landing and headed for the center of the city, he broke away with a small group of men, turning onto the winding road that led up Church Hill. The air was rank with smoke, and the roar of the fire was still punctuated by the sound of exploding shells.

There was something eerie about Church Hill that morning, a bizarre, unnatural peace, poised as it was between the ravaged countryside and the burning city core. It might have been Sunday in the old slave days, the houses all still and the sidewalks empty, except for small clusters of black people who waved from the front yards or ran out to greet them. *Is the army behind you? Is Mr. Lincoln coming? Is it true we're free now?* Things he expected them to say, and things he didn't expect. *See, I told you, they don't have any horns, they're just like our own folks. Lord almighty, look at them horses, what do they feed 'em to get 'em so fat?*

"Colonel, look."

A soldier leaned over to him, drawing his attention away from the Negroes, and pointed up the street, toward a high, pillared mansion with beautiful Greek porticos. Floating above the front gable, magnificent and defiant against the wartorn sky, was a huge American flag.

"I guess we don't have to ask anyone which is the right house," the soldier added.

They rode into the Van Lew yard. Several black people waited there as well, rushing to surround them as they dismounted.

"Are you all there is?" one of the small ones demanded.

"Hush your mouth, child, and say good morning to the colonel. We're mighty glad to see you, sir."

"Is it over?" asked another. "You here to stay?"

"Yes, you can depend on it, we're here to stay. I am Colonel Parker, from the staff of General Grant. The general asked me to convey his compliments to Miss Elizabeth Van Lew, and to arrange for the protection of her property."

"Miss Van Lew ain't here, sir. She went uptown."

"Uptown?" Parker stared at them, not believing.

"Oh, yessir, she went more'n an hour ago. She said she was going to the War Department. Said there was no way the Rebels could get rid of all their papers before they left, or take them along neither. She wanted to get to them before anybody else did."

"God in heaven. . . ."

Parker swung back onto his horse. "Jackson, Heinz, stay here and guard this house. The rest of you, come with me!"

The streets were a nightmare, thronged with looters and refugees, with people pouring out of their homes, dragging what few possessions they could, scarcely able to see, scarcely knowing which way was more dangerous to run.

Parker soon caught up with the main column. They marched in good order, quiet and restrained, except for the bands, which played all along the line. They played "John Brown's Body" and "The Battle Cry of Freedom"; most of all they played "Kingdom Coming," and they sang it, too, their voices soaring above the chaos. It was their one liberty, their single arrogance as conquerors. The war was all but over now, and they would act accordingly, but they had taken the Rebel capital, and by God, they were going to sing; *The Union forever, hurrah, boys, hurrah . . . ! . . . Say darkies, have you seen the massa with the mustache on his face . . . ?* On Church Hill the white folks had stayed indoors, but in the heart of the city they were everywhere. No trains were running, but some people fought their way to the stations nonetheless, hoping still to get away. Others thronged toward the open ground in Capitol Square, trying to find safety from the fires. There were loyalists among them, more loyalists, probably, than Richmond's citizens would care to remember afterward, waving hats and handkerchiefs and small painted flags, half crazy with joy and relief. But it was the Negroes who truly made it a day of jubilee. They danced. They sang. They ran alongside the soldiers and offered to carry their packs; they said "God bless you," over and over, "God bless you, God bless Mr. Lincoln." Starving and ragged, some of them, others in the trim servant garb of the great houses, it didn't matter. Fire all around, cinders in their hair, the air so thick they could hardly breathe, it didn't matter. This was freedom's army and they would cheer it till both strength and voice were gone.

It was a day of triumph for the victors; it could be nothing else. Yet for Parker—perhaps for many of them—it was a day as appalling as any he had lived through. Mobs like wolf packs prowled the streets, laden with plunder, their faces grimy with soot and vacant with exhaustion. They smashed in storefronts and homes with makeshift battering rams and axes. They dragged out hams and silk dresses and furniture, laughed, cursed, fought over it, and then left most of it in ruined heaps, to go raiding somewhere else.

Some were undoubtedly ruffians, but Parker suspected that most were simply angry and poor. Others, black and white alike, were too honest to plunder, and ran alongside the soldiers, begging frantically for food. A gaunt woman in a few thin rags, with two small children clinging to her skirt, just skin and bones themselves, grabbed at his reins: "Please, sir, please, for the love of God, can you give me something for the children, just a little bite, they've had nothing for days, oh, please. . . ." In the ranks, hardened men with many battlefields behind them lost their composure in the midst of their victory march, and cried at what they saw.

As they neared the city's heart, even the bands surrendered and fell silent. Men wrapped handkerchiefs across their faces; some stumbled as they marched, barely able to see. The heat was unbearable. The whole central core of Richmond was on fire. The Bank of Virginia, the courthouse, the newspaper offices, the splendid shops of silk merchants and jewelers, all were destroyed—some already smoking ruins, most still wrapped in sheets of flame. Men and horses alike had to pick their way through rubble, and abandoned plunder, and the lost belongings of a ruined world.

What in God's name was it for? Parker wondered. To keep from the hated Yankees a few munitions they didn't need? A few supplies they had by the shipload at City Point? A few bridges and train stations they would simply rebuild? For that a city died, and charred bodies were lying in the streets, and desolate women wandered homeless and hungry, clinging to the only possessions they had left in the world?

Secession had come full circle, he thought, from Sumter to Richmond; here was its signature, in this final, chilling act of folly.

He drew in his horse, and beckoned a man who stood smiling and waving as the soldiers passed.

"Morning, Colonel," the civilian said.

"Morning. You're a Union man, I take it?"

"I sure am, sir, I sure enough am." He looked sly and well fed. Parker wondered how long he'd been a Union man.

"Can you tell me where the Rebel war office is?" he asked.

"Gone up," the man said. He pointed vaguely. "You rode right by it, a ways back. They was burning papers there all night long, in the street. They could've saved themselves the trouble."

Parker wiped his face. For a moment he had no idea what to say. "Was anyone . . . inside?"

"Damned if I know," the civilian said. Then, seeing Parker's troubled face, he added, "I don't think so."

Directly ahead, Federal troops were pouring onto Capitol Square; several were running for the building itself, one of them clutching a flag. All at once, everything around Parker seemed to stop, turn, fall silent. A small dark figure appeared on the roof. Quickly, without any fuss at all, the Rebel flag came down, the Stars and Stripes went up, and a great, swelling cheer rose from the blue ranks, hoarse and sustained, absolutely deafening.

Parker allowed himself a small smile, a flutter of regret that General Grant wasn't there to see it. Then he headed for the Capitol himself. He would need help to search for Miss Van Lew.

But even as he waited to get General Weitzel's much divided attention, a young captain came hurrying up, flustered and dismayed.

"Begging your pardon, sir, but there's some crazy woman and her nigger in the president's office, taking everything apart, and she won't leave and she says she has authorization from General Grant, and what the devil am I supposed to do with her?"

"Forgive me for interrupting, General," Parker said, "but I think she might be one of our agents. With your permission, I'll take care of it?"

For the briefest moment, Weitzel simply stared at both of them. There was a war going on. The city was burning down around his ears. He did not quite believe he was having this conversation.

"What? Yes, of course, Parker. Do it."

The government chambers were a shambles. General Lee had warned his superiors repeatedly that Richmond might have to be given up, and talk of evacuation had been in the air for months. Yet these offices, like most of the others in the city, looked as though they had been abandoned on ten minutes' notice. Records had been burned in huge barrels in the backyard; many were still smoldering. Drawers hung open, only half empty; papers lay all over the floor, and rifled boxes cluttered the floors and the hallways. A pistol had been forgotten in the president's desk, along with his gloves, several photographs, and an untouched bottle of Napoleon brandy.

There the young captain led Ely Parker, and there he found a black man and a pale, exhausted woman, systematically going through papers they had piled up on the desk.

They glanced up at his approaching steps, but they did not stop what they were doing.

"Are you Miss Van Lew?" he asked, and introduced himself again. "The general sent me to see to your safety."

She brushed wild hair out of her face with her arm. Her hands were still full of papers. He had finally got her full attention.

"You're with General Grant's staff? *He's here? In the city?*"

"No, ma'am. He's hard on Bobby Lee's tail, and he isn't stopping or turning until he has the old fox up a tree."

Fox up a tree. Bad imagery, he thought. Lovely prospect. He couldn't help smiling. Gently he took the papers from her hands.

"You can leave these here, Miss Van Lew. This is Federal property now."

"Yes. Yes, of course."

She didn't want to surrender the papers. There was something fierce in her eyes, something fierce and perilous. Then she looked away, and afterward, it was gone. He thought probably it was only stress. She must have passed a terrible night.

"It's over, then," she said. "Here."

"Yes, and it'll soon be over everywhere. You're quite safe now. There'll be soldiers guarding your house as long as you need them."

She said all the right things. She thanked him graciously, and said he must thank the general on her behalf. But her eyes were troubled, full of darkness and a strange, incomprehensible unease.

He would see the same look in his commander's eyes, but he didn't know it yet. Six days from now, outside the house of Wilbur McLean, Lee's signed surrender in his hand. *It's over, thanks be to God. The nation is secure, and nobody else has to die. But what do I do after all this? What do I do for the whole rest of my life?*

Parker didn't understand. He saw only a faithful ally of his chief, exhausted and disheveled and amazingly brave. If she had been a man, he would have saluted her. If she'd been a girl, he might have risked his good name for a kiss. But she was neither, and all he could do was take her arm gently, and lift her onto his horse, and take her back through the smoke and ruins to the quiet house on Church Hill.

So it ended, in Richmond. The Federal army battled out the fires, and saved most of the city. All the rest you know about: the fighting at Five Forks and Sayler's Creek, which broke off still more pieces from the disintegrating Rebel army. The race to Amelia Court House. The supply train that never arrived, because the daringest scout in the whole Union army put on a gray quartermaster's uniform and rode along with it, stopping it here and slowing it there, watering the horses, resting the mules, until Sheridan's cavalry gobbled it up, and Lee got to Amelia Station and there was nothing there, only ravaged countryside and Yankees and surrender.

For a while, right after the war, my life was utterly wonderful. The exiles returned home, my brother John among the first of them, and Tom McNiven not far behind. Everyone came to see me. George Sharpe came, of course, now a brevet brigadier general, as debonair and handsome as an actor from the New York stage. Marsena Patrick came, the provost marshal for the Army of the Potomac; he was a stern old Puritan, appalled by everything he saw, but he was very nice to me. Captain McEntee, who looked after Sharpe's band of scouts and couriers, took me riding all over Richmond, and out to City Point. Men I'd never met stopped by to thank me for a box of food I'd sent to Libby Prison, or for helping a kinsman or a comrade to escape. Then, in May, Grant himself came to Richmond with his wife, and called on me one lovely, sun-drenched afternoon.

In your world, I've been given to understand, Ulysses Grant is not much thought about, or cared about—not like Lincoln, or Lee, or Stonewall Jackson, or even a battered old war horse named Traveller. About the only thing most of you seem to know about him is that he drank. Oh, yes, and one other thing: You seem to think he was big and beefy.

I can't imagine where this notion came from. But I'm told you make plays sometimes about the war—not very many plays, really, which is peculiar—and they are never about Grant, or anything he did. And if he's in the play at all, a little walk-on part, you find an actor who's fifteen years older than he was, and a hundred pounds heavier, and who looks, except for the uniform, like a back-room faro dealer in a waterfront saloon.

But as anyone who knew him could tell you, General Grant was a young man, only thirty-eight when the war began, a mere five foot eight, and slight of build. And yes, as the newspapers often said, he was careless of dress, and had no style about him, neither military nor any other; but clothing says no more about the body than it does about the soul. He was very well made, lean and fit, and his face, though serious, was decidedly attractive. I don't doubt for a moment that Julia adored the ground he walked on.

Years after, in the decades of guilt and sentiment, people began to say he hated fighting—hated warfare altogether, despised military pomp and pretension, never wore a sword, told the marching bands to go play somewhere else; had no appetite for mastery or for blood, no taste at all for putting other men down. It was all true. They were right about everything except the statement they were trying to prove. No man was this good at something he hated.

Therein lay the mystery, the never quite answerable question. How did it work, this improbable combination of quiet decency and methodical violence? Certainly he never tried to explain it, and those who did try never convinced me. In the end, I settled for a platitude: He was one of a kind, and there were no explanations.

Our visit was a quiet one. Grant never talked much in large groups, or in the presence of people he didn't know well; and because of it, there were some who thought he was sluggish of mind. Such people, of course, never paid any attention to what the man actually *did*. And they never looked carefully at his eyes. His eyes were gray as a winter sea, and had the same self-sufficiency, the same relentless depths. Behind the soft hum of other voices, the soft curls of gray smoke, they watched and waited and measured, and they missed almost nothing. Here, I reminded myself, was a man who moved a hundred thousand soldiers out of their trenches in the dead of night, whispered them over fifty miles of enemy countryside, across a broad and bridgeless river, and two days passed before anyone knew they were gone. This was the silence of the hawk, and of the hare. The silence of survival.

He didn't say much at my place, either. He drank tea and ate a piece of cake, and asked my permission to smoke.

"General, if you didn't smoke one of those famous cigars on my veranda, I'd feel positively hard done by."

He lit up. Julia and I did most of the talking. She was a charming woman, not beautiful at all, but wonderfully gracious. She was from Missouri, and seemed to have about her all the poise and tact of the well-bred South, and all the spirit and good sense of a frontier woman.

He asked a couple of brief questions about affairs in Richmond. About my work, he asked only one. And it wasn't even a question, merely an opening.

"General Sharpe tells me you got information from people close to the Rebel leadership itself."

"Yes, sir."

I hadn't told anyone about Mariel yet, not even Sharpe. But I told him. He didn't say a word. At one point Julia did; I had the feeling she was reading his mind. Her words came out in little bunches, with a question mark after each bunch: "They hired? the freed slave? of a suspected Federal spy? and let her serve dinner? in Jefferson Davis's *house?*"

"Good help was hard to come by," I said.

The smoke rings swirled grayer, and the gray eyes grew more impenetrable still. I would have given a great deal to know what he was thinking, but of course he never said. God knows his opinion of Mr. Davis was never very high.

It would be presumptuous to say that General Grant was my friend. But he was and he remained my ally. I didn't apply to the government for compensation for my work, at first, even though we had nearly impoverished ourselves in the service of the country. I considered my work a duty, and I imagined that all the Southern loyalists would soon restore their situations in the ordinary course of things. We were safe now, and free to get on with our lives; we were the friends of the victors; surely we would be fine.

Such folly. Southerners closed ranks against us as they never had in the war. Many a man who thought the real Confederacy absurd, and never served it, allowed himself to be conscripted by a mythical one. Many a woman who once knew the old order for the stifling, unjust world it was chose to forget, and gave her time and her pennies and her soul to the Daughters of the Confederacy, covering our landscape with monuments and the pages of our books with treacle.

The Van Lew household got poorer and poorer. John reopened the hardware store, but it barely made enough to pay for the merchandise he stocked. So, in the spring of '69, a mere fortnight after he was inaugurated president, General Grant asked the Congress for fifteen thousand dollars to repay myself and my family for our services. With all of his prestige and authority behind it, and a letter of support from George Sharpe so glowing it made me blush, the request was nonetheless refused. It was too late. The war was four years over, and Congress was tired of paying its unending bills. Besides, I was just an old maid, anyway, living in some rambling big house on a hill, and said to be a little strange in the head. What could I possibly have done to deserve all that money?

Grant did the only thing he could for me then; he gave me charge of the Richmond post office. It was a coveted patronage appointment, with high status and good pay, and one of the few that could be offered to a woman. But you would have thought he'd committed murder, or worse, there was such a fuss. Unthinkable, people said. An outrage. He was trampling on the feelings of every honest person in Virginia. Et cetera, et cetera. Neither of us could afford to care. He had a whole new fight on his hands, just trying to keep what he'd won at Appomattox, and I needed bread on my table. I took the job gladly, and until he left the White House, and his successor gave it to someone else, I kept it. . . .

The night is almost over, and I am alone on Church Hill. My house is gone, of course. I never could get rid of it while I lived; no one would buy it for a fair price, or even a cheap one. No one would have anything to do with me. For all those dark years, after Reconstruction ended and Grant was gone, I lived without means and mostly without friends. Survivors of Libby and Belle Isle sent me money for my bread, or else I might have died in the streets.

I shiver, remembering, and blame it on a gust of wind. I got strange at the end; I admit it. It wasn't pretend anymore. The isolation grew too much for me, finally. The hatred. The growing sense of failure as the old elites quietly grew powerful again, and took everything back: took back the legislature and the courts; took back the country roads, the guns, the lynching trees; took back the social rules and the public space. They decided who prospered, and who was welcome on the streets. They decided what reconciliation meant. They might take the hand of a Northern officer at a veterans' reunion, but the hand of a loyalist? A Southern spy? Never. We were the snake in the Confederacy's sainted garden, the knife in its heroic back. There was nowhere we could hang our heads that would have been low enough.

Does it surprise you that many denied they had ever been loyal? You might think it was the traitors who should have covered their tracks. But no, it was us. The unsuspected passed the compromised on the street and did not speak. We burned our papers, or buried them in our backyards, ten feet deep. We petitioned our files from the War Department and destroyed them. For some, it worked. Tom McNiven kept his cover for a hundred years. Mary Bowser's family quietly avoided mentioning that she'd ever known the Van Lews or worked for Jefferson Davis, and soon no one else remembered, either.

But for Sam Ruth and Will Rowley and me, it was too late. Will bought a farm with the money he received for his services, but he was never able to pay it off, and in the end he lost it all. Sam was dead by '70, exhausted by the war and by his own divided soul. Before another decade had gone by, Grant himself was ruined and penniless, writing magazine articles about the war to put food on Julia's table.

So I got dark-souled with the years, and bitter, and I talked to the moon. Little boys followed me on the street sometimes, in little packs, and called me witch, and even threw things. But they ran like the devil every time, when I turned around. They didn't like my eyes.

✳   ✳   ✳

Pink dawn is breaking in the east as Will Rowley makes his way slowly up the hill, and settles into the grass beside me. You might think ghosts don't get tired, but they do, after a fashion, and he is very tired indeed.

"Figured I might find you here," he says.

I know why he came, and I am grateful. He takes off his old bowler hat and brushes it, thoughtfully.

"Seems Jubal Early introduced a motion to the gathering tonight. Did anybody tell you?"

"No. What was it?"

"He said we don't belong here. He said we should go reven somewhere else, and if we don't go willing, we should be driven out. Apparently we're soiling something, but I'll be hanged if I know what."

Trust Old Jube to come up with such a notion. He's mean clean through. When he was still alive, he used to say he dreamt every night of fighting Yankees, and was always sorry when he woke and found it wasn't so.

"And will his motion be accepted, do you think?"

Not that it matters much. In one sense, it's already been accepted, passed, written on the books. What Old Jube really wants is to make sure it doesn't get rescinded.

"Accepted?" Will murmurs. "Heaven knows, but it will give them something to argue about for years. After they've chosen the quintessential Southern lady, that is."

"They ought to choose Miss Scarlett."

"She isn't real."

"Precisely."

He says nothing, only spares me a dry look, like many he gave me when we lived. The pink dawn has turned gray with cloud. I feel the tug of melancholy, as I always do in the early morning, when the living world awakes. But I feel something else, too, something that's been stirring softly in my consciousness for days. John Fairfield would no doubt call it an appetite for mischief.

"They've had their way too long, Will," I say to my old friend, quietly.

"They have. A mighty long time too long."

"Suppose we started rattling tombstones? In earnest, I mean. Suppose we woke the whole howling country up?"

We could unbury them all, I tell him, all the Union dead who've been sleeping too long; waken them to memory again, give their names and their long struggle back to the people. And then Jubal Early can make motions all night long, and Miss Scarlett can wag her fan, and Cooper can name his quintessential lady, this one or the other one, just as he pleases. Like Ulys Grant said long ago, it isn't what your enemy is going to do that really matters; it's what you're going to do.

The imps are back in Will Rowley's eyes, and tiny bits of smile are playing on his mouth. "Well," he says wryly, "it sure would liven up the landscape around here."

"So you'll come with me? And talk to the others, maybe?"

He gets to his feet slowly, and lifts me to mine. Just gallantry, of course; I'm a tough old ghost, tougher than he is, probably, and I don't weigh a feather. But I take his arm nonetheless.

"Do you have any idea," he murmurs, "how many ghosts we might stir up, if we go about this proper?"

"I do indeed."

"Some people are going to be real upset."

"I'm sure they will be."

All kinds of people will be upset, no doubt, among the living and the dead. And I don't care a fig. The Rebels rode the finest horses in the war, maybe, and they claimed the finest blood, but we were the real adventurers, the risk-takers, the ones who dared to believe that freedom might be for everyone, the ones who cherished ordinary blood. And yes, we had numbers on our side, but they had all of history on theirs, forty centuries and more of lordlings and slaves, forty centuries of pyramids and rules and every dog in his place. They already had the past, and they wanted the future; they still had Europe, and they wanted America.

And we said no.

That is the real story, and we're getting awfully tired of the other one. Tired of hearing how grand the Old South was, and how the Rebels were more interesting than we were, more daring, more romantic. We gave you a country, you admit it now, but you still say they were the heroes, and you say it without a whisper of a blush.

So we're going ghosting. Our stories lie everywhere, just like our bones, more wild rides than you ever dreamt of, all the daring you want, and all the beauty. Freedom wasn't dull and plodding; it flamed across that Victorian sky like a rocket, it sang in the wind, it made a whole generation into world-changers. And we're going to tell it, if we have to howl in through your keyholes and the cracks in your walls; if we have to haunt your children, and steal across your borders to whisper legends in the ears of strangers.

As for us, the Southerners who were part of it, the most forgotten ghosts of all, we're going to make the most noise. Will Rowley and Marty the Shovel and Mariel and all of them and me, Crazy Bet to the last, plotting in the shadows and digging up dead people, just like they say. I'm not going to be quiet and I'm not going away. Heaven knows they tried their best to get rid of me. They walked past the big house on Church Street as though it wasn't even there. And as fast as they could get their hands on it when I was gone, they tore it down. It was a grand old house, echoing with history, and famous long before it was ours, but they tore it down anyway—ripped out the secret room, drove off the lingering spirits of my sheltered friends, turned to firewood the veranda where Grant and I lingered over tea. They took it all away, and covered the ground over, not with salt but with lies, with a school where history was taught without us.

A school. The irony was almost unbearable. Generation after generation of small, scrub-faced Rebel offspring, trooping through my library and my garden, learning that a cotton plantation was just a great big family farm, and Bobby Lee was just another name for God.

I could hardly restrain myself sometimes. I wanted to slither up and down the aisles, blowing icy breaths down their collars and upsetting their inkwells.

But I got over it in time. Ghosts learn to take a longer view of history. We are alike, after all, ghosts and history: if you forget us, we always come back.

This story, and this war, aren't over yet.

———————— ✳

AUTHOR'S NOTE

This is a work of fiction based on historical fact. The existence of a large and successful Union spy ring in Virginia is a matter of record, and the exceptional contribution of Liza Van Lew is confirmed both by General Grant's chief of intelligence operations, George Sharpe, and by Grant himself. Samuel Ruth, Mary Elizabeth Bowser, William Rowley, and Thomas McNiven, among others, have all been identified as members of her network. Her servants, and a great many other African Americans, most of whose names have been lost, also served the cause, and it could not have prospered as it did without them.

This network supplied, in Grant's words, "the best information" the Union commanders received out of Richmond. But since most Union spies continued to live in the South after the war, Grant, in an effort to protect his agents from reprisal, sequestered the files of the Bureau of Military Information. They were not rediscovered until 1959. These documents, along with a number of postwar claims and depositions, demonstrate beyond question the importance of the Richmond network. At the same time, for obvious reasons, they are often vague about names, sources of information, routes of delivery, and other secret matters, none of which can be recovered now, from any conceivable source.

Only occasionally, therefore, do we know precisely what information came from which individuals, or how it was acquired, or what military actions it supported. On these questions I took full benefit of the novelist's right to speculate. When the details of their work were available, I used them. When they weren't, I took my best guess. I am entirely satisfied that, whatever Liza and her comrades did, it was at least as remarkable as anything I have suggested.

A number of things in the story are factual in essence, but altered in detail. I have occasionally combined minor events and altered minor chronology, though never in such a way as to create a cause-and-effect relationship where one could not have existed. David Todd actually served at Libby Prison, and his replacement moved into the Van Lew house, but all of this took place before 1863. Erasmus Ross (Agent Kiley) helped a Federal officer to escape in a manner much as I describe, but the officer of history was one Captain Lounsbury of the Seventy-fourth New York, not the young man in my tale.

In personal matters I almost always put the interests of storytelling ahead of strict adherence to fact, even when the facts were available, and quite often they were not. Little is known about Elizabeth's early life, except for the barest biographical details, and less is known about her extended family. The Foxes of Philadelphia and the St. Clairs of Devon Hill are fictional. Although a number of slave children were orphaned after the Nat Turner rising, my linking of this tragedy to the life of Mary Elizabeth Bowser is also fictional. John Fairfield is entirely real; and while there is no documentary evidence that Elizabeth ever met him, her spy system resembles the Underground Railway so much, not merely in its tactics and dedication, but also in its style—that is, in the combination of brazen openness with exquisite discretion—I think it certain she must have known, and been influenced by, members of what was surely one of the greatest resistance networks of all time. A young man named

Knight was indeed one of Sharpe's elite scouts, and said to have been "Miss Van Lew's favorite," but the background and personality I have given him is invented. And although I based Liza's character on her journals, and on the records of the time, both the journals and the records are sketchy; the final interpretation could not be other than my own.

As for the really important truths about the Civil War—why it happened, and what it really meant, and why it turned out the way it did—these I have adhered to as faithfully as I could, according to my own judgment, and the evidence accumulated by those scholars who seem to me most credible. The war was indeed a tragedy, but it was not an accident. It came, and it resolved itself, through thousands of conscious decisions by men and women on both sides. While the men and women may have been much alike, the decisions they made—and the reasons for those decisions—were not. Slave-owning and free labor created two societies in America. For all they had in common, these societies also embraced profound differences—differences that both led to the secession of the South, and contributed significantly to the South's defeat.

And that, I think, is the most important truth of all.

———————※

About the Author

Marie Jakober grew up in a log cabin on a small homestead in northern Alberta, Canada. Her home schooling by correspondence, and her imaginative flair for storytelling, brought her international recognition at age thirteen with the publication of her poem "The Fairy Queen."

Marie graduated from Carleton University in Ottawa, Canada, with distinction, and has toured, lectured, and served on numerous panels, including the 1988 international panel of History and Mythology in the Modern World.

Only Call Us Faithful is Marie Jakober's sixth novel. Her previous novels include *The Mind Gods*, 1976, a finalist in the Search-for-a-New-Alberta-Novelist Competition; *Sandinista*, 1985, winner of the George Bugnet Award for Fiction; *A People in Arms*, 1987; *High Kamilan*, 1993; and *The Black Chalice*, 2000.

Ms. Jakober lives in Calgary, Alberta, Canada.

WITHDRAWN